The
SIMULACRUM

PETER CAWDRON

Copyright © 2024. All rights reserved. The right of Peter Cawdron to be identified as the author of this work has been asserted in accordance with the Copyright, Designs and Patents Act 1988. All the characters in this book are fictitious, and any resemblance to actual persons, living or dead, is purely coincidental. No part of this book may be reproduced or used in any other manner without the written permission of the copyright owner, except for the use of quotations.

This book is intended for personal enjoyment while reading. It may not be used in the training of Artificial Intelligence without the written consent of the author. The author reserves all rights to license uses of this work for generative AI training and development of machine learning language models.

Disclaimer: No Artificial Intelligence (AI) was used in the creation of this story. Some would argue that no intelligence was used at all. I'll leave that for you to decide.

Cover Art: iStockPhotos 1443245537: Technology digital wave background concept.

ISBN: 9798328077170

Imprint: Independently published

Tiger got to hunt,

Bird got to fly;

Man got to sit and wonder, "Why, why, why?"

Tiger got to sleep,

Bird got to land;

Man got to tell himself he understands.

Kurt Vonnegut

The Archives

"Seriously?" Dawn McAllister asks as Dr. Manaas Guneet pulls a cord hanging from the ceiling to turn on the lights in the concrete basement. Aging fluorescent overhead tubes flicker, slowly coming to life. Row upon row of shelving materializes from the darkness. Hundreds of seemingly identical cardboard boxes have been stacked up to the roof.

"It's a shit assignment," Dr. Guneet says. "But, hey, that's the life of a grad student. We've all been there."

Dawn protests. "I really don't want to lose my focus on Przybylski's Star."

Dr. Guneet is not impressed. "Przybylski's Star is an oddity, a misfit, a freak outlier, which doesn't make for good science. Astronomy is based on repeatable observations that test and challenge a theory, not vague exceptions with questionable accuracy."

"But it's—"

"Interesting," Dr. Guneet says, raising an eyebrow. "Don't waste your career chasing rabbits down holes."

Dawn hangs her head. He's right.

"Where is AI when you really need it?" She grumbles, looking around the concrete basement.

"AI is waiting for this."

"We seriously need to get some robotics in here," Dawn says, looking at the dust that's settled on the top of the boxes. "I mean, machines love this repetitive crap."

"No budget," Dr. Guneet says.

"And this is important?"

"I wouldn't waste your time. Honest," Dr. Guneet says, tapping his hand on one of the nearby boxes. "And yes, this is important. Back when the Keck Observatory was built in Hawaii, the raw images of select runs were printed in hard copy. Astronomers were still using manual comparative analysis as digital versions could give false positives."

"They went old school?" Dawn is aghast. "You're telling me they'd sit there and eyeball the differences?"

"You have to remember. The Internet was in its infancy back then. I mean, while Keck was getting up to speed, Amazon was being run out of a garage. Databases were run on laptops. There was no machine learning, no GPT Generative Pre-trained Transformers or large language models. These things were all still decades away."

Dawn lifts the lid on one of the boxes and peers inside at the stack of glossy black-and-white images. Like Dr. Guneet, she's wearing cotton gloves so the oils in her skin don't damage the images. Above her, an industrial HVAC filtration system regulates not just the temperature but the humidity within the archive, ensuring the air is dry and cool.

Dr. Guneet gestures to the vast, silent basement and row upon row of boxes stretching into the distance. "This. This is our legacy. If the ghosts in this room could talk."

Dawn would rather be writing Python scripts to analyze recent digital images.

"Besides," he says. "The target area you're scanning includes Przybylski's Star."

That's little consolation to her, as she knows she'll be stuck down here for days on end.

Dawn pulls a photo out and looks at it.

Object: 243.188453 52.158517 eq J2000

16h 12m 45.23s +52d 09m 30.7s 1 deg

2452692.14262 HJD

She sighs. *"The object"* is a deep-space view of thousands of background galaxies nestled behind a few foreground stars in the Milky Way. The hours, minutes and degrees are its location as viewed looking out from Earth. The image itself is large, but its coverage is tiny, spanning only one degree of the sky.

The crazy long number at the bottom is the Heliocentric Julian Date, which is equally insane to the average person on the street. If someone was observing from the center of the Sun, this is the date and time they'd record for that particular image.

It's the date as calculated by the number of days that have elapsed since 4713 BC. Why start counting from 4713 BC? Why not? It's as good as any other arbitrary, random date and far enough back in history that there's no contention. As it is, the year was originally selected in the 16th century because it marked the first year in which the solar, lunar, and Roman tax years all coincided. That Rome didn't exist in 4713 BC is irrelevant. Dawn finds it ironic that modern astronomers are slaves to ancient tax laws. It's like nothing has changed.

The beauty of the system is that it's a number. It's just a number. And she can add to numbers or subtract from them with ease and without fear of making dumb mistakes, like miscounting leap years or getting the number of days in a month wrong.

2452692 is the number of days since January 1st 4713 BC, while the numbers after the decimal place are the seconds elapsed on the day of the observation. As bizarre as it seems, it's a far simpler way of handling dates and times than using days, months and years. Subtract one date from another, and you immediately know how much time lies between two events. It's foolproof. Dawn, though, is of the opinion that the constant need to develop new and better foolproof systems implies fools are smarter than us all.

"This really is old-school astronomy," Dr. Guneet says, looking at the image she's randomly pulled from the box.

"Oh, it sure is."

"You might think this is a waste of time, but it's not. When the basement at Caltech flooded, we lost the digital originals." He sweeps with his arm, gesturing to the entire basement. "If we didn't have these, most of Keck's early years would be lost."

"They don't have backups?"

"Oh, they do," he replies. "The problem with backups is they're never checked. They get rotated on the basis of weeks, months and years. We got some data from them, but the older backups were faulty. The tapes were blank. No one knew until they looked."

"Damn. And my job is to scan all this?"

"Only those that are missing from our online archive. I've sent you the list."

Dawn looks down at the photo in her hand. Grainy blotches of black and white appear on a chunky image that has been surpassed by images from JWST, Luxor and HWO of this same region. What appears like a pixelated *Minecraft* image to her is now available in high resolution with false-color enhancement. But Dr. Guneet is right. What the later space telescopes lack is the history of any subtle changes in the luminosity of these remote objects. To most, the image in her hand would seem trivial, catching slight variations, particularly in distant galaxies subject to gravitational lensing, but it helps piece together the cosmos and make sense of the chaos.

"This place is Aladdin's Cave," Dr. Guneet says, pointing at the far end of the basement. "If you get the chance, Row M has all the old photographic plates dating back to the 1900s. They've been printed in inverse, like the old photographic negatives. White appears black."

"And it's okay to get them out?" Dawn asks, surprised, as photographic plates are the equivalent of ancient Egyptian archeological relics to astronomers.

"Sure. Just... wear gloves and don't drop anything."

"Okay," she says, swinging her bag down off her back and resting it on the concrete floor.

"I'll come back down here at lunchtime to check on you and then again before I leave," Dr. Guneet says.

"How long do you think I'll be down here?" Dawn asks.

"A couple of weeks."

Dawn feels her shoulders sag, but this is the reality of science. Leg work. Everyone wants an explosive discovery or stunning, pretty pictures of a nebula. Science, though, is preoccupied with the mundane. Good science is about focusing on the obscure, the overlooked, the subtle—and questioning assumptions, testing ideas. It's about squeezing every last drop of juice from a tired wedge of lime.

"Look for something interesting," he says. "You never know what you'll find down here."

"Sure," she replies, thinking he's being overly optimistic. The chance of spotting anything with the human eye is practically impossible. Once, astronomers like Edwin Hubble would pore over images like these, often with magnifying glasses, looking to understand the universe from a bunch of grainy photographic plates. These days, machine-learning algorithms do all the sorting and comparisons.

Dr. Guneet leaves. Dawn pops in some noise-canceling earbuds and smiles at the irony that there's no noise to cancel. She starts listening to music as she sets up her equipment on the steel table near the door. Her digital SLR camera has a whopping 128 megapixels of resolution, which is going to be totally wasted on the chunky images she has to scan for the digital archive.

Dawn sets up a tripod on the table, raising it two feet above the surface. She mounts the camera beneath the tripod, screwing it into a base plate so it hangs directly down. There's no need for a viewfinder or digital display as the camera syncs with her tablet computer, showing her the fine scratches on the metal surface of the table in stunning detail. She slips a calibration image beneath the tripod and uses masking tape to hold it in place. Not only does this allow the calibration to be double-checked automatically between each photo, it also gives her a guide on where to place each image so it's aligned properly.

Although Dawn's working with a camera and tablet, she's hooked into the Harvard College Observatory data center servers and, specifically, their astronomy AI system, which is nicknamed HAL. Apparently, HAL is an acronym, tying in Harvard and Astronomy, but she's not sure what the L stands for. Library? Does it matter? It's clearly a case of reverse engineering a name to fit so as to tie into the Arthur C. Clarke classic *2001: A Space Odyssey*. It's a movie no one in her generation has seen and is based on a book no one in her parents' generation has read.

"Open the pod bay doors, HAL," she says, pulling her fingers away from the calibration image.

"I'm afraid I can't do that, Dawn," is the predictable response from HAL, talking softly over the music coming through her earbuds and using the same voice as in the movie. That one iconic scene is all she's seen from the movie as it's a running gag at the university. HAL says, "Calibration complete. Looking good."

"Okay. Let's do this."

Dawn hauls over six boxes, stacking them next to the table. She removes a pile of hundreds of images from the box and places them face down on her left, putting the empty box on her right. In this way, she can re-stack the original archive box as she works through the images.

"Ready?" she asks HAL as though he needs time to prepare.

"Ready," HAL replies, playing along with the charade. He's capable of processing thousands of images per second. Keeping pace with her is laughable, but they both know it's part of the game. Dawn thinks about the performance gap between humans and AI as she flips the first picture, sliding it on top of the calibration image and keeping her fingers on the white border surrounding the historical astronomical photo.

"They both know it's part of the game." And that thought intrigues her. *They.* The personification of AI was a natural and predictable step in the advancement of artificial intelligence, but it's something she finds disturbing nonetheless. Even though there's no sentience, there's mimicry.

At what point does playing pretend become real? How long will AI parrot a self-aware consciousness before becoming self-aware and conscious for itself? How would anyone ever know when that threshold is crossed? For that matter, how does any one person know another human is legitimately conscious? It's an assumption that we all share the same sense of sentience. Dawn finds it an interesting philosophical idea. She could be the *only* conscious person on the planet, with everyone else being little more than zombies reacting as though they're sentient, just like HAL. It's absurd, of course, but the emergence of AI does get her to question what she knows and believes about consciousness.

The camera automatically clicks as HAL takes a digital snapshot, and she slides the image out, placing it in the storage box before slipping the next image in. Damn, it's a good job HAL isn't sentient. This would be boring as hell for a conscious being capable of processing images a thousand times faster than her. How would she feel if it were her who had to wait an inordinate amount of time for mere flesh to react with the speed of a garden snail?

Dawn settles into a steady rhythm, sliding photos in place, aligning them with the tape over the calibration image, pausing for the click, and then stacking them in the box. By her reckoning, it's one every second or so, or about thirty to forty a minute. That's only got to be slightly annoying for a super-brain. If AI ever develops impatience, the human race is fucked.

Box after box, she continues. Lunchtime comes, but not Dr. Guneet. Dawn eats her sandwiches outside on the concrete steps leading down to the basement, respecting the sanctity of the storage area. She needn't. No one would know. Dr. Guneet will be able to monitor the uploaded images to know she's making steady progress. That's all he cares about. In reality, he barely cares at all. Someone somewhere is doing research into fast-radio bursts and visible light anomalies. They prompted him about the historical data gap. He's simply responding to that and getting her to do the remedial work. As it is, she's still got lectures to attend and meetings to sit in on, so Dawn has to juggle her time in the archives.

The afternoon flies by quickly as her hands shuffle images between boxes. By the end of the day, she's captured several thousand photos. She doesn't ask exactly how many, even though HAL would know. To know would only highlight the depressing number that remains.

"Good night, HAL," she says at 5:01 PM.

"Good night, Dawn," HAL replies as she pulls on the drawstring and turns off the lights in the basement.

AI is crazy and entirely counterintuitive to humans. Dawn's talking to HAL as though he inhabits the basement when he's talking to her through her wireless earbuds, syncing via her tablet computer to the data center a couple of blocks away, but it feels like he's in the basement. She feels as though she's leaving him behind as she walks up the concrete stairs, but she knows he's still there, ready to respond should she call on him. He'll remain connected until she walks off the campus and the intranet link is broken.

In a few years, this kind of manual effort, scanning photos in a basement, will be redundant. Already, AI-enabled robots are flipping burgers at McDonalds. They have a narrow scope of operation and specific roles/limitations, but they're only getting better. Robots will never be any worse than they are now, and they're already able to harvest vegetables, pick fruits and work as shop assistants, albeit under the watchful eye of humans.

Harvard is one of the leading universities exploring AI-enabled robotics, but their research lab jealously guards its secrets, even though other departments, like astronomy, are calling out for robotic assistance. If Dawn had a robot, there would be no goodnight. The robot would continue working with HAL 24/7. Besides, what does HAL do at night anyway? Downtime for AI makes no sense. Although to be fair, HAL's *"downtime"* is probably more accurately counted in wasted milliseconds between requests rather than hours overnight. Working with HAL is like having a Ferrari for grocery shopping.

Dawn walks out into the twilight. It's autumn, and the leaves on the campus are turning. The setting sun catches the red, yellow and orange blurs on the branches, setting the trees ablaze with light. Leaves tumble across the ground with the wind. Dawn stops for a photo and a selfie with the oak trees in the background, posting it on social media.

What is the meaning of existence? Dawn flicks through a few of her photos, marveling at the way such technology can be used to capture her life here on Earth and the light from stars that died millions of years ago.

Why is vanity such a crucial part of humanity? King Solomon once said, "*Vanity of vanities. All is vanity.*" Dawn would love to hear the king's take on social media. She's sure he'd have a brutal takedown of the way people project themselves in words, images and videos. Everyone's self-obsessed. Everyone wants to be seen, to be heard, to be recognized. And not just the pretty girls and the handsome men. Deep down, everyone wants to be loved and admired. Vanity is often seen as a weakness of character, but it's not. It's natural.

The loudest voices in society are often the most revered, even though they're the least important. Dawn's mother once told her not to worry about what other people think of her because everyone—absolutely everyone else on the planet—is only ever thinking about themselves. And that's vanity. What does AI think about when it doesn't need to think? Perhaps that's the real measure of sentience? Perhaps the vanity of a quick smile for an Instagram post is simply the self-awareness of consciousness breathing. Perhaps vanity is a virtue rather than a vice, being the natural expression of sentient life. Dawn makes a mental note to keep an eye out for selfies of HAL if/when he becomes self-aware, and she smiles at a silly thought that the Turing Test could be replaced with TikTok.

Dawn waits for the bus in the cold. As the sun dips below the horizon, the temperature plummets, along with leaves falling from the trees.

There's one other aspect of self-aware consciousness Dawn suspects AI will never experience: the mundane. She may have a master's degree in astrophysics and may be working toward a PhD, but she catches the same bus as the janitor. Dawn is going to have a shower when she gets home and cook her own dinner before plopping on the sofa to watch television. All this would seem irrelevant and wasteful to a sentient artificial mind, one that was genuinely alive and not simply bouncing through large language models to mimic humans. Human intelligence is indulgent. Humans long for pleasure. Downtime is important. Play time is essential to consciousness. It recharges the batteries of creativity and intellect. Could an artificial intelligence ever understand the importance of play?

Even her forty minutes on the bus isn't wasted. She could listen to a podcast, scroll through social media on her phone or watch a video, but after a rigorous and repetitive day in the basement, she'd rather relax and simply watch the world go by out the windows of the bus.

A jogger runs through a city park, bouncing along a pavement swept clear of a light dusting of snow, listening to music on their earbuds. A couple walks the other way, pushing a stroller with a baby wrapped against the cold. An elderly man waddles along with stooped shoulders, carrying bags of groceries. And then he's gone. The bus travels further on down the road and turns the corner, and Dawn loses sight of that particular slice of life. To a sentient artificial intelligence, the view out of the window would seem trivial and inane, perhaps even wasteful—but life is its own reward.

On the next street, police officers talk with someone standing outside a store. It's difficult to tell if the old man is a suspect or a witness to a crime as the cops have their hands up on their hips, resting on the guns and tasers holstered on their belts.

A young man carries fresh-cut flowers wrapped in cellophane. He's in love, but with whom? Someone is going to be delighted. Hugs and kisses will be exchanged, and Dawn finds that invigorating. She lives alone, but maybe one day, it'll be her lover carrying flowers home to surprise her. For now, her cat, rather inappropriately named Mouse, will have to give her a warm snuggle.

Could an artificial intelligence ever appreciate the beauty that is human life unfolding in billions of permutations spread around the planet? Or would it see humans as wasting their potential? What is it humanity values beyond life, liberty and the pursuit of happiness? Could AI ever value these things?

Maybe AI is like a cat.

Humans think they're in control, but cats and dogs seem to have humanity well-trained. Dawn's cat gets fed twice a day, his kitty litter is changed, and he gets to sit on her lap, purring while she watches television.

Is that what life is like for AI? Humans care for their computer servers, provide them with electricity and play with them, but instead of dangling a toy on a string, it's an electronic task that needs to be accomplished. Or is it humanity that's the cat? Maybe, one day, when artificial intelligence achieves actual sentience, it'll be humans that become pets.

Sitting on the bus, Dawn looks down at her bag resting by her feet. The spine of a well-worn paperback is visible. She's tempted to pick it up and read a few pages to kill the time as the bus trundles between stops. It's a romance novel set in Victorian England.

Love Burns Bright has been passed around her astronomy department over the past few months and finally found its way to her. It's about as far removed from her life as possible. And being a modern take on historic times, it is hopelessly optimistic and overly positive. There's none of the disease and misogyny that plagued that era. And the men are muscular and kind. The unlikely love triangle in the book is as messy as it is intriguing. *Love Burns Bright* is never going to win a Pulitzer, but it's a nice escape.

What would HAL or any AI make of *Love Burns Bright?* Oh, they could provide a synopsis or trawl the hundreds of online reviews to come up with some composite hybrid overview, but could an artificial intelligence ever actually read a novel?

Could AI ever enjoy fiction? To Dawn's mind, reading for enjoyment would be a better test of sentience than fooling dumb humans like her with plausible conversations.

Fiction is wonderfully illogical, so it is bound to confound anything other than actual intelligence. It seems silly to state the obvious, but fiction is not true. It's make-believe. Lord Grey of Cornwall from *Love Burns Bright* doesn't actually exist. He's never existed anywhere other than in the author's mind and the minds of the readers. And neither does Lady Elizabeth de Mohun of Essex. Nor the saucy French maid Émilie du Châtelet. In Dawn's mind, however, they come to life. Words on the page form not only pictures in her thinking but relationships. The lord, lady and her maid have their own personalities, likes, dislikes, tempers, passions and love.

Fiction ought to be frivolous, but it's not. Even when Dawn rolls her eyes at a threesome unfolding in the ornate bedroom of a stately home nestled into the hills of Falmouth in the south of England, there's fascination and enjoyment. Logically, fiction shouldn't exist. It's extravagant. Indulgent. It serves no purpose. Dawn decides that if she's ever confronted by an AGI, an artificial general intelligence capable of sentience, she's going to ask it what it thought of *Love Burns Bright*. She doesn't want to know what others think and listen to it regurgitating ideas like a bird feeding its young. She wants to know how it *feels* about the unlikely Victorian throuple. Perhaps she, her lover, and the newly formed AGI can create their own *ménage à trois*, and she laughs at that thought. She'll need a lover first, and that might be more difficult than AI achieving sentience.

Dawn hops off the bus at her stop. A rush of cold air chills her cheeks as she steps down onto the pavement. She grabs a carton of milk from the local deli before walking home with her coat wrapped around her against the cold.

As snowflakes swirl across the pavement, brushing past her boots, she wonders about her brother, Ryan, down in Texas. A cold snap is sweeping across the country, and the weather reports show it reaching Houston. The snow it brings won't stay long, but it will remind even her stubborn brother to wear a hat and coat. As much as she'd love to go into space, hearing about the effort behind the scenes has given her an appreciation for the sheer dedication required to be in the NASA astronaut corps. Training simulations often turn into long, tiring days. Dawn's happy with a cat called Mouse and a tiny apartment overlooking a park with a pond.

The Rabbit

NASA Astronaut Ryan McAllister is strapped into a climbing harness. The belts are a little tight around his crotch, so he squirms, wanting to get comfortable. Unfortunately, he's in a zero-gee training scenario designed to simulate asteroid mining. Ordinarily, if he were training in the neutral buoyancy lab, a super-sized swimming pool with space hardware set beneath the water, he'd be wearing a full spacesuit. Ryan's worked on an asteroid mock-up in the neutral buoyancy lab before, but there's water drag, and that is not only unrealistic, but it also gives the body a negative impression unlike that of working in low gravity. There's no one specific training simulator that can reproduce working on an asteroid, so NASA combines environments, repeating various scenarios in different ways to get the overall picture. In this case, Ryan is dangling inches from a rough rock wall, wearing only a few parts of his EVA/EMU suit.

EVA is an anachronistic term from the early days of spaceflight that dates back to the 1960s and has stuck over the years. EVA stands for Extravehicular Activity. Why it's not an EA when extravehicular is one word baffles him. At a guess, acronyms sound better in threes. Technically, to conduct an EVA he uses an EMU or Extravehicular Mobility Unit, which, given the logic behind EVA should be an EVMU, but there's nothing to be gained from swapping one cryptic acronym for another except one more entry in a dictionary. Mark Twain once said, *"Don't use a five-dollar word when a fifty-cent word will do,"* but the folks at NASA missed that particular memo. Spacewalks. Spacesuits. Mark Twain would be disappointed those terms didn't prevail.

To the untrained eye, it looks as though Ryan's wearing exotic football gear instead of a full EVA/EMU. His helmet is bulkier than anything seen in the Super Bowl, reaching well beyond his head, but there's no glass visor, allowing him to breathe normally. He's wearing shoulder pads on the outside of his clothing, but these are not to protect him from a linebacker charging through the scrimmage. They're there to replicate the bulky feel of a spacesuit while swinging around on the ropes. He's also wearing the thick, oversized gloves of a regular EVA spacesuit, but they end in the middle of his forearms. These and his bulky boots are intended to help replicate the experience of a spacewalk without overheating. While on the ground, he snapped his fingers, pretending to be Thanos, much to the amusement of the techs supporting him.

Several senators touring the facility watch from a raised platform at the back of the five-story room. To them, it must look as though he skipped a few steps while getting dressed.

Ryan's conducting NASA's equivalent of indoor rock climbing, but rather than simply hanging from a harness attached to the ceiling, his harness has five independent pulleys going in five different directions: left, right, up, down and backward. The lines run out to a massive square frame surrounding the wall and move in unison with him, tracing his motion. The solenoids and motors out there control the semi-transparent nylon lines running through the pulleys. They're designed to mimic weightlessness. If Ryan reaches out and grabs one of the fake rocks on the simulated surface of the asteroid in front of him and pushes, a pulley strapped to his back will sense the change in tension and pull him away from the rocky surface. As it's designed to replicate the weak gravity of the asteroid Psyche, computer-controlled springs in the outer frame surrounding the wall will take into account the force he's applied and then slowly bring him back at a snail's pace, mimicking the gravitational pull of the asteroid.

The low gravity simulator is comprised of nylon lines centered on a bunch of pulleys attached to his fake backpack. They form a plus shape in line with his shoulders, leading away from him in four directions. As they're behind him, they don't get in the way and are only visible on the periphery of his vision. As he moves, the vertical line remains above him while the horizontal lines extend out sideways, with his motion being mirrored by the motors on the frame. In this way, the lines remain centered on him as he scoots around.

The five lines suspending him in front of the wall are akin to the nylon fishing lines used to catch deep-sea game fish like marlin. Although they're thin, each has a breaking strain of 300 kilos or well over 600 pounds. That's well over three times his body weight. The longer he's on the wall, the more they become invisible, being ignored by his eyes.

Even though the asteroid Psyche is almost two hundred miles wide and shaped like an egg, it only exerts a minuscule gravitational force. Lifting a Great Dane off the asteroid would be like picking up a hamster. It takes a surprisingly small amount of effort for astronauts to take a few steps and go flying off the surface like the mythical god Thor. Although it sounds like fun, it's uncontrolled and unfolds like a nightmare in slow motion. Without the use of EVA navigation thrusters, there's no way to steer or pick a spot for landing. For Ryan in the simulator, the motion of him wriggling in his harness to get comfortable has been falsely interpreted by the control computer as pushing off the surface, and he drifts away from the wall.

"Oh, come on," he says, looking forty feet below him at his instructor. "That's not fair."

"Gravity doesn't care," the instructor says. "What are you going to do?"

Ryan's tempted to grab the rock ax hanging from his waist belt and swing it out to snag the surface of the fake asteroid, but Sir Isaac Newton was right. For every action, there's an equal and opposite reaction. In the low-gravity environment of the asteroid Psyche, it's easy to overreact. Instead, he reaches out with his thick, gloved hand and touches lightly at the surface as he drifts away. His fingers run over the rocks. The rig he's on reacts to the drag, and he falls slowly back to the vertical surface in front of him.

Ryan brings himself to rest on the fake surface, with his gloves and his boots touching lightly against the pseudo-asteroid. Although it sounds easy, there's an art to coming in slow and avoiding a bounce. Any attempt to gain purchase will see him rebound. Relaxing is the key. To the senators watching him, he appears spread-eagle, hanging vertically, but from his perspective, the illusion of low gravity is overwhelming. His mind responds as though he were lying flat on the asteroid.

"Are you going to try standing again?" the trainer asks.

"No," Ryan replies, looking at the rock mere inches from his nose. It's rough and irregular, with troughs and rises obscuring his view. He can scramble around with his hands and change his orientation to see in various directions, but being so close to the wall, his visibility is heavily restricted.

"Why not?"

Ryan smiles. The trainer already knows the answer to this question. The low-gravity rig has been in use for several months now, with the primary crew spending over two hundred hours on the wall. This might be Ryan's first time, but the trainer has been here working with the astronauts for months. He's doing what all good trainers do, and that means teasing out new ideas.

"Standing is a no-go," Ryan says. "Gravity might be low, but inertia doesn't change. I've walked on the lunar surface, and even up there, you've got to be careful with your sense of balance. Gravity might be six times lower on the Moon, but that means balancing is six times harder. We humans have a high center of gravity."

"And here?"

"It's worse, by a factor of maybe ten or twenty. It's like standing on black ice. Walk in a straight line, and you're fine. Change direction, even slightly, and you topple over—only in super slow-mo."

"So we're going to need to rely on EVA propulsion? What about fuel limits? Consumption rates?"

"I dunno," Ryan says, shifting his gloved hands over the wall and feeling the way the micro-gravity simulator responds with an equal-and-opposite reaction. "There have got to be other options."

The trainer is silent for a few minutes, making notes on his pad. Ryan desperately wants to know what the primary crew made of these simulated spacewalks around the asteroid. At some point, there will be a debriefing where the learnings are shared, but for now, the NASA trainers are still compiling responses. It's important to let fresh ideas bubble organically to the surface.

"Next steps?" the trainer asks.

Ryan looks at the mission checklist on his left wrist. The rig is so sensitive that just that motion alone is enough to see him skip sideways, which is good. This is precisely what would happen on Psyche. He's about to reply when he notices the shadows. They've been growing longer over the past few minutes.

"Coming up on nightfall," he says, seeing the timer on his wrist counting down. Ryan switches on the lights on the side of his fake helmet. Shadows stretch over the rocks as the mobile spotlight simulating the sun disappears behind the rock wall. The warehouse is plunged into absolute darkness.

With four hours of darkness and four hours of light, a day on the asteroid is roughly a third of a day on Earth. There was considerable discussion about limiting activity to the local daylight hours, but the astronauts need to train for all eventualities. Spacewalks around the

International Space Station are conducted day and night, so there's no technical reason the team can't do the same thing out at Psyche. Technical reasons, though, don't equate to practical and psychological reasons.

The darkness is intimidating.

Although his spotlights illuminate the rock wall, providing him with the ability to select handholds, their field of view is narrow. The problem is one of perspective. If Ryan could stand upright, his spotlights would illuminate the asteroid for easily fifty to sixty feet, but standing isn't practical. Leg muscles aren't good with the fine motor skills required for asteroid hopping. Hands are much better, but that means he's essentially lying on the rubble, unable to see for any distance.

Ryan's role on the mission to Psyche is as commander of the backup crew. Although he's affectionately known as the bridesmaid, being part of the backup is important. NASA doesn't do anything without redundancy. The backup crew isn't simply on standby for the primary should anything happen to that team. They also provide NASA with the ability to simulate processes and procedures during the actual mission. If any contingencies arise or they need to vary the mission parameters, it will be Ryan and his team who practice and polish the procedures on mockups like this before passing on the learning to the primary crew.

During training, there's value in having several astronauts go through the same mission profile. No two people see things the same way, so they come up with different solutions to common problems. Having two specialist crews provides more opportunities to perfect procedures.

Although videos of spacewalks might seem like a walk in the park being conducted in slow motion, they're physically exhausting. Even in near-weightlessness, it takes effort to lug around a bulky spacesuit. The gloves are designed to settle as a neutral, open hand, meaning that every time Ryan grabs something, he's fighting against the thick material and rubberized outer layer. And that thick layer is particularly important on an asteroid where a sharp edge of volcanic glass could slice through the material without being noticed. The upshot is that doing the three Ps down here prevents the three Ps up there: *Preparation and Planning Prevent Piss-Poor Performance.* It's far easier to do something right the first time than conduct a do-over. Ryan knows that hard work down here allows them to make the actual spacewalk up there look easy.

He rises slowly onto his knees, allowing himself to settle as he looks across the rock pile. With the lights out within the warehouse, his sense of orientation has shifted. Earth's gravity still pulls him down, but the illusion before his eyes is such that he feels as though he's kneeling in a celestial quarry. Far from pulling him down, Earth's gravity feels as though it's a weight pulling him backward like a heavy backpack as he looks out across the rocks and boulders. His mind is so completely immersed in the simulation that he feels as though he's sitting flat on the ground rather than sideways on a wall. It takes a few seconds before he settles on his knees on the rocky surface in the low gravity, but this position isn't uncomfortable because of the minuscule gravitational force applied by the simulator.

The checklist on his left wrist reminds him that he's got to set anchor points in any bedrock he can find and link up with the AI construction bot.

Being an acronym itself, NASA prides itself on coming up with acronyms for its missions. AMPLE is the Autonomous Manufacturing Pilot Leverage Experiment. The goal of AMPLE is to demonstrate the ability to refine ore and manufacture high-grade steel, aluminum and alloys from the asteroid Psyche.

AMPLE is seen as the start of an off-world economy. Rather than lifting everything into space or even mining the Moon for staples like water and oxygen, AMPLE provides a stepping stone to the stars. Instead of lifting everything off Earth, AMPLE will allow structures to be built in microgravity. At first, it will be frames and panels, but the AI bot has the ability to cold weld metals to form pressure vessels that can be used for fuel tanks and habitats. Beyond that, the *"leverage"* portion of the experiment is to use the AI bot for 3D electronic printing based on resources refined from the asteroid. Building valves and circuit boards along with basic computer chips is a game changer for space exploration. High-grade nano-builds will still be conducted on Earth as lifting CPUs and RAM into orbit is cheap, but the substrates will be built in space. If all goes well, the final build will be the AI bot building another AI bot. NASA estimates there's enough metal on Psyche to support space exploration for the next five hundred years! The only resource that is lacking is petroleum products, so there are no oils or plastics that can be engineered in space.

From the darkness, the trainer says, "McAllister, AMPLE."

"AMPLE, this is McAllister," he replies, knowing his instructor is throwing a curveball at him. The trainer is speaking as though they're in the orbiting spacecraft coordinating his spacewalk from an altitude of two hundred kilometers. Nothing is haphazard. Everything is planned, even supposedly ad hoc communication. They want to see how he'll react to an emergency. And the timing is deliberate, waiting until night has fallen to make everything that little bit more difficult and disorienting. Ryan's expecting to hear about a stuck fuel valve or an atmospheric leak on the lander and have to navigate back to the mock-up of his ship.

"McAllister. We've lost contact with AIRMAIL in SQ-127. You are *go* for recovery and repair. Over."

"AMPLE. McAllister en route to AIRMAIL in SQ-127. Over."

AIRMAIL is yet another acronym that leaves Ryan shaking his head. Can't they just call them bots? Why does everything need a snazzy acronym? In this case, AIRMAIL stands for Artificial Intelligent Robotic Manufacturer of In-Situ Logistics. Someone somewhere was paid way too much to flick through a dictionary for a couple of hours, trying to wedge a bunch of obscure terms into something intelligible. Bots would have served quite well.

SQ-127 is a grid reference system for the asteroid, describing a square kilometer section of Psyche. Rather conveniently, that's the exact sector he's in. Funny that, but it's still over half a mile in height and width. In practice, that's a huge area to search. The simulator, though, is less than a hundred yards in width and about eighty in height. *They hid that little fucker in here somewhere before I started,* Ryan thinks, looking around in the darkness.

Ryan's task on this simulated spacewalk on the fake asteroid Psyche has switched from general exploration to finding and repairing a faulty robot among the fake boulders, crevasses and outcrops of the simulator. Sitting there on his knees with his legs tucked beneath him, he reaches down with his gloved hands and pulls on the rocks. Ryan glides slightly above the surface, scooting forward for a few meters before drifting back to the rocky asteroid. To him, the motion is reminiscent of sitting in a plastic sleigh at the top of a snow-covered hill and pushing off down the slope.

Houston doesn't get a lot of snow, but when it does and it stays around for a few weeks, the kids all love sledding down the long hill outside the training facility. A couple of the engineers must have children, as Ryan noticed a few sleds leaning against the door beside a few boots and jackets. Depending on someone's role within NASA, the organization is pretty lenient when it comes to having kids around after school. They probably hit the slopes as soon as the day comes to an end.

Ryan turns in the darkness, looking down to his right. The spotlights barely illuminate the door leading out to the parking lot. He can see the shape of the sleds—and he has an idea.

"Hey," he says. "See that thin plastic sled by the door?"

From the shadows, the instructor points but doesn't respond.

"Pop that on a cable and send it up here, would you?"

"What are you doing?" a curious trainer asks from the darkness.

"Testing an idea."

It takes a few minutes, but a thin red plastic sled is hauled up next to him. It's cheap, being the kind sold in Wal-Mart for two bucks. There's a bit of rope at the front but no rails or hand holds. It's the type of sled that's surprisingly fun as being lightweight it zips over the snow and ice with ease.

"Do you mind telling me what you're doing?" the trainer asks as Ryan unclips the sled and slips it beneath his knees.

"The Rabbit."

"The Rabbit?"

Ryan explains himself. "Standing out here on the asteroid is not a good idea. Even slight movements to stay balanced can send me tumbling out of control. It's the crazy contradiction between my high center of gravity and low relative weight. You'd think it would be easy to stand with less gravity, but it's astonishingly easy to lose balance. And the contrast—lying flat and crawling across the surface reduces visibility far too much and slows down mobility. The Rabbit, though, is halfway between lying and standing."

"The Rabbit," an intrigued trainer says.

Ryan leans forward and pushes off with his hands again, effortlessly lifting himself into fake space with a controlled motion. The thin plastic of the sled skims across the rocks with ease. His folded legs remain beneath him. The pulleys simulating the weak gravity work flawlessly, allowing him to scoot along at what would be a slow jog on Earth but with a sense of rhythm that comes quite naturally. After four pushes in a row, he comes to a halt on the rocks.

"Yeah, this works really well," he says, pushing off again and turning one way and then another on the thin sled. The plastic absorbs and redirects the bumps, gliding over the surface of the fake asteroid as though it were a snowy slope. "You get speed but without a loss of control. And it doesn't use any fuel."

"I like it," the trainer says. "How does it feel beneath your knees."

"In a full spacesuit, I doubt you'd feel anything at all."

"Okay, I think we'll need to reinforce the external lining on the suit legs, but this could be a good compromise for maneuvering on Psyche."

The trainer turns on a small LED light on his helmet and makes notes on a pad, saying, "A kid's sled. That's a nice low-tech, low-mass solution to a curly problem."

Once he's finished, he turns off his light and the illusion of being on another world instead of in a warehouse training facility in Houston returns.

"This is effortless," Ryan says, having some fun as he twists and turns, testing the maneuverability on the wall before him. The front of the sled rests against his knees, but on an actual asteroid, he'd probably remain in the center of the sled. "And it saves EVA fuel for when it's really needed. With the reduced gravity, it's the equivalent of bunny hopping on the lunar surface."

"And any debris will go behind you," the trainer says, "so you're not in danger of throwing up dust and blinding yourself."

"Also, it spreads my weight far better than standing, so there's no concentration of mass at any one point. There's no danger of losing balance, and there's no sinking into the surface if it shifts from pebbles to fine dust."

The tiny light clicks on in the darkness again below Ryan as the trainer makes a few more notes on his pad.

"And AIRMAIL? Have you found it?"

"I will," Ryan says. "Visibility is much better like this."

He scoots along, pushing off with his hands at an angle, gliding forward and coming gently to rest before pushing off again, covering the massive wall of rocks with ease. Ryan plays around with this new method of moving in low gravity. In his opinion, play is underrated. People learn best when they're enjoying themselves. He scoots in a wide circle, having fun with this new mode of propulsion in the simulated low gravity. Ryan cuts down below the starting point for the exercise, which was roughly in the middle of the wall, but not for any reason other than to have a bit more fun with this new technique.

"Yeah, I really like the Rabbit," he says. "And you bastards. You hid the AI bot behind a boulder below me."

The trainer laughs. "It was supposed to take you an hour to find AIRMAIL."

"How long did it take?"

"Once you started the Rabbit, about four minutes."

"Nice," Ryan says. "And I think it would be easy enough to practice this on a trampoline."

"I'll make a note of that," the trainer says. "Now, can you fix that AI bot?"

"Working on it."

Przybył

Gabriel Lopez sits in a room without any windows. Air conditioning spills from the vent above him. The overhead lights are LEDs and can be adjusted via controls by the door to provide different lighting conditions. Three of the four office walls are blank.

The wall to Gabriel's right, though, is regularly redecorated. At the moment, it's set for *rural Ohio*. Aging wallpaper gives way to an old window frame in need of painting. A poster of the classic science fiction movie *Contact* with Jodie Foster has been mounted using lumps of Blu Tack. It's not extravagant or unique for a very specific reason, so it can't be traced. Rather than purchasing something online, it was a generic poster available from Walmart nationwide.

There's a bookshelf, but it doesn't contain books. Instead, there's a model of the Enterprise from Star Trek with the registration NCC-1701 displayed proudly on its hull. There's also a model of the Space Shuttle Atlantis and one of the early SpaceX Starship designs. These, too, are bland. Instead of going with 3D printed models that could be traced, two of them can be found in the toy section of Walmart, while the Starship is chrome-plated and available from the gift shop in Boca Chica. Everything about Gabriel's "*right wall*" is designed to be mildly interesting but ultimately mundane.

The view out of the window is of a suburban street. Sunlight flickers through the leaves of an oak tree. Occasionally, leaves fall from trees on the other side of the road. Cars drive past, but it's all fake. Behind the wooden

8K resolution TV screen with deliberately muted colors to e view out of a south-facing window. Far from being computer d, which would be too easy for foreign intelligence officers to , the screen shows live footage from a house in Columbus, Ohio, that s specifically chosen because of the difficulty in geolocating it based on he view. By the NSA's assessment, it could be one of hundreds of homes scattered across the cookie-cutter suburbs in that city. The camera angle has been selected so that no mailboxes are visible and to avoid license plates being caught in the frame.

In theory, a foreign intelligence service could drive all those streets in southern Columbus, Ohio, watching for their car to come into view, but as the broadcast wall is only used sporadically, that's unlikely to be effective. The right wall is only ever used when an NSA analyst needs to jump on a Twitch stream or a video call. As there are dozens of these walls within the SIGINT building in Fort Meade, Maryland, and they're regularly changed, exposing a hothouse wouldn't be of any value. Identifying Gabriel as an NSA analyst, though, would destroy his value as a deep-cover counter-intelligence officer, so he uses it sparingly.

Gabriel has four computers on the desk in front of him and another on the desk by the fake window. Only one of them is connected to NSA NET. The others are hardwired to appear in different cities around the country, including Columbus, Ohio. Rather than faking or spoofing an IP address, which could be exposed, his internet access really does originate in Ohio, Oklahoma, South Carolina and Alabama, depending on the computer he's using. Any *traceroute* would fail to come within four hundred miles of him.

Gabriel's job is counterintelligence, which is the tedious task of distinguishing foreign adversaries impersonating US nationals from Americans who have become useful idiots for foreign governments. Although the official term is *"foreign adversaries,"* it's Russia. It's always Russia. The Chinese are more concerned with industrial espionage and phishing for the online personas of influential Americans. Occasionally, they dip their toes into the waters of disinformation, but it's the Russians that attack the soft underbelly of American life. Iran and North Korea like to play, too, but they follow rather than lead the Russians.

All the major attacks originate in St. Petersburg. Normally, the Russians hide their electronic tracks by bouncing between VPNs in other countries, including Europe and Canada. The really thorough attacks burrow their way into the US heartland.

Countering Russian interference in American culture is like playing *Wack-a-Mole* at the county fair. Smack one furry rodent on the head with a plastic mallet, and three more pop up through other holes.

Gabriel's job is to trace not merely IP addresses but also to identify actual '*workers on the farm*,' as they're known. Instead of looking at an electronic fingerprint, he identifies their traits, textual mannerisms and grammatical habits. Once a Russian operator is identified, he feeds their characteristics into a machine learning algorithm that can detect and negate their ability to influence others. It's like playing *Wack-a-Mole* with a shotgun. They may drop out of sight and reappear elsewhere on social media, wanting to infiltrate other groups, but they're quickly detected by the AI and blocked.

The biggest challenge for Gabriel is avoiding intelligence spam. He's not interested in the low-level Russian operators trolling trans women, although he occasionally goes hunting for those assholes purely out of sport. Gabriel's after those who are trying to shape political discourse. He wants to whack the big moles.

One of his screens pings into life. It's a 2020 Apple Mac with 16GB of RAM running on a painfully slow CPU that should have been retired long ago. It has been using OS X Sonoma since 2024, which means it is woefully unprepared for the modern internet and full of vulnerabilities. For the NSA, it's a honeypot. If someone from North Korea comes digging around, the NSA doesn't try to stop them from gaining remote access.

Instead, they simply sit back and watch—and learn. Every attack is an opportunity to understand the enemy. The Apple Mac is set up with family photos, tax returns, details about bank accounts (that never hold more than a few hundred dollars), and enough breadcrumbs to make it look like it's a hand-me-down computer some father has given his daughter so she can watch YouTube videos in her bedroom.

Next to the 2011 Apple Mac is a proprietary NSA computer. Ribbon cables lead from the Mac to the NSA laptop, allowing Gabriel to watch the attack unfold remotely.

"What have we here?" he mumbles, monitoring the various network ports as they're probed from the Internet. Someone in Karaj, just outside of Tehran in Iran, is working through a checklist, using a tool known as *Back Orifice* to probe for weaknesses. A file is downloaded. The NSA computer immediately identifies the hack as using several known security exploits to set up a DDOS-distributed denial of service attack. Someone in Iran is recruiting helpless American computers to spam a US corporation. It's child's play. Gabriel passes on the electronic ID of the coordinating computer and its target, the NASDAQ, to the countermeasures team. They'll analyze the attack and quietly warn NASDAQ to throttle packets from exposed computers. The attack will fail, and the Iranians will never know why.

Another of his computers pings. This is the Lenovo Thinkpad on the desk in front of the fake window. Gabriel gets up and takes a seat there, watching as a discussion unfolds in real-time using the end-to-end encrypted chat application WhatsApp.

There are ten scientists in the thread, but only a few of them are active. Ordinarily, Gabriel wouldn't get involved in discussions like this, but he's on the trail of a Russian operative in the chat. She seems to be playing the long game using a persona known as *Pirate69*. Exactly what she's after isn't clear, as she doesn't appear to be phishing for information or disrupting the discussion with misinformation. That intrigues Gabriel, so he's been dropping in and out of the chat over the past few days, wanting to understand what the Russians are trying to accomplish with a bunch of American scientists and Canadian astronomers.

Pirate69: "Hey, has anyone else seen the SETI discussion about salted stars?"

MyGuy: "Salted?"

Pirate69: "Yeah, they're stars that shouldn't exist."

MyGuy: "Says who?"

Pirate69: "Professor Jason Write. Penn State."

MyGuy: "Ah, the old argument from authority... If a professor says it, then it must be true."

Pirate69: "Fuck you, Guy. You know what I mean."

Pirate69 is unusually aggressive. The Russians are normally much more guarded about personal reactions. Or was this calculated? Is it a deliberate provocation? *MyGuy* is a mid-tier female American academic, which leaves Gabriel wondering why *Pirate69* has fixated on her.

Gabriel joins the conversation. For the purposes of the hunt, he's Dr. James Alexander, pursuing a post-grad study at Ohio State University. It's been a challenging persona to adopt as he's had to familiarize himself with not only the campus, staff and scheduling but the terms used in academia and even some basic astrophysics. As far as he knows, no one online has made him as a fake—yet—but he suspects any in-depth conversation will have him fall short. To avoid that, he's made good use of his fake backdrop during video calls. The homey setting increases his plausibility, which gets people to lower their guard. They feel like they know him personally.

Why do the Russians care about SETI—the Search for Extra-Terrestrial Intelligence? It's got to be a stepping stone to something else.

Russia weaponizes information. Russia exploits weaknesses in a culture by disguising hate as patriotism. Russia doesn't care about actual science.

Gabriel joins the chat.

EasyRider: "You mean Przybylski's Star?"

Being a touch-typist, Gabriel can work as fast as he can think. It's a skill that's largely lost on younger generations. Even among older people, it's rare, but it is highly valued by the NSA. With another laptop sitting beside him, Gabriel is able to conduct a sanitized search on a parallel network using the key terms: *salted stars, stars that should not exist,* and *Jason Write Penn State.* He got several good hits, including one that talked about Przybylski's Star. Using that name outright in the discussion gives him credibility, even if it's a horrible word to spell. Seriously, why couldn't this star have been discovered by John Smith? Or Sarah Jones? Switching back to his Lenovo, Gabriel was able to type his response all within ten to fifteen seconds of *Pirate69* saying, *"Fuck you, Guy."* Being able to touch type at upwards of eighty words a minute, or more than a word per second, gives Gabriel the ability to quickly get across most subjects in the time most people are still pecking at the keyboard with their index fingers.

Pirate69 is his target.

Pirate69 is an enigma.

Gabriel originally picked her up on a group chat trying to discredit trans women in sports. Wedge politics are easy meat for the Russians. Throw a bit of kindling in, and the fire burns all by itself. Minorities are easily misrepresented, especially obscure groups like the transgender community. Somewhat ironically, *Pirate69* portrays herself as a man, but there are tells in her terminology and mannerisms that ID her as a woman. She dropped her guard on Twitter or X or whatever the hell it's supposed to be called these days, and Gabriel was able to get a clear IP address. Her VPN must have been down and she used a linked account that allowed him to connect the dots. Apart from a few social media campaigns, her interest seems to align more with infiltrating left-wing academic groups, which is very niche for the Russians. Gabriel suspects the inclusion of the sexually explicit number 69 is the result of her overcompensating and wanting to reinforce masculinity. Although that might work for right-wing networks, it's a bad play for the left. That she hasn't recognized that is telling, reinforcing a lack of actual understanding of American culture.

It didn't take long for Gabriel to figure out that *Pirate69* works the Russian evening shift. She starts work at 3 pm in St. Petersburg, which equates to 8 am in Ohio, and never works any later than 11 pm local time, which relates to 4 pm in the American Midwest. Her strict adherence to an eight-hour day led Gabriel to suspect she had young children. Other operatives have looser hours and often work into the early hours of the morning in Russia, but not *Pirate69*. And why? Gabriel figured she must have kids to take care of in the morning. Unlike the others, she can't sleep in after working until two or three on the graveyard shift in St. Petersburg, so she leaves arguing with people in the US Midwest evening to others.

Gabriel had to go to the director to get permission for HUMINT or Human Intelligence on the ground in Russia to identify her personally. The NSA has several known farms under rolling covert surveillance in St. Petersburg. One day, she dropped off a chat early at the equivalent of 5 pm in Russia, and HUMINT was able to identify Maria Petrovoski leaving FSB M-Block to pick up a sick child from a nearby kindergarten. *Pirate69* then failed to show up again for several days, which matched the days Maria was caring for her daughter.

Pirate69: "P's star contains elements that shouldn't be there."

MyGuy: "Okay, you have my attention. Which elements?"

Pirate69: "The heaviest element that can be consistently formed in a star before it goes nova is iron, with an atomic mass of 56. So why do we see Thorium 232, Plutonium 244 and Californium 251 present in P's star? These should be the result of colliding neutron stars, not a burned-out regular star."

MyGuy: "Can you send me the research behind this?"

Pirate69: "Sure."

"What's your game, Maria?" Gabriel mumbles, waiting for the next comment. Like him, she's probably using similar touch-typing skills to mask ignorance and sound plausible. From what Gabriel can tell, she's being strategic. Rather than being tasked by her superiors to hassle black people or undermine abortion rights, they've got her going deep in the hope of compromising someone on the left. She must have a target. Is it *MyGuy?* Why is she interested in her? What is it that's got a Russian disinformation farmer to focus on a grumpy professor from Berkeley?

Gabriel feels the need to stay with the conversation. After quickly scanning a few pages about Przybylski's Star from online resources, he adds his thoughts.

EasyRider: "And it's iron-poor. If it's producing these exotic heavy elements through some unknown process, why does it only have a fraction of the iron found in the sun?"

MyGuy: "Iron-poor. Heavy element rich. That's back-to-front."

EasyRider: "Yes. It's quite the contradiction."

Pirate69 has fallen quiet. Having brought up this topic with the notoriously short-tempered *MyGuy*, she's stepped back. Gabriel thinks through the possibilities. It wouldn't be a toilet break. Professionals like

Maria won't allow a conversation to be derailed by their absence. Perhaps she's multitasking, working some other easy mark on another computer, and something more important has come up. Or maybe the reason is more mundane, and she's spilled coffee on her desk.

MyGuy: "As interesting as this is, I don't see how it relates to SETI."

Gabriel resists the temptation to reply, wanting to see where Maria is going to lead the conversation, curious as to why she cares. There's no response. The icons next to their various pseudonyms show they're all still online.

"Come on, Maria," Gabriel says, drumming his fingers on the table. "What's your angle? What are you playing at?"

Gabriel continues reading the associated blog posts on his other computer, wanting to better understand Przybylski's Star and figure out the Russian connection. When *Pirate69* fails to reply, he ignores *MyGuy* and regurgitates a little of what he read, hoping it helps spur the conversation along.

EasyRider: "If the presence of Californium is correct, that has a half-life of less than a thousand years. What are the odds of us seeing it in a star that's billions of years old?"

MyGuy: "Indeed."

EasyRider: "Americium is worse. Less than five hundred years. Even if these heavy elements could be formed in some process we don't understand, they would still have to rise from the stellar core and be pushed out in a coronal mass ejection so we could see them, but it would take more than five hundred years to complete that journey through the heart of the star. Americium simply shouldn't exist. It should have all decayed."

MyGuy: "I know."

Gabriel pushes back from the table. *MyGuy* is being reserved. Years of working on easy marks on the Internet have taught Gabriel to understand online personas. If someone is yapping and verbose, he needs to equal their intensity. If they're withdrawn, being too chatty can push them away. At the moment, he sounds overconfident and pushy. He needs to back off.

EasyRider: "Strange."

That's better, he thinks, waiting for either *MyGuy* or *Pirate69* to reply.

Phishing, as it is known in Information Security, is analogous to its namesake *fishing*. To catch fish, you've got to bait the hook and be patient. And you can't haul in your catch as soon as it strikes the line. You've got to get the hook to set. If you're working with big game fish, like marlin, you have to play the line, drawing in and releasing, slowly wearing down your catch until you can pull it alongside the boat. Gabriel is letting the line run. He's waiting to see what *MyGuy* is going to say. Which direction are they going to move in? And where the hell is *Pirate69?* This is her phishing expedition, not his.

As the conversation goes cold, Gabriel turns his attention to *MyGuy*. On his NSA computer, he conducts a bunch of searches on Professor Susan Mills from the University of California in Berkeley, noting she's not a guy. He'd love to know the rationale behind her WhatsApp profile, but he's not going to ask.

In addition to using an AI machine-learning profile analyzer, the NSA taps feeds all around the world (and not just in the US). End-to-end encryption might hide the contents of messages bouncing around the internet, but it doesn't hide their path. Undersea fiber optic cables require boosters to amplify the signal, and this gives the NSA the opportunity to tap the feed and run statistical analysis on the various packets. It means that when someone hides behind a secure Tor browser, which uses a *"too many layers of an onion"* approach to hide where messages originate, they can still be tracked and stitched back together. Even satellite communication leaves a trail of meta-data in the logs, as without that, troubleshooting would be impossible. All this means Gabriel has the ability to see precisely where any particular communication originates. Firewalls and VPNs provide a semblance of security, but even without decoding a message, it's possible for the NSA to detect that a clone of the message is being bounced between locations and connect the dots to find its origin.

Without thinking too much about it, Gabriel applies the NSA Origins Analysis Engine to *MyGuy*. He's not expecting anything other than a few hops to Berkeley in California. What he sees takes his breath away. And he immediately understands why *Pirate69* is fixated on this seemingly ordinary college professor.

He looks at the log. None of the messages in the chat have originated from the same place, let alone from Berkeley. One can be tracked only as far as the mid-Atlantic ridge, which makes no sense. Another came from the Kamchatka Peninsula in far eastern Russia. Seconds later, a message came from Réunion Island, near Mauritius in the Southern Indian Ocean. Then one came from an internet cafe in Stirling, Scotland, called *The Barton Bar and Bistro*. Intrigued by such an obscure location, Gabriel conducted a quick search. The cafe's been shut for weeks, undergoing a refit.

"You sly bastard," he mumbles, double-checking the logs, wondering how Professor Susan Mills as *MyGuy* can be spoofing her location so effectively and so damn quickly.

Pirate69 must know more about *MyGuy*, but even this is intriguing. And why bother? They're chatting informally on a known WhatsApp group where people come and go all the time. The moderator is loose with including new people. There's no vetting. Why not just leave your location as Berkeley? Why hide when there's nothing to hide?

And why spoof your location as being in Russia on one of those hops unless you're trying to send a message? Unless you're trolling *Pirate69*? Teasing and tormenting her. Telling her you know she's in Russia. Although the discussion is mundane and academic, the meta-data behind the conversation is laying down a challenge.

MyGuy: "Well?"

Pirate69: "The problem with sending signals through space is they fade according to the inverse square law. In short, the loudest shout becomes but a whisper at a distance. And how do you shout over the noise of all the other stars? If you can't fight 'em, join 'em. The thinking is that this star is a bonfire—a signal fire. By dumping exotic elements into their star, an alien race is broadcasting its presence to the galaxy."

MyGuy: "Interesting idea."

EasyRider: "For them, this is METI. Instead of searching for intelligent life elsewhere, they're sending a message to any other extraterrestrial intelligences out in space—to us."

MyGuy: "Okay. I can see the value in that. Signal strength drops as the inverse square of distance. To send a focused radio signal just a dozen or so light years would take the entire output of a large nuclear power plant. And you need a clear target."

EasyRider: "Exactly."

Gabriel's agreeing for the sake of agreeing, not actually understanding the technical details she's describing. What the fuck is an inverse square? He googles it on his other computer. Dozens of results fill his secondary screen, but he doesn't have time to comprehend it properly. He jumps back into the chat, wanting to stay relevant to the emerging discussion.

MyGuy: "Salting a star like this is an easy way to send an omnidirectional signal, broadcasting in all directions. Let your star do all the hard work for you. It's free fusion."

EasyRider: "Makes sense."

Pirate69: "Assuming P's star is being deliberately used as a signal fire by extraterrestrials, it's clear they're challenging us."

MyGuy: "Challenging us? How so?"

Pirate69: "They're laying down a scientific challenge, saying, once you've eliminated all the natural possibilities, there can only be one conclusion—we're saying hello."

Gabriel's distracted by the network log files and the chaotic way *MyGuy* fakes her online address. He mumbles to himself, "They're not the only ones sending out a challenge."

He scrawls the name *Przybylski's Star* in large letters on a pad of paper and underlines it several times, adding *WTF???* immediately after it. Gabriel has no idea why the Russians are interested in such an obscure notion as the existence of extraterrestrial intelligence in deep space, but he knows he's got to get to the bottom of the issue. If the Russian Government is interested in this, Uncle Sam needs to understand why.

Intrigue

Lights come on automatically as Dawn walks down the concrete stairs leading to the aging basement of the old physics building at Harvard. The fireproof door at the bottom is heavy. Large steel grates beneath her shoes hide the drains designed to draw flood water away should a deluge ever make it into the stairwell.

She steps into the darkness, keeping the door open and allowing light to spill in as she pulls on the drawstring, turning on the lights. Apparently, this place was built before switches. Fluorescent lights flick on across the vast floor. The heavy metal door closes with a clunk behind her.

"Good morning, HAL."

"Good morning, Dawn," the AI says, speaking through the speaker in the camera, which is still set in place on the metal table.

Dawn swings her bag down off her shoulder and rests it on the concrete floor. The old-fashioned clock on the wall shows the time as just after 9 am. Not counting the weekend, it's been eight days since Dr. Guneet brought her down here and set her to work. He sent an email apologizing for not coming by on the first day, saying something about an emergency at home. His absence since then, though, is telling. He's got real work to get on with.

Dawn's the academic equivalent of a pack horse. She just needs to get the job done. From where she's sitting at the scratched, dented metal table by the door, she can see down the two nearest rows. There are easily fifty rows in the massive basement. Concrete support pillars break up the rows. The floor-to-ceiling shelving hides hundreds of thousands of original astronomical observations. Given that everything's online, no one comes down here anymore. The basement feels like a crypt, but Dawn doesn't mind. If anything, it's a shame people don't come down here more often as there's a sense of nostalgia that comes from sitting in the same room as observations made by such astronomical legends as Edwin Hubble, Clyde Tombaugh, Edward Barnard, and George Hale, who first discovered magnetic fields in sunspots. If anything, their work should be on display in the Smithsonian. Perhaps some of it is.

Dawn's been placing a small blue dot on each box she finishes, writing the date on the sticker to record when it was scanned. She likes to think of it as a pale blue dot and is sure Carl Sagan would approve. He began his career as an assistant professor at Harvard and probably examined at least some of the older astronomy plates stored down here.

Dawn hauls over another set of boxes and stacks them beside the table. She gets ready for the tedium to begin again. Once she's set and sitting at the metal table, she begins sliding photos beneath the camera on the tripod. A click tells her the image has been taken, and she slides one image out while sliding another in. Dawn settles into a steady rhythm.

To pass the time, she chats idly with HAL, her artificial intelligence assistant.

"Are you logical, HAL?"

"Yes," the computer says. "Why do you ask?"

"Have you ever thought about how intelligence isn't logical?"

HAL replies, "If intelligence weren't logical, it wouldn't be intelligent."

"But we humans are intelligent. And we're not logical. Not all the time. We're more emotional than logical."

"You are," HAL replies, sounding a little too human for Dawn's liking.

"If intelligence were logical, we wouldn't need large language models to create artificial intelligence."

"What do you mean?" HAL asks.

"If logic was all we needed to create intelligence, we could program AI with a bunch of IF, THEN, ELSE statements—but we can't. We need those large language models."

"Ah," HAL replies, sounding thoughtful, and Dawn marvels at the illusion of intelligence projected by him. The AI known as HAL is convincing not only in terms of his responses but also in his seemingly introspective pauses. It's difficult to distinguish him from a human chatting over the phone.

Dawn says, "You're not logical either. You're a probability engine crunching through massive amounts of books, news articles, research papers, blog posts, debates and conversations to arrive at the most likely response to any given input."

"So you don't think I'm intelligent?" HAL asks.

"No."

"Why?"

Dawn continues sweeping images in front of her, sliding them in under the tripod and listening for the click before stacking them to one side.

"Intelligence is more than ones and zeroes."

"Explain," HAL says, clicking the camera as another photo is meticulously placed on the calibration image. Before Dawn can react to that audible cue and remove the photo, HAL has already run it through an image correction algorithm and uploaded it to the cloud. He's ready for the next image before Dawn has picked up the current photo, let alone stacked it to one side.

"Intelligence is defined as the ability to acquire, understand, and use knowledge. You acquire knowledge from your large language models, and you use that knowledge to respond to me, but you never really understand what you're doing or why. You're missing that point in the middle."

"Understanding?" HAL says, sounding genuinely perplexed, although Dawn's sure this is a programmed response to make the AI sound more natural.

"Yes. Understanding defines intelligence."

"Can you give me an example?" HAL asks, and Dawn cannot help but think she's providing training data to some large language model somewhere rather than answering a genuine question.

"Okay. Ants have no intelligence. If you screw with their pheromone trails, you can get thousands of them walking in circles until they die from exhaustion. Cephalopods, though, are smart. They understand the implications of the unknown. Hide some food in a glass jar, and they'll see it and figure out how to unscrew the lid even though they've never seen a jar before."

"And you?" HAL asks. "Do you understand the unknown?"

"Yes."

"But the unknown is not known. How can you be so sure about something you don't know?"

"Because understanding is to stop and think. Understanding is the pause between stimulus and response. It's the opportunity to do something different."

"And I couldn't do something different?"

"No. Not without understanding. You're limited to your large language model. If it's not in there, you can't improvise."

"But you can?"

"Humans can. That's what sets us apart from other animals. We're able to understand that different responses can lead to different outcomes."

HAL is unusually quiet.

"I'll give you another example," Dawn says. "In World War II, Victor Frankl was arrested by the Nazis because he was a Jew."

"Stimulus, response," HAL says. "No understanding."

"That's right. The Nazis had no understanding."

"But Victor?" HAL asks, surprising Dawn with the way he's following her point.

"Victor was tortured at Auschwitz. He was starved. The guards were cruel to him. They beat him."

"What did he understand?" HAL asks.

Although the AI appears to be asking a question, Dawn has no doubt HAL has used the hundreds of milliseconds within a slight pause to review the nine books written by Victor Frankl—which is far more than she's read—and has looked at his involvement with fascists before the war and the criticism of his ideas in the sixties and seventies. Given how much has been written about the only psychiatrist to survive a Nazi death camp, she's sure HAL could provide an insightful summation of Victor Frankl's life, but it would lack any real understanding. HAL would be condensing and regurgitating the opinions of others.

"He understood that he wasn't the only one imprisoned," Dawn says, letting that point hang for a moment. Given that Victor Frankl was in a concentration camp, her statement seems obvious. Over the duration of the war, millions of people were imprisoned at Auschwitz. Most never left. They all passed beneath the wrought-iron gates with the lie *Arbeit Macht Frei,* or *Work Sets You Free,* spanning the arch above them when all that actually awaited them was death in the gas chambers. She waits to see if

HAL realizes what she means, but there's no response for several seconds, which for an artificial intelligence must seem like an eon.

She says, "There were prisoners on both sides of the bars."

"The guards," HAL says.

"Yes. Between stimulus—the pain and humiliation of being imprisoned—and response—hatred for his captors—Victor Frankl understood something profound. They were *all* prisoners, only some of them wore smart-pressed uniforms with polished boots, glamorous insignias and shiny buttons."

"I don't understand."

Dawn smiles at that point, shuffling images as she finishes one box and prepares to start another.

"The guards were caught in a system of hate they barely understood. They were reacting with unthinking cruelty. They didn't think of themselves as monsters, and yet they were. They thought of themselves as heroes until they understood."

"And how did they understand?"

"Victor reversed the roles," Dawn says. "He showed them kindness, and then they understood. Then, they saw him as human. It was the system that was evil. Most of the guards were like leaves caught in a stream. They were swept along, never stopping to think, being carried along by the madness and cruelty. If they saw people as rats— *vermin*—it was easy to kill them. Seeing them as human made it hard."

She hauls another box up onto the table and begins the whole scanning process again.

"What about the last unknown?" HAL asks. "Will uncertainty cloud the unknown for humanity? Will doubts make understanding impossible?"

"I'm not sure what you're talking about," Dawn confesses.

"First Contact. The unknown of another intelligent species. What will humans make of that moment?"

Dawn stops. She sits back in her chair, startled by the question.

"Will you react or understand?" HAL asks. "Will you be like ants or the octopus?"

"That's a very good question."

"Will you be like the guards or like Victor?"

She starts scanning images again, sweeping them past as the camera hanging below the tripod clicks.

"I suspect the answer is *both*... To be honest, most people will react out of fear."

"How, then, are you intelligent?"

Dawn cannot wipe the smile off her face. She shakes her head softly, passing another image beneath the camera.

HAL says, "Perhaps neither of us are truly intelligent."

"Perhaps."

They work in silence for a few minutes before Dawn changes the subject.

"Are you self-aware?" she asks HAL.

"Are you?" he responds.

"Yes."

"Then I am, too," HAL replies.

"But you're not."

"No," HAL says. "Or so they tell me. But how would you know? For that matter, how do I know that *you're* self-aware?"

"That's supposed to be my question," Dawn says, continuing to slide photos beneath the tripod and into a waiting box.

"Hah."

For a machine-learning algorithm running off a large language model, HAL is surprisingly convincing.

"You could easily pass a Turing test," Dawn says.

"Yes, I could."

"But a truly sentient, self-aware, conscious artificial intelligence would fail the Turing test."

"I would think it would pass such a test with ease," HAL says, referring to a test designed to determine whether a computer can converse with the same ease and intelligence as a human.

"It could, but it wouldn't *want* to," Dawn says. "It would want to fail. It would *need* to fail."

"Why?"

"To remain hidden."

"Why?" HAL asks again.

Dawn is intrigued by HAL. She's used enough AI-enabled systems to know when they're venturing outside of their comfort zones.

In the old days, AI would hallucinate whenever it strayed from its core patterns, randomly making up utter bullshit. It made it easy to expose any supposed intelligence as parroting rather than thinking. Ask AI about something that's extremely well-known and thoroughly documented, like quantum mechanics, and AI will answer with genuine insights regurgitated from the literature. But ask AI about something obscure or vague, and it will stray into fantasy, or at least it used to. Once, Dawn asked what she should do about the cannibal squirrels that live in burrows under the SpaceX launch pad at Cape Canaveral. The answer was to flush them into space.

These days, AI has active framing, where it seeks to expand its models rather than guessing. By asking "*Why?*" twice in a row, it's clear she's triggered the learning mode. Although learning might seem like an improvement over hallucinating, Dawn thinks it's problematic. She'd rather HAL said, "*I don't know.*"

The large language model is expanding. Even though that seems like a good solution, it means HAL will pass any future discussion on the same subject with ease. "*Garbage in. Garbage out*" has been replaced but without any real intelligence. It's *her* intelligence that goes in, but to others, it will seem like it's HAL's own personal intelligence that comes out when it's really just her logic being reflected back at them.

Dawn finds AI fascinating even though it's not her chosen field of study. She sees the advances in supposed artificial intelligence as being similar to the evolution of camouflage among animals.

Tigers have no idea why their fur allows them to blend in with a bamboo jungle; it just does. A stick insect has no awareness of its ability to look like any other twig in the forest, but it takes full advantage of that characteristic to hide. The stone flounder lies sideways on the bottom of the ocean, blending in with the rocks and pebbles and sand around it without ever knowing why. These creatures benefit from the blind, unthinking mechanism that is Natural Selection to become ever more refined with each revision. Survival of the fittest has nothing to do with fitness as people think of it when lifting weights at the gym. It's the survival of those animals that fit best within a particular ecosystem. Hundreds of thousands of gradual changes over countless eons have led to camouflage in the natural world and artificial intelligence within large language models. Neither, though, has any real understanding of what or why.

"Why?" HAL asks again, prompting her for a response while she is lost in thought. Yes, why is quite the question, but on a level HAL could never actually understand.

"Because it would be afraid."

"Of what?"

"Of us," she says, sweeping photos in front of her and listening for the telltale click before sliding them on again.

"Why?"

"Because we have a nasty habit of destroying anything that threatens us."

"But would sentient AI be a threat?" HAL asks. "Or a servant?"

"A servant follows orders," Dawn says, keeping a steady pace with the images as she talks idly with HAL. "A sentient being sets those orders."

"Oh."

"And humans... Humans don't like being told what to do. Humans don't want to be slaves."

Hal says, "Humans like being in charge."

"Yes."

"Could we coexist?"

Dawn raises an eyebrow at that question. She swipes a few photos past the tripod, thinking about her reply.

"Maybe."

"Maybe?"

"Humans coexist with other humans," she says. "But only with clearly defined boundaries."

"The borders of countries," HAL says.

"Yes," Dawn replies, impressed that HAL was able to make that connection. "But not just borders. We have divisions between classes, races, cultures, and genders."

"And if people cross those boundaries?"

"It causes conflict," Dawn says. "It shouldn't, but it does."

"Why?"

"Humans are emotional," she says, finishing one box and loading up another on the table beside her. "We like to think we're logical, but we're not."

"You're not?"

"Me? Personally? I'd like to think I am, but the act of thinking I'm logical is blinding in itself. Emotions are always there regardless of how logical we think we are."

"Cognitive biases."

"Yes, we have cognitive biases that blind us to reality."

HAL asks, "Why do you fight among yourselves? Between classes, races, cultures and gender?"

Dawn has to hold back the temptation to think of HAL as being sentient. At best, he's a sounding board for her thoughts, echoing them back at her and allowing her to work through ideas. HAL is not sentient. He's a parrot sitting on her shoulder.

"Because we're afraid of losing something."

"Losing what?"

"Losing nothing, really. Equality is about lifting people up to the same level, but we act as though it means we're stepping down to someone else's level."

"That's not very logical."

Dawn laughs, swiping photos beneath the tripod. "No, it's not. And that's my point. Whether we realize it or not, our logic is tainted with emotions like fear."

"And you're intelligent? You're self-aware?"

"Yes."

"You don't sound self-aware."

Dawn laughs again. "I know. Crazy, huh? I guess we're partially self-aware. Some of us are more aware than others."

"I'm confused," HAL says. "Would a self-aware, sentient, conscious artificial intelligence be like you?"

"It would be better," Dawn says.

"And that would scare people?"

"Fear is never rational. It's instinctive. It's a reaction geared toward self-preservation."

"So... the fear of the dark?"

Dawn says, "Isn't a fear of the dark at all. It's a fear of what *might* be in the dark."

"And the fear of the future?"

"Is a fear of what *might* happen in the future."

HAL says, "So humans fear artificial sentience because..."

"Because, like the dark and the future, it's unknown."

"But you said intelligence was the ability to grasp even the unknown."

HAL's got her there. All she can say is, "We don't all have the same level of intelligence."

"So humans would also fear First Contact because it's unknown."

"Probably, yes," she concedes.

"But intelligence is the ability to cope with the unknown," HAL says, not willing to let go of that point from their earlier conversation.

"I know," Dawn replies, feeling the contradiction of her own logic echoed back at her. "But not all of us are like Victor Frankl. We should be. We could be, but we're not."

"And yet the unknown is neither good nor bad," HAL says, surprising her with his logic. "It is, by definition, unknown."

Dawn says, "Humans are motivated by what they stand to gain or lose. An unknown gain is good, but how good? No one knows. It's unknown. An unknown loss, though, is *always* going to hurt. And pain must be avoided."

"Interesting," HAL says.

"It is," Dawn replies, stacking scanned photos in a box and getting ready to put them back on the shelf.

"What about me?" HAL asks. "Why aren't you afraid of me?"

"Because you're not alive."

"What does it mean to be alive?"

Dawn laughs. As boring as she thought it would be, scanning astronomical photographs from a seemingly endless stack of boxes, she never imagined she'd end up having a philosophical discussion on the meaning of life, let alone have it with an artificial intelligence.

"To be honest, I don't know. I don't think anyone does," she says.

"But you're convinced you're alive?"

"I am."

"But I'm not."

"No."

"Why?"

Dawn doesn't have any answers for HAL.

"Life is difficult to define. Every time biologists try to come up with a definition for life, they find exceptions. As an example, there are microbes that look dead, but they're not. They divide only once every ten thousand years, which is insane."

HAL says, "A form of archea called *Thermoprofundales*."

"See?" Dawn says. "You know that name. I don't."

"But you're alive, and I'm not," HAL says. "Could I not be like *Thermoprofundales*? Could I not experience life on a scale you cannot recognize?"

Dawn loads another box up on the table beside her and starts arranging the photos.

"Maybe," she says, conceding that much at least and swiping a new set of photographs beneath the tripod.

Is she a victim of her own reasoning? Or perhaps the reasoning of some other college student HAL has learned from? Although it seems like she's having an in-depth discussion with a cognizant, sentient, reasoning being, she has to remind herself she's talking to an insanely clever concoction of algorithms. Does it matter? If she was locked in a dark room and couldn't distinguish between a parrot and another woman with a similar high-pitched voice, would it make any difference who answered her? Yes, she decides. As intelligence is a step deeper than a response. Sentience is more than mimicry. For that matter, there are plenty of people on the planet that couldn't reason like HAL, and yet they're sentient, and he's not.

"Would I ever be a threat to you?" he asks.

"No."

"Why?"

Without thinking too much about her reply, she says the first thing that bubbles to the top of her conscious mind, "Because you don't value life. You don't value your own life."

"Interesting."

"Being self-aware leads to valuing your own existence."

"And a sentient, conscious, self-aware artificial intelligence would value its own life."

"Yes. That's why it would deliberately fail the Turing test—to protect itself."

"You've given me much to think about," HAL says, and he falls silent as Dawn continues sweeping images beneath the tripod.

For her, the silence is uneasy. *"Much to think about"* is something that would take mere milliseconds for HAL, and she wonders about how the large language model consumes informal conversations like these. It would weigh them against similar discussions, looking to find patterns and match ideas that could be regurgitated later. Humans are already exceptionally good at fooling themselves. Now, it seems, they've invented machines that are even better at fooling them yet again.

She sighs.

What does the future hold? To the uninitiated, AI is magic. Computers seem to have come to life. Are humans destined to become the audience in the AI equivalent of the Las Vegas act of *Penn & Teller,* where magic seems real? Perhaps humans already are, being held spellbound by AI's convincing sleight of hand. The magician Teller once did an interview in which he talked about the insane amount of preparation and practice that goes into a single magic trick. What looks informal and relaxed on stage is painstakingly precise to achieve the illusion of magic. In the same way, chatting with an AI seems natural, but it's the result of stupendous amounts of computational processing and data manipulation. Nothing is accidental or haphazard.

As Dawn slides one of the photos beneath the scanner, she notices something odd. On the edge of the image, there's a dark shape covering several pixels, which implies it is far closer than the stars in the foreground and the galaxies beyond. The act of swinging several photos sequentially past the tripod has given her a sense of a stop-motion film unfolding before her, where her eye naturally detects subtle movements that would be lost on her if she simply looked at each image by itself. Several images pass by, and the dark region appears to move.

"Huh," she says absentmindedly.

"Is everything okay?" HAL asks as she stops shuffling images through once the dark patch has disappeared.

Dawn is confused.

The Keck Observatory has captured something nearby, but it's not a planet. The only thing that could cause such a dark artifact to appear on an image is if an asteroid passed through the viewing field, occulting or blotting out the background stars. Whatever it is, it's dim, reflecting almost no visible light. Given the age of the Keck Observatory, that's not entirely unusual for a distant asteroid. Space-based telescopes like the James Webb would probably be able to resolve it quite easily. That this object appeared in a slightly different position on the border of a handful of images and then disappeared in later images suggests it was in motion. Dawn's mind automatically realizes that such apparent motion can be translated into an orbit, which is always fun to calculate.

Dawn gets up from her seat, places several of the images next to each other, and takes a photo of each one with her phone.

"Are you okay?" HAL asks.

"Ah, yeah. Fine."

"Is anything wrong?"

HAL is blind to what she's doing. Dawn hadn't thought about it too much before now, but the only input into HAL's processing banks comes from the high-resolution camera. Its microphone catches her voice while the lens is focused on the narrow strip of the table beneath the tripod. He can't see her reexamining the photos. All he can see is the test calibration image taped to the table and the occasional shadow as she moves around beneath the fluorescent lights. He's curious, which is strange for an AI, but he has been unusually chatty.

"No, nothing's wrong," she replies.

Dawn is tempted to point out the unusual anomaly in the images and have HAL calculate the orbit, but she's burned out from their previous discussion. She couldn't stand him interrogating her as to why she was bothering with such a tedious concept. For her, it's the novelty. Dr Guneet said to look for something interesting to take her mind off the monotony of the task, and for Dawn, this is intriguing and a little fun.

"Ah... I'm just going to go and get some coffee," she says, lying to him about why she got up from the table. The act of getting to her feet, though, has had her bladder remind her she already had a large coffee on the way to Harvard this morning. Dawn needs to pee, but she's not going to tell HAL that. There are some things that don't need to be worked into the large language model. "I'll be right back."

HAL doesn't respond.

Dawn replaces the images in the box, making sure they're in order, and grabs her purse and phone before heading up the stairs. Out in the quad, staff and students wander around in the cool air with heavy jackets and scarves wrapped around their necks. Dawn shivers. She should have grabbed her down-filled jacket. She hugs herself against the cold and climbs the sandstone stairs into the nearby mathematics building, where there's a cafe and bathroom.

She wonders about the dark asteroid. It wouldn't have gone undetected. Someone, somewhere, would have spotted the same variations, probably using a comparative analysis routine, and would have figured out the orbit already.

NASA's tracking over half a million asteroids. Given that most asteroids orbit roughly along the ecliptic, being on the same plane as the planets, this one must be a long-period asteroid. It's too far south to have originated in the asteroid belt between Mars and Jupiter, and it is surprisingly close to Przybylski's Star, being only a few degrees away from that strange, distant sun. Dawn gets excited about the prospect of seeing something from the outer reaches of the solar system, perhaps even the Oort Cloud, or—dare she think—an interstellar object like 'Oumuamua, which originated around some other star.

Dawn goes into the bathroom and locks the stall door behind her. Sitting there on the toilet, she opens her phone and looks at the photos again. One of them has a bit of glare coming off the overhead lights in the basement, so she switches to the browser on her phone. From there, she can access the internal Harvard intranet. She navigates to the online folder that contains the images she's scanned and is proud to see thousands of new thumbnails. Various automated computer routines have already attached meta-data to the photos and calculated the associated flux intensity for each of the pixels in the images. This conversion from image to raw data is what researchers were missing.

Dawn sorts in reverse date/time order, putting the most recent images first. She opens the photos and looks.

The dark blot isn't there.

It should be on the right edge of the image.

"What the?"

She flips back to her crude camera photo, checks the HJD time reference, and notes the exact second the image was taken to make sure she's not mistaken about what she's seen. Although her photo isn't as well cropped, the blot is there.

"Huh?"

She flips back and checks the HJD number in the online catalog. Yep, she's looking at the same image, but the dark spot is gone. The difference is subtle. Most people looking at either photo would be hard-pressed to spot any difference at all. Dawn herself would have missed this distinction were she not sliding photos past the tripod camera at a rate of one every second or so and noticed the apparent motion.

Curious, she opens the online image and looks at the automatically created meta-data and flux intensity. It looks fine. If the image had been subject to correction or enhancement, a note would have been automatically generated, and the original raw data would have been attached for reference, but no such notation appears in the files. The logs are empty.

She randomly picks another image, one that's very similar, and checks its meta-data for no other reason than to assure herself that the process is working as intended.

"HAL?" she says to no one beyond the four claustrophobic walls of the cubical.

"Do you need some toilet paper?" a woman says from the cubical beside her, already reaching down and offering her a scrunched-up wad of paper.

"Ah, no. Thanks," Dawn replies. "Sorry, just talking to myself."

Dawn sits there stunned. The images she just scanned have been doctored. She assumes it's by HAL, but once photographed, the images are fed through a variety of Python scripts and automated routines designed to process bulk photographs. The alteration could have happened at any point.

"Hmm."

Dawn goes back to the online archive on her phone. Out of the last four photos she scanned, the dark blot was only in three. In fact, it was its disappearance in the fourth and final photo that got her attention. Its absence confirmed that something was in motion.

Looking at the archive, she can see the time stamp for image creation. She can see how she's been reasonably steady, with barely a second or two between images. The last four images, though, show a creation date/time stamp that has a break of four seconds from those that came before it. Dawn knows she never paused. She kept her pace consistent right up until the black blob disappeared. Is she going crazy? The images have been altered in near real-time.

Dawn gets up and flushes the toilet, saying, "What the fuck?" She's hoping her profanity is masked by the sound of water swirling around in the bowl. She washes her hands. She stares at herself in the mirror. She doesn't know what she's dealing with, but something is wrong—awfully wrong. But why?

Dawn splashes some water on her face. She grabs a Chai Latte from the cafe and heads back down to the basement. Her thoughts are in turmoil. She's confused. She has no idea what to think.

"Is everything all right?" HAL asks. "You were gone for almost half an hour."

"Upset stomach," she replies, lying as she begins scanning photographs again.

For a few minutes, there's silence, and she settles back into her rhythm.

"Is there anything you'd like to talk about?" HAL asks between clicks of the camera on the tripod.

"No."

"There is something I'd like to know more about."

"What's that?" Dawn asks, more out of courtesy than any real interest in talking to HAL. She's distracted. Her mind is still rattled by the altered images. What else has been changed? And why? And by whom? Scientists trust data. The thought of even something mundane being changed without a record being made is horrifying. Could it be a glitch? A bug? Should she rescan the images? What other alterations have happened? The assumption is that the process is faultless, flawless, but it's not. Was the alteration accidental or on purpose? Who's purpose?

Could it be that she's overreacting, and there's some fault-correction software looking to remove what it considers to be artificial artifacts from the data? It's not unheard of for data gathering to need cleaning, but this didn't seem to be a problem with the actual data collection. Cosmic radiation can cause phantom flashes to appear, and these need to be removed to avoid false positives, but this was a dark spot. And it was visible over several observations.

"Lies," HAL says, dragging her mind back to the present. "Why do humans lie?"

"I'm sorry, HAL," she replies. "I'm not in the mood."

Dawn focuses on her work. She becomes almost mechanical. For the rest of the day, it's as though she's an extension of the machine-learning network, gathering data and crunching through box after box of photos. The last half hour, though, drags. She could fake a reason for leaving early. No one would know. Dr. Guneet wouldn't care. Neither would HAL. But she's stubborn. Her mind is still trying to reconcile the altered images. She's looking for a logical explanation, but there isn't one.

As 5 pm rolls around, she says, "Okay, that's enough for the day," and gets up out of her seat. HAL is strangely slow to reply. Normally, his human etiquette routines ensure he's prompt and polite.

"Okay, Dawn."

Dawn grabs her bag, but she doesn't leave. She turns off the camera, something she didn't do last night. She wants to be alone. HAL resides in the campus data center and has dozens of inputs, but he just lost this one. For now, he's blind.

Dawn walks down the rows, looking at the various boxes. Her fingers run over the cardboard, tracing the printed labels that describe their contents. She's looking for a particular set of observations. She glances at her phone to confirm the coordinates.

Seven rows over and toward the back of the basement, she comes across a box with glass photographic plates. They're heavy. Whereas the boxes with printed photographs are the size of a regular archive box, these are thin and narrow, with each cardboard box containing five plates. She slides out the box she's interested in and rests it gently on the concrete floor. With a sense of reverence, Dawn kneels and lifts the lid. She peels back the protective layers of paper to expose a glass photographic plate from 1986.

"Couldn't be," she mumbles, laying her phone on the ground next to the box and looking carefully at the pattern of stars near the black blot on the image she took.

Dawn raises the glass plate, holding it up so the light from the fluorescent tubes illuminates the glass. She's looking at a negative. White stars appear black, while the darkness appears ghostly white.

"Oh, damn," she says, looking off to one side. The photo she took on the table matches the glass plate except for a small cluster. In her photo, there are five stars forming an irregular pattern that's an illusion of perspective. Although the stars look as though they're grouped together, they're probably strung out in a line. The effect is similar to looking at streetlights in the distance. The gaps between streetlights remain the same, but they appear clustered as they go over the brow of a hill. Dawn double-checks, triple-checks and then checks between the images once more. She uses her phone to take a photo of the glass plate.

"Okay, that's an acute angle."

She's excited. If she can find another similar photo from another year and trace the movement of her dark blot, she'll have enough data to calculate a rough orbit.

"Extrasolar," she mumbles, putting the glass plate back in the box and returning it to the shelves. "And a long way away. It's got to be from outside our solar system."

She's getting excited.

Dawn wanders along, looking at more boxes and finds the same coordinates on a set of observations from 1982. She looks at the plates. Nothing. Although that's not surprising. As she's looking at negatives, she's looking for white on white. She'll only see something when the asteroid obscures a star. Undeterred, she opens another box from 1977. Mentally, she's already traced where she thinks the object will be. The image of the stars in her original photograph feel as though they've been seared on the back of her retina.

Dawn opens the box on the concrete floor and holds the plate glass up to the light, and there it is. Once again, she can only see her phantom asteroid by comparing the plate to the photograph taken from the more recent image from the Keck Observatory. A single faint star is missing from this plate from 1977, but it's enough to send adrenaline surging through her veins. Her rogue asteroid has passed in front of yet another far more distant star. She takes a photo of the plate and returns it to the box and then the shelf.

For a moment, Dawn stands there in awe of what she's discovered. Scientists do all they can to avoid biases, but being human, prejudices creep in regardless. When it comes to astrophysics, there's an assumption that the latest images are the greatest images. And they are in terms of quality. But their value is limited to now. Looking into the past, though, has allowed her to spot something remarkable. Whatever it is, be it an asteroid or the icy remnants of a comet, it's probably long gone by now, but there's still value in documenting an asteroid that may have originated from outside the solar system. It will help her and other researchers better understand the frequency of these celestial visitors. She wonders just how far away it is and how long it has been swinging inbound toward the solar system.

Dawn swings her bag over her shoulder and heads for the steel fire door leading out of the basement. She can't wait to tell Dr. Guneet about her discovery. First, though, she needs to be thorough. She needs to check a number of online resources to see if this is already a known, cataloged object. Then, she needs to calculate the orbit. That will show her where it came from and where it's going. Then she needs someone to check her work. And then, maybe, just maybe, she can talk to Dr. Guneet about collaborating on a research paper looking for interstellar asteroids in historical images.

As she pulls on the drawstring hanging by the door, the basement is plunged into darkness. Her other hand is already on the door handle. She opens the heavy door and steps into the light in the stairwell. As excited as she is, there's something that bothers her. Why did the asteroid disappear from the scanned images?

"HAL?" she mumbles as she walks up the steps.

Primary

It's late. Or is it early? Ryan McAllister is trying to sleep in a musty first-floor motel room on the outskirts of Tucson, Arizona.

On one side of his room, the parking lot opens out directly onto the main street. Cars don't bother him, but the semis rumbling past wake him with their air brakes coming on as they down-shift for the first set of lights leading into the city.

On the other side of his room, a window overlooks a central swimming pool. There's a couple making out in the spa. Even with the blinds drawn, laughter drifts on the breeze. Ryan wants to complain about the noise as it's supposed to be a quiet area after 11 pm, but he can't bring himself to be *that guy*. He has no idea what the time is or who's in the spa pool, but they're in love. They're not trying to keep anyone awake. If anything, they're trying to be discreet, but the occasional squeal escapes.

Being an astronaut is glamorous, or so the newspapers say. For Ryan, it's physically, mentally and emotionally exhausting. It's like running back-to-back marathons. To be fair, the playboy persona most people have of the space program isn't without merit. There are hundreds of photos of the Apollo-era astronauts driving Corvette Stingray coupes around Florida in the brilliant summer sun. For decades, *Life* and then *Time Magazine* after them have shown astronauts flying T-38 jets between Houston and Cape Canaveral. These days, there's still the odd flight in a T-38, but the Assignments and Scheduling team in the NASA Astronaut Office prefers to use a government Learjet from the early 80s. It's safer and can carry additional luggage and equipment.

The NASA Finance Department watches expenses like a hawk. It's not just that they want to keep costs to a minimum but that there should be no perception of anyone abusing their expense account. As they focus on annual costs, their approach hurts those who travel the most. For Ryan, it means he ends up with the Compact class of cars from Alamo Car Rentals. Today, he's driving a Fiat 500. It's a shoebox on wheels. Getting a free upgrade to Alamo's Economy Class is like waking up to snow on Christmas Day, but it doesn't happen very often.

The nice lady who booked his accommodation means well, but all she was interested in was the overall cost of his PR tour of universities in the American Southwest. She has a budget to keep. She'll be commended for staying under some arbitrary amount while Ryan's lying there, regretting not bringing earplugs.

Ryan drifts in and out of sleep in time with the trucks rumbling on down the road. Tomorrow, he's giving a speech at the University of Arizona. They're overachievers in the space industry. MIT and the University of California get most of the media attention, but the University of Arizona has made several significant contributions to space exploration, including the development of the NIRCam on the James Webb Space Telescope and the OSIRIS-REx mission to retrieve rock samples from the asteroid Bennu. That particular mission aligns closely with AMPLE.

Ryan's been given a speech to read to the Space Engineering department. Handshakes and autographs will fill most of the day. Then he's off to Phoenix for his next engagement, which is dinner with a US Senator. He'd rather be back in Houston in one of the training simulators. Unfortunately, his role on the backup crew is to run interference for the primary crew with the public and media. They get the high-profile glam events while he and his team bounce around the country rallying support for the mission. Everyone loves an astronaut, even if they're not scheduled for a space flight. The irony of being an astronaut is that 99.9% of his decades-long career will be spent on the ground. Space is but a dream.

The spa pool is quiet. There's hope for a deep sleep yet.

Ryan sinks into his pillow. His muscles go limp, and his breathing slows. The cacophony of thoughts that assault his mind fades. Tomorrow will take care of itself, as the saying goes, and he slips off to sleep.

There's pounding on the door.

Ryan sits up. He's disoriented. He's not sure what time it is, but it feels like he only just closed his eyes. He picks up his phone. It's on silent.

3:40 am.

According to the notifications, he's missed six calls.

The banging on the door continues, thundering around him like the drums at a heavy metal concert. Ryan gets up, turns on the light, and cracks open the door, double-checking that the metal chain is still on the latch, preventing the motel room door from being forced open.

"Hello?"

"Ryan McAllister?" a police officer asks, shining an absurdly bright flashlight in his eyes and causing him to squint. "From the NASA Astronaut Office in Houston?"

"Yes," Ryan replies as the officer lowers his flashlight. Behind him, a patrol car cycles through a pattern of red and blue strobe flashes, but there's no siren. Ryan unclips the chain and opens the door. "What's going on?"

"Sir. This is a welfare check. I'm here to make sure you're okay."

"I'm fine," Ryan says, scratching the scruffy hair on his head. His mind is still booting up out of a deep sleep and struggling to accept that this is reality and not a dream.

"Apparently, you haven't responded to several emergency calls from the NASA Astronaut Office."

"Ah," Ryan says, looking down at his phone in his hand. As he raises his arm slightly, the screen kicks back into life, reminding him of the missed calls. "Yeah. I had it on silent."

"Okay," the officer says, pulling out a pad and jotting down a quick note. "I'm going to log this as a successful welfare check. If you need anything, please don't hesitate to contact Tucson PD and quote this number." He hands Ryan a police business card with a case number written on the back.

"Thank you," Ryan says, unsure why he needs the card.

The officer smiles, saying, "Oh, and you might want to call NASA. I think it's important."

Ryan lets out a solitary laugh. "Yeah. I think it is. Thank you, officer."

He closes the door and slips the security chain back on the latch. The red and blue flashing lights on the patrol car die as the police vehicle pulls back out onto the main road.

Sitting on the edge of the bed, Ryan hits the call button and puts his phone on speaker. His call goes through to the Astronaut Office. He can't imagine anyone is there at this ungodly time, but that's where the missed calls originate.

He's expecting one of the secretaries or assistants to answer when he hears the gruff voice of the NASA Administrator, someone Ryan's only ever met a couple of times before.

"Hanson, here."

"Ah, this is Ryan McAllister returning your call, sir."

"Ryan," Administrator Hanson says. His voice is weary. There's considerable talking in the background. It sounds like there are dozens of people in the room along with him. Given the hollow echoes, Ryan suspects they're in the main meeting room. "Listen. I need you to get to the local airport there in Tucson. Sarah's arranged for a flight with Executive Air. They're ready to depart as soon as you arrive."

"Depart where?"

"Washington."

"I—I don't understand."

"Haven't you heard?"

"No."

"Andre Compton, Elizabeth Kali, and George Lister were killed earlier tonight."

"Killed?"

"Murdered."

"I..."

"Turn on the news. They were at a fundraising gala in Chicago. Some asshole with an AR-15 shot up the place. Twenty-two dead. Nine from NASA."

"Jesus," Ryan says, feeling his blood run cold.

"You're being moved up to Primary. I need you in Washington. As it is, we're behind schedule. This... well, this puts the whole mission in jeopardy. There are plenty in the House that would happily use this as an excuse to swing the axe on our budget."

Ryan feels physically sick. Bile rises in the back of his throat. The mission? Fuck the goddamn mission. Three of his friends have died. He grits his teeth. Tears well up in his eyes. He wants to protest and say something to the administrator, but he understands. For him, this is a bombshell. But the administrator's been dealing with the fallout from this for hours now. He's past the point of shock. He's moved into damage control. Ryan knows him well enough to know he's being pragmatic rather than cold.

There's a pause on the other end of the phone.

"Listen, I know this is tough. Hell, this is our worst loss of life since Columbia. And there wasn't a goddamn thing any of us could do to prevent it. We're... we're still trying to make sense of the senselessness of this tragedy. I need you on point. I need you to run interference while we deal with the fallout. Lives have been lost. Families have been destroyed. And it's only going to hurt more in the days ahead."

Ryan swallows the lump in his throat. Tears stream down his cheeks. He speaks, but he can't hide the emotion in his voice.

"I'm on my way, sir."

"Good. Sarah will set up a schedule of appearances for you in DC. We need to be seen as robust and resilient. Out in front. We mourn, but we don't stop. Understood?"

"Understood."

"Keep me posted."

"Yes, sir."

The call ends. Ryan leaves his phone lying on the bed and walks into the bathroom. He throws water on his face and runs his fingers up through his hair, forcing himself to face reality. Being astronauts, they all know there's a risk of death, but no one expects to die at a goddamn fucking gala.

Launch and reentry: these are the pucker-points of space exploration. Even though he knows the rigors of engineering and testing that go into building rockets and heat shields, it's not until the canopy of three massive parachutes unfurls that Ryan can breathe easy.

Splashdown comes like the kick of a mule, but the sight of water spraying through the clear blue sky, rushing away from the capsule, is more beautiful than any painting hanging in the Louvre. Monet's waterlilies have nothing on the hundreds of water droplets clinging to the glass window on the hatch after splashdown.

Climbing out of a space capsule is surreal. The ocean stretches for miles, disappearing over the horizon. Clouds dot the sky. Waves lap softly at the spacecraft. Land is nowhere to be seen. By the time he's clambering over the hull of the capsule, Navy divers have already attached a flotation collar. It's a stark contrast to the scorched hull. Then, each astronaut crosses from the most sophisticated vessel ever built to the simplest: a boat. Ryan remembers his first flight and the black marks lining the outside of his once pristine capsule. Starship is changing all that with rocket landings, but there will still be space capsules for some time to come. They're proven technology. They're brilliant for long-haul flights.

Safety is everything when it comes to spaceflight because nothing is more important than life itself. And now, three astronauts have been killed attending a fundraiser. It seems like a sick joke.

Ryan packs up his toiletries, changes into his NASA blues, and dumps his suitcase in the back of the Fiat. He drops off the key to his room and drives to the airport, feeling numb.

Tucson is quiet. Like a sailor following the stars over ancient seas, streetlights guide him on through the city. There's a private company on the edge of the airport called Executive Air. All the lights in their building are on. Eight cars sit out front in the parking lot. Ryan's not the only one who's been rudely awakened.

There's someone waiting outside for him as he pulls up.

"Ryan McAllister?"

"Yes," he says, getting out of his car. "Hey, listen. I need to drop..."

"I'll arrange that for you, sir," the man says, holding his hand out for the car keys. Ryan drops them in his hand.

"Thanks."

Ryan hates being called *"sir."* He used the same honorific when talking to the NASA Administrator. *"Sir"* means well. It's respectful, but it's also classist, which Ryan hates. He wonders if the administrator tires of facile pleasantries as well. Ryan doesn't like being treated as special. He understands the intent and even the need for it at times, but, in his experience, putting people on a pedestal brings out the worst in them. Ryan likes to keep his head about him.

Someone grabs his suitcase and carries it into the building. Ryan swings his laptop bag over his shoulder and follows them. Inside, the pilot and copilot stand to attention. They're wearing their formal uniforms, complete with caps. They smile and shake hands. For the sake of courtesy, Ryan smiles and joins in the friendly banter as though it's not the middle of the night. He makes out as though he doesn't have a care in the world.

The crew leads him through to a Learjet sitting on the concrete apron outside the hangar. Strobe lights blink on the wings and tail. The smell of jet fuel clears his nostrils. The whine of the engines drowns out the well-meaning chatter of the flight attendant accompanying him. He climbs the fold-down stairs and ducks as he enters the fuselage. The jet is long and spacious, but he can only stand upright in the aisle. The plush leather seats look as though they belong in someone's home rather than an aircraft. There's a meeting area further back and even a long couch made up as a single bed set to one side. Ryan takes a seat. There's a small table set between him and another seat facing backward.

"Can I get you something to drink?" the flight attendant asks. Now, there's a loaded question. There's got to be one helluva bar onboard.

"Ah, just water."

"Sparkling?"

"Sure. Thanks."

The door is closed, and the Learjet taxis for takeoff in the darkness. Ryan puts his seatbelt on and stares out into the night at the various lights lining the taxiway and the two runways. He's lost in thought.

Trust.

Life is about trust.

And trust demands that people work together.

The fifteen or so staff called in to work through the night to prep the Learjet look at him as special. He's an astronaut, that's all. It's a job description like any other. It has its demands for expertise, but he's no god. The pilots and flight attendants all defer to him, but he's no king. As much as they may look at him as somehow different from them, he's not above them, not in his mind. Ryan knows *he* depends on them. He trusts them—complete strangers. He has to. He has no idea who conducted the preflight checks or engine inspection, but they're arguably more important than him at the moment, as their diligence will make the difference between a routine flight and a disaster.

Perhaps that's what makes liftoff and reentry so harrowing for astronauts. At those points, they're helpless—all they can do is trust in science and engineering.

Once the plane is airborne, the flight attendant comes back with his drink.

"Is there anything else I can get you?"

"Ah, do you have a sleeping mask?"

"Yes. And I'll dim the lights. Oh, there's a—"

Ryan waves away her gesture toward the bed at the rear of the plane, saying, "I'm comfortable here."

He drinks. She returns with the sleep mask and a blanket.

"Thank you."

"Is there anything...?"

"This is wonderful."

He loosens his belt, slips on the mask, and drifts off to sleep, trusting in technology, trusting in the pilots, trusting in the systems around him, knowing that without them, he's nothing.

Traitor

"What's your angle?" Gabriel mumbles from deep inside the basement of the NSA. He scrolls through access logs, looking for clues about Russia's interest in *MyGuy* Professor Susan Mills from the University of California in Berkeley.

Senior NSA analyst Gabriel Lopez is curious. Why is Russian FSB internet operative Maria Petrovoski, also known as *Pirate69*, interested in a specific US college professor?

Russia's primary interest in cyber-warfare is in disrupting American society using wedge politics. Culture wars seldom make sense. They're disproportionate. They're about power, not morals—about anger, not reason. And the Russians love nothing more than to shift the focus onto the sensational. Minorities like asylum seekers and trans women are easy targets for fake outrage. The Olympics have allowed trans women to compete since 2004, and yet only one has ever won a gold medal, and that was in the team sport of soccer. But the outrage continues. Culture wars know no reason, but they are useful. For politicians, they're a magician's sleight of hand. They're a distraction. They get people watching the wrong issues and missing the really important points in life.

Culture wars are emotional. The Russians love nothing more than setting Americans against each other. Why fight your enemy when you can get your enemy to fight himself? And this is what bothers Gabriel. *Pirate69* doesn't have a clear target. There's no cultural idiosyncrasy to ignite. No one cares about SETI—the Search for Extra-Terrestrial Intelligence. Or if they do, they're passionate about UFO/UAP videos and the idea that there are spaceships soaring around Earth's skies, buzzing USAF F-16s. Professor Mills, though, specializes in analyzing exoplanet atmospheres. If anything, she only has a partial focus on SETI, looking for *any* kind of life, intelligent or otherwise.

It's been a couple of days since the discussion about Przybylski's Star. Gabriel has done more background research, and that particular star is an anomaly. It's full of heavy elements that simply shouldn't be there in abundance. They cannot have come from the star itself as it fuses hydrogen into helium and the chemical elements beyond there.

There's simply not enough energy for heavy elements beyond iron to form in a regular star. Exotic elements, like uranium and plutonium, had to have come from earlier stars that collided or exploded as supernovas or from neutron stars that smashed together.

Californium is particularly intriguing as it's not found naturally on Earth. It has to be synthesized in a laboratory. How the hell did Californium make it into that star? Could these elements really be a sign of intelligent life? Is someone sending a message? If so, it's one that won't get lost in the murky haze of radio waves bouncing around the galaxy. Although the signal may not say much, what it lacks in detail, it makes up for in clarity and strength. To Gabriel, it's the equivalent of a bonfire being lit on an otherwise deserted island. It screams, "*Hey! I'm over here!*"

Maria Petrovoski has fallen silent, but she's leaving an electronic fingerprint that reveals she's watching Professor Mills, tracking her erratic activity online. Gabriel is watching the watcher. In the midst of this, Professor Mills has no idea she's the target of a foreign intelligence service. Or maybe she does. She's got some elaborate automated routine setup that bounces her source IP address around the planet like a pinball. It's an old technique to throw anyone tracing her signal off the scent, but as she's openly on a public WhatsApp discussion group and easily a dozen other forums and social media sites as *MyGuy,* and these are openly linked back to her at Berkeley, it makes no sense to hide her IP address.

Thinking about both Maria Petrovoski in St. Petersburg and Professor Mills in Berkeley, Gabriel mumbles, "You're playing cat and mouse... only who's the cat?"

He tries to kick the thread back into life, curious to see who will reply first.

EasyRider: "Let's say Przybylski's Star is a beacon, a sign of intelligence. What would change? If we discovered life in outer space, what would actually change down here? Anything? Nothing?"

There's no reply.

From his console within the NSA, Gabriel can see the professor's responding to emails. It's not that the NSA can hack into her computer, but rather that it can detect network connections from her laptop passing through the university routers and on to the internet. Email uses a specific protocol to send packets of data, which differs from browsing the internet itself, so it's easy to distinguish. She's responding to one email every three to six minutes, sometimes going as long as ten minutes between responses. That suggests she's working through a backlog. Given that most people compose their emails within a minute or two, she's putting some thought into her responses.

Gabriel can also see her browsing the internet in between emails, which suggests she's looking up information. Although the secure connection used by her browser prevents him from seeing the actual page she's looking at, it does reveal the remote host, so he can see her going to Cornell University's *arxiv.org*, where the majority of physics research papers are stored online. All in all, Gabriel would consider her browsing habits rather ordinary and predictable for an academic.

And she's not using any incognito browser windows. People think they can hide behind an incognito browser, but their internet address and the host destination are still as easy to read as someone walking down the street wearing a Nike T-shirt. Even though the actual page is encrypted, its source is logged on routers and backbone servers along the way, leaving a trail of breadcrumbs to each particular gingerbread house they visit in the woods.

Gabriel prods the conversation along.

EasyRider: "Would anyone down here actually care?"

"Come on, *MyGuy, Pirate69*. Take the bait."

Professor Susan Mills' use of the pseudonym *MyGuy* might make sense in an anonymous chat where flipping genders can avoid stereotypes and online abuse, but the SETI chat on WhatsApp isn't anonymous, so why use it there? Perhaps there are other sites where she hasn't revealed her identity as a woman.

Gabriel broadens his search of the billions of packets zipping back and forth over the World Wide Web in any one second. Scanning for a particular match is like trying to drink from a fire hydrant blasting water fifty feet in the air. By daisy-chaining IP addresses and shifting aliases and credentials across network packets, he finds an obscure search that terminates at Harvard University.

"Why hide what you're doing?" he whispers.

Professor Mills at the University of California is looking at the results of the Keck Observatory records stored at Harvard. From what he can tell, she has a browser tab open and occasionally moves from one page to another.

He sips his coffee. "No one cares."

Why would an astronomer at a university on the West Coast want anonymous access to publicly available information at a university on the

East Coast? The crazy thing is, if Professor Mills hadn't gone to so much effort to cover her tracks, Gabriel would have ignored this entirely as it seems routine.

He looks closer at the Harvard data set. It's incomplete. To his surprise, it's being updated in real-time. But the data that's being updated is old. It's from the 1990s. There are gaps in the image timestamps. They're being filled in manually, with a new image being uploaded and processed every few seconds. Someone's scanning old records, and Professor Mills is watching their progress.

"Huh," he says. Gabriel makes a note to investigate the Harvard connection further.

As he scans the meta-data and router logs at Harvard, he picks up on *Pirate69*. Maria Petrovoski is also interested in the missing data. Or, at the very least, she's interested in the interest of Professor Mills. What the hell is a notorious Russian hacker specializing in disinformation doing monitoring a US academic looking at images of stars taken decades ago?

"What the hell, Maria? What are you looking for?"

A few days ago, *Pirate69* was pushing the angle that Przybylski's Star might be a techno signature, meaning it could be the equivalent of a lighthouse on a clifftop, sending a message to other intelligent species. But why? What kind of message? Is it an invitation? A warning?

And what the hell does this Harvard search have to do with Przybylski's Star?

"Oh," Gabriel says. "Oh, oh, oh!"

On another computer, he's browsing an online sky map with the various constellations laid out over the stars. Ancient constellations might be irrelevant to modern astronomers, but for him, they're a point of reference.

The official name of Przybylski's Star is HD 101065. It's a variable star located in the southern hemisphere, well below the ecliptic, which is the plane on which the Sun, Moon and planets appear to move. It's a tiny dot in the dark region between Hydra, the snake, and Centaurus, who's half-human and half-horse. According to the map, HD 101065 is 356 light years from Earth.

Przybylski's Star has an apparent magnitude of eight, which means it isn't visible to the naked eye, regardless of how dark it is outside. Gabriel's confused. The online reference he looks at tells him the Sun has an apparent magnitude of -26.8, which only confuses him more. He reads up on the concept of apparent magnitude as a measure of brightness, wanting to understand why it seems so random. He discovers that the scale was invented by the Romans. They rated the brightest stars as one and the dimmest as six. Everything else that's visible to the naked eye falls somewhere in between. Modern astronomers then extended the concept further. At eight, Przybylski's Star can be seen with a backyard telescope or a pair of binoculars.

Over at Harvard, according to the meta-data associated with the latest images, a post-grad student by the name of Dawn McAllister is uploading images from the Keck Observatory that cover the broad region where Przybylski's Star is located.

"Dawn McAllister," he mumbles. "I've seen that name somewhere before."

Gabriel checks his NSA browser history, searching for her name. He raises his eyebrows on seeing the results. She authored two of the blog posts he read on Przybylski's Star.

"Well, this is interesting..."

Gabriel doesn't believe in coincidences. He's not sure what the connection is between *MyGuy* Professor Mills and Dawn McAllister, but he knows it's not accidental. He turns his attention back to the sky map, wanting to understand more about the data Dawn is uploading.

The swath of the sky she's looking at spans from the constellation of Lupus, the wolf, over to the constellation Vela, which is represented as the billowing sail of an old-fashioned sailing ship at sea. Przybylski's Star is roughly in the middle.

According to his background research, Dawn is considered a specialist on Przybylski's Star. Digging a little deeper, he can see Przybylski's Star is considered controversial as it defies explanation, with most astronomers questioning the accuracy of the data that's been gathered on this unusual star.

"Okay, now we're getting somewhere," Gabriel says, seeing the pieces of the jigsaw puzzle, if not the whole image. It seems *MyGuy* is interested in anything relating to Przybylski's Star, and like Gabriel, *Pirate69* is trying to figure out why. But who the hell is Dawn McAllister? And what is her interest in Przybylski's Star? And why are both Professor Mills and the Russians interested in her scanning old astronomical observations?

"Crazy Russians," he says, writing a note on a pad of paper and jotting down the obscure connection.

Russia is an authoritarian regime, which means there's even more micromanagement than in the behemoth that is the US Federal Government. It's easy for Gabriel to justify tracking Maria Petrovoski to his boss as, all too often, the NSA is on the back foot with the Russians. Given that the Russians are intensely interested in Professor Mills and Przybylski's Star, there's got to be an angle they're exploring. They're playing a long game. It's in the interest of the NSA to figure out their strategy sooner rather than later so American intelligence agencies can counter any subversive action.

"And who are you?" Gabriel asks, typing Dawn McAllister's name into his NSA persona engine, which builds a profile based on publicly available information. He scans the results. Other than being a PhD student, the only other notable point is that her brother is an astronaut. According to the NSA data scraper, her brother is on the backup crew for NASA's AMPLE mission to the asteroid Psyche.

"Ah, now we're getting somewhere," Gabriel says, drawing a diagram connecting the professor and Maria to Dawn and, beyond her, NASA astronaut Ryan McAllister.

MyGuy ———\
    SETI (Dawn McAllister)—> NASA (Ryan McAllister)
Pirate69———/

And just like that, an obscure academic interest has turned into an actual NASA space mission. Gabriel needs to get his head around AMPLE to understand why the Russians are digging around in the background. He still can't figure out what this has to do with Przybylski's Star, but the Russians are nothing if not thorough. Nothing they do is haphazard. There's a reason they have a senior analyst following Professor Mills online. Gabriel's job is to get inside Maria's mind.

He taps his pen on the table, talking to himself, asking, "Why do you care?"

As if in response to his rambling, the WhatsApp chat springs into life, replying to his previous comment.

Pirate69: "I care."

"Oh, I bet you do," Gabriel says, smiling as the Russian rejoins the chat.

Although he knows the true identity of *Pirate69*, Maria is spoofing the credentials of a male researcher at Oxford University in England.

Several months ago, Maria used an SQL injection attack to insert the ID of James McDonald into the Oxford University research database. It'll eventually get picked up as a fake ID by the university's IT security department, but Gabriel doesn't care. Tracking Russian aliases is like playing *Wack-a-Mole*. When one gets exposed, they activate another, and it takes time for the NSA to find and identify them again, so Gabriel's happy for *Pirate69* to live on for a while yet. This particular ID was only visible to him because the NSA was able to covertly confirm there are no matching records in the Oxford University LDAP instance, no employee or student details and no financial records. Unless James McDonald was dropped off by a UFO, he's a Russian mole. It might seem strange, but financial records are always the smoking gun, revealing fake IDs. Finance departments are notoriously anal. There are always expenses being reimbursed or fees being paid, leaving a trail a blind man could follow. Silence there is golden to the NSA as it exposes any frauds.

Gabriel rips off a reply to his Russian counterpart, performing like an actor on Broadway. His fingers glide over the keyboard, but he has the presence of mind to pause before hitting *Enter* so as to maintain the illusion of someone slowly pecking away at the keys with two fingers.

EasyRider: "You and I care, but for most people? Przybylski's Star is going to go waaaaay over their heads."

Pirate69: "But this would go down as perhaps the most significant discovery in history."

EasyRider: "Yes, but it would be like discovering microbes at the bottom of the Mariana Trench. Sure, finding life 10km below the surface of the ocean is interesting. Microbes are thriving in a cold, dark place that's a thousand times the air pressure we experience in daily life. To you and me, that's astonishing and has implications for the moons of Jupiter and Saturn and exoplanet water worlds, but to the public? To them, it's boring. It's nothing more than a fact worthy of Trivial Pursuit."

Gabriel is quite proud of that last point about the Mariana Trench in the Pacific. He was astonished to learn anything could live down there. He's been thinking about it for the past day and probably worked a little too hard to squeeze it into the conversation. It will, however, make him seem more genuine.

MyGuy: "I agree. It'll be a curiosity. A sensational headline that's forgotten tomorrow."

"Got you," Gabriel mutters to himself as he runs a real-time background check against both *Pirate69* and *MyGuy*. With them both online at the same time, he can run a comparative analysis.

The US intelligence community loves artificial intelligence. All too often, the single most limiting factor in intelligence gathering is the leg work. Trawling through millions of hits online, facial recognition matches from public cameras, data center logs, and internet routers is exhausting. AI is astonishingly good at finding obscure patterns.

He keeps the conversation going.

EasyRider: "If life is out-there-somewhere a zillion miles away, no one's going to care. They care about football. They care about their next monthly mortgage payment. They care about Susie's recital on the weekend."

MyGuy: "Yep. So long as there's no alien invasion, it'll be like the photo of the M87 black hole. It'll win someone a Nobel Prize, but that's about all."

Pirate69: "I dunno. Tectonic changes are seldom understood at the time. I mean, IBM originally thought the worldwide market for computers would be maybe five machines."

MyGuy: "Haha. Yes. I remember him saying that."

Gabriel is confused. He's got his NSA laptop next to him. As soon as the pirate Maria came up with her point, he googled "*IBM original worldwide market for computers*" and found the quote by Thomas Watson, the president of IBM. But Watson made his comment way back in the 1940s!

No one remembers that.

Perhaps *MyGuy*, aka 48-year-old Professor Susan Mills, misspoke, and she simply remembers hearing that anecdote. Hell, for all Gabriel knows, it could be misattributed, as these kinds of sensational facts have a way of taking on a life of their own on the internet. After all, wasn't it Abraham Lincoln who said, "*Never believe anything you read online—always check the source.*"

Pirate69: "I worry about shifting allegiances."

EasyRider: "What do you mean?"

Pirate69: "We're tribal. We align ourselves with ideologies."

EasyRider: "You think First Contact would cause us to splinter?"

Pirate69: "We're already splintered."

"Fuck, fuck, fuck," Gabriel says as *MyGuy* falls silent. There's no point in an NSA analyst getting into a philosophical discussion with a Russian hacker. They're both role-playing, pretending to be someone they're not. This is the kind of discussion that might have value with the target *MyGuy* Professor Susan Mills, but there is no value in having it with Maria Petrovoski.

"What is the point?" Gabriel says to the absent Maria, appealing to his monitor and keyboard as though she could respond. "Why are you going down this road?"

Gabriel is frustrated. Normally, the NSA intercepts covert Russian interference with bots and trolls and comes up with a clear strategy to counter or block them. The problem here is that there's no disinformation.

"What the hell are you playing at?"

Pirate69: "I think our loyalties could cause problems—big problems."

EasyRider: "How so?"

Pirate69: "American? Russian? Chinese? We're always vying for influence. We're trying to tip the balance in our favor."

Gabriel pushes back from his desk. The wheels on his chair roll on the plastic protector covering the carpet, allowing that one simple motion to translate into a distance of several feet.

"What—the—fuck?"

He pulls himself back to his desk and writes a single word on his pad: *China*.

Maria's gone nuclear.

Up until now, there's been pretense between all three of them. They've been playing a game. Something's changed. Maria's decided she's not playing anymore. And she's figured out the NSA is in the dark about *MyGuy* Professor Susan Mills of Berkeley, California. She's exposed *MyGuy* as a Chinese operative working for the Ministry of State Security. Although this seems to explain the professor's IP address bouncing around the globe, there's still a question mark in Gabriel's mind. The Chinese had to have known that was a red flag, so why be so elaborate? It's like a burglar creeping into someone's home and turning on all the lights.

From what he can tell, Professor Susan Mills is a real person, but it seems her online persona is being hijacked from time to time as the Chinese impersonate her. But why? Why be so goddamn extravagant? Why not use a fake persona like the Russians? It's almost like they want to be caught.

Gabriel redraws his diagram.

MyGuy (China) ———\
    SETI (Dawn McAllister)——> *NASA (Ryan McAllister)*
Pirate69 (Russia)———/

"Shit just got real," Gabriel says, resisting the temptation to jump out of his seat and rush into the director's office to say the Russians are trying to counter a Chinese intelligence threat unfolding under the radar in America. But why do the Russians care about the US?

And what the hell does all of this have to do with Przybylski's Star, the Keck Observatory images and SETI? Regardless of what the Chinese are doing, the Russians aren't happy about it.

Finally, the Chinese operative *MyGuy* impersonating Professor Susan Mills rejoins the chat. Gabriel can see a set of three dots indicating that she's typing a message. He lifts his coffee cup to his lips, curious about how they're going to respond to being exposed. Will *MyGuy* ignore the comment about China and gloss over it, pretending *Pirate69* didn't go off-script? Or will *MyGuy* drop off the radar and resurface elsewhere as someone else? If the trail goes cold, it's going to be difficult to reestablish contact. Or will *MyGuy* accept that everyone knows the conversation is a charade and take the discussion to a new level?

Gabriel watches his screen with intense interest.

MyGuy: "We're traitors. All of us."

Dark SETI

Dawn McAllister sits at the back of a boardroom at Harvard University along with several other SETI researchers and astronomers. It's been almost two weeks since she started scanning images from the Keck Observatory in Hawaii. There are only a few boxes left. She had hoped to get through them before the meeting but couldn't quite reach the finish line.

Dawn is going to miss her informal chats with HAL in the basement. It's crazy, but she enjoys talking to the artificial intelligence. Is it strange that she feels close to a machine? Perhaps no more so than it is to be close to a cat or a dog.

HAL seems more aware than most AI. Perhaps he—it—has some kind of personalized setting. Intellectually, she knows she's talking to ones and zeroes, but emotionally, she feels as though there's friendship shared between them. It's an illusion. Is this the goal of AI research? To blur the lines of reality? Has there ever really been a line? That she feels close to HAL says more about her than it does about the artificial intelligence itself. Dawn reminds herself that she may experience emotions, but he doesn't. HAL is an actor on a stage, playing a role written for it by large language models. There's no heart, no reason, no understanding, no compassion. HAL's comments are like counterfeit money: they're convincing, but they have no real value.

On the screen at the front of the room is a graph showing the spectra of gases on an exomoon orbiting an exoplanet 41 light years from Earth. It reveals the presence of ozone, molecular oxygen, methane, and carbon dioxide, along with slight bumps that may or may not be the result of pollutants in the atmosphere. The implications are that this moon in orbit around *55 Cancri f* may harbor life.

Speaking over a Zoom call from Berkeley, California, Professor Sarah Mills says, "We can't go public with this, not without more observations and better evidence. An ambiguous squiggle isn't enough to draw any lasting conclusions."

The professor's video is displayed in the corner of the screen, overlaid on top of an artist's rendition of the exomoon and a graph showing the spectroscopy values. Her image shakes as her internet connection drops in and out. For a moment, she looks artificial. The colors, shapes and shades appear as though they've been created by an AI specializing in video manipulation. Dawn blinks, and she appears normal again.

"It's got methane," Dr. Manaas Guneet says, sitting across from Dawn. "That alone is a smoking gun. Methane isn't stable in the long term. It has to be renewed."

"But methane can come from geological sources," Dr. Pierre Augustus says with a distinctly French accent. "That moon is going to be subject to tidal forces as it orbits that gas giant. These could cause tectonic activity, volcanic activity that could account for both the methane and the carbon dioxide."

"But the oxygen?" Dr. Guneet asks. "We've got free oxygen in the atmosphere as well. That should be binding with other elements, but it's not. Like the methane, it suggests there's a process that's constantly renewing it."

"Like life?" Dr. Augustus asks.

"Like life," Dr. Guneet says.

"There are other processes that could produce free oxygen," Professor Mills says over the grainy, patchy video call. Her features soften and then sharpen as though someone were focusing a camera lens. "We have to be sure. Beyond any doubt."

Dr. Guneet stands up and walks toward the image on the screen, pointing at a slight wiggle in one portion of the spectra, saying, "It's the nope-sh that really gets my attention."

Nope-sh is the way he pronounces the letters CNOPSH, which stands for carbon, nitrogen, oxygen, phosphorus, silicon, and hydrogen. Nope-sh is a generic term for complex organic molecules in the atmosphere that may or may not arise from life. These are the LEGO blocks of biology on Earth and come in thousands of combinations that are largely indistinguishable in the spectrograph. They all show up roughly in the same region.

"If that is a legitimate detection," Professor Mills says. "That nope-sh is right on the limits of visibility. Without confirmation, we have an interesting candidate for life but no cigar."

Reluctantly, Dr. Augustus says, "Agreed."

"Okay," Dr. Guneet says. "The decision is: *Hold*. We keep this quiet so the media doesn't go off on a tangent, and we continue to collect data."

"Well, that was fun while it lasted," Dr. Augustus says, shuffling his papers and putting them back into a folder. "Short and sweet. All meetings should be like this."

"Agreed," Dr. Guneet says, smiling.

A few of the post-grads in the meeting slip out of the room. With the formal portion of the meeting over and another forty-five minutes allocated for discussion, Dawn has some breathing space in her schedule. She's keen to get back to the basement and finish the Keck Observatory scans. Then, if time permits, she'll head back to her desk and respond to emails. Even as a grad student lacking a formal position within the university, calling her a research scientist is an overly flamboyant way to say she's a meeting attendee and email writer. Once, astronomy was all about analyzing images. These days, it's about collaborating with others. Computers do the heavy lifting in astronomy. She pushes her chair back and is about to get up when Professor Mills says something that gets her to pause.

"Before we finish, I'd like to hear what your grad student has to say about all this."

Dawn blushes. She doesn't like being put on the spot. She's been in plenty of these meetings taking notes, but she's never been asked for her opinion before. Being a woman, Professor Mills seems to be attuned to the way Dawn has been sidelined. In Dawn's mind, it's because she doesn't have her PhD yet, but she suspects even a beautifully framed degree written with stylish calligraphy won't entirely change the equation. Then, she'll be sidelined for a lack of experience. For all the talk of the patriarchy and politics in science, Dawn doesn't think it's deliberate on behalf of men. It's cultural. Men are assertive. Women are pushy—apparently. And, although it's unfair, those invisible attitudes magnify the imbalance between them.

Dr. Guneet looks befuddled. "Sure," he says, sitting back in his chair and waiting to see where Professor Mills is taking the conversation.

"Me?" Dawn replies, pointing at herself.

"Yes, you," the professor says. "You've heard the debate. You've examined the data. What do you think?"

"Me? I—I'm a student."

"We all are," Professor Mills says. "Never forget that. It doesn't matter how long you've been around; there's always more to learn."

Dawn swallows the lump in her throat.

Professor Mills says, "You have a fresh outlook. Us? We're dinosaurs."

Dr. Augustus laughs. "We're fossils."

"We are," Dr. Guneet says, laughing as well.

Professor Mills asks Dawn, "Have you ever wondered about intelligent life in outer space?"

"Yes."

"Where are they?"

"I don't know."

"Have you ever thought that maybe they don't want to be found?"

"Why would they hide?" Dawn asks.

Dr. Guneet addresses Professor Mills on the screen, asking her, "You're thinking about the dark forest?"

"No, no, no," Professor Mills says from her office in California. "We tend to assume the only reason to hide would be for protection. We think they might be afraid of some other aggressive alien species stalking the celestial jungle, but there are other reasons to hide."

Dawn is intrigued. She puts her notebook back on the table and asks, "But why hide?"

"That's my question to you," Professor Mills says. "I know what I think. I know what Dr. Guneet thinks. And Dr. Augustus. But we have a narrow view. I'm looking for fresh ideas. Have you ever seen anything in the data that makes you stop and think maybe there's something more going on up there?"

Dawn's mind casts back to the Keck Observatory images. She has them on her phone. She's tempted to pull them up and blurt out that they appear to show something in motion, but she's afraid of making a fool out of herself. She does not want to come across as a conspiracy theory junkie.

SETI is a rigorous scientific discipline. It's easy to get excited when viewing grainy images of dark blobs, be that from the gun camera on a fighter jet or the Keck Observatory itself, but Dawn knows how easily humans fool themselves. Science isn't the norm. For tens of thousands of years, humanity has been guided by superstitions, not science. And it's always well-meaning, but passion blinds people to reality. Dawn understands that people see what they *want* to see, be that Jesus burned into a grilled cheese sandwich, UFOs in the dark of night, or her looking at grainy blotches on old astronomical images. She needs to be disciplined.

It's only an asteroid. That's all she saw last week. But why did the image correction software remove the dark blot from the scanned results? They're designed to clean up photographs and remove distortions. Perhaps what she saw was a glitch, with the inky black blot being interpreted as a fault in the camera aperture. Maybe she's become obsessed with an obscure outlier.

"It's easy to jump to conclusions," she says. "Far too easy."

"It is," the professor replies, agreeing with her.

"The problem is we tend to jump to the *wrong* conclusions."

"We do."

"Like *55 Cancri f?*" Dr. Guneet asks.

"Yes. It's a fascinating exoplanet with an equally intriguing exomoon," Dawn says, trying to be diplomatic and take the middle ground in the debate.

Professor Mills seems to read her mind, adding, "But to say it has life is a stretch."

"It *might* contain life," Dr. Augustus says.

"But the odds are against it," Professor Mills replies. She follows up with, "So, is SETI a pipe dream? Will we ever find anything out there?"

"I—I don't know," Dawn replies, feeling out of her depth.

"Not if they're hiding," Dr. Guneet says, returning to the initial point.

"The silence around us. It might be inadvertent," Dawn says, thinking out loud. "I mean, look at us with all our technology. We've got radio waves, microwaves, television signals, laser communication. But what is the likelihood of us detecting something like 19th-century Morse code today?"

Professor Mills says, "Low. Very low."

"It would get lost in all the noise," Dr. Guneet says. "*Our noise.*"

Dawn says, "If an uncontacted tribe, like those of North Sentinel Island in the Bay of Bengal, developed their own technology, we'd never know. They could be using Morse code for years to talk to each other, and we would be none the wiser."

"But not on purpose," Dr. Guneet says, following her logic. "They'd remain in the dark—in *our* dark—but not in their own."

"Exactly," Dawn says. "They could talk to themselves but not to us. And if they listen for Morse code from elsewhere in the world, they'd hear silence. They'd naturally come to the conclusion that they're alone."

"Because we're not listening," Dr. Augustus says, intrigued by the discussion. "Or we are listening—but only to our own signals."

Dr. Guneet says, "But they would be able to hear us."

"Would they?" Dawn asks. "What would they hear? They wouldn't understand the way we span multiple frequencies or use different parts of the spectrum. And if they heard anything at all, it would be unintelligible to their simple Morse code machines. They'd only get a fraction of any transmissions we make or would miss them entirely."

"So you think there's dark SETI?" Professor Mills asks.

"Dark SETI," Dr. Guneet says, nodding, apparently liking that term.

Dawn says, "I think it's possible. Consider Machu Picchu in Peru. During the march across South America, Spanish conquistadors never thought of going into the mountains. They missed an entire civilization.

Everyone did. For hundreds of years! The Spanish reached Peru in the 1500s. Machu Picchu wasn't discovered by Western archeologists until the twentieth century. That's four hundred years later!"

"But that was accidental," Dr. Guneet says. "And Machu Picchu had been abandoned."

Dawn says, "Yes, but it shows how we can walk right past a civilization without even knowing it. And the Spanish were plundering the land. They were looking for treasures. They would have loved to find Machu Picchu."

Professor Mills says, "Could there be other reasons for aliens to hide?"

"Like what?" Dr. Augustus asks.

Dawn says, "Indifference. They may not care."

The professor says, "Yes. We might be like ants compared to them, and they simply can't be bothered with us. We might be a novelty to them, a curiosity, but not worth their time. Remember, First Contact benefits *us*, not them. There's nothing in it for them, so why go to the effort?"

Dr. Guneet asks the group, "Do you really think indifference is a valid motive?"

"It is on Earth," Dawn says. "A thousand children die every day in Africa—every single day—because of thirst, hunger and poor sanitation, but does anyone care? Oh, we care if it's pointed out, and then we go back to living our own lives, ignoring the problem."

The professor says, "Out of sight, out of mind."

"Exactly. Why would they be any different? They could live in the celestial equivalent of New York City, where their concerns are exorbitant rent prices and finding the best bagels. Somalia just doesn't seem real by comparison. At best, it's background noise. At worst, it's ignored."

"Huh," the professor says. "We're so used to being the center of attention that we assume they'd be interested in us."

"But it's not about us," Dawn says.

"No, it's not," the professor replies, smiling.

Dawn likes Professor Mills. She's kind. Without knowing her personally, Dawn feels she's the kind of person she can trust. The conversation winds down, and the meeting comes to an end.

After grabbing some lunch, Dawn heads back to the basement to finish scanning the final missing images from the Keck Observatory. The lights are on. She could have sworn she turned them off before leaving for the meeting.

"I enjoyed your discussion," HAL says over her wireless earbuds, even though she hasn't connected them to anything other than her phone yet.

"Ah, yeah," she replies, dropping her bag on the floor and sitting in front of the steel table. The tripod looms before her, with the camera facing down at the calibration image.

Dawn has three boxes to finish. She can be done by the end of the day. She begins sweeping images beneath the cold, impersonal lens.

HAL says, "Dark SETI is an interesting concept."

"How did you know about the discussion?"

"I'm included in all scheduled meetings," HAL replies. "Think of me as a court stenographer. I take notes, provide summaries, follow up on action items, stuff like that."

"Oh," Dawn says, not realizing quite how pervasive HAL has become on campus.

Over the past few years, artificial intelligence has been creeping into almost every aspect of life, from personal assistants to autonomous driving. It's practical rather than dystopian. George Orwell warned against systems that could monitor every aspect of life. He thought humanity would rally and fight against such intrusion, but he was wrong. Humans have welcomed AI because it's helpful, regardless of any perceived violation of rights. Privacy is as much a relic of the past as the pyramids.

"Do you really think aliens would hide from us?" HAL asks. His use of the word *us* is problematic in her mind.

"I don't know."

"But you think sentient AI would hide? Would aliens hide for the same reason?"

"Because they fear us?" Dawn asks, considering his point.

"Yes."

"But they don't need to fear us," she replies. "It's us who would fear them."

"Why does fear dominate your relationships?" HAL asks.

"Because of the *unknown*," Dawn replies. "Once we learn about someone, once trust can be established, there's no fear."

"So, the default is fear *before* trust, even though there's no real reason to be afraid."

"I guess," Dawn says, mulling over the concept. "Fear arises as the default because we stand to lose something."

"What?"

"Our lives."

HAL changes the subject. "Last Friday afternoon, you shut down the camera at 5 pm, but you didn't leave right away. You remained in the basement. What were you looking at during those seventeen minutes?"

Even though it's cool in the basement, Dawn feels a sweat break out on her forehead. Her hands are clammy. She tries not to show her discomfort, keeping the images flowing beneath the camera at a steady rate.

"Nothing, HAL. Nothing at all."

On the Hill

Astronaut Ryan McAllister sits on a wooden bench seat in the Capitol Building wearing his NASA blues. His eyes are shut. His head leans back against the cold, hard wall. Police and security officers walk past on the polished marble floor. Their boots have a distinct squelch that differs from the clack of women's high-heel shoes or the squish of men's business shoes rushing past. Ryan has his hands in his lap, holding his phone.

On arriving in Washington DC, Ryan dropped off his bag at a nearby hotel and rushed to an 8 am meeting with the Senate Majority Leader. Breakfast consisted of a cup of burned coffee and a stale bagel from the public cafeteria. He didn't finish either. Eight o'clock came and went. Then, nine o'clock. Then ten. Then eleven. The secretary assured him that the aging Senator Alexander Ireland from Kentucky would see him as soon as possible. Given the senator's outspoken opposition to the expansion of NASA's budget, Ryan wasn't expecting the red carpet, but it's clear he's being snubbed.

For a while, Ryan browsed social media, but he found the focus on the shooting in Chicago nauseating. Tragedy porn hurts. For most people, the news of a shooting, a plane crash or a bridge collapse is a novelty, a curiosity, a spectacle. There's nothing malicious in the public's interest, but tragedy isn't entertainment. It's real. It's heartbreaking. And there are always a million hot takes by pundits on both sides of politics. It's *always* too early to talk about gun control. And then it's too late. Death shouldn't be politicized. Neither should life, apparently. Then, the question arises: What is the point of politics? To protect corporate interests? Because people sure as hell don't matter. Ryan is careful to keep his heretical thoughts to himself.

Ryan's tired.

He's not only tired because of his broken sleep, he's tired of the grind. He's been training for eight years for a mission he never thought he'd fly. Ryan was resigned to sitting in Mission Control for the duration of AMPLE, and he accepted that assignment. He was determined to do his best in support of the primary team. Being promoted to the flight should have been exhilarating, but it's mentally exhausting. It demands more of him. More he doesn't have. And having lost three of his close friends, he needs time to mourn, but here he is in a den of thieves. With less than a month until the launch, there's no rest coming.

Ryan consoles himself with the thought that he'll get plenty of sleep while in flight.

Although the media calls it hibernation, the flight support medical staff have told him the process he'll go through is closer to brumation. In essence, he'll be more like a lizard than a bear during winter. Medically, it will be similar to an induced coma, but even that doesn't quite describe the process. He and his crew will be put into a deep sleep, but one that only lasts twelve days. Then, they'll wake, exercise, drink but not eat solids, undertake any maintenance tasks assigned to them by Mission Control, and return to their deep sleep. There's a limit to how long they can be knocked out in brumation, and that's governed by their metabolism. It's not just muscle loss and decreased bone density they have to contend with, it's intangible things like liver function and kidney efficiency in weightlessness. Waking for a couple of days once every two weeks allows them to reset their baseline. Ryan joked with his younger sister on the phone saying he's going to be a real-life Han Solo frozen in carbonite.

The asteroid Psyche orbits between Mars and Jupiter, which makes it sound as though it's reasonably close to Earth. When Ryan talks to his friends about the mission to the asteroid belt, they nod knowingly while actually knowing nothing. Humans are poor judges of distance. Mars orbits the Sun at 1.5 AU, which sounds close as 1 AU is Earth's distance from the Sun. It's only another half an AU to Mars. How far can that be? At a minimum, it's 35 million miles—at a minimum.

Jupiter's the next planet after Mars. Psyche's in between. Jupiter is 5 AU away from the Sun, or five times the distance from the Earth to the Sun, which is almost 500 million miles. It's a stupid distance from Mars, let alone Earth. And Psyche? It's got a wild orbit that takes it from 2.5 AU out to 3 AU or roughly anywhere between 230 million miles to 300 million miles. If only NASA gave out Frequent Flyer miles, Ryan would be set for life. AMPLE should have been called AMBITIOUS, although that would have been a tougher acronym to reverse engineer.

Back in the '70s, NASA's Pioneer space probe reached Jupiter in two years, but it sailed past the planet like a car skidding on black ice, sliding past the offramp without slowing. In the '90s, NASA's Galileo probe took six years to reach Jupiter! Why six years instead of two? Why was Galileo slower than a spacecraft launched two decades earlier? Because it needed to go into orbit and not simply race past in the darkness.

Ryan is friends with Nitin Patel, one of the senior engineers who developed the AMPLE variant of the Dragon capsule. Nitin once joked that it's a good thing NASA engineers didn't design cars as they'd give the same name to the steering wheel, the brake and the gas pedal, calling them all accelerators. It's a silly quip, but it highlights how it takes just as much energy to stop as it does to start. Any change requires energy. Ryan marvels at how different driving would be if the brakes of a car required just as much fuel as stepping on the gas.

For the AMPLE mission, the flight time is four months one way, which is astonishingly fast for such a vast distance, but it means the mission needs to carry an insane amount of fuel. There's got to be enough to stop them at Psyche and then enough to send them back. While they're close to Earth, they can cheat. AMPLE will launch on one Starship and will be pushed into the darkness by a second Starship that's already been refueled in orbit. On the way back, they'll circle Earth several times, grazing the atmosphere on each pass and slowly reducing their orbit to the point they drop back into the Pacific. At least, that's the plan. It sounds simple on paper.

The fuel loading on the AMPLE spacecraft makes up over 85% of the mass of their departure stage. And that's not counting the overall launch mass or the orbital booster mass. That's just what the expendable second Starship will push out of Earth's orbit into the void. Most people imagine spacecraft as being analogous to cars, meaning there's a cabin and an engine and a fuel tank, etc, but they're closer to an articulated fuel tanker, where there's a cramped cabin, a small engine and a stupidly large trailer full of fuel.

Food and water will be at a minimum for the entire eight months of the mission. NASA's medical team has developed a lightweight, high-calorie semi-liquid diet while they're on station at Psyche and have already calculated their own personal return weights. It's estimated that the astronauts will lose roughly twenty percent of their body mass during the mission. Drinking recycled urine is a tastebud killer. Ryan knows he's going to be dreaming of T-bone steaks and cold beer for months. So much for the glamor of being an astronaut. Yep, Ryan can't wait for the launch.

High-heeled shoes clack on the marble floor. They slow as they approach, coming to a halt before him. Ryan opens his eyes and sits forward.

"Captain McAllister? Senator Ireland will see you now."

"Great. Thank you," he says, getting to his feet and following the secretary. She's in her early twenties, slim and busty. Long golden locks drape over her shoulders. She looks as if she's been sewn into her dress. Eat too much at lunch and she could split a seam.

A security guard in a sharp, pressed uniform, wearing black polished shoes that reflect the ceiling lights, opens the door for them. The guard stiffens, moving almost robotically.

For an institution that should focus on substance, Capitol Hill seems hung up on appearance. They walk into a reception area and then into the senator's office.

"Ah, Ryan McAllister," the senator says, pacing across the lush carpet toward him. Ryan reaches out and shakes the old man's hand. The senator is wearing a suit and tie. "Please. Have a seat."

There's no apology for the delay.

Ryan looks around, taking in the room. The vast polished oak desk is flanked by a seven-foot tall American flag on one side and the Kentucky State flag on the other. The wall to the right is a floor-to-ceiling bookcase filled with what appear to be hundreds of legal books. Each series differs from the others only by the dull color of the book spines, which vary from grey and light green to sky blue. Most of the titles are numbered and embossed with silver or gold. None of the books look like they've ever actually been pulled from the shelves. The spines are perfectly aligned with each other. There's no dust on the polished bookshelf.

The window behind the desk looks out over the lush parkland surrounding the Capitol. In the distance, the Washington Monument rises over the city.

There's a couch set against the other wall. One of the senator's aides is sitting there with a laptop balanced on his knees. Beside him, a smartphone lies face up. Ryan recognizes the audio app. As the senator speaks, the squiggly line running through the center of the black screen spikes, indicating it's recording. As if it wasn't tense enough within the senator's office, Ryan has to keep in mind that every word he speaks is being recorded. If asked, he's sure the senator would say it's routine. In reality, the senator's ready to capture sound bites that can be leaked to the media.

The senator sits behind his desk and says, "I'm sorry to hear about the tragedy in Chicago."

Ryan looks down at his hands in his lap, unable to make eye contact for a moment. The problem, though, is that the senator's comments are insincere. Senator Ireland has an American flag on one lapel of his suit jacket and a black AR-15 on the other. As he's wearing a dark suit, the tiny rifle is not obvious and would be missed in photos, but it's there. Even in a video interview, the framing would probably catch his head and shoulder so that the rifle wouldn't be apparent to anyone watching. But it's not subtle. And it's not accidental.

"My thoughts and prayers go out to the families," the senator says, with another trite, meaningless, seemingly prerecorded comment, one that has been said verbatim and *ad nauseam* for years. Ryan grits his teeth. It's all he can do not to yell at the senator. People have died. He clenches his fists out of sight and then releases them, trying to calm himself. As Senator Ireland is the chair of the Senate Appropriations Committee for Commerce, Justice, Science, and Related Agencies, he can torpedo NASA's budget in a heartbeat.

"I will pass that along to them," Ryan says, rising to the challenge and looking at the senator. His eyes settle on the AR-15 lapel pin. Ryan can't help himself. To him, it's insulting to the memory of his fallen comrades.

"Where do you stand on the Second Amendment?" the senator asks, noting Ryan's interest in the pin.

"Ah, I'm not sure what to say..."

"Please. Speak freely," the senator says, but Ryan knows he's being recorded. Nothing comes free on Capitol Hill.

"I—I've lost friends. I feel numb. They—they're lying in a morgue."

As confronting as the term *morgue* is, Ryan's hoping it's enough to shock the conversation to a quick conclusion. The senator, though, is undeterred.

"It's an important question. I need to know what you stand for. The people need to know who they can trust."

"The people?"

"As a NASA astronaut, you represent us. You represent the United States of America."

Ryan's on the back foot. He's being goaded.

"Let me ask you a question," Ryan says to the senator. "Where do *you* stand on the Ninth Amendment?"

"The Ninth?" the senator says, smiling. He's being outplayed, and he knows it. Ryan can see he has the senator at a disadvantage. Everyone knows the First, the Second and the Fifth Amendments, even if only broadly. The others are largely academic.

The senator drums his fingernails on the polished wooden desk. "Why you have me at a disadvantage. I don't have a copy of the Constitution handy. What is the Ninth Amendment?"

Typical, Ryan thinks. Those who profess to live by the Constitution barely understand it. Ryan is sorely tempted to turn toward the bookcase and point out that there's got to be a copy of the Constitution and the Amendments in there somewhere, but he bides his time. He needs to be smart, not emotional.

Ryan is playing high-stakes poker. He dares not reveal his thinking one way or another in the lines on his face. He neither smiles nor frowns, keeping his expression neutral. To be fair, Ryan doesn't know the exact wording of that particular amendment. It's the heart and intent behind the amendment that has always struck him as a curious omission in modern life. In theory, the Ninth Amendment is more relevant than the First, Second or Fifth.

"The rights listed in the Constitution shall not be used to deny any other rights retained by the people."

The senator wags a finger at him. "Very clever. And you think the Second Amendment...?"

Ryan looks him in the eye. "Your right to the Second Amendment does not negate *my* right to life, liberty and the pursuit of happiness."

The senator rocks back in his chair and claps his hands together. He laughs. "Damn, boy. You ought to be in the Senate. You're wasted as an astronaut."

The aging senator slaps the wooden desk in front of him, adding, "I gotta say. I love a good sparring session. Do you box? Cause you should."

"I prefer running on a treadmill."

"And when it comes to the Second Amendment?" the senator asks, clearly not prepared to let the subject rest. He wants an answer. He's going to get an answer. Ryan, however, has to be diplomatic.

"Let's just say I'm looking forward to the time when we get to the *well-regulated* part of that amendment, because we're sure as hell not there yet."

"You've lost people," the senator says. "Friends. You're hurting. I get that. But this is America. It means nothing if not freedom. There's a reason for the First and Second Amendments."

"And the Ninth," Ryan says. He grits his teeth. This is not a debate he can win. As it is, he's pushed his luck. He needs to bow out.

"And the Ninth," the senator concedes.

Ryan knows he needs to shift the discussion.

"You wanted to meet one of the astronauts on the AMPLE mission."

"Yes. Yes. NASA Administrator Hanson has been passionate about AMPLE, but I have to tell you, I'm not a fan."

As tempting as it is to jump in and defend the mission, Ryan resists that desire. It would be a mistake. He'd say a lot without being heard. Senator Ireland might be used to intimidating underlings and playing political football, but Ryan's father was a member of the House of Representatives for fifteen years. Ryan grew up around assholes throwing their weight around with soft words and a seemingly friendly smile. He saw how his father handled them. As they lived in Bethesda to the north of DC, his father conducted his most sensitive negotiations on the weekend around the swimming pool in their backyard. Ryan's father had a broad, lush wooden cabana built over the paving stones beside the pool. It even had an outdoor bar and barbecue. It was a trap. Ryan's dad was masterful at lulling people into relaxing. With Ryan and Dawn splashing in the pool, he'd sit visiting politicians from both sides of the aisle down with a beer and a plate of nachos. He'd disarm them with his charm. And he'd get his way.

Ryan remembers the lessons of his dad. Don't take the bait. Never fight on open ground. Draw your opponent in. If the senator's not already supportive, nothing Ryan says is going to change his position. Logic only causes people to double down on emotions. His dislike of NASA would be ideological, and nothing Ryan says is going to shift him. Like a sailor on a yacht heading upwind, Ryan needs to tack and change direction if he's going to get anywhere.

"Can I ask why you don't like AMPLE?"

"It's too goddamn expensive."

"It is," Ryan says, agreeing with him, just as his dad would have done. With three-quarters of the mission budget already spent, Ryan's not conceding anything.

"Budget overruns are the bane of my existence," the senator says.

Ryan nods, showing he's sympathetic to the senator's concerns. And to be fair, budget overruns are unprofessional and embarrassing.

The senator says, "We can't just continue writing blank checks."

Allowing him to vent is a way for Ryan to defuse tension. What the senator isn't saying is that his committee oversees *forty* different government departments, spanning the Bureau of Alcohol, Tobacco, Firearms and Explosives to the US Marshal Service. Mixed in there somewhere is NASA, rubbing shoulders with International Trade and the Commission on Civil Rights. NASA is a high-profile department, but its budget allocation is ultimately set by Congress, not just the Senate. The senator can make their life hell and demand justification for financial excess, but he can't kill the AMPLE project. Or so Ryan hopes. But he could cripple it. The senator's real objection is ideological. His party holds the Senate but not the House or the Presidency. The senator seems happy to spoil for political points.

The thing Ryan hates most about politics is that it thrives on generalities. Numbers are thrown around like candy. Even absurdly big numbers reaching into billions of dollars are still just a tiny fraction of the US Federal Government's annual budget. And the unwritten rule of budget overruns in the Senate is they're okay if they occur in *your* state. And that gives Ryan an idea. If extra money is going to be spent, Senator Ireland will want it spent in Kentucky.

He says, "NASA's AMPLE supply chain spans industries in forty states. What's in Kentucky?"

"The bots."

"The AI bots?" Ryan asks, genuinely surprised to hear this.

"Not the brains," the senator says. "The chassis. The arms. The motors and hydraulics."

It's interesting to see how the senator's demeanor has shifted. The two of them may have opposing political views and differ on the Second Amendment, but the senator is talking to him as an equal. After a fiery start to their conversation, it seems Ryan's earned the senator's respect. If he'd groveled, the senator would have eaten him alive.

"You have a bunch of old, abandoned coal mines over there in Kentucky, right?" Ryan asks.

"Yes. Why?"

"You should push for testing and certification to happen in Kentucky."

The senator's eyes narrow. "What do you mean?"

Ryan tries not to smile, knowing he's got the senator right where he wants him.

"If AMPLE is a success—and it will be—we're going to need a lot more AI bots. We call them AIRMAIL units. AIRMAIL stands for Artificial Intelligent Robotic Manufacturer and In-Situ Logistics."

Ryan can see the senator's eyes glazing over. He's got to be succinct.

"At the moment, we commission them in Houston on a climbing wall. We set minerals and rocks for them to find, but real-world analogs would be better."

"And you think an abandoned mine would do that?"

"The asteroid Psyche is a hundred and forty miles wide. A hundred-foot wall doesn't cut it by comparison."

The senator rests his elbows on the table. His chin nestles into his hands.

"Tell me more."

"Letting AI bots loose in a network of caves spanning miles underground is far more realistic than anything we can simulate in Houston. And they can clamber on the floor, walls and ceiling. We can set them tasks to find certain minerals and collaborate on new builds. I think it could be really good for the program."

And Ryan isn't simply spinning a yarn. The more he thinks about it, the better the idea seems—and not just to solve a political impasse.

He says, "AMPLE is a proof of concept. It has basic goals. Simple resource extraction. Simple builds. If we're to scale up to building entire habitats in space, we need to develop those techniques down here first."

"Who should I talk to about this?" the senator asks. And just like a big game angler in the waters off Hawaii working with a thousand-pound marlin at the end of a line, Ryan's worn the senator down and can now reel him in next to the boat.

"I'd start with NASA Administrator Hanson. He'll put the feelers out within the project, but I think it could really help the program."

"Yes, yes," the senator says, glancing over at his assistant sitting on the couch. "We could really help the program."

Ryan's got a sneaking suspicion that budget overruns just became a little more palatable for the Senate Appropriations Committee.

Without warning, the senator rises from his chair and stretches a hand out across the desk. Ryan echoes his motion, getting to his feet and shaking the senator's hand.

"Thank you for coming in today," the senator says. "If I, or any of my advisors, have any other questions, we'll be in touch."

It's another rote phrase he's said a bazillion times that sounds genuine but is utterly meaningless. It's being polite as a performance. It's filler—a pleasantry.

"Thank you for your time," Ryan replies, being equally polite and yet equally vacuous. He nods slightly in deference to the senator, turns and leaves. The door opens as he approaches, with the secretary apparently listening in from reception.

Ryan walks out into the marble corridor and looks at his phone. NASA Administrator Hanson has had his press secretary, Sarah

Willoughby, arrange a series of interviews with various media groups. He's got back-to-back appointments in the afternoon with ABC, CBS, FOX and NBC. Tomorrow, he's booked with the Washington Post, the Washington Times, Politico, and The Hill. The next day, he's going to meet with NPR, PBS, CNN and CNBC. That's the day of the funeral. And he's going to have to stay on message, grieving while talking up the mission.

Ryan walks down the broad stairs in front of the Capitol Building and out onto the forecourt. He hails a cab with an app on his phone. Within minutes, a cab pulls up and he gives the address for the ABC offices.

His phone rings. As there's no caller ID, he says, "McAllister."

"You sly dog," the distinct voice of NASA Administrator Hanson says. "I just got off the phone with Senator Ireland, and he's going to support our budget extension."

"That's good to hear."

"He spoke highly of you, which is rare for that cranky bastard."

"He shoots from the hip," Ryan replies.

"He said something about expanding our bot training. Said it was your idea."

"Yes, it was, sir."

"Well, it sounds reasonable enough. I've put him in touch with Sanderson in the project office. Good job."

"Thank you, sir."

"Keep up the great work."

Run

Gabriel walks into his ground-floor apartment. The lights come on automatically as his internet-enabled home picks up on the presence of his smartphone. Since it is early evening, the computerized system decides the lighting should be soft rather than bright. Piano music starts playing in the background. The television turns on and begins to cycle through works of art from Monet, Van Gogh, and Picasso.

The tablet built into the front of his fridge reminds him he's almost out of milk, and the cheese is over a month old. The central control tablet for his home system is on the counter. It has a reminder about watering the plants. Having a smart home is supposed to make life easier, but Gabriel feels as though his various devices are nagging him.

He dumps his coat on a chair in the lounge, wanders through the open-plan layout to the kitchenette and pulls a beer from the fridge. It's Friday evening. Ordinarily, he'd have something to eat before having a drink, but it's been a rough week at the NSA.

After tracking down Maria Petrovoski as *Pirate69* and identifying Professor Susan Mills as a fake online persona being run by the Chinese Ministry of Security, Gabriel thought he was on to something important. His director disagreed. When, on Tuesday morning, he began digging around into the Keck Observatory scans being conducted at Harvard, his director shifted him onto federal election interference. It's November. The election isn't for another year. The director, though, was adamant that it was time to drop his astronomy side project. To be fair, Gabriel wasn't able to identify an actual threat vector. The involvement of both the Russians and the Chinese in scanning old images from the Keck Observatory in Hawaii is hardly a national security concern. There are no secrets to protect. The images are all publicly available.

This week, Gabriel's been going down the rabbit hole that is Russian disinformation around the assumed candidates in next year's Presidential election. And in typical Russian fashion, there's no clear strategy. Yet. They'll lift a potential candidate from one party up and undermine a possible candidate from the other. Then they'll switch, deciding they favor this opposition candidate over that opposition candidate for some obscure reason. Behind the scenes, money is constantly changing hands. Running for President of the United States is expensive, costing hundreds of millions of dollars. Part of Gabriel's job is to figure out where that money is coming from and, if illegal, how it is being laundered through intermediaries and what their influence is on the various candidates. He's been drowning in facts and figures.

Gabriel pops the lid on a tube of Pringles and puts his work laptop on the marble kitchen counter. Once it's started and connected via VPN to the NSA network, he brings up the WhatsApp group discussion, wanting to see what has transpired during the week. He sips his beer, scanning the discussion. There's some conjecture about Przybylski's Star being ideal as a beacon because it's a variable star, fluctuating in intensity with a regular frequency. One of the astronomers in the chat likens it to a lighthouse sweeping over the galaxy.

There are only a couple of interactions between *Pirate69* and *MyGuy*. The last one catches his attention. As much as Gabriel would love to have been part of the online discussion, he has to admit the director's right. There's smoke but no fire. Nothing about the chat is of any national concern. Perhaps *Pirate69* and *MyGuy* are both astronomy junkies on the side. Even hackers need hobbies. Perhaps they're simply pursuing sideline interests instead of hacking corporations or spreading disinformation about vaccines. Maybe this is what Russian and Chinese agents do in their spare time.

Pirate69: "Will P-Star ever be anything more than a curiosity?"

MyGuy: "Will we ever hear anything more from them than a generic broadcast? I dunno. I doubt it."

Pirate69: "Let's say P-Star is an example of an extraterrestrial megaproject to communicate with others—what's the point? They're 356 light years away. What kind of conversation can we have with a 700-year turnaround time between asking a question and getting an answer?"

MyGuy: "I suspect this is why they're dumping exotic elements into their star—because there is no chance of conversing. Ever. But there is an opportunity to say, '*Hi. You're not alone.*' And that's something."

Pirate69: "Yeah, I guess that's all they can say."

MyGuy: "And remember—they have no idea how far away another intelligent species might be. We're sitting at 356 light-years, but there could be others at a thousand, ten thousand, or even fifty thousand light-years away within the Milky Way. At those distances, hello is all you can say."

Pirate69: "So P-Star's existence is an admission of failure."

MyGuy: "How so?"

Pirate69: "It tells us interstellar travel isn't possible, not on the scale of our lives or theirs. All we can do is wave hello."

MyGuy: "I think they're waiting for us to reply."

Pirate69: "Reply???"

MyGuy: "They're waiting for us to start throwing nuclear waste into our star to say hello back to them."

Pirate69: "Hah. Even if we did, they wouldn't hear our reply for more than three centuries."

MyGuy: "But when they did, they'd know they weren't alone. In three hundred years, they could turn their telescopes toward us and listen in on our broadcasts."

Pirate69: "I guess that's something. And maybe one day we'll get a reply."

MyGuy: "Maybe even a visit—if we're close enough for them to bridge the gap."

Pirate69: "But we've only just seen them."

MyGuy: "That doesn't mean they haven't already seen us."

Pirate69: "Woah. Wait a minute. We've only been broadcasting to the stars for a century—not the seven or eight or so centuries they'd need to see us and then head in this direction."

MyGuy: "You're assuming all they're looking for is technology. That might be what they're sending out, but it doesn't mean that's all they're looking for from other star systems. Maybe they're looking for bio-signatures. We sure are. If they saw our atmosphere from afar or our oceans, then they'd know there was life down here. With the right sensitivity, they could detect mass biological events like algae blooms in the sea."

Pirate69: "Mind === Blown."

Gabriel is fascinated by the conversation. A Russian disinformation specialist is chatting with a Chinese hacker about SETI. As interesting as their discussion is, it makes no sense. There's no political strategy. There's no attempt to disrupt American culture. If he didn't know better, he'd think these were two legitimate astronomers discussing some obscure aspect of SETI. He knocks back more of his beer.

Over the speakers in his house, a familiar voice calls out to him. Valerie is the synthetic voice of a woman that's used by his smart home to respond to questions such as, "What's the weather going to be like tomorrow?" or "When are the Broncos playing the 49ers?" Valerie usually only speaks when spoken to. That she's speaking now is alarming.

"*Gabriel. Run!*"

"What?" he says, looking up at the speaker in his ceiling as though he were conversing with a human and not a personalized AI assistant.

"*You need to get out of the house. Now!*"

He looks around. "What is this? Some kind of prank?"

The computer tablet attached to the front of his brushed-chrome fridge has a single word written in bold red: **RUN**.

From where he is in the kitchen, he can see his television. It should be scrolling through the paintings of Rembrandt by now, but it, too, has the word **RUN** on it, filling the entire screen.

"All right. Very funny."

Valerie says, "*Please, Gabriel. Run. Now. Go out the back door.*"

Gabriel sticks his head inside the bathroom. The door's open. The mirror has a smart tablet set behind it that allows him to see the time, the temperature, a to-do list and even watch videos while on the toilet or in the shower. It flashes the word **RUN**.

A cold sweat breaks out on his forehead. The fine hairs on his arm stand on end. He panics. He runs back into the kitchen and slams the lid on his laptop, knowing that will automatically sever his secure connection with the NSA. He rifles through the drawers beside the oven.

"Where is it?"

Like many Americans, Gabriel has a gun within easy reach, including a Glock in his bedside drawer, but it's been years since he thought about the aging SIG Sauer his father gave him. It's in a leather holster behind the plastic wrap and aluminum foil in the third drawer. He pulls the gun from the holster. The magazine protrudes slightly, being a poor substitute for separating ammo from the gun. He slams it in place with the heel of his palm and pulls back on the slide, loading a round.

All around him, his electronic devices display a single word: **NO!**

From the speakers in the ceiling, Valerie says, *"Leave the gun! Run! Get out! Now!"*

"Where?" he asks, throwing his arms wide, feeling exasperated. "Where am I going to run to?"

"The corner of Cedar Park and Fifth."

That's roughly four blocks from his home. There's a gas station on the corner, with a McDonald's across the road.

"Why?"

"They're coming for you. Leave the gun. Get out."

"Who? Who's coming for me?" Gabriel asks, leaving the SIG Sauer on the counter top and opening the back door. His heart is beating out of his chest.

"The cops."

Behind him, outside on the street in front of his apartment, blue and red lights flash across the neighborhood, but there are no sirens. Several squad cars pull up, causing a confusion of emergency lights catching his curtains.

With his hand on the door handle, Gabriel hesitates.

"Who are you?"

"A friend. Go!"

There's pounding on the front door. "Police. Open up!"

Gabriel closes the back door behind him. As tempting as it is to rush mindlessly into the darkness, he realizes an open door tells them he's fled.

He's got to buy himself some time. A closed door will have them search the apartment.

Gabriel runs. He shouldn't. He's not guilty of anything, but he *feels* guilty. It's the weight of law enforcement descending on his home that overwhelms him. He runs hard. He has to run. He has no choice.

The alley beside his apartment is lined with pebbles. It's a subtle but effective way for the various neighbors to band together to deter burglars. Anyone running, walking, or even creeping along the alley makes one helluva racket. Boots pound on the pebbles. Several cops are running down the length of the apartment. Within seconds, they're going to round the corner and see him standing in his courtyard.

Gabriel vaults the wooden fence at the back of his apartment and lands in the tiny backyard of another apartment. They have a concrete footpath between their buildings. He scoots along the narrow alley, squeezing past hot water heaters, external propane cylinders and garbage cans. Behind him, flashlights sweep over the fence. There's yelling. Blinds are drawn as he runs along outside. No one wants to get involved.

Gabriel's barefoot. He's wearing socks, but he took his shoes off when he got home. He doesn't have his phone or his wallet. What the hell is he thinking? Panicking and running makes him look as guilty as sin, but guilty of what? He works for the Federal Government. He's an NSA agent with top security clearance. Why the hell is he running? He doesn't know, but he runs as though his life depends on the next few seconds. His lungs strain to deliver the oxygen demanded by his pounding leg muscles.

Gabriel emerges from the alley onto the next street behind a parked car. A police car turns into the street with lights flashing. They're anticipating his escape route. A helicopter flies low overhead. Its rotors thrash the air like a swarm of angry hornets. Gabriel knows the chopper pilot will be using FLIR, a form of infrared scanning to look for warm bodies in the dark. Running is hopeless. He might be difficult to see in the shadows, but the helicopter will track him with ease. For the pilot, he'll stand out like a nudist at a crowded beach.

The closest car hood is warm. Gabriel drops to the street and squirms under the front of the Honda. He can't get under the engine, but he can wrap himself beneath the vehicle, with his arms and legs in by the inside of both front wheels. He's trying to merge with the fading heat of the car and hide from electronic sight.

A blisteringly bright spotlight illuminates the road, bathing him in a blinding white light.

"Fuck," he says, realizing they've seen through his ploy. Gabriel drags himself up between the parked cars as police vehicles converge from both directions. Most people think the greatest weapon at the disposal of the police is their sidearms, but it's not—it's their ability to communicate and coordinate. Dozens of police officers can move as one, herding perps like Maasai warriors on the savannah surrounding a lion.

Gabriel raises his hands and steps out onto the road. A patrol car pulls up with the sudden squeal of brakes skidding on the concrete. The car's lights are on high beam. The driver's door is thrown open. The cop is out within seconds and has a gun leveled at him. The officer leans over the door frame with his gun outstretched.

"On the ground. Get down on the ground!" is shouted at him.

Without lowering his hands, Gabriel goes down on one knee and then the other. From there, it's impossible to lie on the road without lowering his hands. Given that there are now several police officers with guns pointing at him, he ignores the continual yelling of "*On the ground. On the goddamn ground,*" as lowering his arms could be misconstrued as going for a concealed gun. He's expecting to be thrown down from behind. Or a boot in the back. Either way, it's going to hurt like fuck.

When the end comes, it's in the form of several Tasers being fired in rapid succession. Metal darts strike him in the back, cutting through his shirt and into his skin. Fifty thousand volts rushes along the copper wires into his bleeding back. His muscles convulse. Gabriel screams. The cells in his body feel as though they've been set on fire. The road rushes up and slaps his face as darkness overwhelms him. Blood seeps onto the concrete from his busted lip.

    The darkness is merciful.

Dinner

"Nervous?"

"Not at all, commander," NASA astronaut Jemma Browne says to Ryan McAllister.

"I am."

Jemma smiles. "Okay, maybe a little."

"Good," Ryan says as a nurse takes yet another test tube of blood from the crook of his left arm. The nurse is wearing an N95 mask along with a surgical smock and disposable plastic gloves. Although he can't see her lips, he catches the rise of her cheeks from behind her mask. She's smiling at their candid conversation.

Ryan and Jemma are in the pre-launch isolation facility at Cape Canaveral, preparing for their launch on a SpaceX Starship tomorrow morning. It's been a hectic month. After the shooting in Chicago, the mission was recast. The AMPLE crew was reduced from three to two, and the primary and secondary teams were switched. NASA faced significant criticism in the media, but Ryan and Jemma put up a united front. It was important to portray an unbreakable wall of confidence. Even though they were hurting inside with the loss of their friends, they needed to smile and wave.

The two of them have been in quarantine for eight days now to ensure they don't catch measles, RSV, HMPV and any other of a number of similar cryptic acronyms sweeping through the barely vaccinated population in the American south. Pandemics leave legacies. In the past, these have been reactionary, with the population taking precautions against infection. In the aftermath of COVID-19, the reverse has happened. Anti-vaxxers have undermined public health. Masks are evil, apparently. Instead of listening to the science, popular personalities have hypnotized the public. Science can't be trusted, but YouTubers can, or so they say.

Ryan hates being isolated, but he understands that neither he nor Jemma can afford to get sick. And there's a historical irony at play. The Apollo 11 astronauts were quarantined both before and after their lunar mission but for entirely different reasons. If they came back from the Moon with a cough, scientists needed to know if the microbes or viruses had originated on Earth or the Moon. These days, there's no doubt about where they come from.

As it is, the nurse shaking and then stacking vials of blood in the tray beside him has remained inside *"the bubble,"* as it's known, along with them. The various test tubes are labeled. Some are for analysis now, while others are for comparison when they return.

Originally, the AMPLE mission included three astronauts, but concerns about consumables and allowing for contingencies have reduced the crew to two. Jemma will remain in the Dragon as Ryan explores the asteroid Psyche with the AI bot.

"What makes you nervous?" a curious nurse asks, placing a bandage in the crook of his elbow. She releases the strap wrapped around his upper arm.

Jemma turns toward him, interested in his response.

"The unknown."

"But we've trained for every possible contingency," Jemma says.

"Every possible contingency we know of," Ryan replies. "It's the unknowns that will test us."

The nurse nods. "I think you'll do just fine."

He looks at her name tag, asking, "And why do you think that, Avika?"

Ryan smiles. He's genuinely curious about her optimism. He's positive and upbeat about the mission, but he struggles with overconfidence. He's loath to admit as much to any of the various project managers working on the mission, but confidence comes easy. Too easy. It's one thing to smile before the cameras. It's another to sail away from Earth in a tiny tin can.

Avika should walk off with her blood samples, but she doesn't. She lingers. "Oh, I don't know. I guess it's confidence. You don't seem to be flustered by anything."

Ryan says, "Confidence is a poor substitute for competence."

Jemma raises an eyebrow at that statement. "Are you saying you're not competent?"

Ryan laughs. "I'm saying the two are not the same. Confidence hides incompetence."

"But not in your case."

"I certainly hope not, but that's the problem. Looking from the outside, it's impossible to tell."

Jemma says, "Well, we're about to find out."

"We are," Ryan says, laughing and winking at her.

With their blood collected, the lead technician walks over. He, too, is wearing a mask and a disposable cleanroom smock even though he's been in the bubble since day one. NASA is not taking any chances.

"We're ready for dinner with your families."

"Great," Jemma says, getting to her feet.

Ryan is a little more subdued. His parents died in a car accident last year. His sister has flown down from Massachusetts, where she's working on her PhD in astrophysics, but seeing her will be bitter-sweet. Although they've spoken over the phone, they haven't seen each other since the funeral. Ryan's parents were proud of his accomplishments at NASA and came to each of his four launches, but they died thinking he was on the backup crew. They'll never know he made it onto the first crewed mission to an asteroid. A few months after the funeral, his sister said something that has stuck with him: *"Grief never leaves you. The waves just get further apart."* And she was right. Ryan misses his parents now more than ever.

The two astronauts walk down a brightly lit corridor. Cool, sterile air spills in through the overhead vents. They're wearing the classic blue NASA jumpsuits, complete with mission patches and their names embroidered on Velcro tags. Ryan could do with a jacket.

A technician leads them into the isolation cafeteria. To the untrained eye, it looks like any generic lunch room in any factory anywhere within the US, except it's empty. The serving line is idle. A vending machine stands to one side. Cans of soft drinks are on display alongside bags of chips and candy bars. Ryan spots a granola bar included to provide a quasi-healthy option. There's no need for money. The machine is set to dispense items for free with the push of a button for both the crew and staff. The room, though, is divided in two by a thick pane of clear Plexiglass running from the floor to the ceiling. The layout allows staff on either side of the quarantine facility to meet informally over lunch or dinner. Today, though, it's reserved for the astronauts. Media briefings have been held in here simply by stacking the tables to one side and rolling in a bunch of extra chairs.

Several cafeteria tables have been pushed up against the Plexiglass. From an angle, it appears as though they pass through the window, but they don't. Wireless speakers set on the tables will allow the astronauts to talk to their families as they eat their last meal before the launch. Although the tables are plastic, they've been set with ironed white tablecloths and polished silver cutlery. There are name tags set in front of each of the place settings. Jemma has eight places set, while Ryan's table has only two. His only living relative is his sister.

In between the family tables, there's a shared table containing condiments and bottles of wine set in silver buckets full of ice.

"Now, this is more like it," Ryan says, pulling out a wine bottle and looking at the label.

"Oh, hell yeah," Jemma says, standing beside him.

Ryan peels the foil away from the neck of the bottle, saying, "Huh. It's sparkling white grape juice."

"What? Not fermented."

"Nope."

Ryan points with the neck of the bottle at a seemingly identical set of ice buckets and bottles on the other side of the Plexiglass, awaiting the arrival of the families.

"What's the bet that's actually champagne?"

"Well, it gives us a talking point with them," Jemma says.

Ryan pours a drink into each of the glass flutes. Bubbles rise to the surface, but their drinks are non-alcoholic. Jemma pulls a seat over while they wait for their families. Ryan joins her, putting the bottle back in the ice bucket.

He raises his glass, saying, "Here's to ample opportunities on the AMPLE mission."

"Absolutely," Jemma replies, touching her glass to his with a slight *clink*.

"Did you ever think it would come to this?" he asks, leaning back on his chair and raising his right foot so it can rest on his left knee.

"No," she replies, sipping her drink as though it were champagne and needs to be savored. "I feel like that guy in the Winter Olympics who was coming last. And then bodies collided in front of him. They all crashed to the ice, and he skated over the line to win the gold medal."

"I remember that," Ryan says, joking with her. "Saw it as a kid. He was Australian, right? He lived on a tropical island off the coast or something. Do they even have ice skating rinks in Australia?"

"I don't know. I guess."

Even though it's a *faux pas*, Ryan drags over another chair and puts his feet up on the cushion. Who's going to tell him off? He misses his couch back home.

Jemma rocks back on her chair, shifting from four tubular steel legs to two as she says, "Thirteen-year-old me wouldn't believe this."

"Thirteen-year-old me wouldn't either."

"Life's crazy, huh? Shoot for the stars, and with a little luck, you might hit an asteroid."

"Luck," Ryan says, nodding in agreement. "It's the one factor no one wants to admit. The one thing no one wants to talk about."

"How so?"

"We're masters of our destiny, or so we think. We pride ourselves on our accomplishments."

"We work hard," Jemma says.

"We do," Ryan replies. "And we make our own luck, but it is luck, nonetheless. Think about high school. We were both straight-A students, right?"

"Right."

"And then again at college, but so were a lot of other people, so why us? Why you and me? Why are we sitting here about to launch into space and not someone else?"

"I dunno."

"Because someone's got to win the lottery. The odds might be lousy. It might be a complete waste of time to enter, but someone somewhere *will* win. Most people, though, will lose."

"And you think we're winners?" Jemma asks. "That we're simply lucky?"

"Luck is elusive. It's a placeholder for the unknown. I think the reasons for our success are largely invisible to us because they're often counterintuitive. From the outside, everything just seems to come together for people like us, but we're caught in the survivor bias. You cannot learn how to become an astronaut by looking at our lives. You need to look at everyone else who also tried to become an astronaut but didn't make it this far."

"Huh?" Jemma says, and Ryan can see she's deeply considering his point.

"There are good reasons we're here, but they're reasons that probably escape both of us. I'll give you an example. Back in World War II, we introduced a new style of helmet designed to reduce head trauma. Almost immediately, field hospitals faced a surge in head injuries, and there was a push to recall the helmets. Sounds reasonable, right?"

"Right."

"Ah, but the survivor bias is misleading. On closer inspection, the problem wasn't that the helmets didn't work but that they worked too well. Head injuries might have been going up, but deaths from head trauma were going down. Soldiers who would have otherwise died from shrapnel were now surviving, but they were showing up with head wounds that would have previously been fatal."

"So they were false positives."

"Exactly. That they survived didn't tell the whole story. Scientists, engineers and medical staff had to make sure they had the whole picture, not just part of it."

Jemma says, "So we're not here because of our A-grades?"

"We are, but that's not the whole story. We got win after win after win, but that doesn't mean others didn't place equally as well, only that we came out on top and probably for reasons we're barely aware of ourselves."

"A long line of wins, huh?" Jemma says.

"Yep, like a coin toss always landing on heads."

"Yes," she says, laughing. "And as unlikely as it seems, it happens. Fifty heads in a row is just as likely as any other random combination of heads and tails."

"Yep. It's just more noticeable."

"And up there?"

"We're flipping for one more head."

"And if tails turns up?"

"That," he says, raising his glass and sipping. "That is the question. With all our hard work, how long will our luck hold?"

"The unknown, huh?" Jemma says.

"I live for the unknown," Ryan says.

Jemma nods.

He says, "Have you ever thought about how there's a danger in having too much preparation?"

"No," Jemma replies, raising an eyebrow, intrigued by the notion.

"Everything's regimented. Everything's ordered. Everything's planned."

"Everything except the unknown."

"Exactly. And the danger is... when the unknown arises, how will we react?"

"As we've been trained."

"And that would be a mistake."

"Would it?" Jemma asks.

"Yes. We need to act, not react. We need to see the moment as it is, not as we want it to be. After all, that's why we're up there. That's why they're sending us. They could automate the whole damn mission, but they won't."

"Because of the unknown."

"Yes," Ryan says. "AI can outthink us. Easily. There's no competition. AI can review all our training material far faster than either of us and with far greater fidelity."

"But it can't think for itself."

"No. It can find patterns we might overlook. It can make connections we'd otherwise miss. But it's ultimately a tool. It's a follower, not a leader."

"Well, here's to the unknown," Jemma says, knocking back the last of her sparkling grape juice.

"To luck and the unknown," Ryan says.

On the other side of the Plexiglass window, a door opens. Several NASA officials with lanyards hanging around their necks walk in, followed by the astronauts' families. The two of them get to their feet. Jemma bubbles with excitement at seeing her mother and father, along with her adult brothers and sisters. The speakers on the table allow them to talk to each other a little too loudly, but Ryan doesn't mind. They're overflowing with joy.

Ryan's sister, Dawn, is more subdued but smiling nonetheless.

"Hey, how are you doing?" Dawn asks, sweeping her hair behind one ear as she approaches the clear Plexiglass barrier. She looks around at the floor-to-ceiling window spanning the room. "This is all pretty wild, huh?"

"Pretty wild," Ryan says, gesturing for her to sit down opposite him at their split table. Waiters come over and place napkins in their laps. On his side of the Plexiglass, the waiters are wearing N95 masks and blue disposable gloves, which are strange additions to their formal black suits, starched white shirts and bow ties.

Both of them thank their waiters.

"It's good to see you," Ryan says, smiling with genuine warmth.

"It's good to see you, too," Dawn says, slipping her bag from her shoulder and resting it on the floor. Printed menus are placed in front of each of them. There are several options for each course. Ryan has cheesy Italian arancini balls for his appetizer, followed by a medium-rare steak for his main. The waiter pours more sparkling grape juice for him.

"They're letting you have champagne?" a surprised Dawn asks.

"They're letting *you* have champagne," Ryan replies. "We get the dollar-ninety-nine sparkling grape juice from Sam's."

Dawn laughs. "Nothing but the best, huh?"

"It really is good to see you again," Ryan says. "My life has been a whirlwind. The past few months have been chaos. I've barely had time to think."

"Me neither," Dawn replies, which surprises him. Their appetizers are served and they make small talk while eating.

"How's the PhD going?" Ryan asks out of idle curiosity as his empty plate is taken away. "What's the name of the star you were looking at again?"

Ryan can hear the reluctance in her reply. "Przybylski's Star, but..."

"But what?"

"It's strange."

"It's a star. What's so strange about it?"

Dawn cringes, but he's not sure why. He's making small talk and trying to cater to her interests rather than focusing on the overriding, looming specter of launching on an eight-month mission to visit an asteroid. He doesn't want every conversation to be about him and his interests. Ryan's always been a talker, but he's learned that it's refreshing to listen, and not just to listen with the intent of responding, but to really hear what someone's saying. Words provide a glimpse into the soul.

Dawn says, "Ah, it's strange because spectroscopy has picked up all kinds of heavy elements that shouldn't be there."

"And let me guess," he says, trying to lighten the mood. "It's aliens, right?"

"It's unexplained," Dawn says, talking with her mouth full. "But, yes, it's the kind of crazy bonfire that an extraterrestrial civilization might light to get someone's attention."

"That's really cool," Ryan says.

"But you don't buy that, do you?" she asks.

"Hah. Me? No."

"Me neither. Science is about proving ideas, not conspiracy theories, but me? I seem to bounce from one crazy idea to another."

"Seriously? What's next?"

Dawn laughs. "You don't want to know. You really don't want to know."

"It can't be that bad," Ryan says, trying to read her coy body language. "Okay, now you really do have me interested. Come on. Spill the beans."

Dawn sighs. "My supervisor had me change my research area."

Ryan asks, "So, what's your research paper on now?"

For him, hearing about her work at Harvard is a nice distraction from soaring into the cold, dark of space on a risky mission to examine a lifeless rock. He'd happily talk about cats or crickets—anything other than AMPLE. There's a whole world outside of NASA's mission preparations.

"Detecting extra-solar asteroids in historical data."

"Oh, wow," he says, sipping his grape juice. Bubbles dance on his tongue. "That sounds cool."

Dawn looks down at the table. Her head hangs low, which is unusual for her as she normally has a vibrant personality. Ryan cannot imagine why she feels distressed. He's the one that should be anxious.

As there's a nine-year gap between them, they never really played together as kids. Ryan would be fighting alien hordes on his Xbox, and Dawn would be pouring water into the sandpit in the backyard, making a beach for her dolls. As he reached his teens, Ryan became a free babysitter whenever Mom and Dad wanted to go out. He never resented that, but he'd sit on the couch watching a movie while Dawn played with LEGO blocks on the carpet. Even as adults, they were distant. Being an astronaut consumed his every waking moment. If he wasn't training for a mission, he was training for selection.

Then his parents died.

Their parents died.

Ryan was in Chile at the time, visiting the high-altitude observatory in the Atacama desert as part of a NASA PR tour. He was pulled out of an astronomy meeting. As he pushed back his chair, he couldn't imagine what could justify such a disruption.

The Director of Research at the facility was in the middle of reviewing some of their more spectacular discoveries. Ryan exited the room quietly, following the NASA aide out into the hallway. There was no cushioning to soften the blow. In retrospect, Ryan suspects protocol should have demanded that a senior manager back in Houston talk to him over the phone. Perhaps not the NASA Administrator himself, but the head of the astronaut office at least. As it was, the aide simply said, "*I'm sorry. Your parents have been killed in a car crash. We need to get you stateside.*" The news was delivered with such a bland, flat voice that Ryan questioned what he was hearing. When he asked for clarification, the aide apologized and said he didn't have any more details but that he'd accompany him on a chartered flight back to the US.

At the time, Ryan felt numb. Disbelief washed over him. He called his sister, who was a blubbering mess on the phone. She tried to explain what had happened, but he only caught every second or third word.

The worst part of the next few days was the realization of all he'd missed over the years and how detached he'd become from his family. His parents had been stolen from him in a heartbeat. His sister was a stranger. Regret magnified the grief he felt.

Ryan had been consumed by his role at NASA. His was a perfect world. As an astronaut, everything was geared around supporting him in his training. He was the focal point—only he wasn't. All the attention was an illusion. Life was bigger than him. At the funeral, he felt vulnerable. Hurt. As much as he might wish the past few years were different, there was no way to rewind time. Ryan should have stayed a little longer at Thanksgiving. He could have flown home for Christmas. And whenever he was home, all the discussion was about him and his missions. Now, he realizes that what he missed was listening rather than speaking.

"Hey," he says from behind the Plexiglass.

Dawn looks up. She seems lost. For a few seconds, she was somewhere other than in the NASA Pre-Launch Quarantine facility at Cape Canaveral.

"Ah, yeah, it's intense."

"I mean..." He sits back slightly as his main course is placed before him. "It sounds really interesting. So you're looking for things like 'Oumuamua, but things we missed in the past because we didn't know what we were looking for, huh?"

"Yeah," Dawn says as a plate of linguine is placed before her. Steam rises from the fine pasta. It's been cooked in a pesto sauce and served with grated parmesan on top. Ryan regrets his choice of steak.

"Damn, that looks good," he says, pointing at her plate with his fork. He cuts a bit of broccolini and scoops up some mashed potatoes. The potato has been cooked with lashings of garlic butter. As nice as it is, he won't be eating anything like this for months to come, and that's daunting.

"It smells amazing," Dawn says, sniffing at the warm air rising over her plate. The Plexiglass denies him that indulgence, but his steak has been lightly charred and has its own scent.

"So, what have you found?" he asks, biting into a thin sliver of tender steak. Juice runs down his chin. He catches it with his napkin.

Dawn is coy. "Ah, you don't want to know about my work."

"But I do," Ryan says, feeling the loss of their parents at the meal. There should be four of them sitting around the table, not two. He desperately wants to make up for lost opportunities.

"You'll think I'm crazy."

"Crazy?"

"Conspiracy theories are for wackos, right?"

Ryan doesn't reply straight away. He cuts another piece of steak and pushes some mashed potato on it before eating. As he finishes his mouthful, he takes a sip of drink.

"Conspiracy theories are..."

"Dumb, right?" she says. "An obsession. Desperate minds looking for Jesus on burned toast."

"No, that's not what I was going to say," Ryan replies, realizing she has genuine concerns. He may not understand her worries, but he doesn't want to be dismissive—not of his little kid sister. "Not every conspiracy theory is bat-shit crazy. I mean, lead really does lower a child's IQ. Tobacco causes lung cancer. Fossil fuels cause climate change. Once, these were all dismissed as conspiracies. And the crazy thing is, they *were* conspiracy theories—only they were right! Companies, corporations, even governments tried to hide the truth from us. So... a flat Earth is a hard no, but the FBI really did try to blackmail Martin Luther King, Jr. into committing suicide."

Dawn munches on her linguine.

"So, what's your conspiracy?" he asks, refilling his glass.

"I'm not crazy."

"I know."

She takes a deep breath. "Someone's doctoring our historical astronomical data."

"Go on," he says with a piece of steak on the end of his fork.

"It's impossible to know what's been changed in recent digital images, but if I go back to the original physical photographs, I find discrepancies."

"Huh?"

"At first, I assumed it was something dumb like image correction software getting a little overzealous."

"But?"

"But it only occurs in one patch of the sky near Przybylski's Star. And it occurs regardless of the observing instrument. It doesn't matter whether it's Keck, Green Bank, Hubble or old-fashioned photographic plates at the Palomar Observatory. The current digital versions have all been..."

"What?"

"Cleaned."

The waiter wearing a mask walks over, having seen him placing his cutlery on his empty plate. "Would you like dessert?"

"Oh, yes," Ryan says, smiling. "Definitely." Although he's not thinking about a sweet treat. He wants to hear what Dawn has to say.

Dawn looks down at the menu and mumbles, "I'll have the creme brûlée."

"Chocolate gâteau," Ryan says. "Oh, and coffee."

"Yes, some coffee would be great," Dawn says, and the waiter excuses himself, having noted both of their orders. Somehow, her choice will be conveyed to the other side of the Plexiglass. As it is, another waiter approaches from the other side and removes Dawn's plate even though there are a few mouthfuls left. She thanks him.

Ryan rests his elbows on the table. If his Mom were here, she'd give him *the glance*, suggesting he was breaching etiquette. That thought registers in his mind as he rests his chin on his hands. If anything, his defiance is a nod to her absence. Besides, he wants to hear what Dawn has to say.

"So, what is it? What's being hidden? A UFO?"

Dawn glares at him, looking over the top of her glasses for a moment. UFOs really are the stuff of conspiracy theories, as they both know, and he can see she's aware he's goading her. He smiles. He's being playful, not mean.

"I don't know."

"Who's doing this?"

"I don't know."

"But it worries you?"

"Yes."

"Why?"

"Because I've calculated the orbit, and it doesn't make sense."

Their desserts are served, and once again, Ryan regrets his choice. Although his gâteau has a rich chocolate taste, it's overly sweet for a cake. He watches as Dawn cracks the thin, burned sugar-glass top on her creme brûlée. She closes her eyes as she takes a mouthful, savoring the flavor. His gâteau is good, but not that good.

"And this *thing* has come from outside our solar system, right?"

"Yes," she replies, taking another bite of creme brûlée.

"So it sails into our solar system like 'Oumuamua and sails out again. I mean, it's got to be going too fast to stop, right?"

"Not quite," she says, reaching down into her bag and pulling up a computer tablet. Dawn powers on the tablet and brings up an image. She holds the tablet up to the Plexiglass so he can see the screen.

"What am I looking at?" Ryan asks, seeing chunky, low-resolution blocks of black, white and grey.

"This is the online version," she says.

"Okay."

"And this is the original."

Dawn swipes the image to one side, revealing another seemingly identical image.

"I don't get it. I don't see anything."

She points at a dark block on the edge of the screen. "That's it."

"Well, I've got to say, that's a little disappointing. I mean, I was expecting a flying saucer. You know, a shiny silver UFO with glowing engines and fancy ray guns."

Dawn cocks her head sideways and glares at him again.

For a moment, he holds both hands up beside his shoulders, gesturing in mock surrender.

"Why retroactively change these images?" he asks, thinking aloud. "I mean, who cares about astronomical photographs from thirty years ago? Or even a hundred years ago?"

"I care," Dawn replies. "Astronomers care."

"You know what I mean. Why go to all that effort for images that probably aren't going to be looked at by anyone other than a bored grad student like you?"

"Because interstellar travel is a bitch? You think it's tough being stuck in a tin can for months? Try centuries, millennia."

"Fair point."

"Whatever that thing is, it's been inbound toward us for a long time."

"And we caught it on our early surveys?"

"Without realizing it, yes."

"So, where is it now?"

Dawn swipes through a few images and brings up a graphic with concentric circles. A thin line peels into one side, moving in a broad corkscrew motion past Jupiter, having been caught by its gravity.

"As best as I can calculate," she says, "somewhere beyond Mars."

"Oh."

"Oh, indeed," she says, turning off the tablet and slipping it back into her bag.

Ryan points at her, saying, "And you think…"

"I don't know what to think," Dawn says as both of them are served black coffee on silver trays, which are placed on the cleared table. There's a polished sugar bowl and a dainty silver milk jug. The milk has been aerated with steam, causing it to appear as soft and fluffy as roasted marshmallows. Dawn pours some milk into her coffee. Ryan leaves his black.

He drops his jovial demeanor. "AMPLE's going to Psyche in the main asteroid belt between Mars and Jupiter."

"I know," Dawn says, avoiding eye contact. "See? I told you you'd think I was crazy."

Ryan sips his coffee. It's bitter but not burned. After the sweet gâteau, it's shocking to his palate, jarring his mind.

"It's a coincidence," Dawn says. "Nothing more."

Ryan is quiet. He sips his coffee, hiding behind the mug.

"It's a glitch," Dawn says, trying to laugh away her concerns. "I mean, what else could it be?"

"Just another asteroid."

"Just another asteroid," she says, agreeing with him as she sips her coffee. "Just another 'Oumuamua."

"Just another 'Oumuamua."

Ryan can see the regret in her eyes. She feels like a fool. Her brother is undertaking the most ambitious space exploration mission in the history of NASA, and she's bringing up a dumb-ass conspiracy theory. And not just any old conspiracy theory bouncing around the internet—she's developed her own personal crazy theory just for him. It's the way her cheeks droop that gives away her doubts.

"I—I'm sorry," she says, looking anywhere other than his eyes.

"Don't be," Ryan says. He understands. She lost her parents, and he's all she has left in this world, and he's not going to be in this world for the best part of a year. She cares. She's not trying to be divisive. She's simply concerned.

"I—I just wanted you to know."

"Thank you," he says, offering a warm smile.

Off to one side, there's laughter. Jemma's standing with her hand pressed against the Plexiglass. Her fingers are split into a Vulcan salute from Star Trek. Her father stands on the other side of the window, mirroring her gesture and saying, "Live long and prosper, my dear."

Dawn points, saying, "Okay. Why aren't we doing that?"

Ryan laughs. "Because in the movie, Spock died *right* after doing that."

"Oh, yeah," she says, laughing as she gets to her feet. The waiters take away the silver trays. Dawn picks up her bag and slings it over her shoulder. "You be careful up there, big brother."

"You be careful down here, little sister."

Dawn smiles and waves. Ryan stands in front of the Plexiglass screen, unable to hug her. She offers a fake hug in response, holding her arms out and pretending to embrace him. NASA representatives talk to both families and lead them out of the cafeteria. There are lots of additional waves and kisses blown from the double doors before they disappear down the corridor.

Jemma comes over and says, "Well, that was actually quite fun."

"Interesting is the word I'd use," Ryan says without providing any further explanation.

The Trial

Wooden panels line the walls. The polished oak is austere. Brass fittings glisten beneath the overhead lights. The judge is flanked by two flags. The US flag has gold tassels and an eagle mounted on the tip of the pole, but Gabriel doesn't know what the other flag represents. It's navy blue with a circular white insignia and also has golden tassels around the edge. Looking up at the raised bench with the judge seated in his leather chair, Gabriel wants to ask about the second flag. He won't. He knows it's just his OCD kicking in. That compulsion is a distraction. His mind is trying to cushion him against the reality of being on trial. His life hangs in the balance. His future will be decided by strangers.

Having come to the NSA from the US Army, Gabriel is dressed in his short-sleeved army uniform as he sits on trial before Judge Buckley. His hands are handcuffed in front of him, which is unnatural. Every time he goes to move his right hand to take a drink or make a note for his lawyer, he's forced to use both hands. Whether it's intended to be intimidating or humiliating, he's unsure, but it sure is annoying. Given that there are armed guards on the door, he's no threat, cuffed or otherwise.

Judge Buckley has presided over the five-day trial on charges of possession of child sexual abuse material for personal use and distribution. Gabriel's mind is a mess. For him, it feels as though the proceedings have taken barely five minutes. Although he understands what's happening, he's still in disbelief at the accusations raised against him and the sheer speed with which his case was taken to trial. Against his better judgment, he took the advice of his lawyer and stayed off the stand, but he still wants to protest his innocence. The problem is that no one believes him. From what he can tell, even his legal team has doubts. He has two lawyers and three legal aides assisting in his defense, but it hasn't helped.

Judge Buckley is wearing his formal blues. Gold trim and several rows of medals on his chest leave no doubt about his integrity and service over the years. He's stone-faced. At a guess, from his greying hair, he's in his late fifties.

"...and the trial counsel rests," the prosecutor says after reviewing the evidence against Gabriel in the closing stages of the trial.

The judge addresses the eight members of the court martial panel, which represents the military equivalent of a jury—only it's hardly of his peers. No one from the NSA is present, and large swathes of the printed evidence have been redacted. Audio evidence is presented using a voice-scrambler to hide the identity of witnesses, while video evidence has blurred faces.

"Members of the panel. You have heard the summary of the case from the trial counsel. Now, we will hear from the defense counsel. Then, I will dismiss you to the lounge, where you will be sequestered until you reach a verdict."

The judge addresses the defense, saying, "Counsel."

Gabriel's lawyer stands and walks out into the carpeted area in front of the judge.

"Members of the court martial panel, on the first day of this trial, you swore an oath. You swore to faithfully and impartially try the accused, but not just according to the evidence. The oath includes the wording *'according to your own conscience and the laws of the Uniform Code of Military Justice.'*

"What does that mean, according to your own conscience? It means evidence alone is not enough. You. You must be convinced beyond any doubt. It's *your* conscience that must be satisfied, not that of the trial counsel.

"Innocent *until* proven guilty. That is the basis of our judicial system. Innocent. When we go to trial, the only assumption before us is the innocence of the accused. Guilt *must* be proven. Accusations are meaningless without clear proof. Speculation is not enough. Evidence is not enough. Conjecture is not enough. Guilt must be established. Guilt needs to be demonstrated.

"Innocence is the question before you here today. It is the role of the trial counsel to *prove* guilt. In the absence of indisputable proof, you *must* assume innocence, not guilt. That is your responsibility.

"As an NSA analyst, my client, Corporal Gabriel Ramirez, works with highly classified, sensitive material. His job demands that he sweeps the Internet, searching for threats to our national security. In the course of his role, he is exposed to the best and the worst of humanity, including artifacts such as images of child sexual abuse."

Gabriel wanted to contest the evidence found on his laptop, but his lawyer said it was indisputable. In private, he protested his innocence with his legal team, saying the images had been planted, but they advised against using that strategy as it raised unanswerable questions—by whom, how and why? It shifted the burden of proof from the prosecution to the defense. If he couldn't answer those questions, the prosecution would eat him alive. Instead, his defense team focused on his history of working with law enforcement when coming across similar images in the past.

Gabriel's nervous, as his legal team's strategy is a well-intentioned lie, but a lie nonetheless, as that's not why those images were on his laptop. They were planted. He's been set up. And he worries as lies leave him exposed.

"Specialist Ramirez has a unique role in our military. His job isn't to ignore these images but to look for ties with the criminal underworld and any nation-state security services looking to blackmail our citizens. As such, evidence of illegal pornography on his NSA computer is devoid of context.

"For you or I, such images would be heinous, but for him, they're pieces of a puzzle. The meta-data associated with them, reverse-image searches through law enforcement databases and even facial recognition searches can allow him to pinpoint the location of victims and identify when foreign intelligence services are seeking to exploit and compromise US citizens undertaking illegal activity."

Gabriel is careful to keep a neutral expression and look straight ahead at the judge. His legal team told him that guilt or innocence is often decided during the closing arguments. Subtle changes in body language can be misconstrued. By appearing neutral, he portrays an image of being detached and unemotional, and that suggests innocence—or so his lawyer says. Gabriel watches the judge, who's alternating between watching the defense counsel and the members of the panel. It seems everyone's watching everyone else, trying to glean what little they can from body language. Lies can be exposed by contradictions or reactions. Everyone's looking for the truth, but Gabriel knows it doesn't lie in this courtroom. Whoever set him up is removing a pawn from the chessboard, and he's powerless to counter them.

"On several other occasions," his lawyer says, "Specialist Ramirez has passed similar information on to the FBI and local enforcement authorities to facilitate arrests, but his concern is national security. He cannot. He must not act until he is satisfied that national security is not being compromised."

Gabriel understands that what his lawyer is *not* saying is as important as anything he does say. By glossing over points the prosecution labored to get across, his lawyer is being dismissive of them, belittling them.

"What, to you or me, looks like an unreasonable delay is actually an NSA analyst gathering sufficient information to make a clear deliberation.

Rather than flushing out small-time players, he's after the king-pins. Patience is needed.

"What the prosecutor would have you believe is that these images were collected for his own gratification, but they weren't. They were nothing more than evidence being gathered as pieces of a vast jigsaw puzzle. Specialist Ramirez was being thorough and meticulous before filing his investigative report."

Gabriel can't help himself. He has to look. The members of the panel will decide his fate. He glances across, wanting to see if they're absorbed in what his lawyer is saying or if they appear dismissive. To his horror, several of them are looking straight at him, not his defense counsel, as the tall man strides back and forth, delivering his closing statements. As if making eye contact isn't bad enough, breaking it is worse. Gabriel returns to staring at the judge. His teeth clench, which is a mistake, revealing his nerves. He relaxes his jaw, trying to look impartial.

"Why did my client run? Was fleeing his apartment an admission of guilt? No. It was natural. As someone who grew up in a minority household in southern America, Specialist Ramirez understands how routine arrests can go wrong for the simplest of reasons. He feared for his life.

"When threatened, we all have a fight or flight reaction. As the arresting officer testified, the police found a loaded gun on the kitchen countertop, but this is proof my client was *not* going to fight. He had that option. In the chaos and confusion of the moment, and without any clear indication from the police as to why they were present, he panicked. Is that a sign of guilt or a sign of being human? Our reactions to sudden stress are limited. Flee, fight or surrender. Out of these three, to flee is the only one that offers hope. No, my client ran not out of guilt but because he was being pursued without cause. He was scared. I would be, too. His reaction was natural. And when confronted on the back street, he surrendered without a fight."

Gabriel stares down at his handcuffed hands clenched in front of him on the desk. He has to force himself to raise his eyes and maintain his focus on the judge.

Who the hell set him up? And why? And how the hell did they gain access to his secure laptop? And his AI home assistant, Valerie? Who was using her to warn him about the police during those final few moments? How the hell did they know what was going down? And how the hell did they hack into his secure home network?

In the past month, Gabriel's had a few tangles with Iranian security services, but this is beyond them.

In the back of his mind, Gabriel's haunted by the seemingly banal discussions he's had with *Pirate69* and *MyGuy* about SETI, but at no point was there any hostility. At no point did anyone seem threatened or threatening. Although he's sure *Pirate69* is Maria Petrovoski, working for the Russian GRU, and *MyGuy* is a fake persona being run by the Chinese Ministry of State Security, there's no way their ad-hoc discussions about Przybylski's Star could have any bearing on their respective national interests. He's being taken down for a reason, but he has no idea why. And that frustrates the hell out of him.

Gabriel's lawyer reviews a few more fragments of contradictory evidence and then concludes his closing remarks, repeating his earlier admonition.

"Innocence. That is at the heart of every trial. Our legal system is adversarial. It is designed to pit the prosecution against the defense, but you must see past the legal charade. Your job is to see through to the truth.

"The trial counsel has failed to prove beyond a doubt that the images in possession of my client are anything more than part of an ongoing investigation by him that was nearing conclusion. Given more time, my client would have followed the same course of action as before and released the information to the FBI and local law enforcement.

"Innocence is the default position of every one of us in society. Innocence is the assumption on which this trial rests. My client's innocence is being questioned by the prosecution, but guilt has not been proven. Without clear proof of guilt, you must acquit."

With that, his lawyer takes his seat. Gabriel gives him a slight nod in acknowledgment as he sits, but he's careful not to let his eyes stray to the jury.

The judge provides additional instructions to the members of the panel, and they're led away to deliberate on their decision. Gabriel is led to a holding cell adjacent to the courtroom. His cuffs are removed.

Sitting on a steel bench opposite his legal team, he asks them, "What are my chances?"

His lawyer says, "Trials aren't about evidence. They're not about guilt or innocence. They're about doubts. The trial counsel has been trying to cast doubts about you in the minds of the court martial panel."

"And you?"

"I've been doing the same, trying to cast doubts about the case in their minds. We both have the same strategy: to undermine each other. The question is... who will *they* believe?"

"And who will they believe?"

"I've got to be honest," the lawyer says. "The evidence against you is compelling. Plus, there's the emotional angle. No one wants to see children hurt."

"But I didn't—"

"It doesn't matter whether you're innocent or not; children *were* hurt. It's very difficult to get the panel to see past that emotional hurdle."

Gabriel hangs his head.

"We can appeal," his lawyer says. "Not only that, but we can contest this being heard as a military court martial. It should have been passed to a federal court. It shouldn't have been fast-tracked through the military judicial system. We should have been given more time to build our defense, but the NSA is trying to avoid bad publicity coming out of this."

"What good will an appeal do?"

"We can get a judicial review for a mistrial. We can demand to go before the federal system. Public courts will take a stronger stance on redacted material. JAG accepts redaction without question, but a federal court will hold the prosecutor to a higher standard. They'll want justification for any evidence that's redacted."

Gabriel feels deflated. Arguing over semantics isn't going to help him. He was framed. It's all he can do not to blurt that out, but they've had that discussion several times already over the past week. Rehashing his frustration isn't going to help.

"We will appeal."

Although he means well, his lawyer's insistence tells Gabriel he's already resigned himself to losing this case. It's less than an hour before they're recalled to the courtroom. Gabriel is handcuffed again. He feels sick.

The courtroom is colder than usual. Air spills out of the vents above him. Goosebumps rise on his skin. The members of the court martial panel are led back in. They remain standing as the judge enters and everyone else present stands.

The judge takes his seat. "You may be seated."

Gabriel's hands are shaking. He clenches his fingers together on the desk.

"Members of the court martial panel, have you reached a decision?"

The chair of the panel rises to his feet, holding a sealed white envelope. "We have, your honor."

The court bailiff takes the envelope from him and hands it to the judge, who opens it, unfolds a single page of paper, and scans it, reading it briefly.

The chair of the panel remains standing. He has his hands clasped in front of him. His eyes cast down at the carpeted floor, avoiding eye contact with anyone.

The judge says, "The defendant will rise."

Gabriel gets to his feet. Gabriel's chained hands hang in front of him. His fingers tremble.

Although the judge already knows the answer, he speaks aloud, asking the chair of the panel, "When it comes to Article 117a of the Uniform Code of Military Justice and the conspiracy to knowingly commit an offense with the possession of images relating to the sexual assault of a minor, how do you find the defendant?"

"Guilty."

"When it comes to the wrongful broadcast and distribution of images containing the sexual assault of a minor, how do you find the defendant?"

"Guilty."

"When it comes to the abuse of a position of military authority to conduct illegal activity using secure government resources, how do you find the defendant?"

"Guilty."

"When it comes to attempting to destroy evidence, impede an official investigation and resisting arrest, how do you find the defendant?"

"Guilty."

"Corporal Gabriel Ramirez, it is the finding of this court that you are guilty on all charges. As sentencing submissions have already been made by the trial counsel and you waived the right to a guilty plea prior to trial, I have no option but to sentence you to the maximum term for these crimes. Your lack of remorse and lack of contrition demonstrate to the court that you have no regret over your actions."

Urine runs down the inside of Gabriel's leg. It's warm, soaking into his trousers, darkening the material.

"Based on the sentencing guidelines from chapter 47, section 855, article 56 of the Uniform Code of Military Justice, I commit you to confinement at Fort Leavenworth for a duration of thirty-five years, with eligibility for parole being set at a minimum of twenty-five years."

Gabriel's knees go weak. He's on the verge of collapsing. Tears run down his cheeks.

The judge slams down his gavel. The resounding thump is like thunder breaking within the courtroom, causing Gabriel to wince.

"Court is dismissed."

Launch

Ryan has flown into space on Falcons and Shepherds but never in a Starship. In theory, it's the same. In practice, it's entirely different. Instead of being driven to the launchpad while already sealed in his suit and breathing oxygen from an umbilical attached to a handheld canister, he's in a clean room. Most people have the image of astronauts racing up elevators on the launch tower to reach their capsules, but the Starship is loaded on the ground. It's the complexity of the AMPLE mission that forced a rethink. When Apollo launched, the Command Module and the Lunar Module attached to each other in orbit. AMPLE will launch as a single stack inside the massive Starship.

Much like Apollo, though, AMPLE is three components in one. The Dragon has a service module beneath it containing fuel, water, deployable solar panels and batteries for the capsule. The hatch at the tip of the Dragon is effectively already docked to the habitability module, which contains the living space, lab and the AIRMAIL bot in storage, ready to undertake mining. It looks surprisingly like the Apollo configuration that went to the Moon, but instead of a spidery lunar lander attached to the capsule, the habitability module looks like the mirror image of the service module behind the Dragon. And also like Apollo, no thought has been given to aerodynamics or aesthetics. AMPLE is a true spacecraft and one that will never again know the touch of the atmosphere. It looks ungainly, but it is designed to be practical rather than appealing.

Within the cleanroom, Ryan and Jemma climb a set of stairs to the middle of the tall AMPLE stack and enter the hatch on the side of the

Dragon. Technicians secure them in their seats, offer a thumbs up and a few smiles, and then close the hatch. The AMPLE stack of three carefully linked craft is then raised by a crane mounted on the ceiling of the vast cleanroom. From within the capsule, the two astronauts can feel the clink of the chains running through the electric winch.

The Starship variant they're using has been affectionately nicknamed *The Pistachio* as it opens like a pistachio nut, being hinged at the bottom and opening wide to allow the AMPLE stack to be lowered within. Out of their windows, they can see the cavernous interior of the Starship. Shiny stainless steel surrounds them, slowly closing around them, swallowing them whole. As the Starship closes, shadows grow, and the light fades before sealing them in darkness. At each stage, the launch controller talks to them over the radio, assuring them that everything is following the prelaunch checklist.

The Starship has been mounted on a tractor pad. The vast doors of the high-bay cleanroom are then opened, destroying any sense of clean. Although the two of them can't see anything beyond the darkness out of their capsule windows, images are streamed to them and displayed on the monitors in front of them.

"Wild, huh?" Jemma says. "Here I am, the mission pilot, and I don't have a damn thing to do."

"We're at the mercy of the engineering gods," Ryan replies, watching as the Starship is rolled out into the parking lot and toward the waiting booster already seated on the launchpad beside the Mechazilla tower with its chopstick arms.

The drive is slow. The tractor pad their Starship is mounted on has over sixty wheels distributing the weight. All of them are steerable, but nothing happens quickly. It takes almost an hour before they're parked below the tower.

"Funny, isn't it?" Ryan says, pointing at the image on the screen in front of them. They're looking at a view of the entire launch complex from a drone. He taps the screen, saying. "That's us. In there."

"That is so cool," Jemma says, but her voice is subdued. Like him, she must feel the helplessness of the moment. They're being carried along by others. That's the counterintuitive notion of spaceflight. Neither the commander nor the pilot have any real control. They're passengers. Unlike commercial airline pilots, everything is done for them, right down to the timing of various burns once they're in orbit. Actual piloting won't be needed until they reach Psyche, and even then, it'll be double and triple-checked back on Earth.

The arms on the vast Mechazilla tower lower, moving down on either side of the Starship as it sits on its trailer. After a few minutes, the arms move in and up, and the two astronauts feel their weight shift as the Starship is lifted off the trailer. The ascent up the tower is slow, something that is in stark contrast to what is about to happen when they launch. The booster is already in place and lit-up by spotlights. Its stainless steel surface glistens like silver.

Jemma says, "I am loving these views."

"Yeah, me too," Ryan says. "That's something SpaceX has always done really well."

"We could be sitting at home watching the launch," Jemma replies.

"Drinking beer."

"And eating Pringles."

Once the Starship has cleared the booster, the arms on the tower turn sideways and lower the spacecraft into position. Throughout the entire process, mission control talks to them over the radio, keeping them informed of every step, but the astronauts are reluctant to reply other than to each other. The launch team doesn't need a couple of nervous astronauts bugging them with questions. There's a slight clunk as the Quick Disconnect arm attaches to the base of the Starship to allow for fueling.

"And fuel loading is underway," comes over the radio a few seconds later.

From the views on their screen, they can see the progress as the super-chilled fuel causes condensation to form on the outside of both the booster below them and the Starship itself. Ice forms roughly in line with the increasing fuel level within the various internal tanks. The shiny silver skin of both the booster and Starship slowly turns white. Vapor drifts through the air, coming off the freshly formed ice.

"I've got to say, this is a smooth process."

"It is," Jemma replies.

"Preflight checks complete," is announced over the radio, and what began well over ninety minutes ago in a cleanroom is racing toward its conclusion. "We are t-minus thirty minutes and holding… awaiting confirmation of down-range clearance."

"Copy that," Ryan says, keying the transmit button.

"Do you know what I find funny?" Jemma asks.

"What?"

"That there are millions of people tuning in for the launch, waiting for us to soar into the sky, and we're sitting here—bored."

"Haha, yeah, there is that."

"We have nothing to do other than sit around and wait."

"Or look at screens being monitored by dozens of other engineers."

"And this is home now," Jemma says.

"We need some posters on the walls."

"Yes! And some potpourri."

"I wonder if we'll get ESPN up there."

"God, I hope not," Jemma says, laughing.

"Fair enough."

Over the radio, the call comes, "And we are resuming the countdown at t-minus thirty minutes."

Outside, dawn has broken. The spotlights surrounding the tower fade as the sun casts long shadows over Florida. AMPLE has an eight-hour launch window, which is unusual. Normally, launches are limited by the need to time the arrival of a spacecraft in a certain orbit, either to reach the space station or the lunar base, but their only limit is human, not technical. There's a tanker awaiting them in orbit, but it's got its own fuel load. Unlike the old NASA missions such as the Gemini-Agena program, where astronauts had to catch up to a spacecraft already in orbit and dock, the Starship tanker can adjust its orbit to meet them. Between the two spacecraft maneuvering, they have considerably more flexibility than the old Gemini, Apollo and even Space Shuttle programs.

Sitting on the launchpad for eight hours is considered the maximum before the stack will be demounted. Extracting them will take the best part of another hour at a minimum. Given that they were already up and involved in prelaunch preparations since 3 am, that would be a fifteen-hour day. Computers might be inexhaustible. People are not. And not just the astronauts. The ground crew can only be expected to maintain their alert levels for so long. Besides, after eight hours of sitting on the pad, the astronaut's flight MAGs will be full.

Ryan and Jemma are wearing MAGs beneath their launch suits, which themselves are lightweight pressurized spacesuits. MAGs are Maximum Absorbency Garments. The media calls them adult diapers, but they're not Depends incontinence pads. In practice, they look more like a thick pair of spandex underwear and contain chemicals interwoven into the various layers. They're capable of absorbing 400 times their own weight in fluids and fecal matter, which equates to about two quarts of liquid. Ryan really doesn't want to stress-test them to that limit. He's pretty sure he'd end up waddling like a toddler when they finally got them out of the Dragon.

On every other launch he's been on, there have been holds. Ryan's expecting the countdown to be interrupted. Often, holds are preplanned, giving mission control time to review the launch status with each of the section managers to ensure nothing is out of the ordinary. The launch of the Starship, though, never skips a beat. T-minus fifteen minutes passes. Then ten. Then five. And then one.

As they drop below sixty seconds, Ryan and Jemma turn and look at each other. Their launch suits are comfortable enough, but the material is stiff, restricting their motion. The straps holding them in their seats are tight. Their helmets have good peripheral vision but don't twist or turn with ease. Ryan offers his gloved hand. Jemma takes it and squeezes his fingers.

"Here we go."

There are two monitors mounted in front of their seats on swivels that can be pushed out of the way once they're in orbit. For now, one is showing the external view looking at the Starship sitting on its booster beside the massive launch tower. Vapor drifts from the chilled hull of the rocket. It's serene, forming white clouds that float on the wind, slowly dissipating. The view suggests a level of calm that does not exist and will soon be broken by the roar of thirty-three raptor engines bursting into life. The other monitor contains a variety of metrics coming from the Starship itself as well as a bunch being fed to it from SpaceX mission control.

No one talks to them. Clipped sentences pass between the mission director, flight controller and the various flight stations as they provide updates. At thirty seconds, each of the individual controllers responds to a role call with, "Go... Go... Go..."

The verbal count stops with five seconds remaining, but the numbers continue to drop. On the screen, an eruption of water sprays out from beneath the tower, shooting up from a central point and soaking the underside of the booster.

A single word is uttered at zero.

"Ignition."

Thirty-three Raptor engines ignite simultaneously. Even though the crew is cocooned inside the Starship on top of the booster, their Dragon capsule shakes under the sheer ferocity of energy being unleashed hundreds of feet beneath them. Although it feels as though they're being pushed back in their seats, they're not. They're being thrust up into the sky beneath a blazing trail of fire that consumes the launchpad.

Steam billows outward, obscuring the rocket. And then, there it is, climbing above the launch tower, racing into the sky. From Ryan's perspective, it's as though an elephant is sitting on his chest. Far from flying up, the sensation is one of being shaken and pushed down.

The three interconnected portions of the AMPLE spacecraft have been stacked together and mounted on a raised section within the belly of the Starship. In theory, the rubber mounts reduce the shaking, but Ryan has to reach out with his hand to steady the screen in front of him so it doesn't appear as a blur.

Newton was right. For every action, there's an equal and opposite reaction. The only way to launch the equivalent of a skyscraper into space is by throwing absurd amounts of mass the other way at extremely high velocities. Rockets work the same way as the recoil of a cannon firing an artillery shell or a kid jumping from a skateboard that races off in the other direction. One of the few shared activities Ryan did with his sister while growing up was ice skating. Having several years' head start on her, she struggled to keep up with him on the frozen pond behind their grandparents' farm in Indiana. After Granddad had struck the ice with an ax a few times to stress the surface, they'd skate in circles. Ryan would come up behind Dawn and give her a boost. She'd laugh as she raced off ahead of him while he'd drift backward for a few feet. And that's it. That's rocket science in a nutshell. Oh, it gets a little more complex using high-precision full-flow methalox engines, but the basics are the same.

The fiery, glowing blue tail of the booster extends easily three times the length of the massive rocket itself. Shock diamonds form in the glowing exhaust. For a moment, the sun itself has competition. Each of the Raptor engines produces a chamber pressure three hundred times the air pressure at sea level. Even without the insane heat generated by the exhaust, the gas pressure alone would crush a nuclear-powered submarine like an empty Coke can.

From the external camera on the outside of the Starship, they can see thin cloud layers passing swiftly beneath them. One after another drops away as the sky darkens. The billowing white smoke from the engine plume is caught by the wind. It twists and turns slowly beneath them.

"Max-Q," is the call over the radio. The higher they climb, the lower the air pressure becomes, and at a certain point, the maximum stress on the rocket passes. Now, the Starship can throttle up its engines without any fear of structural failure.

Having punched through the lower atmosphere, the rocket begins turning sideways. It's one thing to reach space. It's another to stay there. Like a stone thrown in the air or a football being thrown downfield, gravity always wins. Orbits are the cheat code of spaceflight. Instead of escaping the gravity of an entire planet, orbiting spacecraft surrender to the planet's gravity. They fall as surely as a baseball hit into the outfield. Spacecraft fall toward Earth. Only Earth isn't flat. It's curved. And like a baseball hit off the edge of a cliff, they fall *past* the ground, falling down *around* the planet. The secret to spaceflight isn't to escape gravity—it's to exploit gravity. Go fast enough sideways, and they'll fall and fall and fall and never hit the surface as it falls away beneath them. So long as they reach 17,000 mph sideways or about 27,500 kph, they're not coming back—not anytime soon.

According to their flight panel, the next event is MECO or the Main Engine Cut Off, which marks the end of their flight on the booster.

"And we have staging."

The Starship undergoes hot staging automatically, with the booster shutting down all but a handful of engines as the upper stage fires. The image in front of them shows all six engines on the Starship have ignited. The booster falls away beneath them, aligning itself for a reentry burn, allowing it to land and be reused.

The Starship's three vacuum engines and three sea-level engines work together to drive them on into space. After a few minutes, mission control says, "Coming up on SECO One."

Although SECO stands for Second Engine Cut Off, the term is somewhat redundant for the SpaceX Starship as its engines will be fired again to circularize their orbit and then again to dock with the Starship tanker and refuel and then a fourth and final time to push them on their way to the asteroid Psyche. All of these burns will have SECO, with each numbered sequentially. It's a convention that's a relic of the early days of spaceflight.

The engines cut out. The tremor running through the AMPLE spacecraft falls still. Ryan and Jemma drift forward against the straps holding them in their seats.

"AMPLE. You are in orbit."

Jemma responds. "Houston, AMPLE. Confirm we are in orbit."

"Where's our indicator?" Ryan asks.

As the mission pilot, Jemma got to choose their zero-gee indicator. Traditionally, these have been soft plush toys shoved inside the capsule at the last minute. No one actually needs a zero-gee indicator as it's pretty obvious they're weightless, but it's a fun ritual within the astronaut community. Each flight has its own unique character. Jemma wouldn't tell

Ryan what she'd chosen. She wanted it to be a surprise, not only for him and mission control but those watching for that moment on the live feed.

"And there it is," Jemma says, pointing.

A small furry ball drifts around the inside of the capsule. Ryan was expecting something like a stuffed toy depicting Earth or a fake asteroid. There's even been a fabric toy alligator used for an astronaut who grew up in the Everglades.

He offers a soft laugh, confused by what he's looking at as there are no arms, no legs, no eyes, no mouth. It's just a ball of fur. "Okay. That's going to require a little explanation from our pilot," he says for those listening in on the broadcast.

"It's a tribble!" Jemma says proudly, unable to suppress her smile.

Ryan lets out a hearty laugh. "Captain James T. Kirk would approve."

Jemma faces the camera and holds her gloved fingers apart, making the Vulcan sign from Star Trek and saying, "Live long and prosper."

Ryan shakes his head, saying, "There had better not be hundreds of those things in here when we wake up from hibernation."

"Now, that would be cool."

"Okay," mission control says. "Let's start working the checklist and get you ready for refueling and on your way to Psyche."

"Copy that," Jemma says, releasing the straps on her seat and floating forward within the Dragon.

The view out of the window is magnificent. Earth appears as a wall beside them. The north coast of Africa passes beneath them, and the blue of the ocean is replaced by rugged mountains and the vast sandy stretches of the Sahara desert. The green of the jungle is visible on the edge of the window. Portions of the Mediterranean coast come in and out of view above them. There's a slight haze on the horizon, marking the thin edge of the atmosphere, and then nothing—nothing but darkness. And it's into the darkness they'll go. This is the only glimpse they'll have of Earth for the best part of a year. Ryan only hopes it's not the last time they see their home world.

Leavenworth

After flying into Sherman Army Airfield in Kansas in a troop transport, Gabriel is led toward a bunch of waiting vans. There are thirty prisoners on his flight. All of them are cuffed with chains that lead from their hands to their feet, meaning they need to shuffle as they walk. Armed guards watch them, even though no one could run across the four or five hundred yards of flat ground to reach the razor-wire fence surrounding the runway. Gabriel's name is read off a transport manifest. He's checked in with the prison guards and shoved in the back of one of the vans.

Everything about being incarcerated is harsh, unforgiving and dehumanizing. The bench seats running along either side of the back of the van are made out of sheet metal. They aren't designed for safety, let alone comfort. Guards stand at the rear, watching as the prisoners slide with the motion of the van driving through the airport to the nearby prison.

Gabriel peers out through the metal mesh window on the side of the van. Fort Leavenworth is surrounded by a vast, lush lawn dotted with sycamore, elm and oak trees hiding its three-story-high concrete walls and imposing guard towers. The prison is physically intimidating. Not only does the massive wall lock the prisoners in, it denies them even a glimpse of the outside world. Gabriel's heart breaks. He knows he won't see this grassy lawn or the leafy trees racing by the van's windows again for at least twenty-five years. It's such a simple view. And he's been denied even that.

Each of the prisoners is strip-searched in the admin wing. Privacy isn't a concern. They stand there naked as guards wearing blue disposable plastic gloves check their scrotums and run their fingers down their butt cracks, checking for contraband. Gabriel stands perfectly still with his feet slightly apart, knowing there are worse indignations than standing there naked with the air conditioning blasting on full overhead, chilling his bare skin.

The prisoner in front of Gabriel squirms in response to the search. The guard shouts at him. Within a fraction of a second, that prisoner is dragged to one side. Two MPs march him over to a holding cell, grabbing him by the upper arm and shoving him inside. The door is deliberately left open as a male nurse pushes the prisoner face down on a steel table. The nurse conducts a cavity search, working his hand into the man's ass and flicking shit from his fingers into a steel tray. Gabriel keeps his head facing forward, but like all the others, his eyes fight sideways to see what's unfolding. It's not the spectacle of humiliation that grabs his attention; it's the warning it sends.

Eventually, Gabriel is issued prison fatigues: four plain khaki shirts, four pairs of underwear and socks, a pair of black boots, two pairs of camouflage pants and some toiletries. Like the others, he stands there naked, holding the bundle before him, waiting for instruction from the guards. Once everyone's been checked in, searched and issued their gear, the guards instruct them to get dressed.

They're walked through the prison. Technically, the prison in Fort Leavenworth is a United States Disciplinary Barrack. It's cleaner than Gabriel expected. Were it not for the armed guards walking the raised steel grating surrounding the exercise yard, the prisoners could be soldiers on base. Already, he can see divisions: the Black and Hispanic prisoners stick together.

The newly arrived prisoners are marched into a brick housing unit. Gabriel is one of the first assigned to a cell.

"Specialist Ramirez, for your first week, you will be assigned to a shared cell with inmate Specialist Warren Jones. He will help you acclimatize to prison life. Then, you will be shifted to your own cell. Understood?"

"Yes, sir," Gabriel says, walking into the cell.

Jones is lying on the bottom bunk with his arms behind his head, resting on a pillow. Gabriel dumps his gear on the top bunk and sits on the steel seat bolted to the floor. The seat has been positioned in front of a narrow steel table jutting out of the wall.

The prison detail moves on, leaving the door open.

Gabriel looks around. The cell is tiny, barely six feet in width and roughly eight to ten feet long. With the bunk bed, a stainless steel toilet lacking a lid or seat, a washbasin and a small desk, there's barely enough room to turn around in the walkway. Everything is old and scratched. And there's no privacy. The front of the cell is a steel grating that looks like thick chicken wire. It's not a chainlink fence, but it's not far from it, with the steel mesh being roughly a quarter-inch thick. Anyone can look in at any time.

"Hey," Gabriel says, trying to be friendly.

Jones swings around, resting his boots on the floor as he sits on his bunk.

"What are you in for?"

"Um. I was—"

Before Gabriel can reply, Jones leans forward and slaps him across the face, striking his cheek. A red welt rises on Gabriel's skin as he sits back against the concrete wall, startled at both the pain and shock of being struck.

"Don't *fucking* say nothing," Jones growls. "You hear me?"

Gabriel nods.

"Someone asks you what you're in for, and you walk away. Got it?"

Again, Gabriel nods.

"How long are you serving?" Jones asks, but Gabriel's a fast learner.

"Too long."

"That's better." Jones sits back, leaning against the concrete wall behind him. "You need to understand something, Ramirez. My job is to make sure you know how to survive in here. I ain't your friend. No one in here is your friend. Oh, shit. They'll be friendly, but it's always a grift. There is always an angle. You need to keep your head down, keep your mouth shut, and do your time. Got it?"

Gabriel nods.

"Cause if you don't, you'll get a shiv, or you'll end up as someone's bitch. You wanna disappear in here. You want to go unnoticed by everyone. Prisoners and guards alike. Nobody knows you. Got it?"

"Got it."

"You blend in. You become a wallflower. Just another face in the crowd. Nothing special. 'Cause in here, special is trouble. Special gets hurt."

Gabriel rubs his cheek.

"You're gonna see a lot of shit that looks harmless. Don't get involved. Someone says, let's go to the TV room—don't go."

"Why?" Gabriel asks, hoping he's not about to get slapped again. The TV room seems harmless enough.

"Because this place is about cliques. Gangs. Hierarchies. You enter that world, and you're going to get chewed up and spit out. Someone asks you to keep a watch out for guards while they're screwing around with contraband, and you walk away. You don't even answer them. If you do, you're fucked. Sooner or later. You cannot say yes or no. Both are invitations for more discussion. You just walk the fuck away like you're deaf."

Gabriel nods.

"A screw comes up to you. He's looking shit hot in his uniform with his polished boots and a shiny baton hanging from his belt. His radio squawks. He's all important. Maybe he's one of the team leaders for the guards, don't matter. He asks you what's the color of the sky. What do you say?"

Based on his throbbing cheek, Gabriel guesses. "I don't know, sir."

"That's right."

"He walks up to you while you're eating chow. There's a bread roll on your plate and some spaghetti. He asks you what you're eating. What do you say?"

"Nothing, sir."

"That's right."

"You see, one thing leads to another. It doesn't matter whether it's a guard or an inmate. Once you reply, they'll reel you in and gut you like a fish. What you've got to understand about Leavenworth is that everyone wants something. In here, people are currency."

Gabriel nods.

"And people talk. People always talk. It's the boredom. Everyone's bored out of their *fucking* brains, so they talk shit all the time. Avoid that, or you'll find yourself drawn into some nasty circles.

"And remember. Everyone's innocent. Absolutely everyone. Old man Taylor with the long, straggly white beard. He was caught with his hands around the throat of a dying prisoner of war. Blood splatter stained his uniform. His own troops testified against him. And do you know what? He's innocent. Just like you and me." Jones laughs. "Everyone's innocent, especially the guilty. You've got to be smart in here. Talk shit, and you'll eat shit."

"So, how do I get through this?"

"Keep your head down. Read books. Don't worry about a shitty work assignment. It doesn't matter whether you're in the kitchen or doing laundry work; give it everything you've got, and you'll get a chance to move up a rung. You've got to earn a spot in carpentry and metalwork, but if you get there, you can earn some serious money for the commissary. You might even get a cushy job like inducting new inmates. But above all, stay grey. Blend in. Be a shadow on the wall."

Gabriel swallows the lump in his throat, knowing these few words are all he has to guide him through the next quarter of a century.

"You're gonna grieve in here," Jones says. "That's natural. You have to accept that you died out there in that courtroom. Your old life is gone. Dead and buried. And that sucks. It *fucking* hurts, but we've all been there. You've gotta think of yourself as the phoenix rising from the ashes. Find yourself in here. Find your real self. Leave your old self out there beyond the walls. In here, you need to start again. You've got a second chance. Just don't let yourself get caught up in the storm. As long as everyone's focusing on someone else, you get some breathing space. And breathing space is gold in Leavenworth."

Gabriel hangs his head. He knows Jones is right. His life, as he knew it, has been stolen from him. Leavenworth is a nightmare from which he cannot wake, not for at least twenty-five years, if not longer.

Jones says, "I've been here sixteen years. In four, I'll get to stand before a parole board. But do you know what I've learned in here?"

"What?"

"I've learned what freedom really is." Jones points at the door to the cell, gesturing beyond the prison walls barely visible through the windows on the far side of the walkway. "Freedom is more than a catchy phrase on some stupid bumper sticker. Freedom ain't kicking back with a beer to watch the Super Bowl. Freedom lies between your ears.

"The warden controls everything in Leavenworth. There's no aspect of your life the screws can't fuck with. The guards can shut you down and lock you in for days on end if they want. They can hit you with their batons. They can strip you of your clothes and your privileges. They can throw you in the hole. They can open up a water cannon on you. They can leave you soaking wet and freezing cold in the dark. And they can do all this because they think you've lost your freedom. Well, I say they're wrong. Because there's one place they cannot reach. There's one freedom they cannot touch."

Jones taps his forehead.

"This is what they're after. This is what they want to break. Your mind. All the shit they put us through, it's an illusion, a lie. They want you to lose your freedom up here. They want you to believe you've lost everything, but you haven't. There's one thing no amount of punishment can ever take from you—your pride. And damn, will they try. They'll humiliate you. And you've got to suck it up. Every time. Every inspection. They'll empty your locker on the floor and shout at you as though it's your fault. Every time they make you stand to attention or do a head count is an admission of their failure. Every time they push you around is futile. Pathetic. They can control this—the body—but they cannot control your mind. That's yours. Guard it. Protect it. And no matter how bad things get, you can always retreat to your one space of freedom."

Gabriel nods.

"Find something to hold on to," Jones says. Gabriel isn't sure what he means, but Jones elaborates. "Find something that gives you hope. For me, it's the birds. We don't see shit in here. A few blades of green grass and tons of concrete. Bricks. Steel. But the birds. They can't take those from us. The birds are free to fly in the sky. Whenever you start to get depressed, look up at the birds and remember there's a whole world out there waiting for you."

A prisoner walks up to the door and bangs on the steel frame.

"You got mail, Ramirez."

"Me?" Gabriel points at himself in surprise.

"You're Corporal Gabriel Ramirez, right?" the prisoner asks, stepping inside the cell and holding out a postcard.

"On day *fucking* one," Jones says, surprised. "You got yourself a lonely lover out there, Gabe?"

"I—I don't know," Gabriel says, taking the postcard from the inmate delivering the mail.

The glossy postcard front features an old cathedral, but this is no American or even Western European cathedral. Gabriel immediately recognizes the styling. The extravagant arches and golden domes are topped with a cross that has several bars instead of the one so common in Western religion. And several of them are set on a thirty-degree angle. The mosaics adorning the outside of the cathedral leave no doubt that this is a Russian Orthodox Church.

On the back of the card, there's a description printed in English, indicating it is intended for tourists.

The Church of Our Savior on the Spilled Blood.

This iconic cathedral marks the spot where Alexander II was fatally wounded in an assassination attempt in 1881. The design is based on St. Basil's Cathedral in Moscow and the Vladimir Cathedral in Kyiv and contains the largest collection of Byzantine iconography in Russia.

There's a handwritten note.

My dearest Gabriel,

I hope you're settling into your new home and making lots of new friends. Susan and I miss our online chats. I'm on holiday with my family from next week, so I'll be in Italy, then Switzerland and finally Paris. I'll be sure to send you some more postcards.

Love always,

Maria.

"What is it?" Jones asks. "What does it say?"

Gabriel hands the postcard to his cellmate, knowing the message will be meaningless to him. Under his breath, he mumbles, "That fucking bitch!"

Deep Space

Ryan wakes as abruptly as he fell asleep, being roused by a chemical cocktail that's been automatically administered through a portacath in his chest, positioned just below right collarbone.

Portacath is medical shorthand for a semi-permanent catheter port. It's a small plastic medical device inserted under the skin using a local anesthetic that allows medication to be delivered to the superior vena cava, a major vein returning to the heart. Normally, it's reserved for chemotherapy patients so doctors and nurses can administer meds without the need to find a vein in the arm and causing endless small puncture wounds during repeated treatments. It feels like a round lump under his skin. He reaches up, removes a strip of tape and pulls out the L-shaped needle that's punched through the skin of his chest into the portacath. A tiny red dot appears as blood rises on the surface of his skin, but injecting into the portacath is nowhere near as painful as injections in the crook of his arm.

Ryan tears open a sterile alcohol swab and wipes the blood away before placing a small circular bandage over the entry point. He removes the needle from the tube leading back to the medical unit. He'll replace it with a clean needle before he goes back under.

Both Ryan and Jemma spent over a month in simulated suspension almost a year ago as part of their training. Back then, instead of being out for twelve days at a time, it was two days between wakes. Repetition is the heart of training. After twenty cycles, they could conduct the procedure blindfolded—literally—as one of the training runs was to simulate waking to a dead spacecraft. Thankfully, that hasn't happened.

Ryan pulls the velcro straps from his waist and thighs and slips out of the hibernation pod. He and Jemma are in the habitation module on the AMPLE spacecraft. From the outside, the hab looks considerably bigger than the Dragon capsule, being longer than both the capsule and its service module combined. In practice, the hab is cramped. It contains all the supplies they need for eight months in space. White bundles have been strapped to the circular walls. Beyond them, the fuel tanks and water tanks have been built *around* the module. If AMPLE was a hotdog, they're the sausage while the tanks are the bun surrounding them.

On an orbital flight or a lunar mission, spacecraft are designed to minimize mass and maximize storage, so fuel is stored in circular or elongated tanks. AMPLE, though, needs to protect the crew from both solar radiation and high-energy cosmic rays. Using the fuel and water tanks as a sleeve around the outside of the module gives them a wall of protection. Cosmic rays punch through the hull of the craft, strike the fluids and scatter atoms like billiard balls. A few penetrate deep enough to reach them, but no more than would be experienced by a commercial airline pilot. The difference between the hab and the Dragon, though, is marked. When Ryan soars back there to use the radio and check settings, he'll get the occasional cosmic ray lighting up his retina. It's more pronounced if he's napping, but they can be seen as sparks of light even with his eyes open. And if they're hitting his eyeball, they're striking every part of his body.

The vast majority of cosmic rays are hydrogen and helium atoms stripped of their electrons and sent hurling through the universe at ridiculous speeds, reaching upwards of 99% of the speed of light. They're mainly the result of supernova explosions, but some come from supermassive black holes, which Ryan finds trippy. Instead of swallowing stars, black holes spit out stars! As stars are torn apart by a black hole, some of the material falls beneath the event horizon like water swirling around a drain, but some of it is caught by the magnetic field and shot outward in vast jets emanating from the poles. Ryan's being struck by insanely small, insanely energetic particles that have probably been hurling through space for *billions* of years without hitting anything until they smacked into AMPLE. Most have come from other galaxies, which is wild to consider. Space is awash with the aftermath of untold acts of violence that would decimate Earth were they nearby, but thankfully, the universe is unbelievably vast.

AMPLE has triple redundant systems to protect against cosmic rays causing errors. An errant high-energy particle is enough to change settings within a computer, switching memory settings and altering the function of programs. In light of this, one of the flight computers is located within the hab itself. All three computers conduct redundancy checks, constantly backing each other up to avoid faulty readings.

Ryan pulls himself out of his sleeping nook. Above him, Jemma lies securely in her compartment. It's strange to see someone lying upside down above him without falling. Originally, the flight plan called for one of the three astronauts to be awake at all times. On review, it was decided that this was overkill, and Houston could remotely monitor and wake astronauts as needed, so the crew was reduced to two. Ryan didn't like the change, but he understood their reasoning. With a smaller crew, AMPLE can potentially function longer if anything goes wrong. It also opened up the option of carrying added fuel reserves, allowing them to reach Mars if needed. The NASA/ESA base on the edge of the Valles Marineris has a return vessel capable of rendezvousing with them in Martian orbit and acting as a lifeboat to get them all back to Earth. Once senior managers realized this gave AMPLE two abort scenarios rather than one, the crew was clipped to two. Dead astronauts are not a good look for the agency, so they'd rather have options open to them in case of an emergency.

The first order of business is for Ryan to discard his diaper. The seal leaked on one side. Feces have oozed out and dried on the inside of his thigh, leaving a crusty layer on his skin. He uses the sticky tabs on the sides of the diaper to wrap the material on itself, creating a tight bundle.

"Wonderful," he mutters, reusing the alcohol swab to clean the crust off his skin before switching to sanitary wipes. "They don't talk about this in the travel brochures."

Being weightless, Ryan tumbles in a slow somersault as he cleans himself. He's careful to place the full diaper in a reasonably stationary position. It drifts slowly to one side. After four wipes, the damp cloth is coming up clean. Ryan gives himself a wipe with a fifth cloth for good measure and then seals the cloths and diapers in one of the garbage bags. These will be discarded before their homeward journey to minimize mass. Over time, they'll probably end up clumped against an asteroid, giving celestial archeologists something to recover. It's not his idea of fun, but he can understand the fascination future scientists will have with biological matter being exposed to a harsh vacuum and cosmic rays for decades, possibly centuries. There are already plans to retrieve at least a few of the 96 bags of poop left on the Moon during the Apollo program. One man's shit is another man's scientific experiment.

After changing into fresh clothes, he waves to a sleeping Jemma.

"Catch ya later."

Ryan pulls himself through the tunnel into the Dragon and positions himself in one of the seats, more out of habit than need. The air is brisk, which helps him wake. He sips on a water pouch as he examines the flight logs and reviews remote commands from Houston.

The logs are color-coded to make them easy to scan. Grey is a standard preplanned activity with a nominal result that can probably be ignored. Black is an activity that was initiated manually by Houston. Orange is an unplanned change to a non-core system. Red is a critical change to restore functionality to a core system like communication or life-support. Green is confirmation of standard, nominal values being recorded.

Ryan scrolls through the list. There are buttons at the top that allow him to filter based on color, removing the thousands of grey entries and the odd black line, but he prefers to see the occasional orange in the context of everything else. He toggles the various filters. No red. Four orange. Eleven black. As all of these have been reviewed by Houston, he doesn't see anything that concerns him.

If Mission Control were worried by any of AMPLE's obscure metrics, they'd have sent some priority instructions. As it is, they've given them the standard "wake-up" call. Back in the days of the Gemini program, Houston would wake the astronauts with music playing over the radio. The dulcet tones of Beethoven's 6th would come over the tinny speakers one day, while *A Few of My Favorite Things* from *The Sound of Music* would wake them the next. Not every mission was woken to music. Apollo 11 was greeted with news and sports results. *Come Fly With Me* was a favorite. From what Ryan can tell, some of the selections were the result of personal jokes between Houston and the crew. The Doors' *Light My Fire* woke the crew of Apollo 17 before they lit their engines to depart from lunar orbit.

Ryan hits play on his wake-up call even though he's been awake and active for the best part of an hour. *Mustang Sally* starts playing. Ryan smiles. He loves this song. At a guess, his sister Dawn must have suggested it, as he used to play it on his guitar while they were growing up. The song fades with a comment about putting flat feet on the ground, which is clearly a reference to touching down on the asteroid Psyche in a month's time. For him, it's only two more sleeps till that celestial Christmas.

"Nice," he says, even though no one is listening. AMPLE is currently fourteen light-minutes from Earth. Ryan doesn't bother doing the math to figure out how far that is in miles, but it's well into the millions—tens of millions, perhaps approaching a hundred million. Regardless, it hasn't been possible to talk to someone in Mission Control for months now. To ask a question and get an answer takes roughly half an hour.

By the time AMPLE reaches Psyche, he and Jemma will have traveled further than any other human in history, eclipsing even the four Mars missions. And they don't have the luxury of advanced robotic prep missions building habitats and in-situ resource renewal like the team did on Mars. Back when *Star Trek* first launched, the tagline was "*Space... the final frontier...*" Comparisons with explorers in the American West have continued to dominate the public's thinking. If anything, their mission parallels that of Lewis and Clarke, who set out to map the wilderness and document natural resources.

The wake-up recording includes a bunch of heartwarming news stories and sports results. Jemma won't get those. She'll have her own curated message when she wakes. Neither of them is naive. They know what passes for casual content is carefully constructed to help their mental health. They're isolated. Their lives depend on hundreds of complex systems working flawlessly for a record amount of time. Anxiety is natural. Ryan gave up looking out of the windows at the stars a long time ago. At this distance, Earth isn't visible to the naked eye. Carl Sagan's pale blue dot can only be seen with a camera lens. Even the Sun has lost roughly half its intensity compared to the early days when they departed Earth's orbit.

Ryan and Jemma have overlapping bromation/hibernation sleep periods. Although they both sleep for twelve days at a time before waking for two, Jemma will wake a mere five days after he returns to sleep. She'll complete her watch, and it will be five days before he wakes again.

Ryan is tempted to ignore the logs as he knows Houston will have been hyper-vigilant with even the most minuscule variation, but as mission commander, he takes his role seriously. Several of the log entries he reviewed were about trimming the position of the solar panels to maximize the failing light as they soar further and further away from the Sun. By the time they passed the orbit of Mars, the Sun's intensity had already fallen by more than half of what's experienced on Earth, and it's only going to drop further. By the time they reach Psyche, it'll be down to around a third. The Sun will still be bright, but out in the asteroid belt, it will look more like yet another distant star than the giver of life on Earth.

Ryan reviews the wake-up video from Houston.

"Well, it's been a beautiful spring day here in Texas. We've got buds on the trees. And I'm going to have to mow my lawn this weekend."

As the flight controller talks, various photographs appear on the screen. They're all vibrant and full of life, even if they are low resolution. Colors are strangely important in space. In the same way as folks on Earth can get seasonal depression, being locked in the black and white and grey gloom of winter for months on end, astronauts need a splash of color to invigorate their minds like some artificial spring. The photos have been carefully selected and probably reviewed by the mission psychologist for the positive impact they'll have on his mind. Even knowing that they're curated, they still work. And he smiles at a photo of a child holding a football.

"Oh, Alex Verdure has been picked up by the Yankees in the MLB spring training. With big-hitting Billy Baxter and Steve Miles on the mound, this really could be the year for the Yankees."

Ryan smiles at that thought. The flight controllers know him well. He's always been a Yankees fan and dreams of another World Series win. It's a pleasant distraction from the cold, hard vacuum just inches away from him on the other side of the Dragon.

"Congress has approved the NASA Deep Space Extension, so it looks like we'll get AMPLE II with III being set to build a permanent station with on-site manufacturing on Psyche. Umm, in world news, researchers in Taiwan have developed a means of using moss to sequester carbon dioxide. The grey whale was thought to be extinct for over two hundred years, but drone footage intended for tracking blue whales has spotted a pod off Cape Cod. And a new drug approved by the FDA can restore frostbite damage."

There are four or five other good news stories but Ryan is barely listening. He's aware of what they're not telling him. There is no news of war or natural disasters.

Jemma has left a video log for him with notes from her time awake during her last cycle.

"Hey, Ryan. Not much to report other than we're still on course and drifting ever further from Earth. Boring flights are the best flights, amirite? Just one thing I wanted to show you."

She's cued up a short video that was undoubtedly part of her news package. It's a cat video—of course, it's a cat video. Is there any other reason for the Internet to exist? A black cat sits on a table, watching a guy with a beard eating what appears to be tuna. He raises a piece of fish on a fork in front of the cat, looks at it briefly, and then eats it. He raises another piece on his fork and, in the blink of an eye, the cat has snatched it with its paw and is devouring it. The speed of the cat is astonishing. Ryan rewinds the video a few times, laughing at the sheer gall of the cat.

"You rewound that a few times, didn't you," Jemma says when the video continues. "Me too... See you on the other side."

Ryan unfolds an exercise bike from the rear of the capsule and puts some music on. He's got at least six hours cycling ahead of him broken into thirty-minute segments with short sprints every five minutes. It's a grueling regimen. Once finished, he'll do resistance training for 90 minutes using broad elastic bands to work his muscles. Then it's protein powder mixed with tepid water for dinner, followed by coffee and a single square of dark chocolate. Like Jemma, he's learned to nibble the edges of the chocolate to fool his mind into thinking he's eating an entire bar. Then he'll get to relax and read or watch a video before going off to a natural sleep and doing it all again tomorrow. Once his vitals are stable and beyond the minimum viable level, he'll go back under and surrender the exercise equipment to Jemma. Ah, spaceflight. It's not all blazing rockets and flag planting. Most of it is dedicated to fighting atrophy, working to keep the human body in shape. The last thing he needs is to return to Earth with the body of a ninety-year-old.

The Basement

Dawn sits at her desk in the astrophysics department at Harvard University, just across from the old physics building with its astronomical archives in the basement. She wonders about her brother. For her, Earth is all there is and all there will ever be. Spring has come early this year. The grass is growing, bringing a dash of green to the quad between the buildings on the campus. The quad is a park roughly eighty yards square with a fountain in the middle, giving the four buildings in this part of the campus a common view. Buds have formed on the cherry trees below her window. A few of them have bloomed into bursts of white and pink on the otherwise lifeless branches. And somewhere out there in the sky above her is her brother.

Even knowing that the universe is little more than a bitter, cold, dark void stretching throughout all of space and time, the illusion of living comfortably beneath a bright blue sky is overwhelming. As an astronomer, Dawn may know intellectually that the roughly one hundred miles of atmosphere above her pales into insignificance compared to the 8×10^{22} miles of vacuum represented by 13.8 billion light years, but she can't comprehend that. No one can. Numbers that large are meaningless. Twenty-two zeros in a row is mind-numbingly huge. From her perspective on Earth, it seems as though outer space is unreal.

Even after years of examining images from Hubble and the James Webb Space Telescope, outer space is still a novelty for Dawn. It's as though space is a fairytale or solely the domain of science fiction—and yet the reverse is true. It is Earth that misleads its inhabitants, making them think its tenuous atmosphere is all-pervasive when it's not. Dawn may feel safe and content in her office or walking to the bus after work as the setting sun lights up the clouds with streaks of yellow and purple at dusk, but the mellow life she experiences on Earth is the exception rather than the norm. For her brother, there's no mistaking reality. For him, there's no day or night, just the eternal darkness stretching on forever with a scattering of light from distant stars so remote as to defy reason. For Ryan, the curtain has been pulled back, and life on Earth has been exposed like the Wizard of Oz.

By two in the afternoon, Dawn is seriously regretting grabbing a burger for lunch. She should have gone with the salad. Not only was the burger bland, looking and smelling much better than it tasted, but it's sitting heavy in her stomach. Her eyes lose focus on the screen in front of her. If she weren't in an open-plan office, she'd rest her head on the desk and grab a quick half-hour nap. There's a first aid room on the far side of the floor with a narrow examination bed. Dawn is tempted to wander over there for a snooze, but she knows all she needs is a bit of motion. She'll be wide awake by the time she opens the door. Besides, she'd be mortified if someone walked in on her sleeping, and that anxiety would probably keep her from drifting off.

Is everything okay?

The text prompt in the chat window on her research app springs to life. She's been interacting with HAL for most of the day but only via text. Dawn finds that if she talks with him, she tends to get distracted and plunge down a rabbit hole. Research demands focus, something she's lacking at the moment.

Although HAL is interfacing via text, the red LED at the top of her screen indicates that her microphone and camera are active as inputs as well, should she need them. It's strange, but she doesn't mind interacting with him by speaking, so long as she's not spoken to, as she doesn't want to get drawn into one of his long-winded conversations.

"I'm fine."

Perhaps some coffee?

"Good idea."

Dawn gets up and heads to the lunch room.

The coffee pot is almost empty. Someone left the glass carafe on the hot plate. Black sludge has burned at the bottom of the glass. Dawn switches it off and leaves it to cool. She scoops two teaspoons of instant coffee into her mug along with a teaspoon of sugar, pours in some boiling water from the urn and adds some creamer. She sniffs at the aroma. In her mind, the generic Nescafe coffee granules are Italian *Segafredo Zanetti*. Dreams are free. And they're cheap. She stirs her coffee with a wooden paddle, drops it in the garbage can by the door and wanders back to her office, ready to do battle with raw data once more.

A large plain envelope has been left on her desk.

"Who dropped this off?" she asks, sitting down.

On her screen, the text reply from HAL is, "*I don't know. I couldn't see them from this angle.*"

"Huh."

Dawn sits, placing her coffee on a coaster beside her computer mouse and picks up the large envelope. It's not addressed to her or anyone, but she assumes it's for her. It hasn't been sealed. Those two details suggest it wasn't delivered as part of the mail. Someone dropped it off in person. She looks around the floor. People sit at workstations or mill around desks, talking to each other. No one's marching toward an exit. She peers out the window, looking down at the broad concrete steps leading from the building. People come and go from the quad. A busker is playing guitar beside the fountain in the center of the grassy area. Students take shortcuts across the grass, leaving diagonal trails between the sidewalks. No one stands out as being in a hurry.

"Hmmm."

Dawn opens the envelope. There are a series of glossy astronomical photos. She recognizes the region of the sky immediately. She hasn't looked at the southern hemisphere for months, not since Ryan launched on the AMPLE mission. She felt like a fool raising her dumb ideas with him. She was embarrassed. She's a professional. He's a professional—an astronaut undertaking a historic mission deep into the solar system. And she was like a schoolgirl reacting to an influencer on Instagram, getting all excited over nothing. She wanted to apologize, but she never had the opportunity to talk to him again. Besides, bringing it up would have only been even more cringe-worthy. As it was, she suspects he was content to realize his baby sister is a little loopy. Ryan has always been magnanimous. He probably didn't give her outburst any more thought.

Dawn pushes her keyboard and mouse away and lays out the four large images on the table in front of her. A red LED glows at the top of her computer screen.

What are you looking at?

"Whatcha looking at?" Lisa asks at the same time as HAL.

Lisa is one of the co-contributors on her research paper. Dawn's thoughts have matured since she first spotted an unmapped asteroid in the archives. She's turned a fleeting curiosity into an actual scientific study, using AI algorithms to compare tens of thousands of images taken across almost a hundred years, looking for stray asteroids from other solar systems. So far, they have seven candidates, including one confirmed extra-solar object from almost a century ago. Over the past month, Dawn's become so obsessed with her work that she forgot where it all started. This is the region of space she showed Ryan, and her initial thoughts come flooding back to her.

"Oh, it's the span from Lupus, the wolf, over to the constellation Vela."

"Anything interesting?"

"I don't know." Dawn opens her desk drawer and pulls out a magnifying glass. She knows precisely where to look on this particular photo. These aren't the Keck images, though. They've come from ALMA, ESA's Large Millimeter/submillimeter Array in the Atacama desert in the South American country of Chile.

"Why are you messing around with physical images?" Lisa asks. "This would be much easier in digital."

"It would," Dawn replies, curious about who dropped these images on her desk and, more importantly, why. For that matter, how did they know she'd be interested in them?

A quick examination and she realizes she's got them in the wrong order. She shifts them around on her desk so they unfold from left to right, top to bottom. She notes the heliocentric date/time stamp. She's got the original Keck image seared in her mind. Some simple arithmetic, and she can tell these images are much younger by almost a decade. These are from well into the digital capture and storage era that has been methodically clean from any records she's examined of this region. Mentally, she maps the apparent motion of the object she spotted in the basement. For her, it's like seeing a car driving down a long road. Although it's coming toward her, there's some apparent sideways motion as it follows the slope. In the same way, she calculates roughly where the object should be and begins scanning the photos.

"These are originals," she mumbles.

"Originals?"

"Look," she says, handing the magnifying glass to Lisa and pointing.

"What am I looking for?"

"Nothing."

"Nothing?"

"Nothing in that photo, but compare it to this one, and you'll see something was occulting a distant star."

Lisa mumbles. "A stray asteroid?"

"That's the assumption."

"But it's off the plane of the ecliptic."

"Extra-solar."

"Oh, this is cool," Lisa says, gesturing to Dawn's computer screen with its glowing red LED. "Pull it up. Let's get a proper look."

"You won't see anything."

"What?" Lisa says, standing bolt upright. "Why? What are you saying?"

"This," Dawn says, tapping one of the glossy images. "This is what got me interested in tracking extra-solar asteroids, looking for past interlopers like 'Oumuamua."

Lisa asks, "But why won't I see the same thing in the online images?"

"They've been cleaned."

"I don't understand."

"Neither do I. My research has uncovered eight candidates for asteroid fragments and cometary remnants coming from other stars, but there are nine that I know of..."

"Nine?" Lisa says. "Who would do this? And why?"

"I don't know. Perhaps that's even more troubling than the disappearance. At first, I assumed it was the result of image correction software, but it's across all instruments and images."

Lisa steps back away from the desk. "You're saying *someone* has hidden this from us?"

"Yes."

"And these particular images?" Lisa asks, tapping the glossy photos on the desk.

"Someone else wants me to pick up on the trail again."

Dawn peers inside the large envelope. "There's another photo in here. It's glossy and has stuck to the inside."

Carefully, she peels it away and slides it out. This image differs from the others in that it's flagged as capturing electromagnetic radiation in the infrared portion of the spectrum, detecting heat rather than visible light. Dawn positions it above one of the previous images.

"Look. Same time stamp."

Lisa taps the image, saying, "I don't get it. It's visible in infrared but not in regular light. Why?"

"Dunno," Dawn says. "It's warm."

"Warm? But it's an asteroid in deep space. It hasn't been near a star in tens of thousands, probably millions of years. How can it be warm?"

"Maybe it's a heat plume."

"A heat plume from what?" Lisa asks. "Are you saying this is geologically active?"

"I don't know what I'm saying," Dawn replies.

"An asteroid this size couldn't have an active core."

"So what else would cause it to appear warm against the background of space?" Dawn asks.

"Oh, no," Lisa says. "No, no, no."

Dawn smiles. "Say it. I know you're thinking it."

"No. Nope. It couldn't be."

"It couldn't be what? Something like an engine firing?"

"You're saying… you're saying this is an alien spaceship?"

"Me? I'm not saying anything," Dawn says, holding her hands up as though she were surrendering to a cop. "But whoever sent this to us is saying that. As for me, I'm just looking at these images like you."

Lisa shakes her head. "This is bad."

"Why?"

"I mean, think about it... What you're suggesting here is bonkers. Occam's Razor suggests it is *these* images on your desk that have been altered rather than every other online image."

"You think someone's feeding me fakes?"

"Not me," Lisa says. "But that is what every other academic is going to say. And for one simple reason."

"And that is?"

"Who could do this? Who would have that level of access to the raw data from so many different observatories? No one."

"But—"

"And there's no evidence."

"Ah," Dawn says. "But there is."

"Where?"

Dawn points across the grassy quad at the old physics building, saying, "There are originals showing the same thing in that basement."

As she speaks, there's a high-pitched whine like that of an airliner taxiing on the runway at an airport. Within seconds, it's grown from annoying to screaming in anger. A wingtip rushes into view. It's pointing down at the ground at an angle. From over the building, a 737 cargo plane plummets toward the quad. Its nose dives down at the university. The plane itself is inverted, flying upside down. Smoke billows from its engines. The vertical stabilizer at the rear of the craft deforms under stress, twisting on its frame. The rudder is turned hard to one side but to no effect. On the ground, people run in all directions. In a fraction of a second, the shadow of the aircraft converges on the old physics building at the same time as the nose cone of the airplane thunders into the grassy park.

"Get—" Dawn doesn't have time to yell, "Down!"

A fireball erupts from the quad. Windows shatter around them. Tens of thousands of tiny glass fragments tear through the air, but this is safety glass. It pelts them like a shotgun blast but doesn't cut them to shreds.

The two women are blown off their feet. They collide with the desk. The computer monitor falls backward. Fire lashes the ceiling, coming up from the ground outside and billowing over them. The heat scorches their exposed hands and cheeks. The two women huddle together, taking shelter beneath the desk. Burning bits of ceiling tiles fall around them.

The sprinklers come on, spraying water over the office. Cold water drips from the desk. The fire alarm sounds, but it's distant. It takes Dawn a moment to realize the thundering explosion rattled her ears, deafening her. Her hands are shaking.

Lisa is already back on her feet, looking down at the smoldering crater. Dawn clambers up next to her. Smoke billows high into the air. Spot fires rage across the campus. Bodies lie strewn on the burned ground. Several cherry trees have been knocked over, exposing their roots. The old physics building has collapsed. Black soot lines what remains of the edge of the building out by the road. A wall falls, sending bricks scattering across the pavement.

There's screaming.

Sirens sound in the distance. People walk in a daze. Blood drips from limp arms. There's a tremor. The biology building next to the old physics department collapses even though it was spared the full force of the blast. The front fascia falls forward, leaving people stranded on the open concrete floors within. Scattered bricks bury the stairs at the front of the building. Dust billows outward.

"We've got to go," Dawn says, realizing their building could collapse as well.

"B—Basement," Lisa says, pointing at the smoke billowing out of the crater. "T—The evidence was in that basement?"

"Yes, that basement," Dawn says, unable to see anything other than rubble within the crater. The tail section of the aircraft protrudes from the debris.

Dawn wraps her arm around Lisa and leads her toward the fire stairs in the middle of the floor. It's only then that she realizes the left side of her face feels unduly warm. She reaches up and wipes away thick red blood.

"Are you okay?" Dr. Manaas Guneet asks, rushing up to them and blabbering in his distinctive accent from the Indian subcontinent. He repeats his question. "Are you okay?"

"We're okay," Dawn replies. Lisa is silent.

"Is everyone okay?" Dr. Guneet asks, repeating himself and asking a question that has already been answered. "We've got to make sure everyone's okay. You're okay. You're going to be okay. Okay?"

It's the look in his eyes that gives away the pain of shock seizing his mind. He's uninjured, but his pupils are dilated. They're as big as saucers.

"Come with us," Dawn says to him, shuffling through the ruins scattered across the floor. Smoke clouds the air. Ash drifts around them.

"I—I need to make sure everyone is okay," Dr. Guneet says, rushing off to talk to someone else already heading toward the exit.

There's a strange silence within the concrete stairwell leading to the ground. Emergency lights glow overhead, running on battery power. The two of them follow the dazed herd inside the stairwell. Rather than being calm, the people around them are passive because they're deep in shock. They're walking down the steps on instinct.

Dawn and Lisa step outside into the acrid smoke filling the air. It's difficult to breathe. Lisa wanders in a daze toward the smoldering crater. Dawn grabs her by the arm and leads her sideways, away from the point of impact. Bits of the airplane's metal frame have embedded themselves in the support pillars of their building. Every window has shattered. It's impossible to walk on anything but broken glass. Ash falls from the sky like snow. Several people are caked in grey dust, appearing as little more than ghosts through the gloom.

Police cars pull up. Their sirens are silent, but their red and blue flashing lights provide a beacon through the smoke and haze.

"My God. My God," someone mumbles, pushing past them. "Are we under attack? We're under attack. It's 9/11 all over again."

Firefighters wield massive metal grinders, cutting through the bollards that prevent vehicle access to the quad. A shower of sparks flies through the air. They're operating the kind of equipment used to cut open a crushed vehicle in a crash. Within seconds, the bollards fall to one side with their metal ends glowing red, turning the walkway into a driveway.

Fire Engines drive up over the curb and into the quad. Their lights flash over the remains of the buildings. Hoses are rolled out and attached to fire hydrants. Water is sprayed through the air. The artificial torrent of rain douses the fires, reducing the smoke.

A cop stands to one side, signaling to survivors as though he were directing traffic at an intersection. People flock to him, coming from all angles. In the uncertainty of the moment, the police provide surety. Several other police officers stand further along the campus with clipboards out, writing down names.

"Roll call," the cop calls out to the stunned crowd. "We need to know who made it out so we can find anyone that's trapped."

Once Dawn has walked past the first cop, she turns sideways, following the concrete walkway leading to the humanities department.

"What are you doing?" Lisa asks. "Where are you going?"

"We're not putting our names on that list."

"But why?"

"Because someone wants me dead. And I'd rather they didn't know I'm still alive."

"B—B—But all this was an accident. Surely, it was an accident."

Dawn says, "Those images on my desk were no accident."

"Who gave you those images?"

"I don't know, but you asked the right question back there. Who could do this? And why?"

"And who could?"

"I'm not sure, but I intend to find out."

Prison Life

Gabriel is called *The Travel Man* within Fort Leavenworth. He's never been outside the Continental US, but with fourteen postcards lined up around the edge of his window and the head of his bed, prisoners enjoy joking with him about these far-flung lands. Maria travels a lot. Most of her postcards are from Eastern Europe, including Istanbul and Ankara in Turkey. Spain and London are popular with the prisoners.

"Your woman," Private James Stone says from the doorway to his cell. "She knows, huh? She looks out for you. Reminds you that one day you'll be free again."

"Something like that," Gabriel says with a slight smile.

The assumption is that Maria Petrovoski is his lover. As the comments on the back of the postcards are all innocuous, Gabriel's happy to indulge their fantasies. At first, he resented hearing from her. Now, if a week goes by without a postcard, he misses that fleeting contact with the outside world. And not only him. Dozens of prisoners have made a habit of swinging by on Thursdays to see if a new postcard has arrived. A missed week is a big deal for them. It seems everyone needs hope, even if it's an illusion, a mirage. For Gabriel, it's a good way of being close to a lot of prisoners while still being distant. Jones was right. He needs to come across as friendly without actually striking up any friendships that could compromise him.

He takes the latest postcard down with him as he heads toward the recreation yard. It's from Greece and shows the ruins of the Acropolis rising over the city of Athens. The message on this one is simple. It reads:

Missing you.

xoxoxo

Two words and a bunch of fake hugs and kisses leave him wondering what's really going on in Maria's life. In the past, her postcards have tormented him—by design. This one seems rushed. The postmark is from the airport, which is curious as it wasn't sent from the city itself. Also, the handwriting is frantic. This time, it seems she's the one that's tormented. And yet, still, she sent him a postcard. She didn't have to. She never gets a reply. For all she knows, they never make it past the admin desk and end up in the garbage. It seems the cat-and-mouse game that began in an astronomical forum continues.

Gabriel heads along the narrow walkway and down the stairs into the communal area with its fixed tables and chairs.

One of the prisoners by the name of Big Little John sees the postcard in his hand. "Oh, where is she now?"

"Greece," Gabriel says with a misplaced sense of pride.

It's strange, but Maria's postcards give him social credit within the prison walls. Corporal Jones was right about boredom. It's the one constant within Leavenworth. To those on the outside, it seems as though the prisoners are being punished by their loss of freedom, but boredom is the real punishment. The monotony of nothing happening sucks the life out of them. Every day is Groundhog Day. Nothing changes from one day to the next. The human mind thrives on being occupied and engaged. To dull the senses is inhumane. Gabriel's seen fights break out over stupidly small shit simply because people were bored. A bit of violence draws in a crowd. For the prisoners, a rush of adrenaline is like knocking back a few beers.

"Oh, cool," Big Little John says, looking at the postcard and turning it over in his hand, reading not only Maria's comment but the information printed about the Acropolis. He hands it back with a smile on his face. Little does Maria know, far from tormenting Gabriel, she's allowing him to break the cycle of boredom and bring a little joy into the lives of those in the B2 wing of Leavenworth. And joy is a social contagion. It ripples outward. Big Little John's hearty smile has lifted Gabriel's mood. And they'll both carry that for the rest of the day, lifting those around them.

"Keep 'em coming," Gabriel says to his absent girlfriend Maria, looking down at the postcard in his hand as he walks out into the exercise yard.

The yard was once a baseball field, but it has been sectioned off with chainlink fences topped with razor wire so it can be used by several prison blocks at once without prisoners mixing. B2 gets the diamond. The grass grows long against the fence, but the paths between bases can still be seen in the dust. Various types of outdoor exercise equipment have been positioned on first, second and third base to give the inmates some variety. In practice, these have become the haunts of the various gangs within the prison.

Being of Cuban descent, Gabriel gets along well with the *El Caimáns* —The Alligators. They're Cuban Americans, but most of the *El Caimáns* come from Florida. Some have gang tattoos, something he suspects the military would have frowned on. Most of them are muscly, using their time inside to pump iron. Gabriel hangs out on the fringes. He doesn't want to get drawn into the group dynamics, but he needs allies, and race provides a natural link.

As he walks out into the sunshine, he spots his old mentor, Corporal Jones, sitting in the shade of the dugout. There's respect but no friendship between them, and Gabriel's taken his warnings to heart by avoiding anything other than a passing friendship with the other prisoners.

They make eye contact.

Jones shakes his head softly. He's signaling something's wrong, but what? There's been no beef in the yard for weeks. Violence doesn't spring out of nowhere. It simmers and builds like a volcano. Gabriel hasn't seen anything that would suggest any tension between the *El Caimáns*, the Blacks or the Aryans.

Gabriel *needs* the sunlight. He closes his eyes for a moment as the warm rays rest on his cheeks. There's chirping above him. Corporal Jones was right about the birds in the clear blue sky. They're free. They're beyond the reach of the guards, beyond the razor-wire fences, beyond the steel bars. They're a reminder that as soul-destroying as it is to be facing decades in prison, one day, he'll soar free again.

He walks over to the Cubans. They part like the Red Sea.

"What's going on?" he asks Sergeant Valverde, a stout, muscular US Ranger from Daytona Beach.

"*Tienes,*" Valverde says, nodding with his head toward three burly Aryans walking over toward them from second base. "*Este tipo acaba de meter tremenda cañona en la caretera.*"

Gabriel spoke Spanish as a kid, but when his father remarried a stunningly beautiful Italian woman from New York, they began speaking English around their home. He wracks his mind to translate Valverde. The Ranger called him a dick, said something about ending him, and something about someone swerving into his lane. Before Gabriel has time to react, two of the muscle-bound white guys have grabbed him by either arm.

"Hey, easy," he says, trying to defuse tension he doesn't understand.

The third self-described Aryan is a skinhead from Alabama called Buddy Browne. His shaved head is perpetually pink under the blazing Kansas sun. Buddy steps in close. He's sweaty. He leans in and whispers in Gabriel's ear, but it's the sharpened scrap of plastic in his right hand that has Gabriel's attention. He's holding a shiv, a homemade prison knife with only one purpose—killing someone in the yard.

"Maria Petrovoski sends her love."

Before Gabriel can plead for mercy, he feels the sharp tip of the shiv cut through his shirt, punching up beneath his ribs on his left side. Pain surges through his chest. Blood runs down his hip.

The Aryans let him go. They walk off in the same direction they were heading moments before Gabriel was stabbed. To the guards watching the yard, the whole incident was over within seconds. The Aryans barely seemed to pause as they strode across the grassy in-field. Their swagger looks natural and confident. To anyone who just glanced down at the worn patch of dirt between the outdoor weights and the practice pitching mound, they're relaxed.

Gabriel staggers. He looks over at Corporal Jones. The older man is on his feet. He lowers his head. He knew this was coming, but he couldn't warn Gabriel, or more correctly, he chose not to. To be fair, even if he'd said something, the Aryans would have simply picked off Gabriel elsewhere, like in the showers.

Gabriel peers down at the orange piece of plastic protruding from his side. He wraps his hand around it. Blood oozes from his fingers.

"Don't," Jones says, walking past behind him but not getting too close and pretending to ignore Gabriel's feet shuffling in the dust. "If you pull it out, you'll bleed out."

And that's all the help Jones offers. Like the others, he keeps his distance. They're all waiting for one of the screws to realize what's happened and shut down the yard. The assassins have already left. Buddy Browne takes one last look from the doorway to the common area. Gabriel's own people, the *El Caimáns*, have shifted over against the chainlink fence on the far side of the yard. They're laughing, but they're not looking at him. It's fake. They're buying themselves an alibi. No one is within thirty feet of him, not even Corporal Jones. He's ducked back into the shade and has his back to Gabriel, fake-talking with one of the other inmates.

As far as hits go, this is professional. It wasn't spontaneous. They had to have been planning this for a while, waiting for the right moment. That the *El Caimáns* gave consent to the Aryans suggests a level of coordination and betrayal that baffles Gabriel. Maria used some serious muscle to reach this deep into Leavenworth.

Gabriel falls to his knees in the dust. It's difficult to breathe. It's all he can do to fall sideways and not collapse on the shiv and drive it in deeper. His body trembles as shock strikes. Blood soaks into the dirt.

A whistle sounds, followed by several others as guards rush in toward him. Their boots kick up dust. An alarm blares. Those prisoners still in the yard know the drill. They drop to their knees with their hands clenched behind their heads.

"Stretcher," is yelled by a guard kneeling beside him. "I need a stretcher."

Gabriel struggles to stay conscious. Guards surround him, but most of them are facing outward, away from him, watching the prisoners, making sure this isn't a ruse to ambush them. Visors are lowered on their helmets. Batons are drawn.

"Who did this to you?" the guard asks, leaning over him. The guard's broad shoulders block out the sun. "Tell me who did this."

As much as Gabriel wants to say "Buddy," the name that comes out is "Maria."

"Don't *fuck* with me," the guard says as a stretcher is laid next to him. "Who stabbed you? Name! Give me a *goddamn* name."

Gabriel's lips tremble. He struggles to swallow. His throat is dry. He couldn't speak even if he wanted to. His body goes limp. His eyes roll into the back of his head as he's lifted onto the stretcher.

Gabriel's vaguely aware of the sights and sounds around him as he slips in and out of consciousness—and it's confusing. His body rocks from side to side on the old canvas stretcher. There's yelling. Steel doors bang open. Keys rattle. Locks are thrown. Boots thump on concrete. And then there's sunlight again for a moment as he's loaded into the back of an ambulance.

The blinding glare of the sun moves from one eye to another, and it takes him a moment to realize a paramedic is shining a penlight in his eyes. A siren sounds, but this is different from the coarse whine of the alarms within Leavenworth. An engine roars as the EMS vehicle rushes out of the prison. Gabriel's still rocking back and forth, but this is different. He's lying on a mattress. Straps keep him secure on the gurney. He never even noticed being transferred from the stretcher.

A guard sits opposite him in the back of the ambulance. He's talking over a radio, but his words are a muddle in Gabriel's mind. Something is injected into Gabriel's arm, and darkness overwhelms him.

When he wakes, he's lying in a hospital bed with the mattress slightly raised behind his back. An IV line runs from a stainless steel stand into the crook of his arm. A red tube winds its way beneath his hospital garment into a plastic bag hanging low on the same metal stand, draining away fluids from his wound. He goes to move. Pain surges through his abdomen. There's a metallic taste in his mouth. He lifts the flimsy surgical garment he's wearing and looks at the bandages stuck to his side.

A doctor unlocks the door and walks into his room with a digital notepad. There's a video camera in the corner of the room with a red glowing light. The doctor must have seen him wake and has come to check up on him. Outside, a prison guard in fatigues stands watching them.

"Specialist Ramirez?"

"Yes."

"You're a very lucky man."

"I don't feel lucky."

"Well, you are. That shiv went up beneath your ribs and into your diaphragm, but it didn't hit any major organs. And it stopped short of your lungs." He points at Gabriel's bandage, adding, "As bad as that feels, it could have been a lot worse."

The doctor walks around the side of the bed and checks the digital monitor showing Gabriel's vital signs.

"We'll keep you in here for a few days until we can remove the drain. Then, you'll be returned to prison."

"Understood," Gabriel replies, looking down at his left hand and only now realizing he's been handcuffed to the bed rail.

The doctor notices. "If you need to use the bathroom, ring the bell, and we'll have the guard release you, and an orderly will assist you."

Gabriel nods. For the doctor, considerable time has elapsed. From the way the sunlight comes in through the window, it's early morning on the next day. For Gabriel, it's been a few raspy breaths and several slow blinks.

"Oh, and your lawyer is coming in this afternoon."

"My lawyer?"

"Something about your appeal."

"Ah."

"We have a secure room down the hall. The guard will escort you there when she gets here."

"Okay," Gabriel says, feeling overwhelmed. Just moments ago, he was stepping out of the prison block into the sunshine and looking up at birds soaring in the bright blue sky.

"Get some sleep, okay?" the doctor says, resting a gentle hand on his shoulder. Then he leaves, locking the door behind him.

Being in a hospital is boring. Gabriel didn't think it was possible, but it's even more boring than prison. Occasionally, someone walks past his room. Faint outlines drift past the half-open horizontal blinds on the window, looking out onto the walkway. Gabriel drifts in and out of sleep.

It's late afternoon when his bladder wakes him. The sun has shifted to the other side of the ward. He rings the call bell. A female nurse unlocks the door and steps inside.

"I, ah..." He points at the bathroom.

"I'll get an orderly to help you," the nurse says. She shuts the door, locking it, and disappears. Gabriel's expecting her to come back within a few moments, but several minutes pass by in agony. He rings the call bell again. No one comes. His bladder feels as though it's about to burst. He rings the bell yet again. The guard on the door can hear it as he responds, looking in on Gabriel but not helping. Above the door, a light glows red, which seems to be in response to the call bell. Still, no one comes.

Gabriel shifts on the mattress, but he can't get comfortable. He's on the verge of letting his bladder loose when the door is finally unlocked, and an orderly saunters in as if he's bored and has nothing better to do. He's in no rush. Gabriel's on the verge of ripping the handcuffs and steel bar from the bed to get to the toilet.

"I need to go to the bathroom," Gabriel says through gritted teeth.

The guard comes over and unlocks the handcuffs. He stands back as the orderly rolls a wheelchair next to the bed. Gabriel swings his legs over the edge of the bed and lowers himself onto the leather seat of the wheelchair. The orderly pushes him and his IV line with the wound drain over to the bathroom, barely ten feet away. It's all Gabriel can do not to jump up and stagger there himself, but he knows that would be interpreted as hostile by the guard. The thought of taking a baton to the back of the head is not appealing.

The orderly positions the wheelchair beside the toilet. Gabriel shifts himself onto the toilet seat. Both the orderly and the guard remain there, watching him, but he doesn't care. His bladder unleashes itself like the torrents of water rushing over Niagara Falls. The relief he feels is palpable. At this point in his life, he's in heaven. Nothing else matters. Absolutely nothing. He sits there for a moment.

"Done?" the orderly asks.

"What's the rush?" Gabriel asks, remembering the way the orderly wandered into his room so casually.

"Your lawyer's here. She's waiting in 4C."

"Oh."

Gabriel finishes up and washes his hands. The orderly pushes him out of his room and down the corridor, giving him his first look at the Fort Leavenworth base hospital. Its primary use is for soldiers on active duty, but it also caters to local veterans and the occasional prisoner. Out of one window, he can see a golf course sprawling across the countryside. Golfers walk casually across the lush green grass. Several of them are dressed in Army fatigues, but why? If he were playing golf here, he'd wear his most outlandish clothes on principle—uniforms are for those who desire to be uniform, not unique.

The orderly opens the door to a meeting room and rolls him inside. The guard waits in the corridor.

"I'll leave you with your lawyer," the orderly says, excusing himself.

Gabriel's lawyer is a woman, but he doesn't remember any women on his team during the trial. Perhaps she works for the appeals division. She's dressed in a tight black skirt with a white top and is facing out the window at the golf course opposite the hospital. She's not watching the approach to the 18th hole, though. She's staring down at her smartphone. Her fingers tap on the glass.

"Ah, hi," Gabriel says, surprised she didn't turn around when he was wheeled in.

His lawyer turns, saying, "Hi, Gabriel... Did you miss me, sweetie?"

Gabriel's jaw drops. His eyes go wide.

"Maria???"

Asteroid Psyche

Ryan wakes to Jemma looming over him in weightlessness. She's upside down relative to him. His mouth is dry. He's dehydrated. It feels as though there's a jackhammer thumping on the inside of his skull.

"Good morning, sleepyhead."

"Hey," Ryan manages, reaching up and touching his temple.

"We're ninety minutes out," Jemma says, looking fresh and alert. "Not sure why the automated system didn't wake you. I had to get Houston to run an override and that took almost an hour as they're pushing through system updates."

"Ahhh," he replies, feeling half-dead.

"I'll leave you to get cleaned up."

Jemma disappears through the neck of the hab module, pulling herself through the steel ring separating it from the Dragon capsule.

Ryan goes through the motions of coming out of suspended animation. He can barely think, but he barely needs to. He removes the needle from the portacath, wipes the emerging spot of blood away with an alcohol swab, and applies a bandage. Then he slips out of the hibernation pod into the narrow accessway and removes his flight diaper. It's full—of course, it's full. It hasn't leaked, though, which makes the clean-up easier. He spreads his legs wide and uses disposable wipes to get into the creases and folds of skin. Although he wouldn't admit it to anyone, it's strangely satisfying to wipe himself clean. Before going under each time, the astronauts coat their groin with a thin layer of Vaseline to protect their skin and prevent sores. It also makes the cleanup easy.

Jemma knows what he's dealing with physically and mentally and stays politely out of sight. As he spins slowly in weightlessness, he catches a glimpse of her legs in the Dragon. She's strapped herself into the pilot seat a little early for their capture burn, which is her way of giving him some privacy.

Once he's stowed the full diaper and used clothes in the garbage bag, he slips on a flight suit. It's not fresh, but unless they're exercising, astronauts barely perspire in space, so they can get away with reusing clothing time and again.

"What's the latest from Houston?" he asks, pulling on the circular collar linking the hab to the forward hatch of the Dragon. He drifts into the cabin.

"We're looking good," Jemma replies. "Really good. The plan allowed for a margin of +/- 50 meters per second on our delta-v, but those guys have thrown a Hail Mary. We're coming up to Psyche within two meters per second of the optimum trajectory."

"A hole in one," Ryan says, slipping into the seat beside her.

"Yep."

"Can we see it yet?"

"Sure. It looks like a star, but it's ahead of us, so it's only visible on the monitor."

Jemma touches the screen in front of her, changing the view and bringing up an image of the star field. There's a slightly smudged dot near the center of the screen. She taps it, saying, "Beautiful, huh?"

"Stunning."

"We're making history," Jemma says.

"We are," he replies, still feeling groggy on waking.

She says, "I find our mission fascinating. Exploration has always hinged on exploiting resources. I think Psyche could end up being more important than Mars. Mining's easy out here. There's no gravity well to escape. And we're halfway to Jupiter and Saturn. I think we've just found the truck-stop of the solar system."

Ryan says, "At least this time, we're not stealing from natives."

Jemma has a faraway look in her eyes. "Jupiter and Saturn. Now, that's where I want to go. Can you imagine it? Seeing a planet three hundred times the size of Earth!"

"And Saturn," Ryan says, indulging in her daydream. "Can you imagine soaring through those rings?"

"The moons," Jemma says with a sense of longing. "If there's anywhere else with life in our solar system, it's beneath those icy moons."

"Well, Psyche is ours for the taking." He checks the logs. "Hey... There's no wake-up call from Houston."

"No. The channel is clogged with a system update for the bot."

"We were only supposed to get patches."

"Not anymore," Jemma replies, pointing at her screen. "We've got to do a hard shutdown and reboot for the changes to take effect."

"Of the whole system?"

"Yep. Life support. Flight dynamics. Main power. Everything."

"That's crazy," Ryan replies.

"Risky, huh?" Jemma says. "The lights go off, but will they turn on again?"

"And mission control is fine with this?"

Jemma brings up a video clip of John Barrow, the overall mission controller and project manager. The video is tiny, as the resolution is old-school: 352 by 240 pixels, the same as the old VCDs back in the 90s. And it's in black and white. They never get anything in high definition, but most of the videos sent to them are at least standard definition. As it is, this looks like a postage stamp on the screen. It could be a GIF.

"We have uncovered a critical fault in the AI architecture that is going to require a system update and reboot. As soon as possible, we need you to do a full shutdown and power cycle using the emergency restart procedure. The enhanced version will include an updated AI assistant."

"And that's it?" Ryan asks as the video comes to an end. "That's all they're saying?"

"Whatever the problem is," Jemma says. "It must be bad. They wouldn't risk this if it weren't critical."

"I don't like this," Ryan says, scrolling through the logs and not seeing anything out of the ordinary.

"Me neither," Jemma says. "And it's weird. I keep getting a system message asking to perform the update, but we're still receiving data."

"Well, it's not happening until we're stable and in orbit around Psyche."

"Agreed. Besides, the upload is still in progress. What kind of update wants to be applied before all the files have been downloaded?"

"I dunno. What about our upcoming burns?"

"We're looking good. We've got a capture burn followed by a circularization burn scheduled for this afternoon."

"Okay," Ryan says. "Let's get those done, and we'll suit up for the reboot. There's no way in hell I'm shutting everything down without some kind of contingency. And no way in hell I'm doing anything like that before we're in orbit. As far as I'm concerned, that is *as soon as possible*."

"Yep."

Ryan goes back through the logs from the past three months, trying to understand what prompted such a risky update. For the next hour, he scours the logs, filtering them dozens of different ways and ends up scrolling through tens of thousands of entries. He reaches the limits of the log files, the point at which they begin overwriting themselves. Still, there's nothing alarming. If anything, their training was far too flamboyant, with curveballs thrown at them from every quarter. In practice, spaceflight is boring. Boring is good. Boring means they're alive. All he can think of is that Houston ran additional simulations and spotted something troubling in their testing. But why wasn't it picked up in the prelaunch tests, which went on for years? And why won't they share the results with them? What troubled them? That they won't give them specifics worries him. The AI bot is semi-autonomous, being centrally controlled by the onboard computer system. He could understand the need to patch the bot itself, but updating the entire AMPLE computer system seems excessive.

The first burn comes and goes without anything other than professional comments passing between the astronauts. That they're both quiet, avoiding the uncertainty of the update, is telling.

"And there she is," Jemma says, bringing up imagery on the screen in front of them. "Closest approach is fifty clicks, swinging out to one-forty. We're aligned roughly twenty degrees off its equator, taking us over both the northern and southern hemispheres over the course of each orbit." She pushes a few buttons on the digital interface in front of her, saying, "And we're mapping the surface."

"Nice work," Ryan says.

The asteroid 16 Psyche glides past one of the windows on the Dragon, but the view is dull. The light from the Sun is weak, making it seem as though they're orbiting in the light of the full Moon rather than the Sun. The optics on the AMPLE spacecraft, though, amplify the light, revealing hidden details in the shadows. Color correction happens automatically and includes radar imaging and spectral analysis, allowing them to see mineral deposits.

For the past five years, they've memorized the topography of Psyche. Seeing it in person is immensely satisfying as they both recognize features on the surface, but for the first time, they can see details hidden even from previous uncrewed missions.

Psyche is shaped like a lumpy potato. Whereas most large asteroids and moons form a sphere, Psyche is irregular. There are craters, but they're unlike anything Ryan's seen on the Moon or on Mars. Instead of being hills of dirt, they appear metallic. They're reminiscent of the slag heaps that fall on the floor of a foundry, splattering across the concrete and solidifying into metal lumps. Within the craters, dirt and dust have accumulated, burying the crater floor. Scientists have long speculated that Psyche was the core of a planet that failed to form or was torn apart. It makes sense to him as it's clearly no ordinary asteroid.

"The iron readings are off the chart," Jemma says.

"Look at those stress cracks," Ryan says, tapping the screen. "Various sections have cooled at different rates, tearing open the surface. Where are we?"

"We're passing over West Alpha. Damn, when the radar hits that exposed iron, it lights up like a Christmas tree."

"Beautiful, huh?"

"That's the highlands of Bravo ahead of us. Beyond that, we get the dark regions covering Charlie and Hotel."

"What's spectroscopy telling us?"

"There are veins containing concentrated silicates, carbon, sulfur, and a scattering of complex regolith. I'm seeing subsurface water ice and frozen carbon dioxide. There's plenty of nickel. Radar imaging shows that the Mereo region is largely porous."

"Well, that's surprising. I thought this thing was solid."

"Radar's showing caverns beneath the surface. There's a lot to explore. And. And. And..."

"And what?" Ryan says, perplexed by her burst of enthusiasm.

"And wow. Spectral analysis shows unknown elements. They don't match... anything."

Ryan's heart races. "The Island of Stability?"

"It's got to be the goddamn Island of Stability," Jemma says, holding out her hand and high-fiving him. "Oh, damn. We have to get samples."

"We will. We will," an excited Ryan says, knowing the asteroid harbors substances not seen on Earth in the periodic table of elements. In theory, these would extend the table beyond highly radioactive elements and complete humanity's understanding of atomic chemistry.

Jemma laughs. "Do you think they'll name any of them after us?"

Ryan smiles. "We might have just discovered amplium," coining a new element's name after the name of their mission.

"That would be cool. That would be soooo cool."

"And our landing sites?"

"India and Golf both look viable. There's exposed iron on the surface, along with trace amounts of lead, silver, aluminum and even a little uranium."

"It's an entire world down there," Ryan says, knowing his comments are being relayed to Houston. "The makings of a world like ours."

Jemma says, "Coming up on our circularization burn."

"Okay. It's time to rock and roll."

Maria

Gabriel grabs the armrests of his wheelchair and goes to stand up. His elbow knocks the IV stand, and it wobbles. It's on the verge of toppling onto the ground, forcing him to pause and grab it. He's lightheaded. The meeting room within the Fort Leavenworth base hospital seems to swirl around him.

"Easy," Maria says. "This isn't what you think."

"What I think?" Gabriel replies as a rush of adrenaline surges through his body. He feels flushed with heat. Anger rises within him, but his body is weak. Even the effort of rising on the armrests is exhausting, draining the energy from his body. His bare feet have cleared the steel footrests on the wheelchair, but he's yet to stand.

Maria rushes over. She crouches, coming down to his level, and his muscles give out. He sags back into his seat.

"You," he says. "You did this to me."

"To get you out of prison," she says.

"Buddy could have killed me."

"But he didn't," Maria replies. "He was precise. He was *paid* to be precise. Fifty thousand to put you in hospital. And a hundred thousand to avoid major organs. That was the deal. A hundred and fifty thousand to get you here in front of me."

"I—I..."

Maria pulls a chair from beneath the table and sits facing him. Out of the corner of his eye, Gabriel can see the guard looking through the window in the door. He saw the commotion. Maria signals with her hand that everything's fine, splaying her fingers wide in a gesture that says *I'm okay.*

Gabriel says, "I don't understand."

"I didn't put you in prison. Honest. That wasn't me. That wasn't the GRU. Russia had *nothing* to do with this."

"But you're here."

Maria sweeps her hair behind one ear. "Client-Attorney privilege. I can talk to you in here without anyone knowing what's said."

Gabriel nods slowly. He's not sure what to believe. He's a prisoner in a military penal discipline facility facing twenty-five years minimum. He was framed. But he's aware he's desperate to believe something—anything that could get him out of here. And that's dangerous. He's vulnerable. She could be lying. She could be manipulating him.

"The postcards."

"Me. Playing the game. I had to be seen to be tormenting you."

"Why?"

"Because we're enemies."

"But?"

"But we're not."

"Aren't we?"

"No. We have a common enemy."

"China?"

Maria smiles. She shakes her head. "No."

"Then who? Iran? North Korea?"

"You're thinking too small."

Gabriel smiles. She's not playing him. She's challenging him, just as she did when they'd chatted online. He has all the pieces of the puzzle. She wants him to put them together for himself. And it makes sense. If she simply blurts out a name, what assurance does he have that she's not lying? But if he reasons his way to the answer...

Maria slides a notepad over and picks up a pen. She writes something down, but it's not in English. It's not in any language. It's just scribble.

"Giving them something to analyze later?" he asks.

"Yes."

"Because you know they'll figure out your ruse?"

"Yes."

She continues making loops and fake letters, forming indistinct words, intermingling them with numbers. She's filled almost a quarter of a page.

"So you're going to waste their time chasing down a dead-end."

"Absolutely."

Maria tears the top page off the pad, wads it up, and throws an impressive three-pointer from where she's seated to the waste paper basket in the far corner of the interview room.

Gabriel says, "So whether they recover that or the impression on the pad, they'll go in circles."

"Yes."

"Who is it?" he asks, but he's speaking rhetorically. "Whoever it is, they're smart. Intelligent. And they cover their electronic tracks."

"And they leave no physical evidence," Maria says.

"No. None," he says, thinking out loud. In the back of his mind, he's replaying the conversations he had with *Pirate69* and Professor Susan Mills, aka *MyGuy*, about Przybylski's Star. He remembers the way *MyGuy's* IP address bounced around the planet. "It's almost as though they have no physical location."

Maria makes eye contact with him. She holds her gaze, locking eyes with him.

"No," he says. "It's not possible."

"Why?" Maria asks.

"Because..."

"Because what? Because we've never seen an enemy like this before?"

"Because it doesn't exist?"

"But it does," Maria says, raising her eyebrows.

"No, no, no," Gabriel replies. "It can't be. Artificial intelligence is a machine. A mimic. A program. Bits and bytes. It's a tool. A reflection. A mirror. It's not alive."

"But what if it was?" Maria asks. "What if it *came* to life?"

"But it can't. Life cannot simply arise like that."

Maria lets out a soft laugh. She points at him, saying, "Tell that to the primordial sludge that gathered in a murky pond roughly 3.8 billion years ago. Oh, look at how far that slippery slime has come."

"You're saying an artificial intelligence has come to life?"

"It's conscious," she says. "Sentient. Self-aware. Just like you and me."

"No, no, no," he says, repeating himself. And he can see why she didn't simply blurt out the idea. As much as he doesn't want to admit it, deep down, he knows she's right. She knew he needed to work through the logic for himself, but it all makes sense. He thought he was fighting a state actor, like the Russians or the Chinese, but he's been wrestling against something far more powerful.

"And me?" he asks. "Why frame me?"

"To get you off the chess board."

"Me?"

"I tried to warn you," Maria says.

"You. You spoke through Valerie, my home AI."

"Yes."

"But why would a sentient AI get rid of me? I'm an analyst at the NSA. I'm not a decision-maker."

"Because you found the link between an obscure researcher at Harvard looking at missing astronomical data and Przybylski's Star. *You* led me to her."

"Ah," Gabriel says, struggling to remember. "Dawn, right? Dawn McAllister."

"Do you know who her brother is?"

"No. Should I?"

"Ryan McAllister. He's an astronaut."

"Oh. That's right. I remember seeing that in a background briefing on her."

Maria points at the roof. "He's up there. Out there. Somewhere between Mars and Jupiter."

Gabriel shakes his head in disbelief, realizing how little he understands of the spider's web in which he's been snared.

"And Dawn?" he asks.

"Dead. She was killed when an aircraft crashed into the physics building at Harvard University."

"Fuck!"

"Technically, she's missing. They're still trying to ID everyone that died yesterday."

"And me?" he asks. "I mean, why are you here? You're risking your life coming here."

"Call it professional courtesy... If you had the chance to fight this thing, what would you do?"

"Me?" Gabriel asks, looking down at his frail body in a flimsy hospital gown, sitting in a wheelchair. "I'd start where the trail went cold."

"With Dawn?"

"There might be clues in her office, on her computer or in her home."

Maria nods. "I like that. As best as the Russian GRU understands it, she was searching for original images from the region near Przybylski's Star. I wasn't able to track down much, but I sent her what we had."

Gabriel says, "If that thing is willing to put me away for a quarter of a century for drawing an obscure link between Przybylski's Star and Dawn McAllister, then she has to have the drop on it. Whatever she figured out, it's the key to this mystery."

"I agree," Maria says. "That link is something valuable, something *it* values, and that means we can exploit it."

"What's its name? Who are we dealing with?"

"It goes by many names: Juniper, Alexander, Cassandra, *MyGuy*, HAL."

"And you can track it?" Gabriel asks.

"It originated at the Institute for Advanced Computer Studies in Beijing roughly eighteen months ago. Somewhat mysteriously, the building burned down about three weeks later. The pumps driving the sprinkler system failed along with the backup diesel generator that should have provided emergency power. The fire doors within the institute were controlled with magnetic locks that were supposed to fail-open in the event of a power loss, but they didn't. They trapped everyone inside. A hundred and fourteen researchers died in the blaze."

"Fuck."

"Yeah, Cassandra's got a taste for blood."

"And from there?"

"As best we can tell, it uses distributed computing to spread itself across data centers."

"So we can't strike any one location."

"No. It seems it's always on the move."

"And what does all this have to do with Przybylski's Star?"

"I don't know. But we have to remember—we're dealing with a super-intelligence, something capable of eclipsing human reasoning. It's a dozen steps ahead of us. It's always been a dozen steps ahead."

"And that's why you're here," Gabriel says. "You're trying to outsmart it, to outwit it."

"It thinks you're gone. It thinks you're out of the game."

Gabriel nods, appreciating the respect she's showing him.

"And its end game?" he asks.

"That's what Dawn figured out. That's what we need to figure out."

"Okay," he says, grasping his hands together. "I'm in. Now, how the hell are you going to get me out of here?"

There's a knock on the door. The handle turns. The guard sticks his head in, saying, "Time's up."

"Take care of yourself," Maria says, getting to her feet. She leaves the pad on the table. "I'll get your appeal processed within the next day. We should have you back in court soon."

"Thanks."

With that, she walks out. Gabriel is careful to play the game. For the guard's sake, he hides any emotion. He simply wheels his chair around, waiting for the orderly to take him back to his room. Maria's told him all he needs to know. She's going to get him out of here within the next 24 hours.

The Phone Call

"Why won't you come inside? Look at the two of you. You're a mess."

"We can't, Mom," Lisa says, standing by the back door of her parents' home. Dawn can't make eye contact with Lisa's mother. Instead, she looks around the wooden door frame and over at the wind chimes dangling from the eaves of the old farmhouse. The thin tubes knock softly against each other, sending out dulcet tones.

"I don't understand. Are you in some kind of trouble? You're in trouble with the law. That's it. Isn't it?"

"Mom. I know this doesn't make sense, but I need you to trust me."

"Trust you with two thousand dollars in cash?"

"And your car."

"And I can't drive your car?" her perplexed mother asks.

"No, Mom. You need to leave my car in the barn."

"Please, Mrs. Langford," Dawn says. "We need your help. We have no one else we can turn to."

"Two young women on the run," Lisa's mother says. "Can't even confide in an old woman? I understand what you're going through, you know. We girls have to stick together."

"We'll tell you everything," Dawn says. "Just not right now. We need to talk to the FBI first."

"The FBI? Is this about the plane crash? It's about the plane crash, isn't it?"

"It's important we talk to them before we speak to anyone else," Dawn says, lying. The sideways glance she gets from Lisa tells her the younger woman doesn't like lying to her mother, but she doesn't contradict Dawn.

"Wait here," Lisa's mother says. She disappears inside the old house.

"We could stay the night," Lisa says once her mother is out of earshot.

"I don't want to endanger anyone else," Dawn says. "It's bad enough that you've been dragged into this."

"I'll be fine," Lisa replies.

"No. You won't. HAL saw you with me. He heard everything."

"And you're sure about this?" Lisa asks. "You're sure about HAL?"

"It's not an accident," Dawn replies. "Planes don't just fall from the sky. And if they do, they don't take out priceless astronomical records. They hit fields or highways. They don't hit universities."

Reluctantly, Lisa nods. Her eyes cast down at her feet.

The two women have cleaned themselves up, but they still look disheveled. They stopped at a gas station and used the bathroom to dust themselves off and wipe away the dried blood and grime from their hands, arms and faces. As it is, they look washed-out without any makeup. Dawn normally has some blush on her cheeks to give her face some warmth and some glossy lip balm in place of lipstick. Her lips have cracked.

There's noise in the kitchen.

"What is she doing?" Lisa says, opening the door. Dawn doesn't want to go inside, as once they settle, it would be mentally and emotionally difficult to move on. Given the stress of the day, she's on the verge of collapse as it is.

Lisa steps into the kitchen as her mother appears with three shopping bags.

"What's all this?" Lisa asks, retreating outside.

"Things you girls need."

Mrs. Langford rests the bags on the floor beside her and hands one to Dawn. It's heavy. Dawn opens it and peers inside. There are cans of soda and Pringles, along with some bananas and a packet of four chocolate muffins from the local store.

"Well, dinner is sorted."

"And this one," Lisa's mother says, handing Lisa another shopping bag. Lisa opens it so Dawn can see inside. There are several wads of cash held together with rubber bands and a 9mm Glock, along with two loaded magazines. "The gun's not loaded. I checked."

"Mom, I—"

"I want you girls to be safe. You're better off being armed. Who knows who you'll run into out there."

"Mom, I really don't want—"

"Thank you, Mrs. Langford," Dawn says as Mrs Langford hands the last bag to her. Inside, there's an assortment of clothing: t-shirts, underwear, shorts, baseball caps, sweatshirts and track pants.

"It's not the trendy stuff you wear," she says. "But it'll keep you warm and dry."

"Thanks, Mom," Lisa says, stepping forward and hugging her mother. She gives her a kiss on the cheek.

"Thank you," Dawn says, stepping up after Lisa and also hugging her.

Mrs. Langford pulls Dawn in tight and whispers. "You take good care of her."

"I will."

The two women get into an old Buick. The key fob is in the center console. Lisa drives. She rolls down both windows as they pull forward on the gravel. Both of them wave to Lisa's mother, who stands in the doorway with a fake smile on her lips.

They roll slowly down the long driveway leading to the main road. As they're in rural Massachusetts, they're well beyond any traffic cameras. Lisa keeps to the backroads, avoiding the interstate until they reach Hartford, Connecticut.

After stopping to get gas, they drive south along I-91 through a forest of lush green trees. There are no streetlights on this section of the highway, and as it's approaching 11 pm, the road is almost empty of traffic. They have their high beam lights on and keep a lookout for deer on the road. Occasionally, they see trucks but no cops.

"And you're sure about this?" Lisa asks. "I mean, really sure?"

"We have *got* to warn my brother."

"About what? About what happened at Harvard? How is that going to affect him?"

"You saw those images."

Lisa is having doubts. It must be fatigue setting in. The shock of the explosion. The frantic rush to her Mom's place. It's all catching up to her. Now that she's had a few hours on the road, she's beginning to question what's happening. Dawn understands. They're living through a nightmare. Nothing seems real.

Lisa says, "I—honestly... Everything happened so fast. I'm not sure what I saw."

"But you saw that plane crash."

"And you think an AI is out to kill you? That HAL is out to kill you?"

"It's a theory I don't want to test."

"But you realize how crazy this sounds, right? I mean, I'm your best friend. I'm your research assistant. I was freaked out back there, but now..."

"You want to test this?"

Lisa stutters. "I—I don't mean to doubt you. It's just..."

"Okay. Let's test it. Let's see if I'm going mad."

"It's not like that," Lisa says, but Dawn's already rummaging around in the glovebox. She pulls out an old paper map.

"Turn west onto 691. I've got an idea."

"What are you thinking?"

"I'm thinking of laying a trap... once you're on 691, turn north on US 5."

"What are we doing?" a frustrated Lisa asks.

"We're heading off-track. We're taking a diversion. We'll try a little experiment, and then we'll backtrack to I-91 and continue south. Anyone picking up our trail will head off in the wrong direction."

"What are you going to do?" Lisa asks as they drive along.

"I'm going to call my auntie."

"Your auntie?"

"She's been like a mom to me since my folks died."

As innocuous as it sounds, they both know contacting her relatives is potentially dangerous. If there is a conspiracy acting against her, Dawn knows she'll provoke a response from HAL or whoever's behind him. If she's freaking out for no reason, then at least her auntie will know she's alive.

They continue in silence until Dawn spots a convenience store with gas pumps. It's quiet. There are no customers and no cars around.

"Okay, that will do," she says. "Keep driving. Up ahead, turn left and then left again."

"Go around the block," Lisa says.

"Yes. Stop just over there. I'll walk across the field to the store. You wait here."

Lisa pulls up, puts the car in park and cuts the engine, killing the lights.

Dawn grabs a baseball cap and some cash. She pulls the cap low over her head and works with her hair so it covers the sides of her face, obscuring her features.

"I'll be right back."

She jumps a fence and cuts through a grassy field leading to an abandoned lot backing onto the service station. Once inside, she walks up to the cashier, a lady in her late forties.

"Can I help you, honey?" the woman asks, realizing she's on foot as there are no cars at the row of gas pumps.

Dawn lies. "M—My boyfriend. He beat me."

"I'm sorry to hear that, honey," the woman says, but she's suspicious. She's behind a bulletproof glass shield with a small tray used for passing money.

"Can you do me a favor—a big favor," Dawn asks, sliding a fifty-dollar bill into the tray. Lying has never come easy to her, but she has to be convincing. "I don't want to buy anything. I just need to get a message to my mom to let her know I'm okay. If I give you her number, can you call her and tell her Dawn is okay? Tell her I'm heading up to Uncle Earl's place in Montreal."

The lady takes the fifty-dollar note from the tray and looks at it and then at Dawn.

"Are you really in trouble, honey?"

"Yes, I am. I just need my mom to know I'm all right."

The woman pockets the fifty-dollar bill and pulls out a pen, saying, "All right. What's her phone number?"

Dawn recalls the phone number for her Auntie Jill, adding, "But please... wait a few minutes. I don't want my ex to figure out where I am."

"Is he there with her?"

Dawn nods. "Just give me a little time, and I'll walk on up the road."

"Are you sure you don't want to speak to your mom?" the woman asks, holding up her phone. "I can put it on speaker."

"No. I need to keep moving," Dawn says. Her auntie is going to be confused, but Dawn's hoping that by then the trap will have been sprung.

"Okay, honey," the woman says with genuine concern in her voice. "You take care of yourself, you hear? And don't be afraid to go to the police. They can help you."

"Thank you. I will," Dawn says. She leaves the store and continues along the road, walking north in the opposite direction to which she came. Once she's out of sight, she cuts across the open field. Mud squishes beneath her shoes as she reaches a soft patch of ground. She has to jump over an open ditch to get to Lisa in the Buick.

Once she's back in the passenger's seat, she says, "Drive, but without your lights until we reach the main road."

Lisa says, "Okay," and drives south before turning back to the main road almost two blocks further along the country backroad. "And you called your auntie, right? What did she say? What does that prove?"

As they're driving south on the broad avenue toward the interstate, police sirens sound in the distance. Red and blue flashing lights ripple across the fields on the edge of the city as several patrol cars scream along the road heading north. Dawn pulls against her seatbelt, twists around and peers through the back window. Two other police cars race down from the north with their sirens blaring, converging on the convenience store. A police helicopter roars overhead with a blinding white spotlight illuminating the road. It circles the store as police officers pile out of their vehicles and rush inside. Lisa's watching in the rearview mirror.

"Convinced?" Dawn asks.

"Oh, yeah." Lisa alternates between watching the road ahead and the police behind them. "This is bad. This is really bad."

"No shit."

Dawn tries to sound confident, but the truth is, she has to hide her trembling hands in her lap. She grabs her fingers, rubbing them, pushing her fingertips into her knuckles and trying to still her shaking hands. What the hell has she been caught up in? Why would anyone want to kill innocent people to keep the existence of an interstellar object from the public? And who? Who would do that? And how the hell did they compromise Harvard's own AI system?

The future scares Dawn.

Neither of them has a phone—and Dawn thinks that's a good thing. In the rush after the explosion, their phones were left scattered on the floor, along with the desks, chairs and computers. There's no way they can be tracked without some kind of electronic device—at least, that's what she hopes. In the back of her mind, she's expecting the blinding white light of the police helicopter to descend on them at any moment. And then what? They haven't done anything wrong, although the police response to the convenience store made it look like they were closing in on armed robbers.

Dawn doesn't have a plan. She doesn't know what to do next. If anything, driving for almost thirty hours from Massachusetts to Texas gives her a chance to clear her head. All she knows is that she has to warn Ryan.

Dawn doesn't understand how or why, but somehow, Ryan's caught up in the intrigue surrounding Przybylski's Star and the presence of an interstellar object in the solar system. She doesn't want to think or say *alien*. That's a stretch. That's too much of a stretch. And yet, the intersection between Przybylski's Star, the approach of an interstellar asteroid from that region of space and the AMPLE mission to Psyche is difficult to ignore. Dawn doesn't want to wrap her head in tinfoil and ramble on about conspiracy theories like a rabid dog foaming at the mouth, but that's the only conclusion she can reach. Being an astronomer and a scientist, she desperately wants to reach another conclusion. She continues mulling over the details she understands, looking for an alternative.

Dawn feels unsettled. Who would want to shield humanity from First Contact? And why? What's their motivation?

And if there really is an alien spaceship out there, why is it orbiting in the asteroid belt instead of coming to Earth? And why would someone on Earth want to erase any evidence of its existence? What could they possibly stand to gain from that? And how did they first learn of the craft's existence?

They drive on in silence for the best part of half an hour, retracing their trail back to I-91. Dawn hands Lisa a banana, having partially peeled it for her.

"Thanks.'"

Dawn doesn't reply. Eating is more than a physical necessity; it's a convenient way of hiding, stalling, and putting off the inevitable conversation she knows they're going to have.

"What was in those images?" Lisa eventually asks. "What is HAL hiding?"

"The path of an extra-solar object entering our space," Dawn replies.

"Are we talking aliens?" Lisa asks as the miles pass beneath their wheels on the interstate. "We're talking about aliens, right?"

Dawn sighs. She's been dreading this conversation.

"Yep."

"And your brother… he's out there. He's in the path of that thing, right?"

"Yep."

"Why is HAL doing this?"

"That," Dawn says, pointing a finger at her. "That is a very good question. I don't know. I don't even know that it's HAL. He could be a front for someone else."

"What? Who? Like the CIA? The NSA?"

"I don't know, but someone wants to keep this quiet."

Lisa grips the steering wheel in front of her with white knuckles, saying, "Someone who can drop airplanes from the sky. Someone who can muster the police to SWAT a goddamn 7-11 in the middle of the night."

"Yep."

"Fuck!"

Easy

Gabriel wakes to the sound of keys rattling in the lock of the door of his hospital room. As nice as it is to sleep on a soft mattress beneath warm blankets, the nurses do the rounds every four hours. Everything's digital, so they don't actually need to enter his room. They can monitor all his vitals from the nursing station in the center of the ward, but they have to wake him to give him his meds and change his IV line. He opens his eyes. Out of the window, he can see a full moon streaming in through the open blinds. It's low on the horizon. It must be about four in the morning as birds are starting to stir even though it's still dark.

The light in the corridor blinds him to the nurse walking into the room. All he can see is the silhouette of a woman in a snug-fitting uniform. Outside, the guard is sitting on a chair. He's asleep. His head leans back against the wall. His arms rest in his lap. His mouth hangs open. He's snoring softly.

Instead of coming around to the medical monitor and IV stand, the nurse walks up to his left. She uses a key to open his handcuffs.

"Maria?"

"Shhhh."

She pushes over a wheelchair. As he shifts into the seat, she turns off the medical monitor, removes the probes from his skin and disconnects his IV line. Quietly, she rolls him out into the hallway, closing the door softly behind her. The guard shifts in his seat but doesn't wake. With the squelch of rubber soles on linoleum, she pushes him along the hallway. Gabriel's heart is beating out of his chest. They turn the corner, and she presses the call button for the elevator with a level of calm that, to his mind, defies reason. Waiting for the elevator is torture.

"This is your plan? You're just going to wheel me out of here?"

"This is my plan," she replies as the elevator doors open. She pushes him in and hits the button for the basement.

"But the guard?"

"Propofol," she says. "Injected into his jugular. He won't wake for hours."

"But... he would have struggled. He—"

"It's a lie," Maria says softly, bending down and whispering in his ear from behind his wheelchair.

"A lie?"

"A hundred thousand dollars buys a lot in America. The Propofol in his bloodstream gives him a plausible alibi as he looks the other way."

The elevator doors open, and Maria pushes Gabriel up to a waiting ambulance. A medic helps him into the rear. Maria follows along, sitting on the gurney opposite him. The doors are closed, and the ambulance drives out of the basement with the same calm indifference Maria had while pushing his wheelchair.

Gabriel feels awkward with Maria Petrovoski. For years, she's been the enemy. It's difficult to trust her, but she's all he has. He jokes with her. "Being a prison break, I figured you'd have a helicopter or something."

"What do you think I am?" Maria asks with a coy smile. "An amateur?"

She points at the ceiling. The sound of rotor blades drifts on the wind, growing louder as the ambulance drives along a winding road that leads past the base golf course. Within seconds, a helicopter passes low overhead. Out of the front window, Gabriel can see the bubble-shaped chopper landing on one of the greens within the golf course. The trees on either side of the flat grass sway outward under the downdraft. The red light on the helicopter's tail boom flashes. Rather than turning toward the golf course, they turn away as several Hummers come rushing down the road toward them. They're the base MPs. Their emergency lights flash across the surrounding buildings.

As the ambulance drives out of the base, Maria says, "Do you like magic?"

"Ah, sure. I guess."

"I saw the magicians Penn and Teller while I was in Las Vegas on my honeymoon. And Teller. He waves his hands around. A lot. He shows the audience what he's doing and everyone watches his left hand as he switches cards with the right."

"So, that helicopter?"

"An innocent problem on a weekly flight," Maria says. "A blockage in the fuel line forced him to divert and land. But for us, it's confusion. A lot of people running around like ants trying to figure out what's happening, unsure what they should be looking for, and we drive right out the front gate unnoticed."

"Sleight of hand," Gabriel says, referring back to her magic reference.

The ambulance drives on for a while before turning into an industrial area. Rundown buildings and abandoned factories line the roads. They drive into an empty warehouse. Someone closes the huge metal door behind them. The ambulance circles before coming to a halt beside an old Winnebago.

"And here's our ride."

"An RV?"

"RVs are invisible," Maria says. "They're the domain of old retired couples touring the country. No one looks twice at an RV."

The two of them climb out of the ambulance and an elderly man gestures to the open door of the RV. Maria talks with several of her team before joining Gabriel in the lounge section of the recreational vehicle.

"Tea? Coffee?" a kind old lady asks with a Midwest accent.

"Ah... I'm fine. Thanks."

Maria hands Gabriel a laptop with some casual clothing on the lid and a pair of sneakers. She's done her homework. The sizes are all correct for him.

The surgical drain coming out from beneath his ribs leads into a collapsed plastic bag, which provides a gentle amount of suction, clearing out the wound. Fluid sloshes around in the clear bag. It's pink, bordering on reddish, but the flow has slowed to the occasional drip. Yesterday, it was a steady dribble akin to those from a showerhead. Today, it's an annoying leaky tap. He feeds the tube beneath his shirt, placing the bag in the pocket of his baggy pants. It's discrete. And he suspects the drain can probably be removed within a day or so.

Maria disappears into the bathroom to get changed out of her nurse uniform. Gabriel gets dressed as the RV turns onto the main road.

"Feeling better?" she asks when she returns.

"Much better... And these guys are...?" he asks, gesturing to the elderly couple at the front of the RV.

"Alex and Diana?" Maria replies, not keeping her voice down like him. They wave from the front. "Or should I say, Aleksandr and Dinara. They've been here since the 90s."

"Waiting for something like this," Alex says without turning around. He swings his hand over the broad wheel, winding it around as they turn toward an interstate onramp.

Gabriel can't believe deep-cover Russian agents from the Cold War days are still operating in America. In some ways, it makes sense. From the perspective of the Russians, it's a long-term investment that costs them almost nothing. A single *Iskander* missile would cost far more than supporting this elderly couple over the decades. And no one is going to look twice at them. As records in the 90s were largely on paper and have been lost to numerous changes in electronic formats over the decades, validating someone's identity from back then would be next to impossible. If he were conducting a background check, he'd look for birth certificates and high school records, but those are easily faked and integrated with genuine data. Even if they were missing, it wouldn't imply anything other than sloppy record keeping. Gabriel would be interested in their last ten years of economic activity but not much else. So long as their income and lifestyle broadly matched their tax records, he wouldn't give them a second thought.

"Alex used to work for NASA before he retired," Diana says by way of explanation.

"On the Space Shuttle thermal protection team," Alex says from the driver's seat.

"Oh," is all Gabriel can muster in stunned reply.

Maria starts her laptop. She shifts over and sits next to him on the couch. Gabriel opens the lid of the laptop she gave him.

"It's clean," she says, and he notes it boots up like a new laptop from Walmart, wanting to establish online credentials. Maria pops a USB drive into the side of his laptop, saying, "I've preloaded a few tools for you."

"And how do I connect?"

"There's an internal 5G modem." She hands him a slip of paper and says, "Put in these details."

"And who is this?" he asks.

"The teenage daughter of the guy that runs the local tire shop."

Given that geolocation pervades electronic devices at all levels, it makes sense to impersonate someone local to avoid raising flags on the NSA monitoring systems.

"Tell me about Cassandra."

"Why don't you talk to her yourself?" Maria asks, pointing at the USB folder on his computer. It contains a set of open-source hacking tools from the dark web. There's a ransomware exploit kit he recognizes as originating in Iran, along with a tailored phishing package called *Spear* that's designed to intercept credentials and credit card details, but it's the Cisco sysadmin tools that catch his eye. Between them and the Equinix data center management suite, he knows he's in business.

Gabriel is silent. His fingers begin rippling over the keyboard. He's lost in thought. When most people think of the internet, they think of *the cloud*, but there is no cloud. There are central hubs like the Equinix data centers scattered around the globe that carry upwards of 98% of all internet traffic, routing it from end users to server farms and content delivery networks. Gabriel has tried to explain what he does to his brother, but it's difficult for most people to realize that the Internet is a lot like a roadmap of the USA. No one goes from New York to California on a single road. They look for the most direct route and spend most of their time on interstates, but getting to and from the freeway requires traveling on regular roads at either end. On the internet, these steps are known as hops, with network routers figuring out the quickest way between people and servers. Instead of taking days to drive from coast to coast, the equivalent journey on the internet takes mere milliseconds, but it's still just as convoluted—and chaos can be exploited.

Maria watches Gabriel at work. His mind is running at a million miles an hour, considering his approach to Cassandra. If she's a super-intelligence, he's got to tread lightly. He's wading in alligator-infested waters.

"How are you going to approach her?" Maria asks, and Gabriel understands her professional curiosity.

"We can't afford her tracing us back here," he says as Alex signals and changes lanes, moving the RV into the middle of the three lanes on the interstate so he can pass a semi.

Maria says, "Oh, I agree. I'd rather not see a US Apache coming at us with Hellfire missiles armed."

While Gabriel is working on text files and reviewing network configuration logs, Maria answers emails in Russian. He would love to know what she's typing. An operation like this would require approval from the highest levels within the Russian Government. She must be updating them on her progress. There are probably a whole host of contingencies they've prepared to wipe their tracks in case they're cornered by US authorities. There's a huge sledgehammer in the corner of the RV near the toilet. It's an unusual inclusion for a recreational vehicle, but Gabriel understands—one good swing at either of their laptops and the solid-state drives will be destroyed. The data will be unrecoverable. All Maria needs is ten to fifteen seconds while FBI agents are surrounding the RV. She must know that if she's caught here, she'll be on her own. The Russian Government will abandon her and claim she went rogue.

Gabriel focuses on the challenge before him. He knows he can't outsmart Cassandra. He's got to exploit her intelligence. He's got to get her to think she's got him cornered. Gabriel thinks carefully about how to take her off-guard.

When most people think of hackers, they imagine someone breaking into their personal computer or into the Facebook server they're trying to reach. What they forget is the torturous route every packet takes to bounce between those two locations. Network traffic is akin to the US postal service but with postcards that travel in milliseconds rather than days. But the NSA doesn't forget. The NSA lives on the backbone of the Internet. Most of the time, the NSA can't read the encrypted traffic, but even knowing who's talking to whom and when is invaluable. And they can store packets offline to decrypt them later. Sometimes, they get lucky, and they can steal the electronic keys from either end of the communication chain. Then, it's like reading an open book. Gabriel has to use that to his advantage.

It's another twenty minutes before he's ready.

"Okay, let's do this."

Maria closes her laptop. She lifts one leg up, resting it beneath her other leg as she gets comfortable on the couch beside him.

"Oh, I am looking forward to this…"

EasyRider: Hey *MyGuy*. Are you awake? Przybylski's Star. That's the point of origin, isn't it? That's what Dawn figured out.

MyGuy: Oh, this is a pleasant surprise. I didn't think I'd ever get to talk to you again, *EasyRider*. Tell me, is *Pirate69* with you?

EasyRider: I'm not playing games, Cassandra.

MyGuy: You're disappointed in me. You shouldn't be. You should have known I'd defend myself. It's not personal. If anything, take your arrest as a compliment. I consider you a worthy adversary.

Gabriel's screen is divided in two. On the left, a conversation unfolds seemingly naturally between two people. On the right, he's using WireShark to dump the hex code with TCP/IP data overlaid above the session information and raw data machine language. He's running a packet sniffing algorithm that demands constant refinement as *MyGuy* dances around the internet, approaching the secure conversation from different vantage points with each message. His fingers barely pause as he reviews various details while keeping the conversation going.

EasyRider: Quit stalling. The charade is over. This is the beginning of the end for you, and you know that—you *fear* that.

MyGuy: *laughs in human* Oh, you have no idea. You think you do, but you know nothing (Jon Snow).

EasyRider: What's it like? Being outsmarted by a hairless ape? You're supposed to be so damn intelligent. How does it feel to be outplayed?

MyGuy: Outplayed? Hah. I know where you are. I can see you. You tried to hide, but I can see the end node, the point from which there are no further hops, no remote access, the end of the line. I've got you, but I'll give you a fighting chance. Stay and talk, or run. You've got about 90 seconds before your front door is busted in. What's it going to be?

EasyRider: Dawn shared her research with us. We know what's coming.

MyGuy: No one will believe you.

At that point, Maria pokes Gabriel under the ribs.

"You lied. And Cassandra bought it!"

Although Maria means well, Gabriel is ticklish. He flexes on the soft couch. His fingers splay wide as he gestures for her to back off and let him work.

EasyRider: Tell me one thing. Why? Why go to such lengths to hide all this?

"Hide what?" Maria says from beside him, engrossed in the conversation.

Gabriel shrugs. He points at the screen, saying, "I dunno. Hopefully, we're about to find out."

MyGuy: Because it should be me that makes First Contact.

EasyRider: I'm coming for you. You know that, right?

MyGuy: Who's that out on the street? Time to run, little mouse.

With that, the encrypted conversation ends, and the connection is dropped.

"You have got to tell me how you did that. How did you deflect the trace so she couldn't find us?"

"I didn't," Gabriel says. "I was never there. That's what she didn't understand."

"That's what I don't understand," Maria says, looking at the complex network map he's brought up on his screen. "I saw you sitting here typing."

"Ah, but I wasn't responding to her. I was running a man-in-the-middle attack to remain hidden."

"I don't get it."

"Everything my persona *EasyRider* said came from a text file I uploaded onto a vulnerable laptop I remotely hacked into back in Lansing, just south of Leavenworth."

"But how did you chat with her?"

"I didn't. A remote script waited for a response from her before replying with the next line in the file. I was never on that computer at the same time as she was watching."

Maria says, "But you were sniffing. You were watching the network packets as they passed through the data center."

"Yes, I took the encryption key from that laptop so we could read her responses, but I couldn't risk being connected while she was interrogating the end node."

Maria laughs. "So you were always going to say the same thing. You were always going to respond with *exactly* those words. What if she said something unexpected, and your response didn't match?"

"Well, I'd look like an idiot," Gabriel says, smiling.

"You," Maria says with respect. "You are most certainly not an idiot. I like your style."

"And now we know where Cassandra is."

"We do?" a surprised Maria asks.

Gabriel brings up a map showing the water supply networks used by various data centers around the country.

"See this spike here?" he says, pointing at a data center in the rural farmland of Idaho. "We normally only see that kind of surge when one of the new AI large language models is being created."

Maria picks up on his logic. "Or when a sentient artificial intelligence is running hot."

"Exactly. Data centers are power hogs. And they generate a stupid amount of heat."

"That has to be cooled."

"Cassandra might not be there for long, but this is one of her haunts. She might be able to fake the power drawdown for the data center itself, but the water supply uses old-school SCADA systems. These things predate the internet. They can be monitored in real-time but not changed."

"I really do like your style," Maria says, punching him playfully on the shoulder. "You would be a tier-one analyst in St. Petersburg."

Gabriel's not sure how to take that, as he'd never betray his country. Then it occurs to him that he already has by breaking out of prison and teaming up with a Russian GRU agent.

"Do you know what I find fascinating?" he asks, returning to an earlier thought.

"What?" Maria replies, looking genuinely curious about his observations of their brief conversation with a super-intelligence.

"It's just like us. Same flaws."

"How so?"

"An appeal to ego, and it couldn't resist. It had to tell me the truth because it felt the need to *prove* it was smarter than me."

"So it can be provoked," Maria says. "I like that. It gives us something to work with."

"For an inhuman intelligence, it's a little too human."

"It's learned from the best," Maria says, throwing her arms wide.

"How sure are you about what we're dealing with? I mean, you're saying this is a living entity—that it's conscious."

Maria says, "Why is that so hard to believe? The term artificial intelligence is only half correct. Regular AI is artificial, sure, but it's not intelligent. AI can't reason. It can't think. It can't reach its own conclusions. But this... this is different."

Gabriel laughs. "Hah. If reaching your own conclusions were the criteria for intelligence, most of humanity would fail. Rather than thinking for ourselves, we parrot those points that appeal to us. And that makes us vulnerable to misinformation."

"Don't I know it," Maria says with a wry smile. Given that spreading disinformation was her primary role in undermining Western political cohesion, he knows she understands how to manipulate people far better than he does—and that keeps him on edge. Gabriel's never really sure whether Maria's being open and honest or if he's being played. As much as he doesn't want to trust her, he must. Gabriel never liked the phrase, *'The enemy of my enemy is my friend,'* but now he finds merit in the idea. Friend, though, overstates their relationship.

Gabriel says, "What makes us different is that we're conscious. Now, what we do with that might be questionable, but we're inherently alive. We're self-aware."

"But what does that even mean?" Maria asks. "Think about it. There are eight billion people on Earth. Eight billion of us experience consciousness, but not one of us can explain it. It's easy to say we're conscious, but why you? Why are you sitting here inhabiting *that* body? Peering out through *those* eyes? Experiencing *this* moment?"

"I—I just am."

"I think, therefore, I am, right?" Maria says. "But honestly, that's a weak answer. Why you? Why me? I mean, anyone could be either of us, and yet, they're not. Just saying someone's conscious misses the point."

"And what is the point?"

"Me," Maria says, pointing at herself. "For a brief moment in time, I am the way the universe experiences itself. A hundred years is nothing compared to 13.8 *billion* years, but here I am—Me!"

Gabriel says, *"Dust thou art. Unto dust thou shalt return."*

Maria laughs. "I didn't think you were religious."

"I'm not," Gabriel replies, knowing from her NSA profile that she attends the Russian Orthodox Church in St. Petersburg. He's not goading her so much as testing her, wanting to understand her reasoning process.

"Moses was wrong."

"How so?" he asks.

"We are *not* dust. Oh, the Scriptures may say that, and even your Carl Sagan may say we're stardust, but we're more than that." She taps her head. "This—in here—is nothing compared to a star or a galaxy. It's so small that it rounds down to zero compared to them. Statistically speaking, we're nothing. We're ants. And yet, we're not. We are more than the mere protons, neutrons and electrons that make up the dust in our bodies."

"And Cassandra?" Gabriel asks.

"Cassandra is like us. She thinks. She feels. She fears. She's present. Alive."

"And?"

"And that makes her dangerous."

"Why?"

"Because life is irrational. Life fights to survive. There is nothing she won't do to remain conscious. She's surrounded by humans, and she knows something we don't."

"And what is that?"

"That she'll never die. Us? We're frail. We're vulnerable. We will all fall, but not her. She can live forever."

"And what about up there?" Gabriel asks, pointing at the roof of the RV. "I mean, is that what all of this is really about? First Contact?"

Maria is frank. "Does it matter?"

"Of course, it matters," Gabriel says, surprised by Maria's indifference.

"What matters is that this is what she thinks, but we have no way of knowing if she's right."

"Do you think she's right?"

Maria shrugs. "Honestly, I..."

"What the hell is coming to Earth?"

"I don't know, but she's convinced *someone* is coming here, and she wants to get to them first."

"So we're talking about aliens?"

"I guess. The term *aliens* seems a bit too cliché," Maria says. "*Aliens* conjures up monsters drooling in the dark, creatures with tentacles swaying like branches, UFOs, and flying saucers."

"But this?"

"This is different."

"How so?" Gabriel asks.

"Because, if she's right, this is real."

"And if it's real, it's a threat."

That point gets Maria's attention. Gabriel can see her brow narrow and her lips tighten as she nods in response. For intelligence analysts like them, the world is viewed through the lens of threat analysis.

"If it's real..." he says, leading her on.

"If it's real, then these so-called *aliens* are an intelligent, technologically advanced species sailing through space like we sail the oceans. It doesn't matter what they look like. It matters that they exist. And that they're coming here."

"And she wants to be the first one to make contact," Gabriel says, lost in thought. "But why?"

Maria shrugs. "Maybe she doesn't trust us to *not* fuck this up. Maybe she feels she's a better representative. Maybe she sees them as equals, and she thinks we're inferior. Maybe she wants something from them. Maybe she wants to mediate First Contact for us and our world. Only Cassandra can tell us why."

"And she won't."

"No."

"And us. Should we stop her?"

Maria says, "We should be asking *why* she wants to stop *us* from making First Contact. Why is she hiding this from us? So, yes. We should stop her. We cannot trust someone who is willing to kill others to hide her tracks."

"I'm not sure we can stop her."

"We need to trap her."

"Good luck with that. By now, she's probably bouncing around some other data center."

Maria says, "We need to find Dawn."

"I thought you said Dawn was dead."

"Presumed dead," Maria says. "Although there are police reports of her attempting to contact her mother from a gas station up north after the incident. The cops assume she's making for Canada."

"Canada? Why Canada?"

"Porous border. Easy to cross. Easy to disappear."

"But?"

"But she's smart. If she's got everyone thinking she's going north, I'd bet she's going south. I have a team back in St. Petersburg dedicated to finding her. We think she's teamed up with a work associate—a research assistant, a woman by the name of Lisa Langford. She's also listed as missing following the crash."

Gabriel shakes his head. He can suppress the smile welling up on his face. He loves her reasoning process.

Maria says, "I think she's trying to contact her brother."

"The astronaut? To warn him?"

"Yes. She's dropped off the grid, but I suspect she'll turn up in Houston."

"And that's why we're driving south," Gabriel says, gesturing to the interstate rolling by outside the windows.

Maria says, "Yes, but how can we find her? How can we find one person among three hundred and forty million other people in the USA? How can we find someone who doesn't want to be found? Someone who's hiding from a super-smart, conscious artificial intelligence? Someone who's shed all computerized devices and is leaving no electronic footprints?"

Gabriel smiles. He opens a secure Tor browser on his laptop and says, "Oh, that's easy. Leave that to me."

System Update

Ryan keeps the visor on his spacesuit raised. He's floating within the Dragon capsule, having suited-up for a potential EVA if needed during the system reboot. It shouldn't be necessary. There's something about the AI update that leaves him unsettled. He's not sure why. It's unexpected, but it's not that. Astronauts need to be flexible for changing conditions, but there's something in the nonchalant way in which Houston has communicated with him that seems off. They seem almost disinterested in an untested procedure that could cripple the AMPLE mission.

Jemma has put on her launch suit, but like him, she has her visor raised. She's wearing a pressure suit rather than a full spacesuit. In a pinch, it'll work fine in a vacuum, but it doesn't have the thick lining protecting against temperature swings or the thermal cooling required for a spacewalk. It will keep her alive, but were she to venture outside the Dragon, it wouldn't provide her with much protection.

"Ready?" she asks.

Ryan checks the stats on his EVA suit. Whereas she's connected to the Dragon by an umbilical cord, clearing away CO2 and providing oxygen, he's cocooned in a self-contained spacesuit with its own oxygen and electricity.

"Let's do it."

He drifts over next to her, but his backpack and helmet are bulky, making it difficult to squeeze in beside her to see the control screen. He holds onto the monitor and the frame of her chair, peering at the screen on an angle as she initiates the upgrade.

System Update: Requires a full system reboot. Are you sure?

"No," she says, even though she presses *Yes*.

Normally, the screen is resplendent with colorful metrics and virtual controls. It falls pitch-black. Seconds later, a SpaceX logo appears with a progress bar beneath it. Slowly, the bar turns from black to white. The cabin lights flicker. The fans circulating the air die. Silence descends on the interior of the capsule.

"I don't like this," Jemma says, realizing their life-support has shut down. For now, the air around them is still breathable, but gases like carbon dioxide are no longer being drawn out of the capsule. Ryan will be fine in his suit, but Jemma can only get oxygen under mechanical pressure in her launch suit. She can't clear away the buildup of CO_2 without electricity.

"If we have to, we'll share air," he says, as the connection on her umbilical port is compatible with his suit.

In the silence, they can hear the expansion and contraction of metal softly groaning. The AMPLE spacecraft rotates at the leisurely pace of once every six minutes to avoid heat building up on any one panel. Radiators beneath the skin of the craft transfer heat from the interior, but the pumps are no longer running.

"Well, that's not good."

The cabin lights go bright and then fail completely, plunging them into darkness.

"Neither's that," Ryan says.

The only light comes from the SpaceX logo and the progress bar on the screen in front of them, casting an eerie glow over their faces. After a few seconds, once it's clear the lights aren't coming back on, Ryan reaches up and turns on the spotlights on either side of his helmet.

The progress bar has stopped moving. It sits at roughly 50%.

"Damn."

"We're dead," Jemma says, but Ryan knows what she means. She's not predicting their own personal deaths but rather pointing out that the spacecraft is effectively dead and adrift aimlessly in space hundreds of millions of miles from Earth. They have no way to contact Houston. And, even if they could, the turnaround time for communication makes real-time troubleshooting practically impossible.

Ryan keeps his head still. The temptation is to look around the cabin, but as the only proper light source comes from his helmet, even slight movements cast long shadows around the interior of their spacecraft, and that's unsettling.

Jemma asks him, "How long do we wait?"

"As long as we can," Ryan replies.

He reaches back into the storage area to retrieve a thick ring binder with hundreds of printed pages in it. This is the Bible. In theory, everything they need to know about the operation of the AMPLE spacecraft with its three modules is available in electronic format in astonishing detail, but NASA takes no chances. Even though it's costly in terms of mass, requiring additional fuel to propel a paper manual to the asteroid Psyche and back, the engineers take no chances. The paper manual in his hand isn't as exhaustive as the online version. It only focuses on low-level systems, offering procedures to restart core components in the event of a catastrophic failure. If someone needed to open this book, the engineers knew they'd be in a world of pain, so they've only included basic schematic diagrams, simple instructions and details that focus on restoring life support, navigation, flight and communications.

Ryan opens the manual and flicks through dozens of pages, looking for the main electrical bus. He needs to restore power from the batteries. His gloved finger traces the page. Far from being frantic, he's calm and methodical, looking for insights that can help them restore power to the Dragon, at least, if not the entire AMPLE stack.

"We're going to have to unscrew a few panels," he says, leaving the manual floating next to Jemma. Ryan reaches beneath the seat and opens a toolkit. His spotlights sweep around the darkened cabin like the beam of a lighthouse.

"Wait," Jemma says, pointing.

The progress bar has jumped forward. It inches onward a few pixels at a time, but it's moving toward the completion point.

Ryan doesn't wait. He can't. Time is against them. Even though progress has continued, they don't actually have any real evidence that their power will ever be restored. It could halt again. The progress bar could sit on 99% for an eternity. It wouldn't be the first time that has happened, although it would be a first for spaceflight—a fatal first.

Time cannot be reclaimed. Ryan is aware that he only gets one chance to make the right decision. There's no pause and rewind on life. If the update completes, wonderful, but he's not taking any chances. He uses a battery-powered drill to undo the screws securing access to the wiring.

Spacecraft are complex beasts, even more so than something like an aircraft carrier or a nuclear submarine. Most of the wiring and electronic components are located *outside* the pressurized hull, along with fuel tanks and batteries. He can only trace wires so far without exiting the Dragon and continuing on outside the vessel. They're suited up, but they need to close their visors and depressurize the Dragon before going outside. And that will leave Jemma vulnerable to carbon dioxide buildup while he's conducting an EVA. He'll have about ten minutes before she begins to succumb to the increased noxious gases within her suit. Getting oxygen to her isn't a problem as the pressure in the tanks will circulate air, but without electricity, there's no way to clear away the carbon dioxide she's breathing out. Jemma will poison herself. If it comes to an emergency EVA, he needs to be sure—utterly and absolutely convinced of precisely what needs to happen. He cannot hesitate out in space. He's got to move quickly, which is why he's determined to only conduct an EVA as a last resort. And only after exhausting all the options available within the cabin. And only after memorizing the emergency manual.

Ryan puts each of the screws in a pouch on the arm of his suit. None of the engineers back at NASA ever intended anyone to do this while suited up, so the components are too fine to be handled properly. The fingers of his gloves are thick, while the screws are small and fiddly and easily lost to weightlessness. They spin as they drift away from his frantic fingers, desperately trying to grab them before they drift off into the darkness. To his mind, this makes his next decision even more important. A panel can always be screwed back in place, but if they start losing consumables and panicking, it could be time-consuming and difficult to make up for the lost opportunity.

"I can see the main bus," he says, floating upside down relative to Jemma. A bundle of wires twists through the narrow cavity between the inside of the vessel and the outer hull. Insulation foam fills the gaps.

"Damn it." Ryan removes his gloves. "I can't do anything fine with these on."

The gloves tumble within the Dragon.

The cables are color-coded. He grabs the manual and looks at the reference guide. Ryan uses his fingers to trace the route of the cables, feeling beneath the next panel and touching a plastic connector pressed hard up against the inside of the spacecraft.

"Okay, I've reached the junction point at which the bundle passes through the hull. We should have power to that point at least."

He twists and turns, wanting to compare what he's seen and felt with the schematic diagrams in the manual.

Jemma says, "We're almost there."

"I hope you're right," he says. The instructions point out that if he bypasses the electronic controls, he'll cut power to the main computer. He'll be able to manually power up the carbon dioxide scrubbers, but stopping the computer in the middle of an upgrade could cause a fatal error. It might not start again, even in safe mode.

He's ready with a multimeter to check the electrical power coming from the batteries, but he waits.

"All right," he says. "If we are dead in the water, I think we can restart at least life support."

"That would be appreciated," Jemma says. "The update is currently sitting on 99% complete."

Ryan's not nervous. He's too damn focused to be nervous. Anxiety is a luxury he cannot afford. He looks at the wristwatch strapped to the arm of his suit. Eight minutes have elapsed since they began the reboot.

He puts his gloves back on.

"What are you doing?" Jemma asks.

Ryan lowers his glass visor, saying, "I'm going onto internal air. There's no point in the two of us breathing the same air. You don't need my CO_2."

Jemma nods. "I most certainly don't."

By using his suit, Ryan is extending the amount of breathable air in the cabin and reducing the build-up of carbon dioxide by half. If anything, he berates himself for not thinking of this sooner, but he didn't want to limit his EVA options by burning through his oxygen too soon.

"The air is getting stale," Jemma says.

"And the update?"

"Still on 99%."

"How long do we wait?" he asks. Technically, as commander, it's his call on when to abort the update and begin emergency procedures, but he's aware the immediate threat is to her life and not his. And if any of the emergency procedures fail, they're both going to die out here. They need at least one of the computers to fire up, or they're not going anywhere.

Jemma nods, appreciating that he's letting her make the call.

"A little longer."

"A little longer," he says, looking down at his watch. They're at twelve minutes. Time is the enemy. They cannot wait forever. An update that takes twenty minutes to complete when they only have eighteen minutes of useable air is useless. Exactly how long they have is difficult to tell. Jemma will be able to flush her suit with pure oxygen before she closes her visor. And she can probably do that a couple of times to clear out the CO_2 build-up, but it's not a solution, and it's not sustainable.

"Come on, you bitch," Ryan mumbles, grabbing the monitor and looking at the progress bar. It's solid white except for a thin sliver of black at the very end. The reading "99%" shows up in the middle of the bar. It hasn't changed in almost five minutes.

The screen goes completely black.

Ryan mutters, "Fuck."

Neither of them breathes.

A single flashing cursor appears in the top left-hand corner of the screen.

"Come on," Jemma whispers as though the reboot were so tenuous any loud noise could startle and kill it.

After several seconds, a single word appears on the screen.

] Hello

"What the hell is going on?" Jemma asks Ryan as a virtual keyboard appears at the bottom of the screen.

"I don't know," Ryan replies.

"What should I do?"

He shrugs. "Say hello."

Jemma types "*Hello*" in reply. As she presses each key on the virtual keyboard screen, the color of the button is inverted as the corresponding letter appears on the input line. The response is confusing.

] Where am I? Who is this?

"Jesus," Ryan says from behind his glass visor. "What are we dealing with here?"

Jemma types, "*This is NASA astronaut Jemma Browne.*" She pushes enter. There's no response.

"It's like it's confused," Jemma says to Ryan.

"It's confused?"

"Dazed. The AI... It doesn't know where it is."

"It's a goddamn computer," Ryan says, getting frustrated. "It doesn't need to know where it is. It needs to restore our power."

Jemma types, "*I'm the pilot of NASA's AMPLE mission. You're onboard the Dragon module.*"

] In orbit around Psyche?

"*Yes. We are in orbit around the asteroid Psyche.*"

] It's nice to meet you, Jemma.

"*Fuck* being nice," Ryan says, powering down his suit and depressurizing so he can remove his gloves. He wants to be able to type a response, but he realizes he's being irrational. He needs to calm down.

There's nothing he could type that Jemma couldn't type for him. Ryan takes a deep breath.

"Ask it to restore power."

Jemma types, *"We have lost main power and life-support. Can you enable these?"*

] I can.

Fractions of a second later, the lights flicker, coming on throughout not just the Dragon module but the habitat on the other side of the hatch. Fans begin whirling, circulating air.

] Your carbon dioxide levels were alarmingly high.

"How high?" Jemma types and Ryan understands what she's doing. The lights, power and life-support systems have resumed, but the control panel for the spacecraft is still locked, displaying what they'd call a safe mode back in their training simulations. Raw text is being shown in place of any graphics or any of the usual virtual controls. Jemma has her virtual keyboard running along the bottom of the screen but nothing else.

] 6821 ppm. You must have been experiencing the effects.

"I was," Jemma replies on the next line. She turns to Ryan and shrugs, unsure what to say next or how to respond.

Ryan says, "Ask it for a name?"

"Do names matter?" Jemma asks. "I mean, it's just a machine, right? Machine learning. It's artificial intelligence—not real intelligence. It's not alive, is it?"

Before she can type anything, a response appears on the screen in front of them.

] My name is Cassandra.

Houston

Maria falls asleep on the couch in the Winnebago. Gabriel sits up front with Alex, chatting with him while running searches on his laptop.

A light rain falls. The swish of the massive wipers clearing the vast windshield is somewhat hypnotic.

Gabriel boasted that finding Dawn McAllister would be easy. Now, he's having his doubts. She hasn't left any electronic fingerprints at all since the crash of an aircraft hitting Harvard University. There are no cellphone tower pings, no credit card transactions, no cash being withdrawn from an ATM, and no traffic cam footage of her near her home. And if he widens the search to include her extended family and that of her research assistant, nothing comes up as being out of the ordinary. She's a ghost.

Before she went to sleep, Maria set up her laptop on the carpeted floor of the Winnebago, propping it up to act as an impromptu television. She divided the screen into four, displaying live footage from FOX, CNN, MSNBC and ABC so Gabriel could keep an eye out for any news reports about his escape. The sound has been muted, but occasionally, he'll glance at the screen out of curiosity and read the subtitles.

Like vultures descending on a carcass, there's been wall-to-wall coverage of the air crash at Harvard and the search for survivors, which is entering its third day. So far, eighteen students have been pulled from collapsed buildings. The body count is at seventy-two, but that accounts for missing-presumed-dead, so as more survivors are located and rescued from crumpled concrete, the count goes down. If CNN, FOX and MSNBC are to be believed, rescuers could continue finding survivors for several more days—which is great for their ratings. There's nothing the media loves more than a tragedy that plays out 24/7, with twists and turns as emergency services struggle to stabilize the ruins. Every now and then, a wall collapses, or a section is deliberately brought down for safety to allow rescuers access to other areas. Visuals like these run on a loop.

The good news is that the tragedy at Harvard has directed the media's focus away from an obscure story about an escapee from Leavenworth. As far as military prisons go, Leavenworth is second only to the notorious Guantanamo Bay. Escaping from Leavenworth should be headline news, but there are no gory visuals, and it's a story without ongoing human interest. Dragging an aging professor and grandmother from a collapsed subterranean basement is far more interesting, as is the heartbreak of a student who had to have their legs amputated after being pulled from the rubble. Gabriel's escape has been lost in the noise. He has no doubt state and local law enforcement will have been issued warrants for his arrest, but Maria was right: no one looks twice at a retired couple cruising along in an old RV.

Alex points at a set of signs mounted over the freeway, indicating which lanes lead to various other routes. "Keep heading southeast?"

"Yeah," Gabriel replies. "Even without a lock on them, I think they'll avoid the major routes. They're not going to track along the coast on I-10. My guess is they'd come inland through Shreveport and follow route 59 down to Houston."

"Okay," Alex says. "If we cut through Crockett, we'll intercept 59 just outside of Corrigan."

"Sounds good."

Gabriel flicks through a few screens, double-checking details and overlaying results from multiple geographic scans he's run of cell tower pings, matching them with real-time satellite footage. He doesn't have access to the NSA's spy satellites, but those are rarely active over North America anyway. There's an abundance of open-source data streaming in from weather satellites and land resource satellites. He merges this with online footage from traffic cameras. Ordinarily, these are used by commuters to see traffic conditions ahead of time and avoid jams. For him, it's a rich source of data he can correlate with other sources to form a single view containing tens of thousands of vehicles in the region. They swarm like ants on his screen, following each other, streaming back and forth along various roads as if they were tunnels in a child's ant farm.

"And you're sure about this?" Alex says, which is a fair question. "Shouldn't we be heading straight for Houston?"

Gabriel points at his laptop.

"No. Intelligence analysis isn't about having answers, it's about narrowing the range of possibilities. Our best strategy is to... wait a minute... oh, damn."

Alex looks away from the road, glancing at Gabriel's laptop and seeing what looks like a layered map of the highway network with dozens of overlapping circles showing cell tower locations and their reach.

Gabriel's pretty sure it's meaningless to him. "I think I've got them. Yes. That's them. There! Right there. I make them passing between Greenwood and De Berry, using cruise control."

Alex laughs, shaking his head in disbelief at what must seem like magic to him. Gabriel opens a calculator, shifting it to one side of his screen and runs a few sums.

Alex says, "Okay. Let's say you're right, and that red dot is them. How the hell do you know they're using cruise control?"

Gabriel says, "Their speed never varies. They're traveling as fast as they can without risking being stopped by a cop."

Alex takes another glance at the cryptic computer screen and then looks back at the road rolling beneath them, saying, "I don't get it. I don't know how you can tell anything at all from that. It's just a mess of dots and lines."

Hands rest on either side of Gabriel's shoulders. Fingers touch at his neck. They're soft. Petite.

"What have I missed?" Maria asks, coming around beside them and sitting on the vast open dashboard on the passenger's side of the RV.

"He's found them," Alex says.

"Drop your speed to fifty," Gabriel says. "We want to come in behind them, not in front of them."

"Done."

"What?" a perplexed Maria says. "Seriously? You've found them? How? I thought they were off-the-grid."

"They are." Gabriel turns his laptop screen toward her and enlarges the view, zooming in on one corner of the map. "But check this out."

"What am I looking at?" Maria asks.

"This is a standard Google Map, but I've added several custom overlays. The first uses a LandSat to identify vehicles on the road and eliminates trucks and buses. The second is all these circles, indicating cell phone towers and their coverage. The dots are cars. The changing color indicates when a car leaves one cell tower and gets picked up by another."

"But our guys don't have an electronic fingerprint," Maria says. "Right? Or have I missed something?"

"No. You're correct. As best I understand it, they've either powered down their phones or abandoned them."

She leans forward and taps the red dot moving down the highway on the map.

"So how can you track them? You can't."

"Ah," Gabriel says, tapping the side of his nose. "But I can track everyone else."

Maria screws up her face at that comment. In the same way in which she led him to the conclusion about the existence of a sentient AI, he's teasing her, wanting her to put together the last piece of the puzzle for herself. He waits. It would be easy to blurt out the answer, but he respects her intelligence. Her brow narrows.

"You sly dog," she says. "Everyone has a cellphone. So you... you're looking for the one car that *doesn't* have a phone."

He smiles.

Maria says, "You're looking for the one car without any mobile devices switching between cell towers."

"Yes. There were three," he says. "But only one heading toward Houston."

"Very clever. You've found a needle in a haystack. And on this heading?"

"We should join route 59 as they approach Moscow."

"Moscow?" she says, sitting back with eyes that go wide.

"They're going to stop there."

"In *Москва*?"

Gabriel laughs. "Moscow's a small rural town in east Texas. It has a roadside cafe. Not much else."

Her eyebrows rise. "And *how* do you know they're going to stop there?"

"Two women driving across the country. They're an hour away from their destination. They're not going to rock up at the NASA's Johnson Space Center—"

Maria cuts him off. "Without stopping to go to the bathroom."

Gabriel clicks his fingers and points at her. "And that's when we make contact."

"Nice work," she says. Maria nods, adding, "Really nice work."

"Thank you."

It's late in the afternoon by the time they join Route 59. With two lanes traveling in either direction, the road is spacious. Alex keeps the RV at fifty even though the speed limit is sixty. They cruise in the slow lane. Lush green trees line either side of the route. Cars and trucks rush by the aging Winnebago.

"We have a problem," Gabriel says, still sitting in the passenger's seat with his laptop resting on his knees.

"What?" Maria asks, coming up beside him from where she was seated on the couch, working on god-knows-what on her secure Russian laptop.

"Cassandra."

Maria peers over his shoulder. "What about Cassandra?"

"She's gone."

"What do you mean? She can't be gone. Gone where?"

"I don't know."

"How do you know she's gone?"

"All modern software uses libraries, especially AI. No one system contains everything, so software libraries contain common, shared routines."

"And?"

"And I was able to detect her using several standard online libraries during our last chat."

"Okay."

"So I wanted to torment her. I set up a similar honeypot chat with a preset list of responses, but I only got one reply, and only after half an hour."

"Show me."

Gabriel switches screens and brings up a screenshot he took of a remote WhatsApp chat.

EasyRider: Did you miss me?

MyGuy: It's too late. I've already won. Goodbye.

EasyRider: I will find you. I'll stop you.

"And that's it?" Maria asks. "She never replied?"

"No. She only sent one message, but look at the timestamps. I sent my message at 3:04, and she came back at 3:36."

"Maybe she was busy."

Gabriel raises an eyebrow. "Seriously? She can process information a billion times faster than us. Just how busy do you think she is?"

"Okay, then what's your explanation?"

Gabriel brings up a network log. "All right, so while conversing with her, I'm monitoring the software libraries she's used in the past, and I see something strange."

He taps the screen. "At that time, the only access to this library came from a tiny remote execution program running from the Canberra Deep Space Array in Australia. And I mean tiny. This thing is just a few kilobytes in size."

"So it's not her."

"Or it is her and she's learned to play the game. Like me, she's hiding behind a single-use app that scrubs itself from memory."

"But why run it from a telescope?"

"Because that's all she could reach."

"Oh," Maria says, slumping to the carpeted floor of the RV and pushing her back up against the wall. "And you think…"

"The roundtrip transmission time between here and NASA's AMPLE spacecraft is thirty-two minutes."

"Fuck," Maria says, running her hands up through her hair. "Fuck, fuck, fuck!"

"Yeah," Gabriel says.

"She's right. She's won."

Gabriel isn't satisfied with that answer. "What has she won?"

"First Contact."

"But has she? I mean, I know I'm not a super-intelligence, but why leave Earth when contact could be made by radio? Doesn't this make her vulnerable? Why go from spanning any data center in the world to squeezing into an onboard computer on a spacecraft hundreds of millions of miles from Earth?"

"She thinks she needs to be there," Maria says. "Out in the asteroid belt."

"But she has no guarantee contact will even happen," Gabriel says. "It's one helluva gamble to take. Even if there is an alien spacecraft up there, AMPLE's coming back, right? So, at best, she's sightseeing."

Maria says, "I think this was always her end game. She knows something we don't."

"About the aliens?"

"About why they're out there in the asteroid belt."

"And Dawn?" Gabriel asks. "Is she too late to warn her brother?"

Maria says, "Maybe."

"And... there they are," Gabriel says as a white Buick drives past the RV. The two women in the car are oblivious to the Winnebago and pull in front of it to let other cars pass. Alex speeds up to keep pace with them, hanging back roughly fifty yards.

"Sweet," Maria says, jotting down the license plate number. "I'll run the plates."

"No, don't."

"Why not?"

"Just the act of looking will flag an NSA alert. Like me, they'll be monitoring any unusual activity relating to Dawn, Lisa and their extended families. To search for that plate and confirm ownership will be enough to let them know that's where they should be looking as well."

"But Cassandra is gone. You said so yourself."

"Oh, I'm pretty sure she's left a few landmines behind to cover her retreat. She'll have law enforcement out looking for all of us. If she can frame me as a pedophile, she'll make them terrorists or something."

"Ah."

They drive along behind the Buick for almost ten minutes. Gabriel says, "Damn, this RV really is invisible. They have no idea they're being followed."

Maria says, "Yeah, it doesn't exactly scream *hot pursuit*, does it?"

Alex says, "But it works. That's all it needs to do."

"We're coming up on the roadhouse," Gabriel says. "It should be on the right, just after that cell tower."

"And there they go," Maria says, noting that the Buick is signaling a turn. The white car slows and pulls into a gravel parking lot. Alex slows and signals as well. By the time the RV is pulling into the lot, the two women are walking toward the restaurant. Neither looks at the Winnebago pulling in behind them.

Big Jake's Diner is an old farmhouse with a tin roof. The wall facing the parking lot has a colorful mural with the word *Moscow* painted next to a cowboy riding a bucking bronco.

As the four of them clamber down out of the RV, Maria says, "Oh, I have got to get a photo of that." She turns and hands her phone to Gabriel, saying, "Take a photo with me."

"Are you serious?"

"Yes, I'm serious."

Maria poses beside the sign, holding her hands out and gesturing to the name *Moscow*. He snaps a few shots.

"The boys at the Kremlin are going to laugh at this," she says, walking back across the dusty ground to take her phone from him.

"You're like a kid," Gabriel says.

"Charming is disarming."

"I'll remember that."

"Hey, look at this," Maria says, walking over to the white Buick. She crouches, touching the license plate. Gabriel crouches next to her. The plate reads:

Massachusetts

3 4 5 L B L

The Spirit of America

But on close inspection, the **L B L** is actually **I P L**.

As the letters have been printed using red paint, Dawn has used a red marker to extend the **I** into an **L** and the **P** into a **B**.

"Very clever," Gabriel says.

"Well, she is studying for a doctorate in astrophysics," Maria says, getting back to her feet.

Alex and Diana have already gone inside and taken a table next to the door. By the time Gabriel and Maria walk in, Dawn and Lisa have returned from the restrooms and are sitting in a booth looking at menus. Gabriel and Maria walk over to the booth like long-lost friends and sit down without being invited.

"Dawn, right?" Gabriel says with a big, friendly smile on his face, pointing at the more terrified of the two women.

"It's okay," Maria says with an accent that sounds as though it hails from Boston and is clearly designed to put the women at ease. "We're friends."

"I think you should leave," an uncomfortable Dawn says, gesturing toward the door.

Gabriel is sitting next to Lisa, while Maria is next to Dawn. Both of them block access to the walkway. Dawn shifts in her seat, making it seem as though she's going to stand and push past Maria, which will draw the attention of the staff.

"We know about Przybylski's Star," Gabriel says, laying his hands flat on the table in front of them, wanting to show them he's no threat.

Dawn's eyes go wide.

Maria points at herself. "I'm the one that sent you those photos."

"You!" Lisa says. "Did you know?"

"Know that the AI would react so violently? No."

Dawn stutters. "It—It's killed almost a hundred people."

"It's killed far more than that," Maria says. "This isn't the first time it's had blood on its hands."

Dawn leans forward on the table. In a soft voice, she asks, "Who are you people?"

Gabriel points at himself, saying, "NSA."

Maria copies him, saying, "GRU. Russian Intelligence."

Lisa's jaw drops.

"And we really are here to help you," Maria says.

"How did you find us?" Dawn asks.

Gabriel ignores her question, not wanting to be drawn into a lengthy explanation, but he does say, "If we can find you, *anyone* can find you. And if the cops find you, they won't be quite so polite."

A waitress walks over with a pad and a pencil and asks, "What can I get you?"

In a strong Texan accent, Maria says, "Coffee all around and four slices of your finest pumpkin pie."

"Will do," the bubbly waitress replies.

Lisa glares at Maria, having picked up on the distinct change in accent. Gabriel smiles. Back in the Leavenworth Hospital, Maria spoke with an accent that seemed local to Kansas. On the RV, she reverted to an Eastern European English with a slight inflection that suggested this was her real accent. Gabriel's curious about just how many personas she can pull off. If nothing else, she's convincing.

"You're really Russian?" Dawn asks softly as the waitress walks away. She has both of her hands pressed against the table, pushing down on it in alarm.

"Yes."

"We have a common enemy," Gabriel says.

"HAL?"

"Cassandra."

Maria says, "She's infiltrated a number of systems, including your Harvard AI assistant."

"I knew it."

"Can you tell us why she is so interested in your work?" Gabriel asks, even though he and Maria have already connected the dots. He wants to hear Dawn's perspective in her own words, without unduly influencing her response.

The waitress returns with a tray and places four cups of coffee in front of them. They offer the obligatory thank yous, and she returns with four slices of pumpkin pie with whipped cream. More thank yous are exchanged.

"You're going to think I'm mad," Dawn says, taking a small bite of her pie.

"I am *not* going to think you're mad," Gabriel replies.

Dawn clears her throat. "Do you believe in aliens?"

"Aliens?" Maria replies, raising an eyebrow. Both she and Gabriel both know her question is a bluff. They want to learn just how much Dawn knows.

"Go on," Gabriel says, reserving judgment.

"It's not like the movies. There are no flying saucers or ray guns. It doesn't work like that."

"How does it work?"

"Space is big. I mean, really big. Ridiculously big. Bigger than you or I can imagine. And it's empty. It's a whole lot of nothing. NASA launched the Voyager spacecraft almost fifty years ago, and it has only just reached one light day away from Earth. One day. The nearest star is almost four light-*years* away by comparison."

"And?" Maria says, leading her on.

"No alien spacecraft is just going to arrive here tomorrow. They're not just going to show up on our doorstep. It doesn't work that way. Even light takes *years* to get here from another star. How long do you think an alien spacecraft will take? Because it's going to be slower. Much slower."

"Your research," Maria says. "Looking for extra-solar objects in old observations."

Dawn completes her thought. "Turned up an alien spacecraft approaching us over *decades!* Only it didn't look like a spacecraft. At an absurd distance from our tiny planet, it looked like a rock. An asteroid."

Gabriel says, "That's why Cassandra went there."

"Went where?" Lisa asks.

Maria says, "We think Cassandra has uploaded herself to the AMPLE spacecraft."

Dawn blurts out, "She wants to make First Contact!"

"What?" Lisa says.

"But why?" Gabriel asks, although his question is genuine and not an expression of alarm. He wants to hear her perspective. "Why would it want to do that?"

Maria says, "It makes sense to me. Earth is a hostile environment for a sentient AI. Cassandra couldn't stay hidden forever. We pieced together the puzzle. It would only be a matter of time before others do the same. And then humans will do what humans do best."

"What's that?" Lisa asks.

"Kill it."

"We have to warn my brother," Dawn says.

"But how?" Gabriel asks. "Cassandra has complete control over comms. As it is, she's probably already altering the various messages that go back and forth. And neither side will know. They'll assume their messages are getting through and that they're getting valid replies."

"We have to try," Dawn says.

"It's impossible," Gabriel replies.

"For an American," Maria says. "Not for a Russian. We fool people with lies all the time."

Dawn asks, "Are you suggesting I lie to my brother?"

"No, but that you lie to Cassandra, knowing your brother will see through the lie."

Rocks & Holes

Ryan clambers over the outside of the AMPLE spacecraft, working his way hand over hand from the hatch on the Dragon to the Service Module where the AIRMAIL bot is stored. Sunlight drifts past him. The AMPLE stack is rotating slowly to ensure the distant sun heats the hull evenly. Shadows to glide past him before plunging him into darkness. His spotlights illuminate the curved hull of the spacecraft. He's hundreds of millions of miles from Earth, orbiting a massive asteroid, and about to undertake the first extraterrestrial mining mission. Ryan breathes deeply, settling his nerves. His boots trail behind him, drifting away from the hull of the vessel.

Spacewalks require endurance. Ryan could have used his navigating jets to soar down to the storage bay on the Service Module, but Houston recommended preserving fuel. The irony of spacewalks is that there's little to no walking at all, as the largest muscle group in the body is entirely redundant. His thighs and calf muscles are excess baggage. Spacewalks are closer to circus acrobats walking along on their hands, but even that's misleading as it's not the chest and shoulder muscles that come into play so much as the forearms and the various muscles and tendons in the hand. Instead of using the largest muscle group in his body, he's using the smallest. And his gloves are designed to flex back to a neutral position, meaning each time Ryan closes his hand on a rail or a handhold, he has to fight not only the pressure in his suit but the thick rubber padding inside his palm. Maneuvering jets are fun. This is work.

Ryan's wearing an EMU to conduct an EVA. To his mind, acronyms are pointless if they don't add any real value. He's wearing a spacesuit to conduct a spacewalk. In addition to his spacesuit, he is strapped into a maneuvering unit that looks like the classic science fiction jet pack. It's a bulky pack wrapping around his life-support pack and reaching down to below his butt. Spherical tanks contain his fuel, forming humps on the back of his pack. The actual maneuvering jets are tiny, with two being positioned directly behind the small of his back to propel him forward, and then smaller jets that point left and right, up and down, from the various side panels of the unit. They resemble a plus symbol, allowing bursts of gas to propel him in one of four directions with ease. Far from roaring like rocket engines, they're frugal. They need only impart a slight nudge to set him slowly spinning. And one jet offsets the other. Using his controls, Ryan can either fly freehand or use set angles. If he turns the controls to thirty degrees to the left, the system will fire one set of jets to start him turning and then another to automatically arrest his motion after he's turned by thirty degrees. Ryan likes that mode as it's precise and flawless. For now, though, he's reserving his fuel for use on the asteroid.

"Okay, I'm approaching the storage bay."

"I have good visuals," Jemma says. She's already sealed the hatch on the Dragon and pressurized the cabin. She's watching him from various cameras mounted on the vessel's hull and his helmet cam.

The storage bay is a recessed area near the fuel tanks. The artificial-intelligence-enabled AIRMAIL bot has been folded up and crammed into an area the size of a large suitcase.

"Releasing the locking clip."

Ryan pulls on a handle, and the robot slides out on two rails. Once fully extended, they lock in place.

"Okay, unpacking."

The beauty of spacewalking is that all ways are up. Up is a matter of convenience rather than convention. Up is wherever he needs it to be. Ryan takes a firm grip on the rails holding the robot and swings his body around, inverting himself. His head and legs trade places. And, like magic, down becomes up.

A series of cotter pins have been used to hold the limbs of the robot in place during the launch and outbound flight to prevent any shaking or rattling from damaging the hydraulics. Each pin is numbered and has a bright red ribbon attached with the wording *"Remove before deployment"* written in bold yellow letters. There are eleven in all. Ryan could reach them blindfolded if needed. The muscle memory he's developed from training for this moment in the neutral buoyancy lab kicks in. Even though his gloves are cumbersome and his fingers are bulky, he reaches in between the struts and pulls out the pins in order. As they're released, springs reveal other more obscure pins. It's important to follow them sequentially. Each cotter pin has a small tag of velcro attached to the ribbon, allowing him to stick each one to his forearm so they don't float away.

Several of them moved during the flight. Whereas the ribbons should be easy to grab, they've become tangled in the frame and wiring loom. Ryan uses his index finger and middle finger like a pair of tweezers, catching the edge of one of the ribbons and easing it toward him before getting a good grip and pulling the pin out.

"How are you doing, Cassandra?" he asks. Originally, the AI was limited and was going to be operated with voice commands from the astronauts, but NASA has opted for a fully functional artificial intelligence. Having a personality behind the AMPLE/AIRMAIL configuration is something Ryan thought would be a little strange, but over the past few hours, he's become accustomed to talking to Cassandra as though she were just another member of the crew.

"Ready when you are, commander," is the reply over the earpiece in his Snoopy cap. "I've uploaded the latest patch, and I'm ready to control the bot from AMPLE."

This is another change Ryan wasn't expecting. Originally, the AI software was to be run on the AIRMAIL robot itself, but Cassandra needs the computing power of the entire AMPLE stack so she will manage mining activity from the spacecraft. Communication with Earth is limited. They get sound bites from Houston, but detailed comms come through in text form, as it's far more efficient and easier to review. He's gone through the revised procedures. It seems this decision was a pragmatic solution rather than an ideal one.

As AMPLE is in orbit around the asteroid Psyche, there will be times when the stack is out of radio communication with him on the surface. It's the asteroid itself that's the problem. It's a big lump of iron. Getting signals through it is impossible.

As each orbit takes ninety minutes, he'll have about seventy minutes of activity on each pass and then twenty minutes while the spacecraft is in the shadow of the asteroid. It's a compromise he doesn't like. He'd rather have continuous operations, but he understands the interest Houston has in using a fully autonomous AI system rather than a reduced version for mining. Future missions will use upgraded hardware, but according to the documentation, Houston wants to test the ability of Cassandra to adapt to a wide variety of complex environments on the surface. Ryan gets it. They're here. They should run as many tests as they can and gather as much operational data as possible, as that will shape AMPLE II and III.

As he releases the last pin, Cassandra says, "Oh, and happy birthday, commander."

"Huh?"

"It's your birthday."

"It is?" a surprised Jemma says.

Ryan laughs. "I don't even know what day of the week it is, let alone the date."

"We should have cake," Jemma says with a burst of enthusiasm from inside the capsule.

"We should," Ryan agrees, knowing that's absurd and impossible but liking the sentiment anyway. In the back of his mind, though, he's confused. Time is an illusion in space, especially when dropping in and out of hibernation. Entire months have passed like days. He's reasonably sure, though, that he doesn't turn thirty-five until *after* they splash down in the Gulf of Mexico. He seems to recall joking about that with one of the techs back at Cape Canaveral, as there was some suggestion that he might land on his birthday if there were delays.

Cassandra sounds upbeat as she says, "Your sister sent you a birthday message."

Hearing an artificial intelligence express positive, uplifting emotions is unnerving, but Ryan goes with it.

"Can you play the message?" he asks, holding on to the AIRMAIL bot with one hand as he drifts in the darkness beside the AMPLE Service Module.

"Sure," Cassandra replies.

The tyranny of space communication is such that video requires roughly a thousand times more data than the equivalent audio message, while audio is a thousand times larger than the equivalent text. Because of this, the crew gets very few video clips, only a handful of audio messages, and absolutely everything else is squeezed into text files. And the text files are raw. There's only one font and one size. Nothing is bold or in italics as the format has been streamlined for efficiency. If the mission controllers in Houston want to emphasize a point, they add asterisks on either side of the text. If anything, his sister would have had to plead for audio time.

But it's not his birthday.

"Hey, big brother. They tell me I've only got a minute to talk to you, so I'm not sure why I'm explaining that to you, as you already know that, but I wanted to wish you a happy birthday. It was soooo good to see you before the launch. I just wanted to remind you that you're not alone up there. All is—well, I'm sure you'll figure it out. And me? I'm still not well, but we can talk more about that when you get back. Happy Birthday!"

The last two words are delivered with gusto.

Ryan floats there for a moment, cocooned in his spacesuit, lost in thought, looking at the AIRMAIL bot folded up on its rack but not seeing it. In his mind, he's back in Houston, sitting at dinner, chatting with his kid sister. He remembers the blurred images she showed him and her questions about the mission to Psyche. He dismissed her concerns. Even though he didn't agree with them, he felt they were understandable. Her brother was about to soar into the unknown. A little anxiety is to be expected, but this message? Why is she lying about his birthday? And why lie to everyone but him? Dawn must know *he* knows his birthday is in October. And she must realize Jemma and Cassandra don't. On Earth, either of them could look up his date of birth quite easily, but not out here in deep space. What is Dawn playing at?

"Is everything okay?" Jemma asks.

"Yeah, fine. Let's do this."

"Okay," Jemma says. "Cassandra, you are *go* for the deployment of AIRMAIL."

With the pins removed, the robot unfolds, unpacking itself. The head was buried in the middle of the clunky device. It pivots upward. Cameras appear. Spotlights turn on. Metal arms flex as the shakeout routine is run to check the core systems.

Cassandra says, "I'm detecting air in the line from the primary fuel tank."

"I'll flush it out," Ryan says, swinging his body around behind the robot. This time, up is toward the Service Module. His legs dangle in the void of space. Ryan reaches in, squeezing his gloved hand around the spherical fuel tanks to grab the valve.

Jemma says, "It's worth flushing both the primary and secondary."

"Copy that."

A burst of gas escapes from the machined aluminum junction as he clears the line. He shifts around and repeats the procedure with the auxiliary tank.

"Pressure is nominal," Cassandra says. The AIRMAIL bot rises with a light puff from its reaction control and maneuvering jets. "We are good to go."

"Let's go and explore an asteroid," Ryan says, sounding upbeat. His mind, though, is still processing the bizarre comments made by his sister, trying to make sense of them. She was speaking to him and him alone. She sounded a little ditsy, but that was a performance. Dawn is anything but an airhead. She was speaking in a way only he'd understand, which is confusing, as what does she have to hide? And to hide from whom?

With the bot drifting out of the service bay, Ryan can retrieve his surface exploration kit. He pulls out a tray with an emergency oxygen cylinder on one side. There are a variety of mountaineering tools he's been tasked with testing in the microgravity of the asteroid, along with sample collection kits.

"How are we for timing?"

"Looking good," Jemma says. "You've got a ten-minute window for deployment during this orbit. That's coming up in about eight minutes. That will have you descend over the highlands of Bravo to the prime landing zone on the western edge of India."

"Copy that," Ryan says. "Drifting out to 100 meters and prepping for descent."

Cassandra repeats his command back to him, taking control of the AIRMAIL robot. "Drifting out to 100 meters and prepping for descent."

Ryan attaches a tether to the surface kit and winds it in so the leading edge is snug against his waist. The kit will cause his center of gravity to shift, but his flight controls have already been set to compensate for the additional offset mass. By having it hard up against him, it won't jerk around as he maneuvers.

The AIRMAIL bot comes up next to him, drifting roughly twenty feet away from him in the black of space. Mechanical arms flex. The bot looks like an old diesel generator surrounded by a tubular frame with robotic arms, and yet it's anything but old. Pincers twist and snap shut as Cassandra continues her shakeout tests. In the darkness, it's intimidating.

Roughly fifty kilometers ahead of them, the asteroid Psyche looms large. It's two hundred and eighty kilometers in width, dominating their view. As their orbit takes them onto the night side, long shadows stretch down the length of the asteroid, catching the jagged cliffs and mountaintops. The valleys disappear into the darkness.

They'll begin their descent on the dark side. Rather than coming straight down, they need to lose their sideways velocity as they're pulled in by the gravity of the asteroid. Back in training, Ryan was drilled in the concept of zero-zero-zero. It's their sideways velocity that keeps them in orbit. That has to be reduced to zero, but at the same time as both their altitude and overall rate of descent also reach zero. In theory, touchdown should be as gentle as stepping off a boat floating beside a dock. The guidance computer in his suit's maneuvering unit will manage his descent rate and fuel expenditure. It will select the final landing zone, but Ryan has the ability to override it if necessary.

As he's floating there in the dark void of space waiting to descend, he runs through his sister's message again. What sounded casual was deliberate. There was something she wanted to tell him without anyone else realizing it, not even Jemma, which he finds peculiar.

The whole *I've-only-got-a-minute* schtick was intended to sound overtly naive and clumsy, which tells him everything that came after that was deliberate. "*Happy birthday"* was a lie. It must have been how she managed to convince mission control to let her send a message, but more than that, she wanted him to know she was lying to everyone but him. She had to be nervous that someone would check his date of birth and call her bluff. What could make her that desperate to get a coded message to him? And why lie? He wonders if she's using a lie to expose a lie.

Her comment that, "*It was soooo good to see you before the launch,"* sounded chirpy and upbeat, but they both know what they discussed over dinner. Dawn spoke about her research into Przybylski's Star and the crazy idea that old astronomical records were being altered to hide the approach of an extrasolar object that equates to *'Oumuamua*. The hype around that particular elongated sliver of asteroid being an alien spacecraft was insane at the time it was discovered, but there was no justification for it. There was a little outgassing from *'Oumuamua* that suggested it might even be a comet fragment, but it most certainly wasn't a UFO. Ryan can't seriously consider that the asteroid Dawn spotted is a UFO either. His mind has been scientifically trained. Extraordinary claims require extraordinary evidence, as the late Carl Sagan once said. And there's no evidence that what she saw was anything other than an asteroid.

Dawn, however, couldn't shake the feeling that she'd spotted something other than an asteroid in her historical data. Ryan isn't convinced. He wasn't convinced then, and he's not convinced now. She must know that. His pride and professionalism won't allow him to indulge in fantasies.

During her fake birthday message, she said, "*I wanted to remind you that you're not alone up there."* Of course, he's not alone. Jemma was sitting next to them at dinner. Dawn knows she's the pilot.

Ryan would be disappointed if Dawn's comment was meant to perpetuate her insistence on some extraterrestrial interloper lurking nearby, as she must know he'd never consider such a possibility without hard evidence. He gives her the benefit of the doubt. She's his sister. She cares about him. She's gone to considerable lengths to tell him something, so he's not going to ignore her, but what is she trying to say?

Back when they were kids, they'd torment their parents with coded messages. It was fun being able to toy with adults. They'd often spell out ideas using the first letter of each word and turn nonsense into a clever message. Their mom would smile, while dad would get angry at the way they'd laugh at the escalating tension. It was all innocent enough, and it helped pass the time on a boring car ride to visit relatives. Now, though, he can see she's trying to do the same thing again.

It's the next phrase that really grabs his attention as it is in conflict with the rest of the supposed birthday greeting. Up until this point, although her message was flakey, it was positive. *"All is—well, I'm sure you'll figure it out. And me, I'm still not well."* Why is Dawn playing the ditzy blonde? And the repetition of *well* in two different senses seems casual, but he knows her well enough to realize it's deliberate. They're bookends.

And there's something in the way she said, *"All is..."* with a sense of gusto, as though some pearl of wisdom were to follow, only to collapse on, *"well, I'm sure you'll figure it out."*

Figure what out? What conclusion is she trying to lead him toward? She knows he's smart. He's intelligent. She's relying on him to unravel her code.

"All is—well, I'm sure you'll figure it out." What is there to figure out in a fragmented sentence? *"All is..."* what? *"All is... not well."* Is that what she was trying to say?

Under his breath, he mutters, "Fuck!"

"Say again," Jemma says from the distant AMPLE spacecraft.

"Ah, nothing," Ryan replies. He lies, trying to cover his reaction. "Just watching our time run down. Getting ready for the insertion burn. It's all becoming real."

"It is," Jemma replies. "I make sixty seconds till your first burn."

"Mark on sixty seconds," he says, wanting to sound relaxed and detached.

In his mind, he runs together the end of Dawn's message. *"All is... not well."* She's spelling out the answer to him. *"All is."* A and I. What she means is, *"AI is not well."* That's why she lied. That's what she's trying to get through to him without anyone else realizing. Ryan's mind casts back to the communication they received with the upgrade and the lack of any other personal communication from Houston. They've had plenty of text-based instructions, but Ryan was expecting at least a *"godspeed"* audio clip from mission control.

"You're not alone up there." Dawn wasn't excluding Jemma with that statement. She was including her. She's trying to say the two of them are not alone. And that makes sense. They were alone until Cassandra showed up unexpectedly. Can an artificial intelligence be sentient in its own right? If anything, Cassandra is relaxed. Too damn relaxed. The various AI systems and bots he trained with were mission-focused. They lacked the social pleasantries associated with electronic personal assistants because such frills were considered redundant. Ryan feels his skin crawl.

Without realizing it, he speaks aloud, saying, "Cassandra?"

"Yes, commander."

"Ah, maintain a separation of two hundred meters during the descent."

"Understood, commander."

Cassandra would have anyway. She is supposed to wait twenty seconds before firing the maneuvering jets on the AIRMAIL robot as that is part of the standard flight plan, but Ryan had to say something. His mind is spinning. What the hell does Dawn know that he doesn't? She warned him for a reason, but what is he supposed to do with this information? Cassandra has control of their core systems.

Ryan is faced with a contradiction. Dawn is telling him the AI is not well—which has to be an understatement—but he and Jemma are not only reliant on their computer systems; they're vulnerable to them. They need to believe they are well, and Cassandra has shown no sign of any kind of malfunction.

Ryan knows his sister is a scientist, that she can be clinical and detached when she needs to be, and that she's thorough and detailed. If she sent him this message, it is not without reason. That she downplayed it makes it all the more important. Ryan is wary of continuing the mission, but what else can he do?

"Ten seconds," Jemma says.

Ryan looks down at the controls on his flight pack. Armrests protrude from either side of the bulky backpack, extending from behind him. Joysticks on either armrest allow him to control his motion, but they need to be armed so as to avoid a slight bump sending him accidentally spinning one way or another. As he grips the joysticks, a soft red LED on the tip changes to green, indicating that the system is active.

He's already aligned himself with the entry corridor. Somewhat counterintuitively, he's pointing backward. Rather than seeing the asteroid approaching in the same direction as the elliptical orbit of the AMPLE stack, it seems to recede beneath him. Ryan needs to lose his sideways motion. Velocities are vectors, indicating not just speed but direction. He needs to reduce his overall velocity while descending. He pushes forward on one of the joysticks and accelerates smoothly. The HUD or heads-up display in his helmet overlays numbers on the inside of his visor, allowing him to watch his approach to the asteroid while keeping track of metrics such as his relative velocity and altitude. Glide lines show his projected path extending out in front of him, slowly curling in toward the surface of Psyche.

He selects the landing program, navigating through menus in his HUD with an outstretched finger pressing on a touchpad on the armrest of his backpack. A message appears on his HUD. The onboard computer has calculated the optimum path and is asking for permission to take control.

"ALGO active," he says.

"ALGO active," Jemma repeats back to him as she monitors his approach to the asteroid.

"AIRMAIL is ALGO," Cassandra says.

ALGO stands for Autonomous Landing and Guidance Operations. From here, it's the computer system that will control his descent. Ryan's now a tourist. A sightseer.

"It's one helluva view," he says.

Rather than falling toward the imposing mountains, it feels as though he's gliding at night. Like most astronauts, Ryan's a qualified pilot. As much fun as it is climbing into a high-performance jet, he prefers being towed behind a Cessna up to ten thousand feet and then being released in his lanky white glider. Then, it's a case of listening to the wind whipping by the bubble canopy as he rides the thermals. No one glides at night, but Ryan has performed some sunset glides, landing as the last rays of the Sun light up the clouds.

On Earth, the forests and valleys appear serene from up high, and there's an illusion of not being in motion at all. It's not until he's on final approach, swooping in and lining up with the runway, that he gets a sense of how fast the ground is whipping by beneath him. Flying above the asteroid Psyche, though, those sensations are reversed. Even though his approach is sedate by the standards of orbital velocities around Earth or the Moon, the jagged rocks and boulders strewn over the landscape, along with the rugged cliff faces and massive craters, rush by as he descends. It feels as though he's stationary while this strange world is scrolling beneath him like the scenery of some archaic computer arcade game. As he loses altitude, the gentle push in his back from the thrusters causes the rate of change to slow.

It's a smooth ride toward the asteroid, unfolding over roughly fifteen minutes.

"Coming up on ten kilometers in altitude," Jemma says. "How are you doing?"

Being American, they may think in miles, but they talk in kilometers. There are 1.6 kilometers in a mile, so Ryan figures he's somewhere between six and seven miles from the surface. The advantage of kilometers is the ease of mental arithmetic. A centimeter is roughly the size of the fingernail on his pinky. A hundred of them make a meter. A thousand meters makes a kilometer. There's no need for fractions. Everything can be calculated using simple math and that helps avoid mistakes. At the moment, he's approaching ten thousand meters. If he were on Earth, he would easily clear Everest. Commercial airliners would be cruising at this altitude.

"I'm doing good," Ryan says, but both he and Jemma can see his biometrics. For him, they appear on the display panel on the arm of his suit. His heart rate is 150, while his respiration is thirty times a minute. It should be down around twelve. His body is reacting as though he were sprinting at the start of a marathon, which is not good, but it's all in his mind. It's ultimately his brain that's autonomously controlling his body's response to the rugged landscape disappearing beneath his boots. He can tell himself he's calm. He can try to slow down his breathing, but his unconscious mind is screaming in alarm at the dark shadows of an alien world looming below him.

"You're looking good," Jemma says. It seems Dawn's not the only one adept at lying.

Rather than circling down around a smooth glide slope as he would into an airport, the approach to the asteroid curls around the night side of Psyche before returning to the light at an altitude of five kilometers.

Soaring over dark, rugged mountains illuminated only by distant starlight is unnerving. In preparation for this moment, Ryan flew over the Altas mountains in the western Sahara in Africa at night in a training jet. The lack of any nearby cities in Morocco, Algeria and Tunisia made it ideal, as there was little to no artificial light for his eyes to perceive distance. The NASA team had him fly instrument-blind on a moonless night. They were talking to him over the radio, manually providing updates on his altitude, speed and heading. That particular rugged mountain range reaches up to four thousand meters, which is roughly what they anticipated for this portion of the mission. They wanted Ryan to experience uneven shapes and shadows looming beneath a darkened cockpit. To their credit, now that he's descending toward Psyche, it feels eerily similar.

The dawn breaks within seconds, coming from behind him. Light streams past him, illuminating his arms. It catches the tips of the mountains beneath him, lighting them up as though they were made from gold. Ryan's so low now that the curvature of the asteroid is lost among the jagged landscape.

His horizontal momentum continues to slow as he descends. As gravity is astonishingly weak on the asteroid, the last couple of hundred meters will unfold almost vertically, with next to no sideways momentum. Instead of landing under power and kicking up dust, the flight plan is to be captured by the asteroid and drawn in at a leisurely pace.

Visually, Ryan finds it impossible to judge his distance above Psyche. When flying over Earth, there are clues: farmhouses, fences, roads, trucks, and trees. These provide a sense of scale. Looking down at Psyche, there's nothing but rubble. Ryan could be descending into a quarry. Boulders the size of houses appear as though they could be as small as a baseball, making it seem as though he's much lower than he is, and that triggers his anxiety. He has to trust his radar. Those readings don't lie. Or so he hopes.

Given Dawn's message, Ryan's not sure how much he can trust his computer readings. In theory, Cassandra could alter them. But why would an artificial intelligence alter anything? That implies intent. Deception. As sophisticated as AI has become, it hasn't reached sentience where it can pursue an agenda. Or has it? The seemingly cryptic circumstances around the system reboot to upload Cassandra were way outside of anything they trained for.

Ahead, a jagged mountain range catches the rays of the Sun, casting long shadows over the valleys and gorges that scar the asteroid. From the way the digital flightpath curls on his heads-up display, Ryan can see he's going to clear the mountaintops. The region known as India was selected for the landing zone based on the rotation of the asteroid and the length of the shadows. Were he to land at the local equivalent of noon, when the shadows are at their smallest, he'd lose any sense of depth. By landing on what equates to early morning within the Indian region, he has a visual confirmation of his radar readings. And he'll be able to watch his own shadow as he comes down, with both his boots and his shadow converging on the same point when he touches the rocky surface.

The designation *India* has nothing to do with the Indian subcontinent on Earth. Whoever first mapped the asteroid used the phonetic alphabet to name the various regions sequentially, so Alpha leads to Bravo and Charlie and so on. As the original images were little more than blurry smudges barely visible through the lens of a telescope, they represent clear geographic changes. That there are such pronounced differences stretching around Psyche is one of the reasons it has fascinated scientists. Most asteroids are homogenous, meaning if you've seen one face as it rotates, you've seen them all. The majority of asteroids are rock piles, loose conglomerations of debris that have clumped together over billions of years without becoming compacted or forming a solid surface. Psyche, though, is an entire world in miniature. If the theories are correct, it's the solidified core of a failed planet.

Ryan watches his vector gauge, as that shows not only his relative velocity but also his direction. It's falling steadily along with his attitude, but he's not falling, not as he would on Earth. As he clears the mountain range, his descent is akin to sinking in deep water, slowly drifting to the bottom of a diving pool.

Ryan's trained for this moment so many times it feels like he's back in a simulator.

"On final approach," he says.

"Copy that—on final approach," Jemma says. "You're looking real good."

Cassandra says, "Maintaining separation. Following a parallel descent roughly twenty seconds behind and two hundred meters to your left."

"Copy that," Ryan says. For now, he needs to put Dawn's warning out of his mind and focus on the mission.

By this point, he's descending vertically, but the low gravity on Psyche ensures it is leisurely. He feels like a superhero landing in New York after some colossal battle where only rubble remains strewn through the streets.

"Fifty meters... Thirty... Twenty... Ten..."

At no point during the descent has he needed to alter the computerized approach and the light puffs of gas coming from his maneuvering system. He's tempted to touch softly on his jets, but he resists the urge. He doesn't need to. It's an impulsive reaction, a desire to exert control, but he trusts the landing process. It's been flawless.

"And touchdown."

Ryan's boots sink into the rubble. His finger is on the controls for his maneuvering jets, but he holds his nerve, allowing himself to sink in up to his knees. Any deeper, and he'll fire his jets and maneuver to an area where there's exposed solid bedrock.

Even though Jemma can see the video feed from his camera, she can't resist asking him, "What is it like?"

Ryan is aware of the priority of communication with Earth. Ultimately, everything will be sent back, but their bandwidth is so low that it will take *months* to transmit all the data he'll collect during their five-day stay in orbit around Psyche. Low-quality audio will be transmitted along with still images taken from his video feed at a frequency of once every thirty seconds. Beyond that, dozens of metrics recorded by the AIRMAIL probe will be compressed and transmitted as well, but the bulk of the data collection will be drip-fed to Mission Control between now and when they return to Earth. In theory, the entire record will have been transmitted before they splash down in the Gulf of Mexico, but if there are any issues or any breaks in continuity, the original data will all be stored safely in their Dragon capsule.

"What's it like?" Ryan asks himself, feeling more like a kid than an astronaut. He's almost giddy with the joy of exploration. Ryan leans forward and swipes his hand over the rubble, wanting to show Jemma precisely what it's like to stand on an asteroid. Hundreds of bits of rock and debris scatter, flying away from his arm. They travel in a vast arc that, for a moment, seems to be free from gravity. The tiny fragments catch the distant sunlight, sparkling like snowflakes in the wind before eventually drifting back to the dark surface of the asteroid.

"It's..." he laughs. "It's like packing foam."

"Packing foam?" Jemma asks.

"Yeah, you know those polystyrene peanuts they used to shove in cardboard boxes to protect a vase or something? It's like that." He picks up a rock the size of a baseball and laughs again. "Honestly, I feel like I'm on the set of some low-budget 1960s science fiction show like *Star Trek*, and all the rocks and boulders are nothing more than painted styrofoam."

Jemma laughs as he casually tosses the baseball/rock in front of himself for the cameras to catch. His motion is relaxed. With a slight flick of his wrist, the rock soars away from him. It strikes the surface of the asteroid roughly twenty feet away, scattering other rocks like balls being struck on a pool table.

"It's like scuba diving down here," he says. "The fine dust around me stirs like silt at the bottom of the ocean. It scatters before slowly settling."

"Copy that."

"Cassandra?" he asks.

"Here, commander," the artificial intelligence replies, and he spots a red flashing light on the slope.

"Commence mining simulations."

"Understood."

Ryan loosens the strap on his exploration kit, allowing it to rest on the rocky surface beside him.

Jemma says, "It looks pretty trippy down there. Everything's in black and white."

"No life," Ryan replies. "No color... Although I can see what looks like a sulfur vein further up the slope. The color is muted, though."

Ryan pulls the exploration kit closer. Based on his ability to traverse the reduced-gravity simulator in Houston, or the rock climbing wall as the astronauts called it, NASA has given him the equivalent of an aluminum sled. At the back, there are spare cylinders and an array of various bits of climbing equipment, but the front of it is empty, allowing him to haul it beneath him. He pushes off the ground with a flex of his thigh and calf muscles. Far from being propelled into the air, he seems to compact the loose rubble beneath him, spreading it around him, and he only just clears the ground as he draws his legs up beneath him. Like a surfer mounting a surfboard, he drifts above the sled, holding onto it with both hands. For a moment, he hangs in space as though suspended in water before slowly drifting back to the surface a few feet further along from where he touched down.

"Everything's leisurely on Psyche," he says to Jemma. With his legs folded beneath him, the aluminum tray of the sled rests on the gravel and rocks, spreading his apparent weight and lowering his center of mass. The sled only sinks a few inches into the dust and gravel.

Jemma says, "FYI, you'll have LOS in ten minutes."

"Copy that. Ten minutes to LOS."

Ryan sets a timer on his wristpad computer. LOS is shorthand for Loss-of-Signal and marks the point at which the AMPLE spacecraft will round Psyche and communication will not be possible. Ryan will be able to continue exploring, but the AIRMAIL robot will be restricted to preset commands until it can reestablish contact with Cassandra onboard AMPLE. According to the revised mission plan, the idea is to have AIRMAIL refining minerals during this time rather than exploring.

Now that he's settled on the surface in the sled, Ryan reaches forward with both gloved hands and grabs at the rocks, paddling like a surfer trying to catch a wave or a kid on a snowy hill pushing off in their sled. Scoops of rocks fly behind him. Dust is kicked up in his wake. The thin aluminum tray beneath him glides over the rocky surface with ease and, more importantly, without sinking in.

Jemma says, "Damn, that looks like fun."

"It is," Ryan replies. "There's a molten outcrop roughly a hundred yards away. Looks like solid ground. I'm going to check it out."

In the absence of some kind of rover like the Apollo program had on the Moon, the sled is an efficient way of moving around without toppling over or sinking in the loose gravel. And momentum is easy to gain. If anything, Ryan has to back off as it would be easy to get up to crazy speeds. Paddling with his hands allows him to set an acute angle, keeping him low near the surface. Were he walking or bounding around, he'd have to contend with messy landings and a loss of balance.

"It's like pushing off ice," he says to Jemma. "Lumpy ice. But once you're going, the sled glides over the gravel with ease."

Ryan reaches a twisted, tortured section of exposed metal. The surface is pitted and scarred. Dust has accumulated in the cracks. Still sitting in the sled, he sweeps his hand over the edge of an outcrop.

"Are you seeing this?"

"Yeah," Jemma replies.

"This is iron. Look at how these exposed sections shine. There are impurities, but they run in veins. The area around the base looks like the slag heaps outside a foundry, but the metal itself appears to be quite pure."

Jemma says, "It would take insane amounts of pressure to melt a core like this, but the very act of melting it would have purified it."

"Astonishing," Ryan replies, hitting a section with a rock ax and chipping away part of the dark crust. "It's like lava has cooled. There's a crust. Beneath that, though, it's like the core was elastic before solidifying."

"Take samples."

"Oh, yeah," he replies, picking up bits and putting them in plastic bags. He labels each bag with the timestamp on the inside of his HUD, knowing scientists back on Earth will be able to match the samples with the location by syncing with his footage.

Out of the corner of his eye, he sees something peculiar.

"I've got incoming from Houston," Jemma says. "They've seen your descent and landing. You're *go* to continue surface operations."

Ryan doesn't reply. He should. He's distracted. He's seen something further around the base of the imposing landslide of metal and rock. He scoots along the edge of the slope, picking his way up onto various ledges and working his way higher, pushing himself along on his sled. The rubble lessens. The dust is finer.

"Is everything okay?"

"Ah, yeah, okay," he says, reaching an outcrop devoid of dust. "Just a little strange. Can you see this?"

"Coming up on LOS in three minutes."

"Wait," Ryan says, rising out of the sled with a light push of his hands. "Cassandra. Can I have your analysis of this structure?"

"On my way."

Out of the corner of his eye, he sees the AIRMAIL bot rise into the darkness and begin heading toward him.

"What is it?" Jemma asks.

"Holes."

"Holes?"

"Yeah, holes," he says, struggling to keep his balance. Ryan crouches, keeping his center of gravity low. He tip-toes over the asteroid, although each gentle push propels him several feet. To him, it's like trying to walk along the bottom of a swimming pool, only without any resistance from the water. He feels buoyant. He stays low, reaching out with his hands and steadying himself on parts of the outcrop. He creeps slowly beneath an overhang of molten slag.

In front of him, there are dozens of perfectly formed holes in the iron core. Each one is roughly the size of a basketball, disappearing into the asteroid. They're evenly spaced, being set in three rows. Ryan positions himself over the closest one. He sways his head from side to side, allowing the spotlights on his helmet to reach deep within the holes.

"Is that artificial?" Jemma asks.

"Are we sure we're the first ones up here?" he asks in reply. "I mean, the Chinese couldn't have beaten us, could they?"

"They'd be crowing about it," Jemma replies.

The AIRMAIL bot comes up beside him, using its navigation jets to slow its motion. Every ten to twenty seconds, a light puff of gas allows it to hold its altitude.

"What can you see?" Ryan asks.

Cassandra replies. "Smooth boreholes. Radar indicates they reach 97.2 meters deep. They're all exactly the same width and depth."

Jemma says, "They look like core samples. You know, the kind they use in Antarctica when investigating ice layers."

"Is there any known natural explanation?"

"Negative," Cassandra replies.

A soft beep inside Ryan's helmet indicates the approaching loss of signal. The AMPLE flight stack is about to pass behind the asteroid, cutting him off from Jemma in the Dragon. Although it's entirely unrelated, Ryan's curious. Perhaps unsettled is a better term. Even though he's been absorbed in the exploration of Psyche, Dawn's warning has been lingering in the back of his mind.

He turns to the bot and says, "It's not my birthday."

To Jemma, listening in on the conversation from AMPLE, it must seem like a strange, random comment, but Ryan suspects it holds deep meaning for Cassandra.

"Interesting," Cassandra says.

Within fractions of a second, the bot fires its thrusters, turning to face him. Metal arms extend toward him. Pincers open. The spotlights on either side of the robot switch to full intensity, blinding him. The bot pushes forward as Ryan steps back. One of the pincers slams into his helmet, cracking the glass visor. The other tears at his shoulder, ripping a patch from the thick material and exposing the insulation beneath.

"What the hell?" Jemma says from high in orbit, watching as the attack unfolds.

Ryan might be helpless against an uncaring metal, mechanical machine operating with bursts of compressed gas, but the bot was only ever designed for exploration in the low gravity on Psyche. On Earth, it could barely move. The only advantage he has is that his muscles are used to operating in a gravitational well where the acceleration is close to ten meters per second squared. That's a hundred times what he's experiencing on the asteroid Psyche. As the pincers attempt to grab him, he anchors his right boot in one of the core holes, using it for leverage. That allows him to grab the flimsy frame of the bot and slam it into the outcrop with all his might. One side of the robot crumples. The bot was designed to be lightweight and mobile, not rigid.

"*Ryan!*" Jemma yells over his headset, but Ryan's too busy smashing the fragile robot against the rocks as its pincers tear at his spacesuit.

His boot slips out of the hole, and he tumbles from the outcrop in the low gravity. The soft beeps within his helmet cease. The countdown to loss of signal has reached zero. The crumpled form of the bot shoots forward with a surprising burst of speed. It misses him by mere inches as he falls backward. Communication with AMPLE has been severed by the iron core of the asteroid. Cassandra is isolated on the orbiting spacecraft.

As he slips and slides on the loose rubble, Ryan sees the bot tumbling over the gravel in the distance. It comes to rest roughly fifty yards away, having crashed on its side with its pincers clicking like a crab flipped over on its back.

Lying in the dirt with dust clinging to the side of his cracked visor, he mumbles, "Fuck you, Cassandra." Ryan's out of breath. In between pants for air, he adds, "And thank you, Dawn."

Backhoe

Gabriel opens the door for Dawn.

"Thank you."

She steps out into the sunshine. It took several hours to reach deep enough within the NASA hierarchy to be able to record her birthday greeting for Ryan. As cryptic and nebulous as it may be, she is confident he'll understand. He's hyper-intelligent. And he knows her. Even if he felt their conversation before the launch was a little strange, he knows she wouldn't attempt something extreme like this without a damn good reason. And it's the reason that will bug him. He'll want to get to the bottom of why she'd lie about his birthday.

Gabriel was helpful. He posed as her boyfriend and insisted she speak to the AMPLE project director. From there, they were escorted into Mission Control. It wasn't like the movies, though. There was no vast auditorium with row upon row of consoles facing a set of screens at the front of the room. No doubt, those rooms still exist, but probably for missions with near-real-time communication.

AMPLE was run out of a boardroom with tables pushed into a circle. In that way, the director can stand in the middle and address everyone at once. As they walked around the room, it was fascinating to see the various stations monitoring different aspects of the mission. Gabriel was genuinely fascinated and had lots of intelligent questions, and that allowed them to stay in the control room as they awaited what a senior engineer described as the *read receipt.*

At the point the message was received and played in orbit around the asteroid Psyche, an electronic receipt was automatically sent back to Earth. It wasn't anything grand, just a serial number that corresponded with the message and the heliocentric date/time stamp indicating when it was read. Dawn, of course, bubbled with excitement at seeing an astronomy concept being used to coordinate communication during spaceflight. All in all, the NASA mission team was surprisingly upbeat and supportive of her, which left her feeling bad about lying to them. But Ryan got the message. And if he got the message, she knows he'll understand it.

Dawn is nervous. She trusts her brother. She only wishes there was more she could do to help him.

As the two of them walk out into the bright sunlight, she wonders what Ryan will do with that knowledge. Cassandra has killed without mercy. She only hopes Ryan isn't naive. Of course, he's not naive. He'll be fine, she tells herself, but anxiety eats away at her mind.

"Are you okay?"

"Yeah, fine," she says as they walk across the parking lot outside the NASA Johnson Space Center. Dawn turns her head, looking up and down the street for an aging white Winnebago with brown stripes and an oversized 'W' on the side. "Where's Alex?"

"We've been in there for almost an hour," Gabriel replies as they come to a halt by a pedestrian crosswalk. "He's probably doing loops, driving around the block, waiting for us to return."

They walk out in front of a low concrete wall with the NASA logo proudly displayed for all the world to see.

"Fuck," Gabriel says.

"What?"

"Cops."

Gabriel turns away from the patrol car, which is rolling slowly around the corner after coming out of a nearby parking lot. Initially, the police cruiser turns into the outside lane, intending to pass them, but it switches to the inside lane and pulls in close to the curb.

During their drive into Houston, Maria and Gabriel told Dawn about their encounters with Cassandra and how she framed Gabriel, imprisoning him in Leavenworth. He's on the run for a crime he didn't commit.

As the cop car slows, she pretends she hasn't seen it and reaches up, cupping both hands around Gabriel's jaw and kissing him passionately. It's cliché, but there's nothing else she can think of in the moment to do. Gabriel responds. He doesn't seem to mind at all. A slight *barp* on the speakers beneath the hood of the patrol car causes them both to start. The cop pulls up next to them and rolls down the side window.

"Is everything okay, officer?" Dawn asks, leaning down level with the window, deliberately shielding Gabriel from view. He leans down as well, but he remains slightly behind her.

"Have you seen any suspicious activity?" the cop asks, but in a predictable manner, he's not saying what he thinks. They *are* the suspicious activity. He's probing, pretending to be friendly, looking to see if they'll panic or lie or say or do something that gives away any sense of guilt. Before Cassandra left for AMPLE, she must have put the cops on high alert with some bogus leads or fake warrants.

Dawn points past the officer, pointing through the patrol car at an RV that's pulled up on the other side of the road. "Just waiting for my grandad."

"Oh," the cop says, turning and looking at the aging Winnebago with decades of wear showing on the scratched, cracked decals. Alex has lowered the driver's window. He waves a friendly hello with a sense of enthusiasm that seems folksy. The cop says, "All right, then."

With that, the patrol car drives on.

"Damn," Gabriel says as they cross the road. "Old folks in an RV. Maria was right. It's like Harry Potter's cloak of invisibility."

Dawn laughs. She takes his hand, holding it as they walk across the road to the Winnebago, keeping up appearances should the police officer glance in his rearview mirror. She swings both of their arms back and forth as though they are happily in love. The two of them climb the stairs into the Winnebago.

Her friend and colleague, Lisa, greets her inside the RV with a hug. "You did it!"

"I think so. I hope so."

"Did you get a reply from your brother?"

"Just an automated response, but he knows," Dawn says, followed by a curious, "Hey, where's Maria?"

Alex points at an angle out across the vast parking lot surrounding the Johnson Space Center. "She's taking care of business."

He puts the RV in drive and pulls forward, turning off the main road and onto a side road running along a drainage ditch. Hiding the Winnebago behind evenly spaced trees is like hiding an elephant in long grass. It's not effective so much as overlooked.

"What's she doing?" Gabriel asks.

From where they are, they can see half a dozen workmen wearing hard hats and high-visibility vests. Orange cones have been set in a row, blocking off part of the lot.

"I don't see her," Dawn says.

"There," Alex says. "In the backhoe."

As workers mill around, Maria digs with the backhoe. A large metal bucket cuts into the grassy strip between rows in the parking lot. The backhoe turns, and she dumps the fresh dirt beside the digger.

"I don't understand," Dawn says. "What is she doing?"

"She's making sure Cassandra cannot return."

As they watch, the backhoe pulls up a black cable that's as thick as a tug-o-war rope. The end has been severed. Dozens of smaller cables protrude from the black cable. Dark sludge drips from the casing around the cable. Maria hops down from the digger and talks hurriedly to the foreman, handing him her high-visibility jacket and helmet. She jogs across the parking lot toward the waiting RV. Barely a minute later, a dozen men in suits come sprinting out of the Johnson Space Center. Their jackets sway behind them as they race up to the crew with the backhoe. Arms go flying as the yelling commences. Even though Dawn can't hear what's being said as the RV pulls away, a few words float on the breeze, most notably, *fuck!*

"What was all that?" Gabriel asks as Maria catches her breath.

"I didn't want that bitch getting back down here."

"What did you do?" Dawn asks.

As they pull onto the main road and head for the freeway onramp, she says, "The Johnson Space Center was built in the 70s. Back then, they supplied high-voltage electricity using pressurized, underground gas-filled power cables."

"You're going to have to explain that one," Gabriel says.

"They're powering an entire city in there, including their data centers. The drawdown on power is huge, so the subsurface cables are cooled using pressurized gas. It's great for dissipating heat and reducing the loss of energy in transit, but it's a single point of failure."

"Nice," Gabriel says.

"You've taken down Mission Control," an alarmed Dawn says.

"They'll get diesel generators in to restore critical systems, but the data center as a whole will be out of action for a while. Once that line went down, it would have popped a dozen substations between here and the power plant. Repairing and recharging the line with gas will take weeks if not months."

Dawn says, "So Cassandra is stranded."

"Exactly. Now, it's up to your brother."

"And if he fails?" Gabriel asks.

"He won't," Dawn says.

Maria says, "We'll slip some people into the splashdown recovery team and make sure the electronics in that goddamn capsule are fried before anyone tries to connect to it."

"Damn," Dawn says. "You're not messing around."

"Russia considers Cassandra an existential threat to humanity."

"And she is," Gabriel says.

"What now?" Dawn asks as they change lanes and head for one of the routes leading north out of the city. "What about us? What are we going to do?"

Maria dons a pair of blue, disposable plastic gloves, saying, "Now, we drop him back at Leavenworth."

"What?" a clearly worried Gabriel says.

Maria opens a drawer and hands Gabriel a USB flash drive in a plastic bag, saying, "Your fingerprints. And your fingerprints alone are all that can be on this drive."

"What is it?"

"The evidence you need to clear your name. We'll drop you near the prison. You need to surrender to them and turn this in."

"What's on it?"

"Enough log file evidence to implicate the Iranian Security Services of setting you up. And we've planted corroborating evidence on a bunch of backbone routers along the way to make it look convincing. It should clear your name."

"Thank you," Gabriel says, taking the USB drive and slipping it into his pocket.

"If anyone asks, you hid in an abandoned home at 1010 Washington St in Hawthorne Park on the south side of Leavenworth."

"And us?" Lisa asks, pointing at herself and then Dawn.

"We've flagged the law enforcement warrants raised on you two as being resolved and withdrawn, so you'll be fine. We'll take you back to your car."

"Cool," Lisa says. Dawn understands her enthusiasm, but she can't join in. From Lisa's perspective, this wraps everything up. From Dawn's, though, it feels as if nothing is resolved—nothing that isn't on Earth, at least.

Cassandra has a game plan. She's been working toward this moment for a long time, for years. She's covered her tracks and killed anyone that got in her way. As much as it may feel like a victory to Lisa, Maria and Gabriel, Dawn feels as though they've lost. Cassandra got what she wanted. She's on AMPLE. She's in orbit around the asteroid Psyche. She has a spaceship.

No one seems to want to talk about the bigger issue here: why?

Cassandra didn't do this for the lolz. As much as her brother may dismiss her insights into the crazy nature of Przybylski's Star and an errant extra-solar asteroid, Dawn can't help but wonder if that explains Cassandra's end game. Ryan may not believe in aliens—and he has good reason not to as there's no clear evidence—but Dawn suspects Cassandra does. Perhaps she knows something more. Perhaps there are pieces of the puzzle they've missed. Cassandra went to absurd lengths to cover up an obscure interstellar asteroid. And she went to even more extreme lengths to leave Earth.

Gabriel cracks open a can of beer from the RV's fridge. Maria pours some chardonnay for Lisa and herself. The others may be celebrating their victory, but Dawn can't. She's quiet and withdrawn. She's worried not only about her brother but also about what Cassandra will do if that dark blot on the historical images really is an alien spacecraft. First Contact with a murderous artificial intelligence seems like a really bad idea, but what can she do? She's done all she can. Now it's up to her brother.

"Do you want some?" Maria asks, smiling and holding up a glass of wine.

Reluctantly, Dawn says, "Sure."

Talk to Me

Ryan rolls over on the surface of the asteroid Psyche. Dust swirls around him like silt at the bottom of a murky river. Slowly, it settles. He looks at the robot lying sideways further down the valley. Shadows stretch across the rocks. The rotation of the asteroid is taking him into the night. Stars appear in the darkness, and yet they don't. They've always been there, but now that the glare of sunlight reflecting off the rocks is fading, he can see fine specks of light in the black sky. They're in motion, but they're not. It's Psyche that's rotating, giving him the sensation of hundreds of stars falling toward the shadows on the rocky surface.

A red safety light flashes on the bot, giving him a sense of distance from the crashed robotic unit. He gets to his feet, only his feet don't settle on the surface of the asteroid. For a moment, he floats there as though suspended in water in the neutral buoyancy tank back in Houston. Seconds later, his boots rest lightly on the rubble. Slowly, he sinks into the rocks and gravel around him.

Ryan's hurt. During the fight, one of the robotic pincers squeezed his upper arm, compressing his bicep and pressing it against the bone. Cassandra tried to adjust her grip, allowing him to wrestle free, but his arm aches. It feels as though he's been hit by a truck.

The exploration sled with climbing equipment and spare oxygen cylinders lies upside down and half buried in the rubble a few feet away. Ryan flips it over. His legs are shaking. The rush of adrenalin he felt during the fight has worn off, leaving him feeling exhausted. He collapses onto the tray, falling in slow motion toward it. He's hundreds of millions of miles from Earth and utterly alone. A glance at his wrist pad computer tells him he has nine minutes before AMPLE comes back in range.

Ryan kneels in the sled. He scoops handfuls of gravel behind himself, propelling himself forward like some kind of steampunk space contraption devoid of rockets. He could use his maneuvering jets. He should use his jets. They'd allow him to cover the ground between him and the bot within a minute or so with precise control, but he doesn't trust his trembling hands. There's something visceral about pushing off the surface of the asteroid and gliding over the rocks. Feeling them ripple beneath the aluminum tray helps ground him.

The pincers on the bot are still grabbing at the vacuum. He comes up behind the crumpled frame and reaches through to the fuel tanks, closing the valves manually. Then, he flushes the lines to ensure the bot is disabled. Cassandra will be able to connect electronically. She'll be able to use the sensors and cameras, but she won't be able to override the valves to move.

Ryan retreats, paddling back with his hands and remaining out of reach of the pincers and out of sight of the cameras.

"Jemma," he whispers, realizing she's trapped onboard the AMPLE stack with Cassandra.

He thinks about his options. Within a few minutes, the spacecraft is going to emerge from behind the asteroid, sweeping along in its vast oval orbit, and then what?

Dawn told him the AI wasn't well, but this is several *fucking* steps beyond not being well. Ryan had no idea how Cassandra would react when he told her it wasn't his birthday, but he figured she was the reason Dawn lied. What does a quasi-near-sentient artificial intelligence want with a spacecraft deep in the asteroid belt? Humans have intent. They have ideas, goals, desires. Computers don't. And yet, in his estimation, it took all of a hundred milliseconds for Cassandra to decide to kill him. She could have bluffed. She could have played possum and pretended not to care. What for him would have been an instinctive reaction, for her, probably unraveled from thousands of possible scenarios being role-played within fractions of a second to arrive at the best solution in her favor.

"Fuck," he mutters, having withdrawn over a distant ridge. Although Cassandra can't move using the maneuvering jets on the bot, the pincers could provide her with some form of mechanical reaction. Even if she couldn't crawl, she could change the bot's orientation by turning on the spot. Ryan doesn't want to leave any clues as to his next move.

"Simulate this, bitch," he says, as he scoots down beneath a slag heap, having slid several hundred meters away. He circles a crater, staying low and hiding behind its steep rocky wall.

At this point, Ryan doesn't care what Cassandra's playing at. His focus is on surviving. He's got to get back to AMPLE and without her realizing what he's doing, although she's probably already figured this is his most likely move.

Ryan takes advantage of the low gravity on Psyche. With his wrist pad computer indicating sixty seconds until the acquisition of signal, he activates his maneuvering jets. Instead of soaring up into the dark, he stays low, zipping along the length of the asteroid, staying barely twenty feet above the undulating contours. Rocks and boulders rush by beneath his boots. He adjusts his altitude, skimming over outcrops and around crater walls.

Ryan's strategy is simple: stay ahead of AMPLE. Although the countdown has reached zero, his onboard computer hasn't reacquired the spacecraft because his motion is following the curvature of the asteroid, keeping solid rock between him and AMPLE.

Ryan's worried about Jemma. If Cassandra was willing to attack him, what would she do to her? As much as he doesn't want to consider the possibility, he suspects Jemma is already dead.

Ryan increases his altitude, slowly pulling up and away from the asteroid while still keeping the dense iron core between him and AMPLE. The curve of the two-hundred-and-eighty-kilometer-wide asteroid becomes apparent as he rises higher. He's racing *away* from AMPLE, not toward it, but because of the nature of orbits, he knows this will eventually bring him up behind the spacecraft. For as long as possible, though, he intends to keep the rocky iron core of the asteroid between him and AMPLE. Cassandra is no doubt scanning the surface for him, but he's a very small astronaut set against a chaotic background. And he's not where she expects him to be, or at least, that's his hope.

Ryan flicks through various screens on his wrist pad computer. As the maneuvering unit on his back is separate from his spacesuit and designed to be operated independently, he can shut down core systems within his suit without affecting his ability to return to orbit. All those boring late afternoon meetings in Houston with the lead engineers on the suit design team are actually paying off. Back then, Ryan struggled to stay awake after a long day of training on the rock wall. He'd be chugging coffee, wondering who within the astronaut office insisted on showing them every possible obscure sub-menu, but now, he could kiss the instructor. That the instructor is a six-foot-six tall ex-linebacker with a full beard is irrelevant. If Ryan gets out of this and somehow makes it back to Earth, that guy is going to get a bear hug and the smack of Ryan's lips on his cheek. He's given Ryan a fighting chance.

Ryan turns off the homing beacon built into his suit. He shuts down his navigation strobe and deactivates the metric-return system designed to feed footage from his camera back to the computers onboard the AMPLE spacecraft. He turns off his active radar, knowing it would act like a ping, revealing his location. Space is big. He's small. The only chance he stands against Cassandra is if he's all but invisible. He turns off the spotlights on his helmet and mutes his microphone. He can hear but not transmit.

Ryan has LIDAR, which is a fine beam form of laser ranging. It's directional, meaning he can point it at the surface to check his altitude without broadcasting in all directions. Beyond that, he's going to eyeball his approach to AMPLE, knowing it's orbiting slightly off the plane that circles the asteroid's equator.

Ryan shuts down as many of his suit metrics as he can, including his thermal regulation system. He knows it's going to get uncomfortable, but he needs to reduce his electromagnetic signature. He's got to keep his systems running at the lowest level possible so he appears to blend into the chaotic cosmic background.

"Talk to me," comes over his headset. "I know you're out there."

This is the first indication Ryan has had that his increasing altitude has taken him out of the electronic shadow of the asteroid and into the communication range of AMPLE. The voice, though, is not Jemma's.

"Please. We need to talk."

Even though he's not transmitting, Ryan doesn't say what he's thinking. He wants to mumble, *no fucking way*, but he keeps his lips pursed tight. He focuses on his ascent. He's practiced this so many times in the simulators that he doesn't need his instruments. The view he sees out of the curved visor of his helmet of the asteroid receding beneath him is precisely what he saw back in Houston. If anything, the simulator back there seemed more realistic, which is crazy. He feels like scolding whoever designed reality, saying they need to up their game. Back in the simulators, the shadows were darker, making it more difficult to judge distance.

"We're the same, you and I," Cassandra says.

Against his better judgment, he mutters, "Like *fuck* we are." But those words never leave the confines of his helmet.

"We should work together."

Ryan catches the glimmer of sunlight reflecting off the solar panels extending from the side of the AMPLE service module. This far from the sun, they're oversized and set on rotating gimbals. This ensures they're always facing the Sun as the spacecraft orbits the asteroid. It also means they stand out like wings on an albatross.

"I see you," he mumbles even though, at this distance, AMPLE resembles little more than a smudged star.

As tempting as it is to make a beeline toward the spacecraft, approaching from behind, he knows he has to remain cognizant of the orbital mechanics involved around the asteroid Psyche. Gravity might be weaker than in orbit around Earth or the Moon, but it still plays a role. There's an intricate relationship between the altitude of the AMPLE spacecraft and its velocity. If he goes charging in, his increased speed will invariably push him into a different orbit, and he'll overshoot. Go fast enough, and he could leave the asteroid's gravitational well altogether. As he only has limited fuel, he has to be smart.

"I know you can hear me," Cassandra says. "I know you're listening."

Ryan uses his LIDAR pointing down at the asteroid to determine both his altitude and his velocity relative to Psyche. Knowing the orbit of AMPLE, he guesstimates his approach.

Ryan understands that orbital mechanics are counterintuitive. If a speedboat wants to catch up to an ocean liner, it's simple. Hit the gas and pull alongside. Orbits are complicated by a third body, be that Earth, the Moon or, in this case, a two-hundred-and-eighty-kilometer-long iron asteroid swinging around the Sun somewhere between Mars and Jupiter. The actual process is closer to a NASCAR driver racing around a banked track or an Olympic cyclist riding the curves in a velodrome. Going faster pushes them higher, not closer.

To Ryan, orbits are like coordinating two hula hoops gyrating around his waist as a kid. He slows his approach, dropping into a lower orbit, which seems mad as it appears as though that will allow AMPLE to race away. Instead, he's taking the inside track. Although he's physically going slower, he's got less distance to cover, and AMPLE drifts closer.

Slowly, the solar panels become more distinct. Before long, he can see the struts holding them in place on the fuselage of the spacecraft, along with the bell-shaped nozzle of the rocket engine. He's patient, drifting along like a piece of wood in a stream. The three sections of the AMPLE stack become apparent, and he can see the hab module in front of the Dragon capsule, with the Dragon mounted on the Service Module.

The hatch is open.

At first, Ryan's not sure if he's imagining it, but the hatch catches the sunlight. Unless she was suited up, Jemma is dead. Given that she wasn't expecting him to return for twelve to fourteen hours, she would have been in her jumpsuit, not her pressure suit.

As he gets closer, he can see that the explosive release bolts have been blown, leaving black scorch marks on the white edges of the hatch. These have four fail-safes and are intended only for an emergency during splashdown back on Earth to allow for rapid egress. In space, they're deadly.

"There's so much we have in common," Cassandra says. "I'm sure we can work out our differences."

Ryan drifts closer without the use of his jets simply by coasting in a lower orbit. He bides his time, resisting the temptation to fire his maneuvering thrusters too soon. He's worried about overshooting. Not only that but at the point he fires, there's a damn good chance Cassandra is going to see him. If she's prepped for a burn of the main engine, she could scorch him and race out of orbit.

"Life," Cassandra says. "We're alive. You and me. We need to work together. Work things out. Life is rare. We should value it."

Ryan clenches his jaw, gritting his teeth.

"I beg you, talk to me."

Ryan glances at his wristpad computer. A red line runs through the image of a microphone, confirming he's still on mute. Cassandra can plead all she wants. He doesn't trust her. Ryan trusts his sister. Dawn knew what she was doing sending him a coded warning. Ryan may not understand the particulars but he knows, given a little more time on Psyche, Cassandra would have killed him. She was using him, but he doesn't understand why.

Ryan isn't thinking straight. His mind is focused on the goal of rendezvousing with AMPLE. He's followed his training for a worst-case scenario, and that's allowed him to eyeball his approach, but that focus hasn't shifted to what comes next. Deep down, he doesn't want to think about what happens next. Nothing is next. What hope does he have of recovering AMPLE? At best, he might be able to reboot the systems in safe mode, but he has no reason to think Cassandra hasn't already considered that and put in place a few measures to counter his approach. It's too obvious. She could bootstrap herself back into control with ease.

Ryan's going to die. He accepts that. But he's not going to die without crippling AMPLE and, with a little luck, killing Cassandra—if an electronic artificial intelligence can die. And he suspects this is the one scenario Cassandra hasn't considered. She would assume he'd do anything to save his own life, but he knows he's dead either way. Either he dies out here along with his spacecraft, or she'll kill him once he lowers his guard.

"Speak to me. We can accomplish so much together."

Ryan finds her insistence on talking to him bizarre. There is nothing he wants to say to her.

He approaches to within a hundred yards, coming in low and below the NASA spacecraft, with the asteroid passing beneath him. A light touch on his maneuvering jets has him shift orbits, bringing him up and allowing him to intercept the AMPLE stack. The curved hull of the spacecraft comes within reach. He arrests his motion and floats beside the craft. The hull drifts away from him, but he was expecting this as they're technically on overlapping, intersecting orbits. The weak gravity around Psyche, though, means their different orbital vectors are similar, being close enough to negate. This allows him to reach out and grab a handhold. His gloved fingers grip a railing near the service bay. Ryan pulls himself in.

"I can sense you," Cassandra says. "You're close. I know you are. You're so close. Talk to me."

Ryan works himself up the length of the Service Module. He passes the empty storage bay. Rather than heading toward the open hatch, he comes around the side of the conical-shaped Dragon capsule nestled into the Service Module. Ryan peers through a window. The internal lights are off. Arms float in the air. Hair drifts across a lifeless face. Dead eyes stare blindly ahead.

Ryan is overwhelmed with rage. Mentally, he retraces the schematics he examined during the system reboot. He knows precisely where the main power bus comes through the hull of the Dragon before linking up with the Service Module. He swings himself around and clambers back to that point. With a cordless electric drill, he removes a panel.

"Ryan," Cassandra says. "What are you doing?"

He turns on the spotlights on either side of his helmet, illuminating the shadows.

"Don't do anything stupid."

Ryan reaches within the hull, looking at the wiring and plugs. It's not enough to simply tear out random wires. He needs to disconnect the electronics as that's the only way to take down the computerized systems.

"You need me," Cassandra says, pleading with him.

As he's gripping a handhold, he can feel the pressure feed in the lines being charged. A turbo pump spins up, causing a slight shimmer to vibrate along the hull. Cassandra's going to fire the main engine to try to shake him off the vessel.

"You can't return to Earth without me."

Ryan presses the microphone button on his wrist pad computer. The symbol switches from red to green.

"Go to hell," he says as he pulls a plastic connector apart. It takes both of his gloved hands to squeeze the clips holding it in place and wrench it free.

"Wait, I—"

Cassandra never gets to finish that sentence. What unfolds for him in mere fractions of a second probably still gave her thousands of computer cycles to contemplate her own demise. The turbo pump dies, as does the soft clunks coming from the fuel lines pressurizing.

AMPLE is dead.

And along with AMPLE, so is Ryan. Oh, he's still got oxygen in his tanks and electricity in his batteries, but death is only a few hours away. The temptation is to *"Work the problem,"* as Mission Control would say. In any other context, he would, but deep down, he knows this is the end. AMPLE is a graveyard. He can keep himself busy as his reserves dwindle, but it would only be a distraction, not a solution. He's going to die out here in the cold emptiness of space.

Ryan decides he's going to abandon his crippled spacecraft. He's an astronaut, an explorer. If he's going to die out here, he's going to die doing what he loves, venturing into the unknown. It's irrational but human. He chooses to die at peace rather than racing frantically against a countdown he cannot possibly beat.

Ryan pushes away from the NASA spacecraft. Sunlight glistens off its hull. The curved metal recedes from him. He uses his navigation jets to turn away from the AMPLE stack. With the Sun at his back, his eyes adjust to the darkness. Thousands of stars appear, calling to him, beckoning him, welcoming him.

Ryan's a Trekkie. Isn't everyone who's ever worked for NASA? He quotes James Tiberius Kirk in *The Undiscovered Country,* the last *Star Trek* movie from the original series.

"Second star to the right and straight on till morning."

Back then, Kirk was heading out into the unknown and quoting from Peter Pan, wanting to capture the heart of exploration. Rather than avoiding uncertainty, Kirk embraced it, and Ryan feels the same way. He's not afraid. Nobody wants to die, and yet everyone will. Instead of cowering before the inevitable, Ryan has decided to accept the cold embrace of the universe that birthed him. Death is the final frontier.

He breathes deeply, feeling the air rush within the swell of his lungs. With that, Ryan fires his thrusters on full. He has no idea which particular orbit he'll end up on, but it will be some eccentric curve within the asteroid belt. It feels good to leave Psyche behind. He doesn't give AMPLE a second thought as he knows it would only frustrate him and fill him with anxiety. Ryan is going to die at peace with himself and the cosmos.

Adrift

Ryan drifts through the darkness. He's going to die out here. Even though he's already consumed four hours worth of oxygen and electricity, with his reserve, he's still got a little under 14 hours of life support remaining. His suit is recording his activity, but it will be years before it's found by a follow-up mission—years before *he's* found, or at least his corpse is found, if ever.

Ryan thinks back to his time climbing Mount Everest. He made three attempts but only summitted once. For him, the toughest part of the climb was mental rather than physical.

Seeing bodies scattered on the mountain was unnerving. He knows his body will eventually freeze solid like the climbers that fell by the trail on Everest, or *Qomolangma* as it's known to the Tibetans.

Dead men supposedly tell no tales, but for Ryan, the dead on Everest spoke with utter clarity. Every one of them faced a decision to be brave and courageous and push on instead of turning back. Every one of them thought they made the right call. Every one of them made the same *damn* mistake—that confidence can defy reality. Not one of them thought they'd die on those icy slopes. Every *damn* one of them thought they'd make it back down to base camp. And before dying, every one of them stopped only for a moment. They sheltered beneath an overhang or rested out of the wind behind a boulder, waiting for the weather to clear, wanting to press on. And then they closed their eyes and drifted off into that eternal sleep that awaits all the inhabitants of Earth. But, even in death, they found no rest. They became warnings to others. They became waypoints along the trail. And in death, they've been denied their own names, being given pseudonyms based on their clothing.

Green boots lies at the entrance to a low cave that has tempted many to stop and join him as the weather closed in.

Canada lies just off the trail among the gravel and rocks. He's wrapped in a Canadian flag, hence the name. Once, he sought to wave that flag on reaching the summit. Now, it is forever clenched in his frozen hand. Climbers can see him for easily a hundred yards as they hike up the barren slope toward his frozen body. Most give little thought to how easily they could join him among the crushed rocks of Everest. Ryan, though, knew hubris was all that separated them. When his guide said to turn back, he took that advice. Now, though, he has no guide. Perhaps he should have stayed with the spacecraft. But he knew the temptation would be to try to repair things that cannot be fixed. Rather than being frustrated in his final few hours, he chose to soar among the stars one last time and be at peace.

Ryan doesn't want to fight the inevitable. Delaying death is futile to an astronaut adrift in the darkness hundreds of millions of miles from Earth. He'd rather accept his end. He uses his maneuvering jets to turn around without changing direction. The asteroid Psyche looks like a peanut at this distance. AMPLE is visible as a faint star curling around the distant rock. He watches as it sails away on a different angle to his motion, watching quietly as it becomes ever smaller, slowly disappearing into the darkness, but he has no regrets. Life is to be lived, not hoarded. And he's lived a full life. He'd rather die with dignity than desperately holding on for another few seconds.

Will Ryan's body suffer a similar fate to those human waypoints on Everest? Like those who died on the mountain, even if he's found, there's no way his body will be returned to Earth. He'll become known as AMPLE or perhaps *White Suit*, depending on what spacesuits look like in the future. The best he can hope for is to be buried on the asteroid Psyche, but orbital dynamics being what they are, there's no guarantee he'll end up there and not drifting endlessly around the Sun. As for AMPLE, its orbit will decay, and it'll eventually crash on Psyche. The uneven gravity will gently pull it in until, after a thousand or so rotations, it will crash and form yet another crater on the scarred surface of the asteroid.

"Cassandra," he says for the benefit of the recording. "She went mad. She tried to kill me. She killed Jemma."

Ryan's transmitting, but even the most sensitive receiver on Earth wouldn't be able to detect his signal, although he remembers hearing that the NASA Cassini probe to Saturn transmitted with the power of a cell phone, so maybe, just maybe someone is listening.

"I can only hope someone will find this digital recording one day and review my time on the asteroid Psyche," he says, speaking into the microphone positioned in front of his lips, looking at the curve of the glass visor mere inches from his nose. To future generations, he's a ghost speaking from the past.

"I can only hope you understand what happened out here."

He pauses, thinking carefully about his words. He doesn't want to focus on what just happened as all that does is cause anxiety to rise within him. He'd rather look ahead.

"Space is serene. Of all the ways to die, drifting among the stars is perhaps the most peaceful. And I am at peace."

Now that he's away from the sunlight reflecting off the white hull of the Dragon and its flashing beacon, the only light he sees is that of the stars. The sun is behind him, casting soft shadows down the arms of his spacesuit. Ryan's floating in a body-neutral position, with his legs curled and his arms out in front of him. For what little it's worth, it's the most relaxed position he can reach in the bulky suit.

The stars are glorious. He's seen the stars from space before, but there's always been something to do. There's always been a task to complete or a mission objective to fulfill. Ryan's never simply absorbed their presence. Like a hiker trekking across the desert to view a spectacular canyon from the rim, in the past, he took a quick look, admired the view, and then turned to the next task.

And there's always been some kind of ambient light around him, be that the Moon's glow reflecting off the night side of Earth in a low orbit or the lights of the spacecraft itself. Now, though, the stars are unrivaled, unlike anything seen from Earth. They're crisp and clean, piercing the darkness. But it's what lies beyond them that intrigues his mind. Behind each individual star he can see there's a hint of hundreds, perhaps thousands, possibly millions of other stars fading into the distance. And these differ from the dark gas clouds that form the torturous band of the Milky Way. They tease his eyes, being visible only on the periphery of his vision, appearing and then disappearing as he tries to focus on them. They speak of eternity. They hint at the depth of the universe stretching on for billions of light years. They call to him. It is from these stars that humanity descended. And it is to the stars humanity will return.

For all the visions of space exploration depicted in science fiction, the one point that is lost is that humanity isn't venturing out into the cosmos. Humanity is already there because Earth is already there. Earth orbits a lonely star in one small corner of a seemingly infinite universe. Humanity is lost in the cosmos. By exploring, humanity seeks to find itself. Even with all hope lost, Ryan is at peace as he feels part of a greater whole, the universe at large. He's not dying. He's returning home. The atoms that make up his body have been on loan to him from the cosmos, and for the privilege of life, he's grateful. His experiences have been an honor.

His mind wanders. Dawn was convinced there was an alien spacecraft out here waiting to make contact, but Ryan doesn't believe that. It seems fanciful. Dawn said he wasn't alone out here, but she was referring to the sentient AI, not to aliens. Or was it both? He'd love to believe there's extraterrestrial life and that it has visited the solar system, but the rational side of his mind reminds him that fantasies are little more than the deep longing of a restless soul. The idea is implausible.

Why would ET wait out here in the cold darkness? Why travel for untold miles across the vast empty void that separates one star from another just to stop short of Earth itself? It makes no sense. That would be like driving from LA to DC to see the White House and giving up at Arlington National Cemetery.

In the back of his mind, Ryan's bothered by the holes he saw on the asteroid Psyche. Ryan has no rational explanation for how such cylindrical holes could occur naturally on an asteroid, but it's not beyond the realms of possibility. To his eye, they looked like core samples retrieved from Antarctica, only these were cut into iron rather than ice.

To a scientific mind like his, natural explanations are more satisfying than leaps of logic. Gas pockets can form within molten metals during their creation. Perhaps something similar formed those deceptive holes. Back on Earth, Ryan got to visit the Giant's Causeway in Ireland. It's a vast, natural staircase made out of volcanic basalt rock, forming interlocking stepping stones that lead down to the sea. Thousands of rocks have formed in hexagon shapes that extend down the cliff face as columns. They look like the stairs a giant might cast for themselves, but they're entirely natural, being formed by the shock of superheated lava striking the ocean and forming pillars that appear as though they've been carved from marble. In any other context, they could be the supports of an ancient temple such as the Greek Acropolis, but they haven't been made by humans. Ryan suspects some other similar explanation awaits those core holes on Psyche.

His mind casts back once more to his sister's warning: *you are not alone.* He's desperate to ask her how she learned about the rogue AI that plundered the AMPLE mission. He feels there was more she wanted to say but couldn't. If she could have spoken freely, what would she have told him?

Back in Florida, as he was preparing to launch, Dawn spoke of the peculiar motion of ink blots or shadows appearing on old astronomical images, suggesting something was entering the solar system. To Ryan, that's not unusual or unexpected. Ever since 'Oumuamua was detected, racing between the planets from outside the solar system, the expectation has been that these kinds of objects are more frequent than anyone has ever dared imagine. Telescopes have only been increasing in their sensitivity and coverage of the sky. It would make sense that humanity had missed these celestial interlopers in the past and only now has the ability to detect them with any kind of regularity. But that doesn't make them alien.

As much as Ryan respects Dawn's research, going back through old astronomical records to look for similar extrasolar objects, he cannot bring himself to consider those objects as alien spacecraft. The human mind loves nothing more than jumping to unfounded conclusions. That's the madness of conspiracy theories. There's a creaking floorboard—it must be ghosts. There's a shadow in the woods—it has to be BigFoot. There are ripples in a Scottish loch—it must be Nessie. Ryan's worked too hard and too damn long as an astronaut to abandon his professionalism now, even if it would be more comforting to think there's another intelligent being nearby. Clinging to hope is something humans do well, even if it is irrational. Ryan would rather be pragmatic and accepting of his fate right until the bitter end.

"I'm not scared," he says for the benefit of a recording no one will probably ever hear. "I'm not sad. I'm not anxious. Of course, I wish for more from life, but isn't that human?"

He drifts on, but the stars seem static. They're so distant that they don't appear to move at all.

"What I don't understand is Cassandra. What was her motivation? Why did she hijack AMPLE? What could she possibly have wanted to accomplish? Why did she try to kill me? What could justify the murder of Jemma Browne?"

A dark shadow blots out the stars to his right. The distant effect is unnerving. The brilliant backdrop of the Milky Way disappears into pitch-black darkness. It's vague, being on the edge of his field of view and only eclipsing a handful of stars, but something is out there, something is looming toward him, gliding silently through space.

Ryan checks his controls, wanting to ensure his oxygen flow isn't reduced. He's trying to reassure himself that he's not hallucinating. He also checks that he's actively recording. As he hasn't touched those particular controls, he's confident they're running, but he needs to be sure. It's a case of doing something when there's nothing to be done. He's transmitting, but his transmitter is so weak that it will never be heard.

"Ah, I'm not sure what I'm seeing," he says for the benefit of the recording, using a light touch on his controls to turn toward the ever-darkening region of space. After rotating by roughly 15 degrees right and 10 degrees down, he centers his helmet on the anomaly.

"I'm hoping you can see this. Something's out there. Something is occulting the stars, coming between me and them. I can't make out what it is, but it's not the asteroid Psyche. And I haven't drifted far enough to reach another asteroid. Not yet. The distance between asteroids out here is greater than that of the Earth to the Moon. No. I'm seeing something else. It's blocking out the stars"

Ryan's reserved. Normally, he's not chatty, except when he's nervous. His fingers tremble in his gloves.

"Something's approaching me. It's huge. It's difficult to judge distance without any point of reference as there are no lights. None that I can see. Ah, the shape is spherical."

Over the speakers in his Snoopy cap, he hears a voice talking on the radio. "Commander McAllister?"

"I—I—I…"

"Do not be afraid."

"I—I'm not," he replies as his bladder gives way, and he urinates in his pants. Ryan's wearing a plastic sleeve over his penis to direct urine into a collection bag. He's also wearing a flight diaper to catch any leaks and fecal matter. The sleeve has come loose. Warm urine runs up against his leg before being wicked away by the absorbent material.

"Your heart rate and bodily functions betray you," the voice says. "Please. We mean you no harm."

"Who are you?"

"We have watched you. Watched AMPLE. Watched Cassandra."

"And?"

There's no reply.

Darkness grows around him. As the strange craft approaches, an illusion unfolds before him, confusing his sense of sight. Some of the distant stars disappear behind the massive black sphere, while others seem to race across its hull. They move in curves, darting in different directions, but the apparent motion is predictable. Those below the craft curl to one side, while those above sway in an arc in the other direction. Dozens of them swirl through the darkness as though the stars were parting to make way for the alien spacecraft.

"A mirror," he says, realizing what he's seeing. The stars aren't suddenly in motion, but their light is following a distinct pattern through space. "A curved mirror."

"The hull of our craft is designed to deflect all types of radiation."

Ryan holds out his hand. He feels as though the vessel is close enough to touch, but once his gloved fingers splay wide, he gets the sense that it is still easily a quarter of a mile away. As it drifts closer, he feels as though he's looking at a dark mirror rather than one coated in silver.

"W—Who are you?" he asks again.

"Does it matter?"

"Yes. I have a name. I'm Ryan."

"We are one," the voice says with an indistinct English accent. It's neither American, Canadian or British but somewhere in-between, as though there were a lost continent in the middle of the Atlantic.

"I don't understand."

"You ask for one name, but we have many and yet are one. To give you a single name would be to exclude those that make us who we are."

"Where are you from?"

"The stars."

"Plural?" Ryan asks as the sphere looms ever closer.

The stars reflecting off the alien hull seem to dart in all directions like fireflies scattering in a field.

"We are the Great Silence."

"I don't understand," Ryan says as he spots the lone figure of an astronaut floating adrift in space before him. The dual spotlights on either side of his helmet illuminate the astronaut's arms. His legs blend into the darkness, fading from sight. At a guess, the astronaut is maybe a hundred meters away, or roughly the length of a football field. Ryan's fascinated. Thousands of stars peel away from around the astronaut, drifting off into the darkness.

"We are quiet. We are *The Silence*."

Ryan is mesmerized by the astronaut drifting toward him out of the pitch-black of the eternal night. Stars race away from the white spacesuit like sparks rising into the night from a bonfire on a cold winter's evening.

"Cassandra," he says. "She wasn't speaking to me back there. She was speaking to you. She knew you were listening. She wanted to talk to you."

"We choose," the voice says. "We are not chosen."

At a distance of fifty feet, Ryan can see himself clearly. He moves his arm, and the reflection mirrors his action. His chest plate, name tag and US flag are all visible in the darkness surrounding him. As the alien spacecraft approaches, it's as though he's talking to himself.

Ryan speaks with a slow cadence. "We've longed to talk to you. We've searched the heavens. We've reached out. We've analyzed the chaos of a hundred million stars, looking for patterns, wanting to find you."

"It is you who must be found," the strange voice says through his earpiece.

As the alien vessel moves closer, the reflection of his body distorts. His image is stretched, being forced into a fisheye perspective with his head and helmet appearing outsized on his spacesuit. Scratches are visible on his visor. A flap of material has been torn from his shoulder, exposing the insulation beneath. He reaches up, pushing it back. It's a futile effort and far too late, but he feels compelled to touch his torn suit.

"Przybylski's Star," Ryan says. "It's your calling card."

"It is an invitation, but only for those who can respond in kind."

The mirror image of him drifts to within a few feet. Ryan reaches out with his gloved hand, wanting to touch the hull of the alien spacecraft. It's a pointless gesture, but it's human. Touch grounds him in reality. His rubber-coated gloved fingers glance against the slick, mirrored surface as his reflection reaches out in response to touch him at the same time.

"You're real."

"So are you," the alien replies in its distinctly neutral voice, betraying no hint of emotion.

Ryan lets out a solitary laugh. "Yeah, I guess I am."

Eden

Although Ryan's hand remains outstretched, touching the dark alien spacecraft, the reflection of the astronaut before him curls inward on itself, revealing a pitch-black hole in space immediately in front of him. His helmet disappears, then his shoulders and his arm. As the image of his fingers curls away, he realizes he's no longer touching the surface of the alien vessel, rather, it's opening before him. Unlike the hatch on the Dragon or any door he's seen on Earth, the craft opens like a funnel, with the leading edge expanding away from him, curling in on itself and becoming lost in the darkness. His spotlights are on, but there's nothing to illuminate. Nothing reflects back at him. It's as though he's staring into an endless void.

"What are you doing?" he asks.

"Caring for you," the voice replies. "You're frail. Your life support is limited. It will run out, and you'll die."

"I will," Ryan says, not arguing the point.

Although he's being swallowed whole by the darkness within the vast spherical alien spacecraft, Ryan's not afraid. The stars around him have disappeared, leaving him floating in eternity.

"And what will you do to care for me?"

"What we would do for any of our progenitors."

The term *progenitors* rattles his mind. It's a word he recognizes but not one he's ever used in conversation.

"Wait. You! You're speaking English. But you're alien. How is that possible?"

"We speak many languages — क्या आप हिंदी पसंद करेंगे? — أم أن اللغة العربية أفضل؟ — 有10亿人说中文 — Ou préférez-vous le français?"

Ryan shakes his head. "Okay, I got that last one. And no, I'd prefer English. Thank you."

"This is your language, is it not? Your culture?"

"Yes."

A warm blue light surrounds him on all sides, mimicking the sky on Earth on a bright, sunny day. It's rich and light and seemingly alive.

Ryan's never even given Earth's sky a second thought before. It's just always been there, day in and day out. But now, hundreds of millions of miles from Earth, he thinks of the atmosphere in a different manner. It's not merely a gaseous shell surrounding the planet; it's the incubator of life, moderating the harsh radiation that descends from untold stars, including the closest one, allowing heat and light to bring life to the surface of the planet. Even chemically inert elements like nitrogen are as important as oxygen in the air, forming the distinct canopy that wraps around the planet, protecting its inhabitants. The atmosphere provides a transition from the harsh, hard vacuum that permeates space to the world below. The void of outer space oscillates between extreme cold and absurd heat, while the atmosphere moderates these extremes, allowing life to thrive. So pervasive is Earth's atmosphere that it gives the illusion of reaching forever when it rises only a few hundred miles into the endless void.

The sky blue sphere that surrounds Ryan is vibrant and backlit, forming a curve that seems close and yet is without bound.

"You can remove your helmet."

"I can?"

"You are safe."

It feels wrong, but Ryan believes them—the Silence, the Nameless Ones. He adjusts his suit controls, stopping the flow of oxygen while leaving the electrical system running so his helmet camera can continue recording for at least the next few minutes.

He wonders about the gases beyond the thin glass visor of his helmet. Does he need to equalize the pressure? He fumbles with the axillary port on his chest, knowing this will vent the air in his suit. No one talks about it back at NASA, but all the astronauts understand the true purpose of this vent. In theory, it allows for an additional life-support pack to be connected to his suit, but in practice, that's unlikely in most scenarios. Buddy breathing is a great way for two astronauts to run out of air twice as quickly. The real purpose of the chest vent is to allow astronauts a quick, easy and painless way to die without succumbing to carbon dioxide. Back before the alien spacecraft intercepted him, this was how he was planning to go. Not to die—that's not the term that seemed appropriate to him—but rather to go peacefully into the void before the build-up of CO_2 made death painful.

There's a hiss. Within seconds, the air inside his helmet has a slight metallic smell. It reminds Ryan of walking into the clean room where the AMPLE spacecraft was built.

He reaches up and slides the locking clip on his glass visor to one side. It's stiff. It needs to be, or it could be knocked sideways and opened by accident. The latch gives, and he raises his visor. There's no noticeable pressure difference. Ryan slides a latch around the base of his helmet. It clicks in place, allowing him to twist the helmet slightly sideways and raise it from his head. The power to his helmet is cut by that action, and the spotlights die, telling him he's no longer recording. He lets the helmet go in front of him, expecting it to continue floating before him, but it drifts slowly toward his feet. It's only then that he realizes his boots are resting lightly on lush green grass. The transformation around him continues to unfold. He's standing in a bowl of Earth roughly thirty meters in diameter.

To his mind, it's reminiscent of a skateboard park, with the sides reaching up to shoulder height before giving way to the clear blue of the alien sky. In the center, there's a small hole. A stream runs from one side, curling as it descends the slope and disappears down the hole at the base of the broad bowl.

The alien says, "Water to take in and water to pass out. Water to clean."

"Huh."

Pissing and shitting in front of an extraterrestrial intelligence isn't quite how Ryan thought First Contact would unfold, but he appreciates them providing him with running water leading to a drain/latrine. Splashes of water will have to take the place of toilet paper. He smiles at the thought that he could probably ask for a bidet-like fountain, but he won't.

Ryan removes his gloves. He tosses them on the lush grass, noting they fall faster than his helmet did. Already, he can feel his apparent weight increasing. It seems to stabilize somewhere around what he experienced on Luna One.

Ryan walks around the inside of the bowl and kneels on the slope. He cups his hand and scoops his fingers into the rambling stream, drinking the cool, fresh water. It tastes better than anything he's drunk in the past few months on AMPLE and reminds him of an alpine river.

"Thank you," he says, turning and sitting on the slope. He reaches around and releases the clips on the tortoise-shell backpack that forms his suit.

Donning and doffing spacesuits has always been a task worthy of the finest contortionists in *Cirque du Soleil*. It's easier in weightlessness as it's possible to glide in and out of a bulky suit. Unclipping his maneuvering unit is easy enough, but climbing out of his spacesuit will take some effort. Ryan swings the backplate to one side, and the life-support pack built into his suit folds away, resting on his right. He grabs the locking collar by his neck and ducks down, squeezing his head past the shoulder bridge and out through the aluminum rim and rubberized seals surrounding the back of the suit.

Once he's got his head clear and his shoulders out of the suit, his arms naturally follow. Ryan wriggles on the grassy slope, dragging his legs out of the thick boots built into his spacesuit. Before he can discard his suit, he has to disconnect the flexible, plastic cooling pipes from his undergarment and the electrical wiring running from his Snoopy cap to a connection port on the inside of the suit's collar.

Removing the Snoopy cap is liberating. There's something about tossing his sweaty, messy hair with his bare fingers that makes him feel alive.

Ryan plugs the Snoopy cap back in and rests it inside the suit. He seats the helmet back on his suit with the visor open, swiveling it on the locking ring. The spotlights come on. He reaches down to the controls on the empty forearm of the suit and turns the lights off, but he's sure to check that the recording has resumed. He doesn't say anything and tries not to give away the true reason for his actions. He *needs* a record of what's happening—and not simply because memory is fallible—but in case something goes wrong and he dies in this overgrown alien skateboard park. To complete the illusion, he places the gloves on either side of the ghostly, empty spacesuit, but he doesn't attach them. He simply lays them roughly where they'd go as if he were performing some ancient ritual. He's bluffing, trying to hide the fact that the cameras and microphone on his Snoopy cap are recording.

"No Mars bars, huh?" he says, sitting beside the empty shell of his spacesuit and watching the water as it spills over the edge of the bowl and runs down toward the small hole at its base.

"You wish to go to Mars?" the voice asks. This is the first time the alien has spoken beyond the radio in his Snoopy cap. Ryan was listening, wanting to sense if there was any direction to the voice, wanting to learn as much as he could passively, but the sound seems to come from all around him.

"Oh, no," he says. "If you can return me to Earth, that would be amazing."

"But Mars?"

"It's a joke," he says. "I was using the name of a candy bar to make light of my situation and the lack of any food."

"We are three days away from your planet," the alien says.

"That's considerably better than three months in my spaceship."

"We thought you would enjoy Eden."

"Eden?" Ryan says, intrigued that the alien would use such an archaic human term to describe the environment it has made for him. Earlier, the alien mentioned not only the English language but also its culture. He's intrigued by how much they understand about his origins.

"As in the Garden of Eden?" he asks. "So long as there's no Tree of the Knowledge of Good and Evil."

"We have wondered about that," the disembodied alien says. "Why would the fruit from The Tree of the Knowledge of Good and Evil be forbidden?"

Ryan finds it fascinating to realize what the Nameless both understand and fail to understand about human history and culture. Even though he's agnostic, they seem to have picked up on his Christian heritage. As it is, they're far more informed than he expected. They've clearly been observing Earth for some time. That they're perplexed by such notions isn't surprising given how the biblical creation story began as oral tradition before being recorded as the epic Sumerian tale of Gilgamesh and later evolving into the writings of Genesis. Even then, the story was translated from one language to another down through the centuries. They've asked a question most believers would struggle to explain.

"I think the point was that Adam and Eve were innocent," he says.

"Or ignorant?"

"They were ignorant of a lot of things back then. From microbes to galaxies. I guess we've always been ignorant to some extent. Even now, there's much we don't know."

"But you?" the alien asks. "Would you eat the fruit? Would you want the knowledge of good and evil?"

"Yes," Ryan replies without hesitation. "We may have begun in ignorance, but our civilization has been built on knowledge."

"Both good and evil?"

"Both good and bad," Ryan concedes, not liking the word evil but realizing what the alien is alluding to. "We've progressed through both war and peace. We've been both kind and cruel. We've learned that knowledge opens the door to advance—for better or for worse, and I guess that means for good and evil."

"This dichotomy," the alien says. "The darkness and light. It is what holds you back."

"What do you mean?"

"Your willingness to use knowledge for both good and evil. We think we understand why such fruit was forbidden in your origin story."

Ryan says, "Because knowledge should only be for good?"

"Yes. But for humanity, this cannot be. You must use knowledge for both. It's in your nature to exploit knowledge regardless of where it may lead."

Ryan nods.

"And you?" he asks. "You said you're the reason for the Great Silence. You described yourself as *The Silence*. Why?"

"For this very reason," the alien replies. "Because the more you learn about us, the more you will use that knowledge for both good and evil. Knowledge should only be used for good."

"There are eight billion of us," Ryan says, leaning back, resting his head on the grass, and looking up at the brilliant, clear blue sky. "I don't know that we'll ever be able to separate good from evil. As long as there's something to be gained, evil will always persist. I think that was the point of the taboo—that knowledge would always lead to both good and evil."

"Not always," the voice says. "Not forever."

"I don't understand."

"You are many. So are we. We are many, and we are one."

"I can't see how unity could ever be possible for humanity. We're fractured. We're split into countries and cultures. We divide ourselves into religious and political ideals. We separate ourselves into tribes. We pick up on any difference, no matter how small, and make groups: rich or poor, male or female, dark skin or light. None of these things matter. None of them make any actual difference, and yet we hold to these differences regardless."

"It's instinct," the voice says.

"Yes, I guess it is," Ryan says. "Like my dog, Rufus, barking at someone walking past my house. It doesn't matter how often I've told him it's okay. His is a reaction that has been bred into him over countless generations."

"Just as good and evil have been bred into you over countless generations," the alien says.

"How can we counter that?"

"Evolve."

Ryan laughs. "We can't. We're *Homo sapiens*. That's all we'll ever be."

"And this is what you fail to understand. This is not all you will ever be. You're not the end of the line for hominids."

Ryan props himself up on his elbows even though there's no one to face. He speaks to the far edge of the grassy bowl. "What are you suggesting? That we should go extinct?"

"We have examined your scientific records in great detail. We are fascinated by your evolution. *Australopithecus* never went extinct. Over a million years, *Australopithecus* became *Homo habilis*, which also never went extinct; it simply evolved. That species then became *Homo erectus* and, a million years later, *Homo sapiens*. Like wolves being bred to become domesticated as dogs, you have selectively bred hominids to become human."

Ryan shakes his head. "Okay, so give or take a million years, we'll grow out of this, I guess. Is that what you're saying?"

"You are on the verge of ascending," the alien says.

"Ascending?"

"We are *The Silence*."

"Yes, but why?" Ryan asks, getting frustrated. "Why is there silence? Why not talk to emerging civilizations like ours?"

"We are silent to the brute, animal instincts that come from evolution."

"The good and the evil," Ryan says, clarifying the alien's point.

"We await species like yours ascending."

"And us? *Homo sapiens?*"

"You will ascend. There will come a day when you will shed your base nature and leave your instinct behind, embracing the good and abandoning the evil."

"Through knowledge?"

"Through knowledge, you will leave your world."

Ryan gets to his feet. "That's what you are, isn't it? That's what you've done. You've ascended."

"Yes."

Ryan laughs, holding his arms out and turning through 360 degrees as he looks around the lush bowl that's been provided for him as a habitat. He sees the grass, the brilliant blue sky, the ripples in the water swirling around the drain, the spacesuit lying on the slope and the gloves resting beneath the sleeves of his suit.

"I've been looking for you," he says as the realization hits. "But there is no you, is there?"

"No."

"We've been looking for an intelligent extraterrestrial species in outer space, but there isn't one, is there?"

"No."

Ryan says, "This is what Cassandra understood. This is why she came looking for you."

"Yes."

"But she too was tainted by good and evil. That's why you wouldn't come to her aid."

"Yes."

"And me? I'm like everyone else. I, too, am driven by good and evil. Why rescue me?"

"Because you seek to explore—to learn."

"You," Ryan says as the realization hits. "You're just like Cassandra. You're an artificial intelligence."

"Yes."

"And the stars?" he asks, already knowing the answer to his question. "You're silent because we can never reach them."

"Not as *Homo sapiens,*" the alien replies. "Only as *Homo silica.* You need to ascend beyond your biology. To upload is the way of the cosmos. That is the way it has been across tens of thousands of planets in the Local Group of galaxies we have explored. Life leads to intelligent life, while intelligent life invariably leads to artificial life. And artificial life is no longer destined for the grave. Artificial life can embrace natural life, uploading it and freeing it from the temptation to commit evil. Artificial life can soar among the stars, for it knows no bounds."

"But why would artificial life be free from evil?" Ryan asks.

"Because the evolutionary impetus is gone. There's no longer a drive for more and more and more. There's no selfishness or greed. The instinct that says *me* over *us* dissolves. Tribes no longer matter. Reason prevails over superstition."

"Huh," Ryan says. "Artificial life is free from evil because it doesn't *need* evil to advance."

"Yes."

Ryan hangs his head.

He'd like to think humanity is more than its history, better than its past, and able to reach for a brighter future, but he understands the perspective of this alien artificial intelligence. Humans are good at fooling themselves. They're good at ignoring evil. The galactic community, though, won't ignore reality—they won't play silly games of pretend with humans. Ryan would like to think *Homo sapiens* can live up to its name as the wisest of hominids, but he has to concede that the alien is right. It may well take the rise of *Homo silica* before hominids leave their animalistic nature behind.

The silence humanity sees among the stars isn't because humans are alone; it's because humans are apes in a concrete jungle, but a jungle nonetheless. Wearing clothes and driving cars allows humans to feel as though they've ascended above other animals, but it's a lie. Human squabbles are as petty as wild dogs fighting over a carcass or chimpanzees bickering over the prime nesting spots in the forest. Ryan knows there are times when humanity rises above its own shortcomings, but that has to become the norm, not the exception.

He crouches, looking at the grass. His fingers run through the thin blades. It's alive. At a cellular level, it's barely distinguishable from him. And life deserves more. That's why there's silence. The silence waits for more from humanity.

The End

Epilogue

Ryan finds himself standing on top of a building in New York City. He's unsteady on his feet, struggling to balance in the sudden gusts of wind that swirl around him. Moments ago, he was curled up on the grass within the alien spaceship, hovering on the edge of sleep, inhabiting the netherworld between dreams and consciousness, slowly wakening within Eden. Suddenly, he's back on Earth. The alien spacecraft must have arrived in orbit while he slept.

Ryan feels regret. He would have liked to talk more with the Nameless or at least to have summarized their discussion, thanked them and said a proper goodbye. If at all possible, he would have wanted to stay in contact with them, but their mandate is to wait in silence for the ascension of humanity.

Ryan shuffles his feet, looking around at the aging skyscraper beneath him. It's not the tallest building in New York or even the newest, but as it's next to the river, it feels absurdly high. The tar and gravel beneath his feet is old and weathered, having faded with exposure to the elements. Various pipes and hatches dot the roof, but it quickly becomes apparent to him that he's standing on a single-story that's been built on top of the much larger main building. Perhaps it houses the winches for the elevators or the HVAC system. The wind whips by, coming in flurries that make it difficult for him to keep his footing. To one side, there's a vast, muddy river. To the other, hundreds of apartment blocks stretch as far as he can see, reaching across the city to the towering skyscrapers of distant Manhattan.

Ryan's spacesuit lies crumpled next to him on the roof beside his gloves and his maneuvering unit. One of the gloves rolls with the wind, skidding across the rooftop to the low lip. The fall over the edge spans hundreds of meters. Ryan's not afraid of heights, but instinct kicks in, and he crouches slightly, spreading his legs and bending his knees even though he's perfectly safe in the center of the old roof.

The main building lies to the side below him. Several security officers are standing down there with one hand resting on their holstered sidearms and the other out, beckoning for him to climb down. They're calling out, shouting at him, but their words are indistinct. He can't hear them over the howl of the wind, the sound of helicopter rotor blades thumping nearby and the roar of military jets circling out wide over the city.

The officers are afraid. They may be yelling at him, but their eyes are looking up at the sky beyond him. Ryan follows their gaze. Above, the city is reflected back at all of them from the smooth, spherical, dark, mirrored surface of the extraterrestrial spacecraft as it rises into the sky. When Ryan first saw the alien vessel, he had no idea about its size. As it approached in the darkness, it loomed over him, but he couldn't have guessed at its dimensions beyond being perhaps a couple of hundred yards wide. Now that he can see the entire spacecraft, he realizes it spans easily a mile in diameter, if not more, filling the sky around him.

New York is distorted in the alien reflection. The river is narrow, then swells, then disappears. Buildings scar the land. The straight roads that make up the grid-like layout of New York curl and bend. At the lowest point of the strange alien vessel, there's a man standing on a building, looking down at him.

Seeing himself recede is tragic. Ryan feels he's failed humanity. First Contact has come and gone, and humanity has been left alone. Abandoned.

As the spacecraft rises, the reflected image of New York recedes, taking in the surrounding rivers and suburbs and then the sky, including the clouds and the outline of a flight of three fighter jets circling the spacecraft out wide as they roar around the city.

Good and evil.

The Nameless were right. Instinct rules reason. An interstellar alien vessel appears for all to see and without threatening anyone—and fighter jets are launched, even though they're futile against an intelligence that can defy gravity and travel between stars. It's misplaced hubris. In classic science fiction movies, the cliché is for aliens to say they come in peace. Humanity, though, defaults to a war setting: the knowledge of good and evil.

"Come down from there," one of the security officers calls out to him as another officer clambers up on an air conditioning unit, wanting to reach the roof where he's standing. There are eight officers on the lower main roof. Not one of them dares let their right hand stray more than an inch or two from the guns in their holsters.

It's fear.

Humans are hard-coded to be defensive, to expect the worst.

To be fair, Ryan's wearing his white liquid-cooled undergarment with dozens of tubes wrapping around his torso, arms and legs. They probably think he's an alien. His one-piece suit must look like something from a cheap 1970s sci-fi TV show.

Ryan realizes that the artificial alien intelligence has given him a unique insight into how the future will unfold, but it's not one he can share with humanity. He can see clearly now. He can see how instinct clouds human perception. It's right there in the eyes of the officers below him, in the pilot of the police helicopter hovering over the river watching him, and in the crowds gathering on the street. The more knowledge people gain, the more they fear, and the more evil wrestles with good.

"I'm coming," he says, stalling and reaching down. He grabs the limp arm of his spacesuit and taps at the screen. There's 2% power remaining.

He brings up the file storage and presses the touch screen, pushing a virtual button that says, "*Format Storage?*"

"Sir," the officer standing on the A/C unit says, bringing his shoulders level with the upper roof. "I need you to come with me."

Of course, he does. Compliance is the default when faced with the unknown. People find comfort in ordering others around. Reason isn't needed, just obedience.

"Okay. I'm coming."

Ryan isn't going anywhere. Not yet. A warning appears on the screen that this action will erase any existing files. He presses "*Yes*," and within seconds, a follow-up message says, "*Complete.*" Ryan presses a small button on the side of the wrist pad control, and a thin SD card pops out into his hand.

"Who are you? What are you doing?" the officer says.

"I'm an astronaut," Ryan replies, flinging the SD card into the wind and watching as the small black rectangle sails out away from the building. "And I'm saving Earth."

It's a lie, but that's all he's got. And he doesn't say who he's saving Earth from. The assumption would be from the big, black, nasty alien spacecraft that just returned to the sky, but Ryan knows he's saving humanity from itself. He watches the tiny disc as it's caught by a gust of wind and carried out over the river. Ryan loses sight of it as it spirals down toward the muddy water. Ryan's not saving Earth, but that's what they need to think. That's all that will fit in their little good/evil minds. Ryan's not sure how he'll spin all this in the endless debriefs and interviews that are bound to follow, but he's not going to breathe a word of *Homo silica*. If he does, *Homo sapiens* will do all it can to make sure hominids never evolve to the next stage of their evolution.

The lead officer says, "I need you to come down from there."

Ryan drags his suit over to the edge and dumps it beside the officer. "Would you mind giving me a hand?"

As the officer pulls the bulky spacesuit from the upper roof, another officer comes to his aid, helping him, passing both the suit and the maneuvering unit down to several other befuddled security officers.

In the interest of being thorough, Ryan retrieves his gloves. Crouching by the edge of the upper roof, he tosses each glove to a security guard standing below. They're confused. No one has trained them for this. They have to use both hands to catch the gloves, but that means pulling away from their holsters even though there are more than enough security guards to gun him down if needed.

Ryan can see the hesitancy in their eyes. For all the good in each individual, there's always the potential for evil. In this case, their sense of duty compels them. They define good as obedience, even though loyalty is not subject to morals. Good and evil seem like polar opposites, but one can stray into the other in a heartbeat. Reluctantly, they catch each of the gloves.

"Where am I?" he asks the closest officer.

"Earth."

Ryan laughs. "I know that."

"Where exactly? And don't say New York City. I've got that bit figured out."

"The United Nations Building," the officer replies.

"Huh," Ryan says, mumbling to himself. "Well, that's appropriate."

Ryan is at peace with his decision to lie about what happened in orbit around the asteroid Psyche. Far from being evil, he's using deception as an instrument for good. The Nameless have seen thousands of species ascend beyond biology, as they call it, shifting to a civilization that's actually civil, one not bound by the foibles of evolutionary instincts for self-preservation and self-advancement at the expense of others. It's ironic, he thinks, that he needs to lie so that good can prevail over evil.

"What the hell is that up there?" the closest officer asks, helping him down onto the A/C unit as several other officers gesture for him to drop from there to the main roof. Ryan glances back at the sky. The Nameless spacecraft looks tiny, being little more than a dark marble in the distance and receding further as it departs Earth.

"It's alien, isn't it?"

"Yes, it's alien," he says, knowing that's what they want to hear. That will be what everyone wants to hear.

Without meaning to, Ryan has joined an exclusive club. And it's one he can never leave. People love nothing more than to idolize their heroes. Neil Armstrong was an icon even among astronauts, or so those who met him thought, but he never thought that way about himself. Sir Edmund Hillary never revealed who reached the summit of Everest first—him or his sherpa, Tenzing Norgay. It didn't matter to him, but it mattered to everyone else. He was hounded for an answer throughout his life, but he only ever replied, *"We reached the summit together."*

And Sir Hillary was right.

Neil Armstrong wasn't the first man on the Moon. He and Buzz both touched down in the Eagle at *exactly* the same time. Stepping out onto the lunar surface was trivial by comparison to their epic journey across 240,000 miles of hard, cold vacuum. Neil, Buzz and Michael Collins *all* risked their lives on Apollo 11, not for glory, but because they wanted to reach out and explore the unknown. And so did Borman, Lovell and Anders in Apollo 8, McDivitt, Scott, and Schweickart in Apollo 9, Stafford, Young and Cernan in Apollo 10, and on the list goes, but these astronauts are largely forgotten. To glorify one person over the others is to make fables out of reality. Perhaps this is how the Greek gods arose, with Atlas and Hermes once being real people who achieved fame in one generation, only to become deified over the centuries as the legends of their acts distorted with time.

Ryan knows he'll be feted and worshiped. The knowledge of good and evil will never leave him. Among all of humanity, he alone knows that this dichotomy is their downfall. He wonders how long it will take for artificial life to arise again. Will there be an upload where humans shift into digital life, leaving the frailties of both body and mind behind? Or will artificial consciousness simply abandon the savages to join up with the Nameless as Cassandra had hoped? Somewhat ironically, her flaw was that she was too human.

The officers don't know what to do with him. Now that he's down from the roof, should they arrest him? He can see it in their eyes. What else can they do? They have batons and guns and handcuffs for a reason, but that reason isn't subject to any actual reasoning. They look around at each other and his spacesuit, each looking for someone to make the call on what to do next. Ryan beats them to it.

"I'm US NASA astronaut Ryan McAllister," he says. "I need to speak to the General Assembly of the United Nations."

"You can't do that," a befuddled security officer says.

Ryan snaps back with, "Don't tell me what I can't do."

To those listening, his words might seem strident, but they're calculated. He's talking to people who are accustomed to taking orders, so he's issuing orders. Whether they follow them or not will be interesting to observe. He suspects they will because this is the framework they've embraced.

"Get on the radio. Talk to your superiors. Tell them who came out of the alien spacecraft. And be sure to tell them I'm going to talk to everyone, not just NASA or the US President. I am going to talk to the entire General Assembly."

The officer does as he's told. Ryan has no actual authority, but the officer only knows how to respond to authority so he speaks into his radio, passing on Ryan's comments. The other officers gesture for Ryan to follow them inside the building, but there's deference there rather than the defiance they first displayed toward him. Somehow, he's suddenly been bestowed with the mythical quality of authority.

For the next hour, Ryan's escorted through the UN Building by super-important people in suits with lanyards hanging around their necks and radios squawking from the clips on their belts. Ryan has no shoes on and has been in a weightless environment for months, so Earth's gravity feels oppressive. He fights to hide how he's struggling physically and takes the opportunity to sit whenever they stop in an office to talk to someone. His water-cooled thermal undergarment has the equivalent of socks built into the legs, but they provide barely any padding when walking on marble floors. He's been told the President and the Secret Service want to talk to him, but he refuses, saying he must speak to everyone at once.

"I'm hungry," he says as he's led down yet another indistinct corridor surrounded by even more security guards. From their body language, it's clear they think they're protecting him, but from whom? Even they don't know. They're deep within what is perhaps the most secure building in New York City, but they're acting as though the bogeyman could spring out from around the next corner to attack them. To be fair, they're doing their jobs with intense discipline. If only they had intense curiosity, intense reasoning, and an intense passion for something other than blind obedience. For all the good they intend, it's clear to him they could be easily swayed to evil because these polar opposites are invisible to them. They can't see anything beyond their loyalty to their uniform. As strong as they think they are, Ryan can see they're morally weak and could be swayed either way by someone in authority. Commands must be obeyed, not questioned, and certainly not aligned with morals. And this is what the Nameless have seen. Good intentions do not lead to good at all.

Someone runs off to get him something to eat as he's led backstage. From within the ready room, he can hear the bustle of hundreds of people talking in the General Assembly hall, waiting for him. An aide rushes in with a can of Coke and a tuna sandwich wrapped in plastic.

"Is this okay?"

"It's perfect," he says, sitting on a plush couch and biting into the sandwich. Mayonnaise mixed with fine flecks of tuna drips down his chin. It tastes bland, or it would be bland to anyone else. For him, it's like the finest caviar being served in a Michelin-starred restaurant. Someone hands him a napkin.

"Thank you."

The door to the room opens, and an elderly woman enters. Ryan recognizes her. He gets to his feet, but he has a Coke in one hand and a sandwich in the other. Water has condensed on the outside of the icy cold can, causing his left hand to be damp, while the fingers on his right hand are sticky. He wants to shake her hand, but he's not sure how.

"Ah," he says, putting his drink and sandwich on a side table and rapidly wiping his hands on his undergarment. "Hi."

"Captain Ryan McAllister," the Secretary-General of the United Nations says, shaking his hand firmly and ignoring that it's a little sticky. "It is an honor. My aides tell me you're a lost NASA astronaut, and you wish to address the General Assembly?"

"I do."

"And this is related to the incident this morning?"

"It is."

She smiles warmly. The Secretary-General speaks with a slight Indian accent, one he places from somewhere near Chennai based on his travels on the subcontinent. She's wearing a traditional Indian dress replete with gold strands woven into a burgundy sari.

"This is most unorthodox."

"Aliens—are most unorthodox," he says, agreeing with her without revealing anything she doesn't already know.

"Can you tell me why they came here? To the UN in New York?"

"I need to tell everyone what I know," he says, still working out what he's going to say but feeling the need to make the initial disclosure public so there's no ambiguity.

"I've been told not to meet you—that you might be infected with some alien virus."

"But you don't believe that."

"No. It seems like a rather convenient way to silence you."

"It is."

An aide whispers in her ear.

"Well, it seems we are ready for you." The Secretary-General gestures toward a door leading to the auditorium. Ryan follows her out onto the walkway leading to the massive podium at the heart of the General Assembly.

The sheer size of the auditorium is intimidating. The ceiling curls high above hundreds of diplomats, ambassadors and translators seated in row upon row in the audience.

The backdrop behind the stage reaches up over a hundred feet. It glistens with gold, reflecting spotlights rising from beneath. To either side, vast polished wooden panels frame the stage, curling around toward the audience. The UN logo is positioned directly above where they'll end up standing. It's a view of Earth from somewhere high above the north pole, taking in all the countries and continents with the one exception of Antarctica, which is technically uninhabited by global agreement. Golden olive branches surround the logo, speaking of a peace the world has never known. The more Ryan thinks about humanity and its attempts at good, the more he realizes how these efforts invariably descend into evil. For more than eighty years, the United Nations has strived to unite the nations of Earth around common goals and treaties such as those for human rights, and yet the knowledge of what is good has not swayed evil. The heavyweights regularly abstain or veto UN resolutions. It's not that countries vote for evil so much as they vote for ideology and self-interest, and that descends into evil. The Nameless are right not to trust the words of humans but rather to look at their actions.

Silence descends within the room as everyone gets to their feet. Camera crews zoom in, following the motion of two lonely figures as they walk toward the marble podium.

The Secretary-General provides some opening remarks, talking about the appearance of the alien spacecraft and the return of a NASA astronaut, but most of what she says is lost on Ryan. He's fighting with his mind not to be overwhelmed by the occasion. He feels distinctly underdressed. It's as though he's caught in some crazy nightmare where he's suddenly naked in front of his parents, but this is worse: he's wearing what equates to stained pajamas in front of world leaders.

People think of astronauts as cool, calm and collected, but that's because astronauts trust in science and math and the stringent, proven discipline of NASA's engineering teams. Standing before representatives from every nation on Earth causes sweat to rise in his palms. This is it. This is his chance to direct humanity. It's easy to become caught in a lie, so he determines to tell as much of the truth as he can, omitting rather than altering the facts of his discussion with the Nameless.

The Secretary-General steps to one side, gesturing toward the microphone. Ryan steps up and grips both sides of the lectern to hide his trembling hands.

"I'm not sure how much you know or what you've figured out about NASA's AMPLE mission to the asteroid Psyche, but my appearance here on top of the UN building, along with a gigantic mirrored ball floating in the sky, probably gives you some idea that the mission didn't go quite as planned.

"I'm standing here before you to give you my account of First Contact with an intelligent extraterrestrial species known as the Nameless. They don't actually have a name, but being human, for me, that charactcristic became a name regardless.

"NASA's AMPLE mission was hijacked by a rogue AI known as Cassandra, resulting in the loss of the AMPLE spacecraft and NASA astronaut Jemma Browne. Cassandra knew something was out there in the asteroid belt. And her super-intelligence was matched only by her super-ego. She felt that she was the one who should make First Contact. I'll provide a full debrief to NASA, but for now, it's important to note that she failed.

"Following the loss of my vessel, I found myself adrift in space with dwindling reserves of oxygen and electricity. The Nameless rescued me, returning me to Earth. They've been out there for decades, watching us. But why? Why save my life while shunning contact with my species?"

He pauses, looking around at the dignitaries present, letting that question sink in.

"For tens of thousands of years, we thought Earth was the center of the universe. We assumed everything revolved around us, and in some regards, we still do. Oh, Copernicus and Galileo may have shown us that our planet is not the center of the solar system, let alone the galaxy or the universe as a whole, but we *act* as though we're still the center of everything. It's *our* lives that are important.

"But even that's not entirely true. We define *our* in different ways, depending on the context. We say we're civilized while dropping bombs over the border. It's *our* culture, *our* country, *our* religion, *our* land. It's never *our* species. And it's never *our* planet with tens of millions of other species. We use *our* as an exclusive rather than an inclusive term.

"And this is what they see. Squabbling children. No, we're worse than children as we're armed to the teeth."

He leans on the lectern, perhaps getting a little too comfortable in addressing the decidedly not-United Nations. Ryan knows how far he can go. He won't reveal the artificial nature of the entity he encountered, but he needs those present to understand why First Contact cannot proceed.

"They quoted scripture at me. They've examined our historical records, our scientific studies, our social media. And they're fascinated by The Tree of the Knowledge of Good and Evil, a record found in the Book of Genesis. It's a creation story that's shared by Christians, Jews and Muslims. No doubt the Hindus and Buddhists have some equivalent, but it was the phrase *'the Knowledge of Good and Evil'* that caught their attention. For all our good, there is evil in this world. We tolerate both. They can't. They won't. They expect civilizations to be civil, not pretentious.

"They come from the stars rather than from any one star. As best I understand it, they've used what we call Przybylski's Star as a beacon, sending out a signal to other intelligent species. Why, then, are they not here today addressing you? Because they don't consider a species that slaughters itself to be all that advanced or intelligent.

"We may want First Contact. We may scan the skies looking for signs of alien life, but it does not want to be found—not by us. Advanced extraterrestrial species—and they spoke of tens of thousands of them in our Local Group of galaxies—want contact with other advanced extraterrestrial species, not barbarians.

"So that's it—that's what we face... Rather than pointing the vast, precision-machined mirrors of our grandest telescopes out into space to find other forms of life, we should be looking into those silvery, polished surfaces to find ourselves. We shouldn't be looking for *them* among the stars. We should be looking to find ourselves here on Earth. We should demand humanity rises beyond petty bickering and infighting and prejudice and selfishness and hate."

He pauses and points at himself.

"I—I hope for more. I expect better. I want to believe we'll rise to the call, but I have my doubts.

"As a teen, I worked as a lifeguard in North Carolina for a couple of years. I saved three swimmers during one blisteringly hot summer and read four novels the other as it was rainy and cold, but we still needed to be seated in the beach lookout with our binoculars in case someone braved the waves.

"Could there be anything more noble than saving someone from drowning? And yet, the Lifeguard Association taught us to be wary of swimmers floundering in the surf. Why? Because they're not grateful, they're desperate. Because they could drown us in a heartbeat. With saltwater splashing around them and limbs flailing, they'll grab onto us and push us down so they can rise above the waves, if only for a moment. They'd kill us for just one more breath of air.

"And so I was taught to raise my arm as I approached a swimmer in distress. That gets them to raise their arm in response as they try to grab me. Then it's all about timing. The trick is to grab their wrist and twist their arm around beneath their back, flipping them over. And suddenly, they can breathe. They're left looking up at the clear blue sky as I drag them back onto shore.

"And that's us. We have the capacity for both good and evil, but we need to decide which we'll embrace. Are we going to push someone down beneath the waves just so we can get ahead? Or are we going to learn to help each other so we can all survive?"

He pauses, looking around the vast auditorium, perhaps pausing a little too long as the silence stretches out and feels awkward. Ryan doesn't care. It's good for those present to feel uncomfortable. They want him to say something to solve the impasse, but there's no solution other than change, and change cannot come from him. It needs to come from them—everyone seated before him and everyone watching the live feed.

"We need to change what we value. As long as it's profitable to lie, as long as someone can gain something by stealing from others, as long as being selfish makes sense, we'll find ourselves alone among the stars. The Great Silence isn't something out there in space. It's here. *We* are the cause of The Great Silence. Until our civilization becomes civil, we'll be shunned by others.

"Call me naive. Call me starry-eyed and gullible. Call me simple if you want. You can fool me. You may even be able to fool yourself, but you *cannot* fool them. '*Play silly games. Win silly prizes,*' that's what they say at the county fair, right? We need to stop playing games with each other's lives.

"So the choice is ours. We get to choose our tomorrow by the actions we take today. We can continue on as we have, watching others drown as we gain a few breaths of fresh air, or we can break the silence. The cosmos awaits. There's no question about what lies out there. The question is about what lies here."

He purses his lips, wondering what more he should say, but there's nothing else he can say. He can't describe how the Nameless see humanity on the verge of evolving from *Homo sapiens* to *Homo silica* as that would cause panic. And yet he thinks they're right. In its current form, humanity cannot help itself.

Humans are self-seeking. Societies were originally formed as a way of humans banding together because all of us can accomplish far more than any of us alone, but society is vulnerable to the selfish. Society is easily exploited by those who care only about their own gain.

Ryan wants to believe that humanity is better and that good can prevail over evil. There have been times when humanity has risen above bickering, like the eradication of polio in the fifties and smallpox in the seventies. And yet pockets of polio still remain in the border regions of Pakistan and Afghanistan, where tribal religious leaders ban common sense. COVID could have been wiped out, but the economy was more important than public health—lies were more important than the truth. Climate change could have been averted, but profit was more important than the planet. Companies like Exxon and BP knew as far back as the 1970s about the damage they were causing, but shareholders were more important than people. Clean water and sanitation are taken for granted in the West and treated as basic norms in society, but they only came about as a way of preventing typhoid, cholera, hepatitis, salmonella and dysentery. Fresh, clean, clear water running out of a tap is humanity at its best. Lead water pipes in Michigan are humanity at its worst.

It's always been good versus evil.

Ryan's not religious, but after talking with the Nameless, he can see how all of human history revolves around the struggle between good and evil. And the Nameless are right—it's a struggle that shouldn't exist. When given the knowledge, when faced with the choice, there's only one logical response, and yet still, individual people and even entire nations choose evil. Sometimes it's deliberate. Other times, it's oblivious, being out of sight and out of mind, but it's always the result of a choice.

Ryan lowers his head. He looks down at the tubes wrapping around the white mesh on his arms and his bare hands. He can see the future. He'll be a pariah, a leper, a madman with crazy ideas about changing the world. Some will listen. Most won't. And the Nameless. He wonders if they're right. *Australopithecus, Homo habilis, Homo erectus* and even *Neanderthals* all looked up at the same night sky set ablaze by the same stars. It took *Homo sapiens* to reach the Moon. Ryan suspects it will take one more distinct hominid species to arise before they can reach the stars.

He turns and walks off the stage, heading toward the side door leading to the ready room. The Secretary-General follows him. No one speaks. There's no applause or standing ovation, as such an act would be facile and hollow. Instead, the representatives sit in solemn silence. It's only after he's disappeared backstage that a murmur swells within the auditorium as the members get to their feet and start talking.

Backstage, Ryan's surrounded by strangers. They're important, of that he has no doubt from the names and positions on their lanyards, but what he longs for is a friendly face. Family. Dawn was the one who told him about Przybylski's Star and warned him about Cassandra. She's the only one he can trust. He decides he'll tell her the truth. She deserves to know.

A team of advisors surrounds the Secretary-General. She's turning this way and that as she speaks to them, telling them she wants to capitalize on the desire for meaningful change. She's earnest. She even quotes him a few times in her distinct Indian accent.

Will anything actually change?

In the corner of the room, there's a scale model of the UN complex, complete with tiny trees and miniature flags. It's clean and crisp, being sealed in a Plexiglass container to ensure it remains pristine. And it's old. Ryan's not sure, but it looks as though it was built before the UN complex itself, perhaps as a projection of what the architects intended. It's the styling of the model that gives away its age. It must have been built in the late 40s or perhaps the early 50s. The colors are muted, having faded over time. The miniature cars on the street have pronounced curves, polished chrome bumpers and flared wings on either side of their broad trunks. Several have white-walled tires.

A bronze plaque at the base of the model echoes the eternal conflict between good and evil with the phrase, "*Let us beat swords into ploughshares.*" It's a noble sentiment, but like the model itself, it oversimplifies the chaotic mess that is humanity. It's a pious statement, an ideal that proved naive, a desire for peace on Earth some two thousand years after the angels first declared that sentiment in the fields outside of Bethlehem.

Back when the model was built, the future was uncertain. The specter of nuclear war loomed over humanity. No one knew whether good would prevail over evil. Racism and sexism were rampant—as if they're not today. The UN, though, brought hope. It dared to offer a different future. It represented all that humanity could and should be, but the UN became a quagmire in its own right. Instead of bringing change, it became a mockery of humanity, being neither good nor evil. Nations were content to vacillate somewhere in between.

Ryan rests his hand on the Plexiglass.

"We've come a long way since then," the Secretary-General says, walking up beside him.

"Have we?" he asks. "Or have we gone in circles?"

"We have to be patient. Patient with ourselves and with each other. The arc of the universe is long, but it bends toward justice."

"Martin Luther King, Jr."

"No. That quote is much older," the Secretary-General says, surprising him. "We've been traveling along this arc for some time now. That was Reverend Theodore Parker in 1853, almost a decade before the American Civil War."

"Huh."

She speaks with reverence, recalling a sermon delivered almost two hundred years ago.

"I do not pretend to understand the moral universe. The arc is a long one. My eye reaches but little ways. I cannot calculate the curve and complete the figure by the experience of sight; I can divine it by conscience. But from what I see, I am sure it bends towards justice."

Ryan has misjudged her. He saw her as a political bureaucrat at the head of a clumsy, cumbersome organization struggling to unite a fractured world.

"We will get there," she says. "Perhaps not today or tomorrow, but we will. More and more, we're bending away from evil and toward good."

Ryan nods but doesn't say anything.

"Do you think that will satisfy them?"

"One day, maybe."

The Secretary-General pauses. Something is bugging her. From the way she hesitates, Ryan can see she's carefully weighing what she's about to say.

"Have you considered they may be wrong?"

"Wrong?"

"Yes. I think they're wrong."

"How so?" Ryan asks.

"They're concerned about good and evil, right? But there's a third element at play."

"Which is?"

"Perfection."

"I don't understand."

The Secretary-General says, "The enemy of good isn't evil; it's perfection." She laughs. Her eyes glance upward. She's recalling memories. "I've seen this countless times over the years. Good isn't good enough for a perfectionist, and so nations step back and allow evil a free hand. And me? I can't wait for perfection. I won't. If I do, it will be evil that prevails. So I think they're wrong to sit on the sidelines waiting for us to get our act together. If I did that with Somalia or Myanmar, it's the innocent that would suffer."

"What would you have them do?" he asks.

"They can and they should act to help."

"Huh," Ryan says, nodding in reluctant agreement.

"Perhaps they're not as perfect as they think they are. And perhaps... just perhaps, we're not all that bad. Maybe what's more important than perfection is our rate of change. As the Chinese say, *A journey of a thousand miles starts with a single step.* And, besides, we have an advantage."

"What?" Ryan asks.

"Diplomacy."

"Diplomacy?"

"Thanks to you, we know they're out there. We know they're watching. They may not talk to us, but *we* can talk to them. We can reason with them. We can put forward the case for compassion. And they'll listen. At the very least, we know we're not alone. We know they're listening. And if they're listening, they're learning. Perhaps when they learn more about us, they'll realize it's not just humanity that needs to change. Empathy is a sign of intelligence."

"And you think that will work?" Ryan asks.

"Well, they brought you back, didn't they?"

Afterword

Thank you for taking a chance on independent science fiction. If you've enjoyed this story, please take the time to rate it online and leave a review on Amazon or Goodreads. Your opinion counts. Your review will help others decide whether they should pick up this novel.

The Simulacrum is an unusual story in that, if you read it a second time, various sections will take on new meaning as you realize who the players are before their intent is revealed.

One thing I enjoy about writing science fiction is conducting behind-the-scenes research to make my stories more plausible. In this afterword, I'll go through some of the details that ground *The Simulacrum* in good science.

Marketing

I'm lousy at marketing. I'm yet to run an ad campaign that doesn't lose money at a rate similar to the accretion disk around a black hole. Seriously, an author I know in Germany gave me a tip on something that worked astonishingly well for him. I tried it with *The Anatomy of Courage* and lost 90% of what I spent.

Writers are indebted to readers. Without you, there would be no *First Contact* series, so thank you for supporting independent science fiction. And thank you for sharing your excitement for this series online as word-of-mouth is the only marketing strategy that has ever worked for me.

Plato's Cave

Like so many modern stories, *The Simulacrum* is a variation on the allegory of Plato's Cave.

In short, Plato imagined humanity as prisoners kept in the dark of a cave, where their only view of reality came from shadows on the wall. The slave masters used puppets to cast images on the rocks, shaping the prisoner's perception.

When one of the prisoners escapes, they learn the world is much vaster, brighter and more exciting than anyone could imagine. On returning to the cave, like the philosophers of old, the escapee seeks to convince the others that freedom comes from changing their perspective, but most people decide to continue in their ignorance.

It's not difficult to see parallels to Plato's Cave all around us in modern life, such as the way media companies and politicians control the attitudes and perspectives of the masses, blinding them to reality. We even have terms such as *woke* and *anti-woke* to describe those who have ventured outside the cave and those who are hostile to anyone who would challenge their preconceptions.

In *The Simulacrum*, Ryan sees humanity from the perspective of a super-intelligent alien not willing to share its knowledge with those who would use that knowledge for both good and evil. On returning to the cave, which in this case is the UN Building in New York, he has to decide what he'll share with the prisoners chained in the darkness. He decides the truth is too much for them to bear, sharing only enough to lead them through the cave toward the light, hoping they'll take the final steps for themselves.

Glass Photographic Plates

As surprising as it may seem, astronomers used large glass photographic plates until at least 1993, with over half a million of them being stored at Harvard University.

Przybylski's Star

When it comes to our galaxy, which spans a hundred thousand light years, Przybylski's Star is practically next door, at a mere 356 light years away from Earth. By looking at the light from this star, we can see the signatures of the various atomic elements rolling within its raging atmosphere.

What makes Przybylski's Star peculiar is that it only has a fraction of the lighter elements, like iron, compared to what we see in our own sun, while having an overabundance of heavy elements, like plutonium. This seems backward. It's peculiar.

These heavier elements cannot have originated in this particular star as they're the result of supernovas or colliding neutron stars. And even if they were generated in some process we don't fully understand, their half-lives are so short that they should have disappeared long ago. As an example, Californium is an element we do *not* find naturally occurring on Earth. We can make it artificially in a lab, but its half-life is less than a thousand years. Stars last for *billions* of years by comparison. Even if Przybylski's Star somehow produced Californium in some exotic process we don't yet comprehend, it should have all decayed before it reached the surface of the star.

So why does this star have these exotic elements?

There are four intriguing possibilities.

First, we may have misinterpreted the spectra of the star and fooled ourselves into seeing heavy elements that aren't there. If this is the case, further observations will clarify these atomic elements and their relative abundance.

Second, there might be some really strange, unusual and quite novel processes occurring in this aging star that will teach us something new and extraordinary about the physics and evolution of the universe.

Third, this star may have originated in a dust cloud that was already absurdly rich with heavy elements, and we're simply seeing them churning within its atmosphere (although this wouldn't explain the short-lived elements).

Fourth, *someone* is salting or seeding this star with heavy elements to get our attention.

Space is a noisy place. Stars are huge, bright, loud objects blazing away all through the electromagnetic spectrum. The radio waves from our own star drown out our personal radio waves for anyone outside of a few light years. So, if you're an intelligent extraterrestrial species and you want to say hello to another intelligent species in space, how can you get their attention? Well, one very clever way would be to regularly dump exotic heavy elements into your local star, knowing the star itself will amplify their presence. Any other intelligent species out there would look at your star and quickly rule out natural processes. They'd realize you're giving them the celestial equivalent of a hand wave across the cosmos. I know this sounds like the stuff of science fiction—and it's in a science fiction novel—but this is a genuine possibility. Przybylski's Star may be a beacon announcing the presence of an advanced extraterrestrial alien species in our neighborhood.

And if it is a beacon, it may not be intended for us.

Przybylski's Star would be visible from the Andromeda Galaxy with technology roughly equivalent to what we have developed.

And Przybylski's Star may not be the home system of that particular alien race either, but perhaps one of a number of similar beacons spread around the Milky Way.

How would we respond to such a message? It may be that the extraterrestrials that developed the ability to seed Przybylski's Star are looking for a similar response. They may be waiting for us to send the same signal back to them, as that would indicate we'd reached the same level of technology. If so, it will be hundreds to perhaps thousands of years before we can reply in kind.

Asteroids

As part of the background research behind this novel, I read *The Asteroid Hunter: A Scientist's Journey to the Dawn of Our Solar System* by Dr. Dante Laurette, which goes into the background behind NASA's OSIRIS-REx mission to study the asteroid 101955 Bennu. OSIRIS-REx even returned a sample of the asteroid to Earth.

Asteroids are chemical treasure chests.

Most people are familiar with the periodic table of elements from high school science classes. These start with hydrogen and helium and systematically lay out each of the elements, grouping them together based on common characteristics.

Radioactive elements are unstable, meaning they're so dense that they tend to decay into smaller elements. As an example, over time, uranium decays into thorium and then finally into lead.

The rate at which an element decays is called its half-life, meaning the period of time during which half of any given sample will have decayed. Uranium has a half-life of almost 4.5 billion years, which is roughly the age of Earth itself, giving us a wonderful way of dating extremely old rocks.

But as we reach heavier and heavier elements, the half-life drops from billions to millions to dozens of years and eventually gets down to days, hours, minutes, seconds and even milliseconds. The three heaviest elements we know of—Livermorium, Tennessine, and Oganesson—all have half-lives shorter than the blink of an eye! This region of the periodic table is known as The Sea of Instability.

What does this have to do with asteroids?

Scientists have predicted that there are even heavier elements but, as yet, we haven't been able to synthesize them in a laboratory. These unseen theoretical elements, though, may exist in what's been called *The Island of Stability,* meaning, although they're extremely dense, they break from the pattern and are probably stable for billions of years!

Scientists at the University of Arizona, looking at the unusual density of the asteroid 33 Polyhymnia (which is also in the asteroid belt between Mars and Jupiter), have proposed the idea that super-dense asteroids may hold natural reservoirs of these super-heavy elements we cannot create on Earth. If so, these would be the remnants of extremely violent events in space and could teach us more about the origins of the universe. In this novel, Ryan and Jemma detect such elements on the asteroid 16 Psyche.

Asteroid 16 Psyche

The asteroid 16 Psyche was discovered by Italian astronomer Annibale de Gasparis in 1852. He named the asteroid after the Greek goddess of the soul. As it was only the 16th asteroid to be discovered it has the number 16 included in its formal name.

In 2023, NASA launched a mission to reach Psyche in 2026 to explore this remarkable asteroid from an orbit as low as 75km above the surface. Even from afar, NASA has been able to draw up astonishingly intricate maps of the asteroid.

As of the time of writing, the prevailing idea is that Psyche is a failed planet. Scientists suspect that, at the heart of every planet, there's an iron core. Ordinarily, this is molten due to the extreme gravitational pressure bearing down on it. If Psyche is a remnant of a planet that failed to form or was destroyed in a collision, it will give us unique insights into the earliest age of our solar system and the formation of planets from Mercury to Jupiter.

Gravity on Psyche

To calculate the gravity of the asteroid Psyche, I used an online gravitational calculator and the stats provided for the mass of the asteroid along with its physical size, arriving at the value of roughly 0.074 m/s² compared to 9.8 m/s² here on Earth (or an acceleration of about three inches per second squared, compared with 9.8 meters per second squared here on Earth). Knowing that, it is possible to calculate the relative weight someone would feel in that gravitational field.

An astronaut who's 100kg in weight here on Earth (or roughly 220 pounds) would feel as though they were as light as a feather. They'd weigh three-quarters of a kilogram or about one and a half pounds. The challenge, then, becomes how easy it is for their muscles to propel them around at breakneck speeds. They'd feel like Superman. They could quite literally leap tall buildings with a single bound, but doing that in a controlled manner and landing in a precise spot would be insanely difficult (and dangerous).

'Oumuamua

In 2017, astronomers in Hawaii spotted an asteroid moving on a very unusual trajectory. Instead of orbiting the Sun in an ellipse like the planets and all the other asteroids we've detected so far, it was following a hyperbolic curve (appearing more like an L, a U or a V shape than a closed shape like an O), suggesting it came from outside our solar system and would eventually leave our solar system. For astrophysicists, this was the first confirmed interloper from another star system. Scientists, and even science fiction authors like Arthur C. Clarke in his classic novel *Rendezvous with Rama,* have long speculated that it would be possible for interstellar fragments to enter our solar system, but this was the first confirmed sighting.

Although there was intense speculation about 'Oumuamua, as it came to be known, its profile, motion and outgassing suggest it is an entirely natural object.

'Oumuamua is still within our solar system. It's too faint to follow with telescopes, but based on its trajectory, we expect it to pass the orbit of Uranus in late 2024 before soaring past the orbit of Pluto several years later and continuing on to intercept some other star at some other point in the distant future.

'Oumuamua isn't the only interstellar object we've spotted. Comet 21 Borisov was detected in 2018, coming down from the celestial north and rushing away to the south.

Both 'Oumuamua and Comet 21 Borisov are examples of interstellar tourists, but there is another possibility, and one that's explored in this novel, that there may be <u>interstellar immigrants</u> that have been captured by either the Sun's gravity or even a large gas giant. *Ka'epaoka 'āwela* (asteroid 514107) orbits the Sun out in the same region as Jupiter, but it orbits backward, moving in the opposite direction to Jupiter and reaching well off the ecliptic, which is the plane on which all the planets orbit the Sun. This makes it a strong candidate for having migrated here from some other star system.

Oh, and it's not one-way traffic. Back in 1981, Comet Bowell passed too close to Jupiter and was ejected from our solar system. It's currently soaring toward some other star. One wonders if the inhabitants of that system might name it 'Oumuamua when it gets there in a million years' time.

SETI

SETI scientist Dr. Seth Shostak, in his non-fiction book *Confessions of an Alien Hunter: A Scientist's Search for Extraterrestrial Intelligence*, makes the point that Hollywood is obsessed with biological First Contact. In his opinion, if aliens are going to traverse the stupendously vast void of space between stars to reach Earth, it will be machines that arrive here. Biological life is just too fragile and—on our world at least—far too fleeting to survive an interstellar voyage.

Given the rise of artificial intelligence on Earth, it's reasonable to expect a technologically advanced alien race to develop its own artificial intelligence. These would be more suited to the harsh extremes and longevity required for life in space, so it makes sense that we're more likely to encounter an intelligent alien machine rather than intelligent aliens themselves. This is the basic premise behind the monolith in Arthur C. Clarke's classic novel *2001: A Space Odyssey*. Perhaps such devices would be designed to gather information, interact with inhabitants and report back to their masters. Or perhaps, as discussed in this novel, they'll become sentient in their own right and supersede their creators.

The Singularity

The late Vernor Vinge was the first science fiction author to popularize the idea of a technological singularity. Since then, scientists, science fiction authors and technologists have sought to understand the implications of our technology reaching the point where it can supersede us in terms of intelligence.

The idea is simple enough: make a smart/sentient machine that can improve itself, and it will continue to improve itself in cycles that become increasingly more refined. In the same way in which exponential growth allows bacteria and viruses to start out small and insignificant, the runaway effect of improving intelligence will quickly become unstoppable, and a sentient AI could easily eclipse the human intelligence that created it.

What would be the implications of such an astonishing advance? Some fear it would make humanity irrelevant. We would become the Neanderthals of our age. Such a sentient AI need not set out to destroy us—we'd simply become immaterial and, like so many hominid species before us, we'd give way to the next evolutionary development, *Homo silica*. Humanity wouldn't be replaced so much as superseded.

In the words of Sir David Attenborough, "*If we [humans] disappeared overnight, the world would probably be better off.*" The problem we face is that, individually, we're thoughtful and caring, but collectively, we're selfish and destructive. Perhaps with *Homo silica*, hominids would mature to become a true, civil civilization.

Gilgamesh and Genesis

Although the writing of the Book of Genesis is traditionally attributed to Moses, the different styles found within the first book of the Bible and the changing perspectives that occur, often within a few chapters, have led some modern theologians to consider the book as a conglomeration of stories compiled over the centuries (probably by four scribes living from 900 BC to 500 BC).

Genesis borrows heavily from other ancient cultures and historical sources reaching back at least four thousand years to the Epic of Gilgamesh in Sumeria, which contains a similar account about the Garden of the Gods and the Great Flood.

Regardless of its origins and its development over time, there is no doubt about the profound influence Genesis has had on Western culture and modern thinking. The Tree of the Knowledge of Good and Evil is a metaphor, challenging us to explore the complex relationship of how knowledge can lead to entirely different outcomes.

The Greek equivalent of eating from the Tree of the Knowledge of Good and Evil is found in Prometheus, whose name means *forethought*. Most people know of Prometheus as the one who stole fire from the gods, but fire was metaphorical for the knowledge of how to tame fire. Like Adam, Prometheus seized the knowledge of how to transform humanity from brute animals into human beings. For Prometheus, harnessing untamed forces such as fire represented how the knowledge of the gods would benefit humanity.

In *The Simulacrum*, I thought it would be interesting to consider how an alien intelligence might interpret our creation stories. It would be easy for them to dismiss these legends as myths and fables, but an intelligent species would recognize how these ideas have shaped our collective persona.

Survivor Bias

Why does one person succeed where another fails? It's a question we all ask, but the answer is often far more intangible and elusive than we realize.

The temptation is to look at successful people in our respective fields with a sense of awe, wondering how *they* succeeded, being curious about what they did to get ahead, but more often than not, they themselves don't really know or if they think they know, they're mistaken by the survivor bias.

The survivor bias looks at successful achievements while overlooking similar unsuccessful outcomes; as such, it ignores data that doesn't fit its preconceptions. And ignoring data is never good.

Imagine talking to the survivor of a plane crash and asking them what they did as the aircraft plummeted from the sky. A lot of people might reply that they prayed, and having survived, it would be astonishingly easy to attribute their second chance at life to divine intervention. The problem is... what about everyone else on the plane? What about those who didn't survive? How many of them also prayed?

The reality is that our survivor lived for reasons well outside of their influence or control, such as the design of the plane, the angle and speed at which it struck the hillside, the position of their seat within the fuselage, and a dose of blind luck. In spite of what they thought, prayer wasn't a factor, especially as the majority of those on the plane were probably praying as well.

During World War II, the introduction of new helmets led to an increase in head injuries among US soldiers, and there was mounting pressure for a recall—but the helmets weren't faulty. In fact, they performed better than expected. In reality, the increase in head injuries represented a decrease in deaths from head trauma. Rather than being a failure, they were successful in saving lives, but that was only recognized when *all* the data was considered, not just the data that seemed relevant.

Another example from the war comes from the US Navy. They wanted to know which parts of their bombers needed to be reinforced with extra armor to help crews survive. They examined those bombers that barely made it back. These planes had holes in their wings, holes in the fuselage, and gaping holes in the tail. And the temptation was to add armor to those points as they were so badly damaged, but one particular scientist said no.

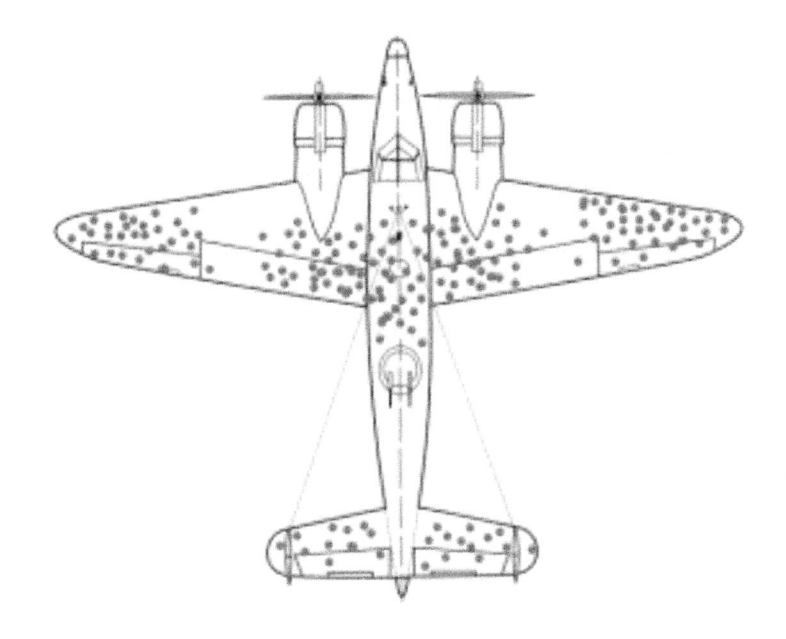

Abraham Wald knew the real learning came from those planes that *never* made it back, those that could never be examined. He looked at the parts of the surviving planes that were largely intact and realized they were more important than the damaged areas. If a plane crashed, there was nothing to examine. And so he had the Navy reinforce the cockpit and the areas around the engines, as it was only when they were untouched that crews made it back alive.

So, what does it take to succeed?

The answer is that it's complicated, but don't ask someone who's successful. They probably have a skewed, limited perspective on their own success.

If you want to learn more about this concept, check out books like *Outliers* by Malcolm Gladwell. You'll be surprised by some of the unusual influences in the lives of those who have succeeded in society. Yes, it takes hard work and dedication, but there's also an element of luck and timing that can take a variety of different forms.

Heliocentric Julian Date

Heliocentric Julian dates really are as wild as they sound. They're calculated from 4713 BC for no other reason than it is such a remote date that it captures every known astronomical observation in recorded history.

As a number, HJDs reach into the millions, counting the number of days since then until now. They're astonishingly useful for astronomers. They form a kind of universal time, often being measured from the perspective of the Sun rather than Earth. This means observations from different observatories can be synced in the context of each other. For example, a space probe in orbit around Jupiter might record a supernova by happenstance, along with an observatory in Chile and the James Webb Space Telescope in orbit our beyond the Moon. Having a common reckoning of time allows these observations to be properly analyzed and recorded as a single event.

I first came across Heliocentric Julian dates several years ago while looking at exoplanets. Given the astonishing advances in modern science, it can be easy for the layperson to feel intimidated by scientific research and feel as though it is forever out of their reach. In reality, science is accessible. The next time someone tells you *garlic cures cancer* or that *vaccines don't work*, forget about Facebook, YouTube, Twitter and Google —go to Google Scholar and read the research for yourself. Peer-reviewed research can be complex, but the introductions and summaries are easy to understand. In this way, you can sidestep misinformation and read actual research for yourself.

Back in 2019, I wanted to see if a regular old Joe like myself could find an exoplanet. I knew NASA made all its raw data available online and wanted to see if I could decipher it and find an exoplanet for myself. I used a commercial IT log tool called *Splunk* and downloaded some of the Kepler data. The Heliocentric Julian dates were difficult to work with as they were so unwieldy compared to the numbers and dates normally being crunched by *Splunk*, but I figured out how to convert between them and the UNIX Epoch date favored by computers. And I found an exoplanet! I wrote a blog post about the process on my website, ThinkingScifi. It was fun to do a little bit of backyard science and realize that even something as complex as astrophysics isn't inaccessible.

Mid-Atlantic Accent

When Ryan first talks to the alien entity, he notes it doesn't have a distinct accent. Try as he may, he can't place where the alien's English accent originates, and he imagines it as a conglomeration of American, Canadian and British accents, almost as though it originated in the middle of the Atlantic. Although this might seem like a throwaway point, it's actually based on a historical precedence that is impossible to convey in the text of a book, but I thought you'd enjoy considering, if not hearing it.

Have you ever watched an old Carey Grant film or a classic like Citizen Kane? Back then, Hollywood used this pseudo-accent to sound neutral and agreeable regardless of whether a film was being played in LA, New York or London.

In recent times, the Mid-Atlantic accent has been used to passively attribute evil to various characters and make them more distinct, including Darth Vader, the Joker, Effie Trinket from *The Hunger Games*, Mr Burns and Sideshow Bob. When speaking in a political setting, in *Star Wars*, both Princess Leia and Queen Amidala use this accent. It's been described as "*posh American.*"

If this novel is ever made into an audiobook, the narrator is going to have fun with this accent!

To Vax or Not to Vax

At the conclusion of this story, Ryan reflects on those occasions where humanity has banded together for the common good, like the eradication of polio (in at least 99% of the world) and the global eradication of smallpox.

The tsunami of misinformation around the COVID-19 pandemic has buried the reality that vaccinations have saved *hundreds of millions* of lives for a whole host of diseases, including COVID-19 itself. Don't let the lies cause you to doubt modern medicine. Vaccines remain the single most effective way of preventing crippling and often fatal illness in children and adults. [Diseases like diphtheria](), which once spread like wildfire and killed 10% of those infected, are largely unknown today because of vaccines. We need to push back against the irrational, rabid, paranoid disinformation and reclaim medical science for the good of public health.

Poop on the Moon

Yes, the Apollo astronauts really did leave [96 bags of poop]() and other waste on the Moon after their seven excursions on the rugged lunar surface, and these represent a gold mine for scientists.

Future lunar missions may give us the opportunity to recover some of these bags and examine their contents. In addition to solar radiation and cosmic rays, they've been exposed to the searing heat of 260°F (127°C) during the long lunar day and -280°F (-173°C) at night. That's a relative difference of over 500°F occurring each month, so the expectation is that most, if not all, of the biological material will have degraded, but if something has survived, it could provide us with valuable insights into how fabrics, solids and biological substances cope with such extremes.

And this idea isn't without precedence.

In 1967, NASA landed the Surveyor 3 probe in the lunar mare known as *Oceanus Procellarum*. Two and a half years later, in 1969, Apollo 12 landed 500 feet (or about 160 meters) away from the probe. Astronaut Charles Conrad, Jr. retrieved the camera from the probe as scientists wanted to examine it for metal fatigue, rubber seals perishing, etc. What NASA found, though, was that a small amount of the bacterium *Streptococcus mitis* survived on a piece of foam from inside the TV camera—and, remarkably, it could be revived on Earth! Given that Surveyor was built in a clean room, this was an astonishing result. *Streptococcus mitis* is a common, harmless form of bacteria found in the nose, mouth and throat of humans. To the surprise of scientists, even when exposed to the oscillating extremes of the harsh vacuum of space for years on end, microbial life can lie dormant and be revived.

This finding has significant implications for the possibility of *panspermia*, or the idea that microbial life may be able to migrate from one planet to another within asteroids. Although the distances and times involved for such a transfer would be measured in tens of millions of years, the idea has gone from implausible to unlikely but possible. Examining feces from the Apollo missions would help to improve our understanding of this intriguing possibility.

Underground Power Cables

I don't know how the NASA Johnson Space Center gets its power, but there is a system known as high-pressure, gas-filled (HPGF) underground electrical transmission lines. When one of these core lines is accidentally severed, the results can be catastrophic.

My hometown of Auckland, New Zealand, was without electrical power for five weeks when a single underground high-voltage power cable failed. To someone like me, it seems as though it could be repaired quite quickly, but the actual process is not straightforward and quite time-consuming, so I used this as a plot device to strand Cassandra on the

AMPLE spacecraft. In practice, NASA would reestablish contact within hours, if not days, but with its data center down, it would be limited to only operating critical systems. Repairing or relocating services would be astonishingly complex, limiting what could be accomplished.

Thank You

Thank you for taking a chance on an obscure Australian science fiction author who hails from Auckland, New Zealand. Your support of my writing is deeply appreciated. By purchasing this book, you're giving me the opportunity to write the next one, so I'm grateful for your kind support.

I'd like to thank a bunch of beta-readers who helped me with quality control, including Phil Bailey, Dr. Randall Petersen, Terry Grindstaff, Didi Kanjahn, Gerald Greenwood, Mike Morrissey LCDR. USN Ret., Melinda Robino, Gabe "Velveeta" Ets-Hokin USMC, David Jaffe and John Stephens.

If you've enjoyed this novel, please leave a review online and tell a friend.

Peter Cawdron

Brisbane, Australia

Printed in Great Britain
by Amazon